IN THE
RED

IN THE RED

CLIVE EGLETON

Hodder & Stoughton
LONDON SYDNEY AUCKLAND TORONTO

British Library Cataloguing in Publication Data
Egleton, Clive, *1927* –
    In the red.
    I. Title
    823'.914 [F]

ISBN 0-340-52394-8

First published in Great Britain 1990

Published by Hodder and Stoughton,
a division of Hodder and Stoughton Ltd,
Mill Road, Dunton Green, Sevenoaks, Kent TN13 2YA
Editorial Office: 47 Bedford Square, London WC1B 3DP

Typeset by Hewer Text Composition Services, Edinburgh
Printed and bound in Great Britain by Mackays of Chatham plc, Chatham, Kent

This is for Ed Kelly.

I owe you this.

'Courage is not an inexhaustible commodity – like a bank account, it can be drawn upon once too often.'

Anon.

1949

SHANGHAI

Friday 20 May
to
Wednesday 25 May

1

The car was a 1936 dark blue Packard four-door sedan with wide running boards and a floor-mounted gear shift. Too many summers in China had taken the gloss out of the cellulose, the suspension was shot to hell and the asthmatic engine definitely needed decoking. There were other major defects like unreliable brakes and a horn which tended to blare every time the driver spun the wheel. But it had been the only vehicle in the station yard when Freeland had alighted from the train at Kweilin and the less obvious faults had only become apparent as they drove out to the military airfield some twelve miles from the centre of town.

The airfield had been constructed during the Sino-Japanese war and was surrounded by a range of beehive-shaped limestone crags which made a low level bombing attack a highly dangerous proposition. Tucked away under the trees on the south side, where they couldn't be seen from the air, were several barrack huts, a control tower, an operations shack and a fuel dump. The perimeter defences consisted of a barbed wire triple concertina fence, numerous slit trenches and a concrete pillbox covering the entrance which was unmanned. The barrier across the access road was secured in the upright position and there was no sign of life in the nearby guardroom. But for the solitary C46 parked on the dispersal apron, Freeland would have concluded that the airfield had been abandoned.

Freeland pointed to the right; responding to his hand signal, the driver put the wheel hard over which automatically triggered the horn. For once, however, its strident note served a useful purpose; as they approached the seemingly deserted barracks, a tall, lean man emerged from the operations shack. The crew-cut hairstyle and the relaxed way he carried himself led Freeland to believe that he was an American. The faded, ex-Army khakis he was wearing clinched that assumption.

The cab driver pumped the footbrakes, applied the handbrake for good measure and finally managed to bring the Packard to a halt in a cloud of dust a good twenty yards beyond the operations shack.

"This okay, boss?" he asked.

"It'll do."

"You pay me two hundred American cigarettes, yes?"

Freeland got out of the car, opened the rear door and retrieved the travelling bag he'd dumped on the back seat. Unzipping it, he took out a carton of Chesterfields and handed it to the driver. No one in 1949 was interested in the kind of money Chiang Kai-shek was printing. With inflation running at a thousand per cent and the Chinese Yuan fetching only one US dollar to three million, people were reduced to bartering for the goods and services they wanted.

"You no going tip me?"

Freeland delved into his pockets, found a half-empty packet of cigarettes and tossed them into the car. The driver acknowledged the tip with something approaching a salute, then made a three-point turn and took off in the direction of the guardroom, the horn still shorting.

"My name's Freeland, Harry Freeland," he said, advancing towards the American. "And you are?"

"George C. Berringer."

Freeland guessed the American was about six foot two which made him almost three inches the taller. At twelve and a half stone however, he was at least twenty-five pounds heavier than Berringer who, close to, looked as though he could do with a good square meal.

"Where have you come from, Mr Freeland?"

"Canton. Is that your plane over there?"

"Yeah." Berringer looked at him hopefully. "You haven't got a replacement compass for me by any chance, have you?"

"I'm afraid not."

"Shit, wouldn't you just know it. I've been stuck in this place three days already and the way things are going, we'll still be here when the Commies march into Kweilin."

"If it's any comfort," said Freeland, "the nearest units of the People's Liberation Army are five hundred miles to the north."

"Don't you believe it. There are a considerable number of guerilla bands operating in this province and it won't be long before they're knocking at the gates once they learn that the airfield is theirs for the taking."

"What happened to the fighter bombers that used to be here?"

"The P51 Mustangs left yesterday afternoon, all thirty-six of

12

them." Berringer scowled. "They've probably gone to join the rest of the Nationalist Air Force in Taiwan. Not that they would have done anything had they stayed on."

Freeland nodded. The Air Force had been curiously reluctant to intervene in the land battle. It was as if, without exception, the pilots found the idea of killing their fellow countrymen utterly repellent. Their only aggressive act had been the sinking of *The Chungking* after the captain and crew had defected to the Communists with their six-inch-gun cruiser.

"The ground crew vanished during the night," Berringer continued. "They literally folded their pup tents and stole away while Joe and I were asleep in the Gooney Bird."

It transpired that the Gooney Bird was an affectionate nickname for the Curtiss Wright C46 Commando and Joe, whose surname was Lander, was Berringer's co-pilot and navigator.

"Joe's an old China hand," the American informed him. "He's been with Chennault right from the beginning, long before Pearl Harbour."

"I've heard of Claire Chennault," Freeland said, but it didn't stop Berringer from delivering a eulogy in praise of his former Commanding General and current employer.

"Did you know that in the 1930s he did more to revolutionise fighter tactics than any other man in the Army Air Corps? 'Course he stepped on a few toes in the process and the Brass in Washington were only too happy to give him a medical discharge in '37. The quacks said he was partially deaf but that was an occupational hazard with flyers in those days."

Chennault's reputation had not been confined to the United States. One important personage to have heard of him had been Madame Chiang Kai-shek, the American-educated wife of the Generalissimo and newly appointed National Secretary of Aviation. It was she who had pressed for Chennault's services in the face of Japanese aggression from Manchuria.

"Joe was regular army when Washington gave Chennault the green light to recruit the pilots he needed from the armed forces. Although they were required to resign their commissions the day they signed on the dotted line, every volunteer was given a solemn assurance that he would be reinstated without loss of seniority the day his contract expired. I don't think Joe was too worried about that; he was looking for excitement, the pay was good and the five-hundred-dollar bonus for every Jap plane he shot down was an added incentive."

The American Volunteer Group, known as the Flying Tigers,

had been equipped with one hundred Curtiss P40 Tomahawks which the RAF had rejected because the experts had considered the plane lacked a sufficiently high performance to take on German fighters over Western Europe. They were, however, more than a match for the Mitsubishi bombers and Joe Lander had earned his first 500 dollar bonus when his squadron of the AVG had tangled with the Japanese over Rangoon on Christmas Day 1941.

"It didn't last. After Pearl Harbour, the Brass went all out to get the AVG back into American uniform." Berringer grinned. "But they had to wait until June '42 to do it. That's when their contracts with the Chinese government expired. Guys like Joe were hard to push around."

"Like their commander?" Freeland suggested.

"No one ever got the better of General Chennault."

Berringer was wrong there. Although he had been largely responsible for General 'Vinegar Joe' Stilwell, the supremo for the China, Burma, India Theatre of War being recalled to Washington, he had crossed swords with too many people to survive. Along the way he had antagonised General Arnold, Chief of the Army Air Corps, an error of judgment which had eventually led to his own dismissal. After the war, he had returned to China with the vision of using the aeroplane as an instrument for winning the peace instead of as a means of destruction. In pursuit of this dream, Chennault had acquired a fleet of war surplus Dakotas and C46 Commandos and with them had formed Civil Air Transport (CAT), his own personal airline.

"I need to get to Shanghai in a hurry," Freeland said abruptly. "The Civil Air Transport office in Canton reckoned you would be able to help me."

"I don't see how I can. For one thing the compass is unserviceable, for another, my ship's carrying eight tons of grain which is destined for Nanchang."

"You might just as well hand it over to the Communists; from what I hear, the People's Liberation Army has the town encircled. The best thing you can do is deliver the grain to Shanghai; the Nationalists could certainly use it if they seriously intend to make the city another Stalingrad."

"Do you work for UNRRA, Mr Freeland?"

It was a perfectly natural question. Much of the freight CAT carried was supplied by the United Nations Relief and Rehabilitation Agency and only one of their officials had the necessary authority to re-allocate supplies destined for one area to another.

"No, I'm with the British Foreign Office."

14

Freeland reached inside his lightweight jacket and brought out an oblong, window-type envelope containing two letters, one from the United States Consul General in Hong Kong addressed 'To whom it may concern', the other from CAT's operations manager in Canton. Both letters requested the recipient to provide the bearer with all possible assistance.

"I've also got a similar note from General Huang Chieh, Commander in Chief South China Front."

"But nothing from UNRRA," Berringer said, returning the letters.

"They don't count any more," Freeland told him. "The man who does is Chairman Mao and he's already made it clear that the new China will have nothing to do with the United Nations Relief and Rehabilitation Agency."

"There's still a problem . . ."

"I'm authorised to hire your aircraft at whatever the going rate might be. Payment can be in US dollars, pounds sterling or in any other currency General Chennault happens to fancy."

"You'd have been better off going by boat or train."

"A boat's too slow and the PLA is sitting astride the only railroad from here into Shanghai."

"I hear what you say," Berringer said, "but it doesn't alter the fact that we've got a bum compass."

"Don't tell me you haven't flown without a compass before. What's wrong with visual navigation? You've got a map and there isn't a cloud in the sky."

"Shanghai is a good eight hundred miles away and we don't know what the weather is like north of here."

"You can always turn back if it gets too bad."

Berringer shook his head. "Boy, oh boy, you've got an answer for everything, haven't you, Mr British Foreign Office man?"

"We could fly into Hungjao; the airfield is ten miles out of town but CAT were still using it a few days ago . . ."

"And I might just pick up a replacement compass from the Maintenance unit," the American said, finishing the sentence for him.

"Or from China Airways."

"I think you've got yourself a deal," Berringer said and started walking towards the C46 transport on the far side of the airfield.

Freeland picked up his travelling bag and hurried after him. "How long will it take us to reach Shanghai?" he asked.

"What's the time now?"

"1035."

"Then we should touch down at Hungjao around 1500 hours."

"That long?"

"The Gooney's cruising speed is a hundred and eighty-three miles an hour. Of course, if you're in a real hurry we could go up to fifteen thou and squeeze another eighty out of her, but she's an old lady and like I said, we've got eight tons of grain on board."

"I'd sooner we arrived in one piece," said Freeland.

"If we're challenged, I'll put you on the air."

"Why me?"

"Because we'll be flying over enemy territory," said Berringer, "and I can't speak Chinese. Neither can Joe."

"Nor can I. French is my other language."

That was due to his mother, whom his father had met in Amiens when his battalion had been resting behind the lines during the First World War.

"What are you doing in China then?"

"You know the saying – a square peg in a round hole."

"Yeah, that's the way our army used to do things." Berringer clucked his tongue. "All the same, I would have thought your people would have made better use of your language qualifications."

There had been a time not so very long ago when they had done exactly that. In January 1941 he had been serving with an anti-aircraft battery on the east coast of Scotland near Dundee which could have been a neutral country for all they saw of the enemy. Bored out of his mind, he had volunteered for special liaison duties in response to an Army Council Instruction appealing for French-speaking officers, NCOs and men. A month later, following a brief interview at St Michael's House in Baker Street, he had found himself on a demolitions course at the Special Operations Executive's (SOE) training school at Beaulieu. They had then sent him on to Ringway, Manchester, where he had made two practice parachute jumps from a captive balloon, followed by six more through a hole in the floor of a converted Whitley bomber. Once he'd got his wings, he might have guessed that SOE would send him into Vichy France on foot from Spain. On his second mission in 1944 they had used a Lysander to land him in a field the Free French Forces of the Interior had chosen near Chartres.

"Were you with the British Embassy in France before they sent you out here, Mr Freeland?"

"In a manner of speaking. I was attached to the War Crimes Commission."

"Which you can't talk about?"

"Right."

16

They walked on in silence towards the C46. As they drew nearer, Freeland could see a figure lying on the ground in the shade beneath the wing.

"That's Joe Lander, my co-pilot," Berringer said, then pursed his lips and whistled.

Lander slowly got to his feet. At a distance, he appeared to have the compact build of many Second World War fighter pilots; close to, Freeland noticed his blotchy complexion and the bulge above his belt, often the tell-tale signs of a man who drank too much.

"This is Mr Freeland, a British diplomat," said Berringer. "We're taking him to Shanghai."

"With or without the grain?"

"With."

"Glad to have you aboard," Lander said and shook hands. More observant than his compatriot, he immediately noticed the mutilated stump on Freeland's left hand but refrained from asking him how he'd lost the little finger. "For a moment there, I thought George was going to tell me we had to unload the ship first. You ever ridden in one of these workhorses before, Mr Freeland?"

"No, I can't say I have."

"They've got a safety record second to none."

"That's nice to know."

Freeland tossed his bag into the plane and climbed in after the two Americans. The sacks of grain were arranged in a neat line stretching all the way from the flight deck to just aft of the side door and were lashed in place by web straps to tie-down points on the floor. Berringer pointed to one of the few remaining canvas seats on the port side that hadn't been removed and told Freeland to make himself comfortable, then went on through to the flight deck. Presently, each of the Pratt and Whitney engines spluttered into life with a wheezing cough to run unevenly for a minute or so before settling down into a deep-throated snarl.

The plane rolled slowly forward, taxied round to the runway and was held there for another few minutes while Berringer ran the engines up to full power. The C46 shuddered like a dog straining at the leash; then suddenly they were thundering down the airstrip, the landscape flashing past in a blur. Seconds after they had lifted off, Freeland heard a dull thump as the co-pilot retracted the undercarriage.

If, against all the odds, the C46 transport made it to Shanghai, Freeland wondered how much time he would have before the People's Liberation Army walked in and took the place over.

Somewhere in Shanghai there was a man called Teale whom London wanted to lay their hands on very badly and he had to find him.

* * *

Imprisonment was not a new experience for Howard Teale. The Japanese had put him into the bag along with all the other British and American expatriates who had been living in Shanghai the day Admiral Nagumo's planes had bombed Pearl Harbour. All the civilians – men, women and children alike – had been herded into the racecourse off the Nanking Road which had served as a temporary internment camp while they were being screened by the Kempeitai. He'd had a hard time convincing the Japanese military police that he was just a simple businessman, but in the end they had accepted his story. Of course, they'd slapped him around a bit and he'd damned nearly died of starvation in 1945 but he'd always known he would pull through. This time Teale wasn't so sure that he would survive.

General Mao Sen had earned the nickname 'Bloody Mao' when he had run the Secret Intelligence Department for Chiang Kai-shek. Since being appointed Commissioner of Police for Shanghai with orders to clean up the city, he had more than lived up to that reputation. On Monday afternoon, three plain-clothes men had called on Teale at his office on The Bund near the Cathay Hotel. Their leader had said there were a number of questions they wanted to ask him about his business connections with the Magic Palace Dance Hall and would he please accompany them to the Central Police Station. Although their spokesman had been very polite and respectful, Teale had been left in no doubt that they would use whatever force was necessary should he refuse to co-operate.

They had bundled him into an ancient Buick parked outside the office and had then driven through the French Concession at breakneck speed before heading north-west to a dilapidated house which backed on to Soochow Creek. On arrival, he had been wheeled straight in front of the Chief Interrogator, a Colonel Li, who had accused him of espionage.

"You run brothel and spy for Communists," Li had screamed at him in broken English. "You write confession, give names of people who help you."

Teale had denied the charge and had earned himself the kind of harsh treatment normally handed out to a petty thief when he had repeatedly demanded to see the British Consul. As little as a month ago, no Chinese officer would have dared to strike a

European but a lot had happened in the intervening four weeks to change all that. On the nineteenth of April, Communist guns had fired on the frigate HMS *Amethyst* as she steamed up the Yangtze towards Nanking, killing twenty-three of her crew and wounding a further thirty-one. The destroyer, HMS *Consort*, guard ship at Nanking, had gone down river to her assistance, all guns blazing, but she too had been hit repeatedly by the Communist batteries massed on the north bank and had been forced to turn back after taking thirty-eight casualties.

Forty-eight hours later, the naval authorities in Shanghai had despatched the 10,000-ton cruiser *London* and the frigate HMS *Black Swan* to escort the *Amethyst* to Nanking where the wounded could receive proper medical attention. Their plan, like their thinking, had been simple enough; unfortunately, they had chosen to mount the rescue attempt on the very day the People's Liberation Army had launched an all-out offensive across the Yangtze. To the Communists it had looked as though the heavy cruiser and her attendant frigate were attempting to disrupt the assault river crossing and they had reacted accordingly. Every gun that could be brought to bear had fired on the *London*, killing eighteen of her crew and wounding a further thirty before she was forced to break off the engagement. In all, the navy had suffered one hundred and twenty-seven casualties with only a muted bleat of protest from the Attlee Government by way of reply. Teale reckoned the lesson had not been lost on the Nationalists.

He felt the stubble on his bruised face and wondered how much longer Colonel Li intended to keep him locked up in this windowless, fetid room in the basement. The guards had done just about everything they could to break him but despite being tortured for hours on end, he had refused to confess. To do so would be tantamount to signing his own death warrant.

Colonel Li was determined to execute him but, for the sake of appearances, he wanted something concrete in the way of evidence to support the verdict and sentence. Teale was equally resolved that the Colonel wouldn't get it from him, but it was more than likely that the prisoner he had seen early that morning would soon be only too willing to become a star witness for Li. When Teale had been taken out into the walled garden for a so-called exercise period, the guards had just finished burying the prisoner up to his neck in the vegetable patch. After a few hours of being roasted alive, ninety-nine people out of a hundred would be quite happy to send their whole family to the gallows if it would put an end to their own suffering.

A key turned in the lock and the door grated on rusty hinges as it opened outwards. The same three police officers who'd arrested Teale in his office escorted him up to the same interrogation room on the second floor where he had first made the acquaintance of Colonel Li. The Colonel was not alone; standing in the corner to his right was the man who had been buried up to his neck in the vegetable patch. His face had swollen to almost twice its normal size and his eyes were concealed by the blisters on both cheekbones. In places his skin had split open like an over-ripe peach. He was also shivering uncontrollably as if in the throes of a severe bout of malaria.

"You not recognise this man, Mr Teale?" Li asked, smiling. "His name is Chien Mai; he used to be barman for you at Magic Palace. You send him through lines with message for General commanding People's Liberation Army."

"That's not true."

"It is all here." Li held up the sheaf of papers which were lying on the table in front of him. "He make full confession. And this," he added, waving a single sheet of paper, "is your death warrant."

Teale stared at the Chinese characters drawn in red ink on the parchment. The bastard really meant to do it; he was going to have a European shot for no other reason than he wanted to impress his superior officer, General Mao Sen, who was determined to sweep the racketeers off the streets of Shanghai.

"Have you informed the British Consul yet?"

"He will hear soon enough."

Teale licked his lips. "Can we make a deal?" he asked hoarsely.

"What you give me?"

"The names of all the Fifth Columnists I know in Shanghai."

Teale had met only two men who might possibly be Fifth Columnists but Colonel Li was not to know that. As for the rest, he would invent them, anything to gain time. All right, so he didn't have a family, but surely someone out there must have missed him by now?

"We give you pen and paper, you make list."

"Right."

"You go now," Li said and looked pointedly at the police officer in charge of the escort.

Instead of returning to the basement, they took him upstairs to a small room in the attic on the west side of the house which overlooked a stone courtyard. There were no bars on the windows and it wasn't difficult to see why. The attic was a good thirty feet above the ground and the flagstones below would make mincemeat of anyone foolish enough to jump.

There was not a stick of furniture but when he tried to point out that he must have something to write on, the police officer in charge merely smiled amicably, then ushered the other escorts out of the room and locked the door behind him. Some ten to fifteen minutes after they had disappeared, a shrill voice drew Teale to the window. Looking down, he was just in time to see Colonel Li pocket the piece of paper he had been reading to the prisoners assembled in front of him.

There were four of them, well-fed young men in smart open-neck shirts and sports trousers, the style of dress favoured by the pimps he'd seen in Bubbling Well Road. They were standing in line six paces apart, their hands tied behind them and facing the house. Nonchalantly, as though out for an afternoon stroll, Li walked behind the prisoners and shot them one by one through the back of the neck with a .45 automatic.

2

The landscape below was a pastiche of paddy fields segregated by narrow bunds which were raised a foot or so above the level of the newly-planted rice. The broad ribbon of the Yangtze meandered across the plain, flowing roughly west to east until it finally merged with the South China Sea.

"Shanghai is that dark smudge on the horizon." Berringer's voice came through loud and clear thanks to the headset Lander had provided when the Americans had called him forward on to the flight deck. "The silver thread is the Whangpoo River."

"How long before we reach Hungjao?"

"Another fifteen, maybe twenty, minutes."

"You want me to go back there and strap myself in?" Freeland asked, jerking a thumb over his shoulder.

"No hurry. I'm going to take a good look at the airfield before we put down. I want to make sure the natives are friendly."

They had map-read their way cross country from Kweilin. Visibility had been good, though the cloud base had been too low for them to cruise along at the plane's most economical ceiling. They had maintained an altitude of five thousand which had put them out of range of the Russian-made 12.7mm anti-aircraft machine-guns the PLA were equipped with but not the 40mm and heavier pieces they had captured from the Nationalists. No one, however, had fired so much as a warning shot at them.

"There's that navy ship of yours up ahead," said Lander.

"Yes."

"What's her name again?"

"*Amethyst*."

"Yeah, that's it, *Amethyst*." Lander sighed, then shook his head, the nearest he'd come thus far to showing any kind of animation. "I guess we're looking at one boat that's going nowhere."

From a purely logical standpoint, it was difficult to refute the co-pilot's assessment. The frigate had come under fire seventy miles up river from Woosun and had run aground on Rose Island after her bridge had been hit, killing her coxswain and nearly everyone else who had been on watch at the time. At high tide that night, she had floated off the mudbank and the acting captain had subsequently moved the *Amethyst* a further eighteen miles upstream in order to put the ship well out of range of the Communist shore batteries. At the same time, the manoeuvre had also taken the frigate deeper into enemy territory.

"Where do you suppose the front line is now, George?" Lander asked.

"Some considerable distance from Hungjao, I hope."

Amen to that, Freeland thought. General Chen Yi had put two field armies across the Yangtze between Nanking and a point east of Rose Island. Above Nanking, another two field armies under Lin Piao had simultaneously established a bridgehead opposite Anking where the river flowed in a north-easterly direction to form what was roughly an inverted letter 'L'. Shanghai was therefore threatened from the north and the west, its Nationalist defenders trapped in a giant vice that was slowly closing on them.

"There's Hungjao to starboard," Berringer said and altered course.

Lander nodded. "So let's do like you said and take a good look at it first."

They began to lose height, the altimeter slowly unwinding as they circled above the airfield. Beyond Hungjao, Freeland thought he could see a number of slit trenches in the grounds of a large isolated house some miles from the outskirts of the city.

"Try calling the tower."

"Roger." Lander checked the frequency, switched to transmit, then said, "Hungjao, this is Civil Air Transport George X-ray 712. You read me?"

There was no reply, and two subsequent calls met with the same negative response.

"Seems no one's at home," Berringer said laconically.

"So what are you going to do, George?"

"We'll go round one more time, then put down. You want to return to your seat, Mr Freeland?"

"Certainly." Freeland removed the borrowed headset, gave it to Lander and left the flight deck.

Berringer had told him that during the Second World War, George X-ray 712 had been on the hump route ferrying supplies from India over the Himalayas to Kunming in China. Apart from having to contend with atrocious weather, the C46 was easy prey for the Japanese fighter planes based in North Burma. To give the slow-moving transport some form of self-protection, selected windows on the port and starboard sides had been enlarged and fitted with a pintle mount so that the freight master and air despatchers could use their small arms to engage an attacking plane. One such adapted window was directly opposite Freeland. Through it, he caught a glimpse of a tracer round curving past the nose of the C46. A split second later, a hole appeared in the fuselage midway between the aperture and the flight deck and he heard a double rap as the heavy machine-gun bullet exited through the roof above his head.

The plane shuddered under the impact, slipped sideways, then went into a steep dive, both Pratt and Whitney engines still on full power. Freeland closed his eyes and braced himself for the inevitable crash. No one had to tell him that his chances of survival were practically nil; the C46 would be doing something over two hundred and fifty miles an hour when it ploughed into the deck and he expected the plane to explode like a bomb. If that didn't kill him outright, eight tons of freight on the move most certainly would.

At the bottom of the roller-coaster, the aircraft suddenly flattened out and started climbing, then dipped, only to rise again, yawing from side to side. Freeland unclipped the seat belt, tried to stand up and fell back as the port wing dropped. Presently, someone up front managed to hold the plane level long enough for him to get to his feet and make it to the flight deck.

Lander was flying the plane with one hand while trying to move Berringer with the other. Freeland could tell at a glance that the pilot was dead; his head was flopping about and there was a gaping exit wound on the left side of his neck where the armour-piercing bullet had also removed most of the shoulder. Lander was shouting at him but his words were inaudible above the roar of the two thousand horsepower engines. It didn't matter because Freeland knew what he had to do; lifting Berringer under the armpits, he hauled the dead man away from the controls and laid him on the floor behind the seat. Then he grabbed the spare headset and plugged it in to hear Lander reciting a litany of four letter words that weren't to be found in Webster's.

"I'm here when you need a spare hand," Freeland said calmly. "Just tell me what to do but keep it simple."

"Okay. Sit down next to me and try not to touch anything." There was still a brittle edge to his voice but Lander was in control of himself again and there would be no more hysterical outbursts.

They were down to about a hundred feet and were flying more or less straight and level. There was no sign of Shanghai, all Freeland could see was a lush but featureless plain which extended all the way to the far horizon.

"Where are we?" he asked.

"South-east of the Whangpoo River." Lander jerked a thumb over his shoulder. "Shanghai's behind us. I'll come round and go into Lunghwa; it's a civil airport and the natives may be a little friendlier."

"Are you saying it was the Nationalists who fired on us?"

"Had to be. The machine-gun fire was coming from the direction of their lines." Lander changed frequency, then said, "May Day, May Day, this is George X-ray 712 calling Lunghwa tower. I have a seriously wounded man on board and am coming straight in. Repeat, I have a seriously wounded man on board and am coming straight in."

"Berringer is dead," Freeland said quietly.

"You think I don't know that? I just don't want any hassle with air traffic control, assuming such an organisation still exists in Shanghai."

Slowly and very gingerly, as though he was afraid to ask too much of the C46, Lander made a wide, hundred and eighty degree turn. As he began the final approach to Lunghwa, Freeland was able to orientate himself by the railway tracks leading to Shanghai's South and West Stations. Recalling details from the aerial photographs of the city which he'd studied in Hong Kong, he identified Siccawei Creek where it joined the Whangpoo and beyond it, the Kiangwan Arsenal. And roughly five miles north-east of Lunghwa airfield was The Bund, arguably the most famous street in all Asia.

"You want to give me a helping hand?" Lander asked.

"I'll do my best."

"Okay. You see that red lever in front of your left hand? That works the landing gear; push it forward when I give the word."

"Right."

"Okay, stand by." Lander trimmed the flaps. "Now."

Freeland moved the lever and heard a reassuring thump as the undercarriage locked in place. The ground rose swiftly to meet them, then with a slight jolt they touched down on the runway. Lander started braking almost immediately and swiftly reduced their landing speed to the point where they were doing a sedate twenty when they turned off the runway to the dispersal apron. A fire tender and ambulance appeared from behind the terminal building and raced past the C46 to execute a U-turn before taking station on either side of the plane.

"Seems the US Cavalry has arrived," Lander remarked laconically. "Trouble is they can't do anything for poor old George." He cut the engines, then stared at Freeland as if he'd never seen him before. "George would still be alive if you hadn't persuaded him to fly you into Shanghai."

"I know. Was he married?"

"Nope. No surviving relatives either, so you got lucky there."

"It's still a waste of a good man."

"Yeah. I just hope your reason for coming to this goddamned place is worth it, that's all."

So do I, Freeland thought, so do I. The time was exactly 1508, precisely eight minutes later than Berringer's estimated time of arrival. It also meant he had a shade under four hours to locate Teale before the curfew was imposed.

*   *   *

There was a great deal of laughter among the guards detailed to remove the bodies, as though they found the task vastly amusing. Teale suspected their hilarity was entirely for his benefit, part of a master plan to soften him up that had begun when Colonel Li had forced him to witness the summary execution of four black marketeers in the courtyard below. Their bodies had lain there all afternoon in the hot sun; now they were being loaded on to a handcart for the final journey to Soochow Creek which was only a few short steps away.

"It is good to pay your last respects."

Teale jumped, then turned about to face Colonel Li, his heart thumping. The Chinese police officer must have been observing him through the spyhole in the door and had silently entered the room while his back was turned. He wondered how long Li had been standing there watching him.

"You have made list for me, Mr Teale?"

They had given him a few sheets of notepaper torn from an exercise book and an indelible pencil, but nothing to write on. He'd had to use the floor as a table and the perspiration had been dripping from his face like a leaky faucet so that the end result was anything but impressive. Mentally bracing himself for the display of anger which the list of names would provoke, Teale reached into his jacket pocket, brought out two stained sheets of notepaper and gave them to Colonel Li. One glance was sufficient to unleash a torrent of abuse.

"Pimps, thieves, gangsters." Li smacked his face with the notepaper, first one side then the other. There was no real force behind

26

the blows but to have to stand there and take it was a humiliating experience for Teale.

"No, Communists."

The fourth person on the list was definitely a Communist sympathiser and probably a Fifth Columnist. Either Li had overlooked his name or he'd deliberately ignored it for some reason.

"No lady here."

"What?"

"Lady with no name not on list." Li's English was incomprehensible, a sign that he was getting very angry.

"I don't know what you're talking about," Teale said, and immediately wished he hadn't been quite so hasty.

The four men who burst into the room when Li snapped his fingers didn't wait for any further orders. Before Teale knew what was happening, they had pinioned his arms and legs at the elbows, wrists, knees and ankles. Then one of them opened the window and they picked him up and threw him out head first. A long drawn-out scream of pure terror changed to one of agony as the ten foot length of rope attached to the cord binding his elbows together prevented him from falling any farther. His arms were drawn back and upwards so that both shoulders were already dislocated when Colonel Li decided to leave him hanging there in mid air, swaying gently like a pendulum gradually running out of momentum. When the guards started to haul him back into the room, the pain was such that Teale immediately blacked out. The respite lasted just as long as it took Li to empty a pitcher of water over his head.

"You tell me now about Russian lady with no name?" Li said.

"Who do you mean?"

Someone tugged on the rope viciously enough to convince Teale that his head was about to lift off.

"You no lie to me," Li told him and instructed one of the police officers to apply even more pressure to his dislocated shoulders.

A Russian lady with no name? It didn't make sense unless Li meant that she didn't have a title. But who among the thousands of White Russians who had fled the Bolshevik Revolution didn't have one? Shanghai was full of princes, princesses, grand dukes and duchesses, counts and countesses, all of them apparently related to the Romanovs. Even some of the Trotskyist Reds who had got out of Russia ahead of the Great Purge of '34 would have the more gullible believe that someone in their family had been a member of the Court of St Petersburg. Nina Burzova: the name came to him in a flash of inspiration and he tried it out on Li in a voice that was barely audible.

27

"Again. I not hear you."

"Nina Burzova."

Teale experienced a momentary twinge of guilt but it soon passed. Apart from a few snippets of information about her compatriots which she occasionally passed on, what was Nina Burzova to him? A forty-nine-year-old tart who'd arrived from Vladivostok in 1919 with the remnants of the Far Eastern White Army in one of three steamers commandeered by Lieutenant General Glebov. What few jewels she had brought with her had soon run out and she had married the first man who had proposed to her, an alcoholic Maritime insurance agent of Danish extraction. It had ended three and a half years later when the Dane had suffered a massive and ultimately fatal cerebral haemorrhage after a bender to end all benders at the Shanghai Club.

After his death, she had reverted to her maiden name of Nina Burzova which was, after all, much more alluring than the one her Danish husband had given her. And without any kind of qualifications that would have enabled her to get a job, she needed to seem alluring. Even in her younger days, Nina had never been particularly attractive but she certainly knew how to please a man in bed.

"Where she live?" Li barked.

"The Villa Mer de la Chine in Rue Clemenceau. That's off the Avenue Lafayette in what used to be the French Concession."

There was, of course, a man in her life, the latest in a small army of lovers, most of whom had paid Nina handsomely for her favours. But he didn't mention Claude Passy to Li. Passy was a man of substance and had a lot of influence. He would make the international community sit up and take notice when he returned to the villa this evening and found that his mistress had been arrested by the Nationalists. Most of the foreign correspondents who frequented the Press Club knew the police had an interrogation centre in the North Western District of the city and with any luck, Passy would find it. Although it was a long shot, the Frenchman was the best hope he had.

"We find Major Fleeman there?"

"At the villa?"

"Yes."

"If he isn't, you'll have to ask Nina Burzova where he's gone."

Teale closed his eyes, waited for that stab of agony to explode in his brain as even more pressure was applied to his dislocated shoulders, but nothing happened and to his amazement, Li left the room apparently satisfied. You clever old bastard,

Teale told himself, you really fooled him. But who the hell is Major Fleeman?

* * *

Freeland walked on, the travelling bag he was carrying getting heavier with every step, the shirt on his back dark with sweat in the humid atmosphere. Until a few days ago, the United States Air Force had maintained a military presence at Lunghwa but within the last twenty-four hours they had suddenly withdrawn all their personnel to Okinawa. No one in Hong Kong had thought to warn him that this was on the cards, and Lander too had been left in the dark. The fact remained however that the Nationalists were now running the airfield and the Army major in charge had given both of them a hard time. Amongst other things, he'd demanded to know why no flight plan had been filed, what had brought Freeland to Shanghai and who had given him permission to enter the war zone.

"Don't give me any of that fucking crap," Lander had exploded. "You're just putting up a smokescreen because you know it was one of your stupid jerk-offs who fired on us."

It had then taken the best part of a pint of bourbon which the American happened to have had in his kitbag to calm the major down and put him in a good mood. After that, he had allowed Lander to use his phone to call the American Consulate in order to make the necessary arrangements for Berringer's remains to be transported back to the States. He'd also agreed that Freeland could leave whenever he felt like it. Of course there wasn't a cab rank outside the terminal building and he had refused to give him a lift into town in a military vehicle.

The Cathay Hotel on The Bund was a good two hours' walk by the most direct route and he could easily lose his way in the Old Chinese City on the edge of the French Concession. He also wanted to catch Teale at his office before the curfew was imposed. From Lunghwa, Freeland had made for the railway, then followed the branch line over Siccawei Creek and on past Kiangwan Arsenal to Shanghai's South Station, a distance nearer to four than three miles.

No trains were running, which was hardly surprising considering the People's Liberation Army were blocking every line out of Shanghai. A freight train, half a dozen locomotives and two eight car units were waiting in the sidings outside the station. One of the locos had a head of steam up but like the rest of the rolling stock, it wasn't going anywhere. It was, however, very apparent to

Freeland that none of the Chinese waiting on the platform shared his opinion. Their optimism was founded on blissful ignorance of the true facts; their patience and calm acceptance of their lot was something he would never understand. Picking his way through the crowd, he walked out of the station.

There were no taxi cabs in the yard, only rickshaws drawn by emaciated coolies. In hiring one to convey him to the Cathay Hotel, Freeland almost caused a riot. Two US dollars, it transpired, was way above the going rate for Shanghai and represented a small fortune. The rickshaw man earned every cent; taking a short cut through the Old Chinese City, he came out on to The Bund just below Avenue Joffre. Head down, sweat dripping from his face and arms, he padded on past the Shanghai Club and the offices of the *North China Daily News* to the Cathay Hotel on the corner of Nanking Road.

Freeland had no difficulty in obtaining a room without a prior reservation. Shanghai had seen very few visitors that year and the desk clerk was able to offer him a choice of suites with marble baths and silver taps. He took the corner one on the ninth floor from where he had a commanding view of both the waterfront and the British Consulate near the mouth of Soochow Creek. In accordance with the emergency regulations then in force, he was required to leave his passport with Reception so that the military police (MPs) could check it when they visited the hotel after curfew that evening. In the space for 'occupation', the Foreign Office had insisted he should describe himself as a government official; it occurred to Freeland that if the MPs were really on the ball, they might wonder why he wasn't staying with one of the consular officials.

London had given him Teale's office and home phone numbers. Glancing at his wrist watch, Freeland saw that it was almost a quarter to six and decided that even the most go-ahead shipping agent was unlikely still to be working at that hour. He tried the home number first and, failing to get an answer, rang his office on the off chance. The engaged tone made a mockery of his assumption. The line was still busy when he tried it again some ten minutes later.

Teale's office was on the third floor of the Yangtze Insurance Building next to Jardine Matheson and Company. According to the desk clerk, it was only a five-minute walk from the hotel which meant he had enough time to have a brief word with Teale before the dusk to dawn curfew was imposed.

The Sikh night-watchman on duty in the lobby of the Yangtze Insurance Building was adamant that everyone had gone home and took some convincing that Teale was working late before he allowed him inside. Entering the nearest lift, Freeland closed the gate behind him and went on up to the third floor. If size was anything to go by, the shipping agency which Teale had founded was definitely modest, the head office consisting of just two rooms on the left-hand side of the corridor at the back of the building. The door of the nearest one had been left wide open.

The outer room was spick and span as though the office cleaners had just been in. The connecting door was locked and there was no sign of a key which struck him as odd. Even odder was the fact that Teale didn't answer when he knocked. He tried the desk in the outer office, found a paper knife in one of the drawers and used it to jemmy the lock.

The phone on Teale's desk had been taken off the hook and placed beside the instrument. The large Chubb safe standing in the right-hand corner of the room had been cleaned out. Lying on the floor in front of it was the body of a young woman.

3

His eyes never leaving her, Freeland carefully put the phone back on the hook. The girl was in her mid twenties, had shoulder-length jet black hair and a face that was more oval than round. Although her long patrician nose suggested that one of her parents had been Caucasian, the almond-shaped eyes left Freeland in no doubt that her origins were predominantly Chinese. She was roughly five feet two and he doubted if, in life, she had weighed much over eight stone, but her body had begun to swell in the heat and the wine-red cheongsam she was wearing had come apart at the seams. Her tongue was protruding because someone had strangled her with a chiffon scarf.

The Chubb safe was roughly four feet by two and a half and would have been big enough to hide a body doubled up except that the shelves weren't adjustable and couldn't be removed. There were no filing cabinets in the outer office but Freeland recalled noticing a large wooden cupboard in the left-hand corner. He went next door, saw with relief that Teale's secretary had left the key in the lock, and opened the cupboard. The shelves from chest level up were jammed with files; of those below, two were empty while the third was less than half full. Working swiftly, he transferred the files to the Chubb safe, closed it up and threw the combination. He picked up the dead girl, carried her into the adjoining room and put her down on the floor in front of the cupboard. Then he removed the bottom three shelves and stacked them on the baseboard before cramming her body into the cubbyhole he had created. After locking the cupboard, Freeland placed the key in the centre drawer of the desk and left the office.

How long had he been? Ten minutes? A quarter of an hour? Long enough at any rate for the night-watchman to wonder what had kept him. The lift was still held at the third floor; entering it, he closed the trellis gate and pressed the button for the ground floor.

The night-watchman hadn't moved from his chair in the lobby

where he could see the main entrance, the emergency exit at the rear of the building and the elevators. Freeland didn't like the suspicious way the Sikh viewed him as he walked towards the main doors.

"The telephone in Mr Teale's office must be out of order," he said casually.

"Sahib?"

Although the night-watchman spoke some English, it was clear that he didn't understand it any too well.

"I got an engaged signal when I rang his office from my hotel. That is why I thought Mr Teale was still working, but now I find he's not here."

The Sikh hadn't the faintest idea what Freeland meant but suspicion had been replaced by worry as he gained the impression that somehow he was to blame for what had happened.

"Never mind," Freeland told him. "I'll report the fault to the phone company myself. Tik hai?"

"Tik hai, Sahib."

The Sikh looked almost cheerful and was moved to salute him as he left the office block.

The Bund was practically deserted, confirmation that there were only a few minutes to go before the curfew was imposed. He walked on swiftly past the Yokohama Specie Bank and the Bank of China and reached the Cathay Hotel without further incident.

He had been ordered to bring Teale out of China and put him on a plane for London by the twenty-third of May at the latest. But that was before the PLA had cut the railway to Kweilin and Mao Sen had put Shanghai under martial law. Teale was a businessman and for personal reasons was apparently in no hurry to leave; consequently he had ignored every signal from London. His disappearance and the dead woman only complicated an already difficult situation. Without the benefit of local knowledge, he was never going to find Teale, so whether London liked it or not, he would have to get in touch with the British Consulate.

Freeland collected his key from the desk clerk, went up to his room and asked the hotel switchboard to connect him with 6912. The number rang out for some considerable time before a languid voice informed him that he was through to the duty officer.

"My name's Harry Freeland," he told the consular official. "I believe you've been warned to expect a call from me?"

"Really? I don't seem to have anything in my folder to that effect."

"I'm the Far East sales representative for ICI and I'm supposed

33

to be dining with the President of the Chamber of Commerce this evening."

"Black tie?"

"Hardly, this is strictly business. The thing is, I'm not likely to make it because of the curfew unless someone can collect me in a car with CD plates."

"Where are you staying, Mr Freeland?"

"The Cathay Hotel. The invitation says seven for seven-thirty."

"I'll have someone there in five minutes," the duty officer told him and rang off.

*　　*　　*

The someone was Frank Matthews, a hard-bitten fifty-two-year-old former Chief Inspector in the old International Settlement Police Force who had returned to Shanghai in 1946 to become the Chief Security Officer at the British Consulate. Many of the Sikh constables who had known him before the war were now employed as guards by the foreign consulates, Jardine Matheson, the Hong Kong and Shanghai Bank and Butterfield and Swire. Freeland liked him on sight.

"Where do you want to go to?" Matthews asked him as they walked out of the hotel.

"Somewhere private. I want some information."

"We'd better go to my flat; there's no sense in driving aimlessly around the city, we'll only draw attention to ourselves."

Matthews ushered him into a black Hillman Minx with CD plates which was parked outside the hotel, then got in behind the wheel and made a U-turn.

"I live in Broadway Mansions," he continued. "That's the other side of Soochow Creek in the Hongkew District."

They went on up The Bund past Jardine's, the Glen Line Building, the British Consulate and over the wrought-iron, hump-back Garden Bridge.

"Do you know a man called Howard Teale?" Freeland asked.

"From way back. He's a freelance shipping agent with a finger in every pie; has an office in the Yangtze Insurance Building."

"I went there earlier this evening looking for him and found the body of a young Chinese woman lying on the floor in front of his safe. She had been strangled."

"How long ago?"

Freeland shrugged. "It's hard to say in this heat; the corpse was bloated and the smell was pretty ripe too. I think she was killed sometime yesterday, but I'm no doctor."

"Twenty-four hours sounds about right." Matthews pulled up outside a dull red brick building and switched off the engine. "Home sweet home," he announced, "all sixteen storeys of it."

His apartment was on the twelfth floor facing the Whangpoo River. The living-room was comfortably furnished but lacked a woman's touch. Matthews' wife had never liked Shanghai and had remained behind in England when they were due to return in June 1939 after home leave. Five years later, she had been killed in an air raid when their house in Clapham had been hit by a V1. He had never remarried.

"Who let you into the Yangtze Building?" Matthews asked.

"The night-watchman, a fairly elderly Sikh, very pointed face, wall eye."

"That'll be Tara Singh. Cross his palm with a few silver dollars and he won't remember your face. I'll make a point of seeing him first thing tomorrow."

"He can be bribed?"

"Of course. Just about everyone and everything in Shanghai has a price tag." Matthews crouched in front of a low teak cabinet. "What'll you have?" he asked. "Gin, whisky, brandy or rum?"

"Whisky with a splash of soda if you have it."

"We lack for nothing except maybe ice."

"Is Teale open to bribery?"

"Probably. He certainly has to grease a few palms in his other line of business."

"You're referring to his part-ownership of the Magic City Dance Hall?"

"And the rest, the gambling dens and whorehouses." Matthews poured two very large doubles from a bottle of Teachers, added the briefest splash of soda before passing the tumbler to Freeland, then raised his own glass. "Cheers."

"Mud in your eye," Freeland responded.

"I tried to nail Teale before the war when I was an honest-to-God copper, but he had friends in high places. Seems good old Howard was supplying British Intelligence with a lot of solid information which his girls obtained from the Jap soldiers they bedded." He glanced sideways at Freeland. "What's he doing these days – spying on the Nationalists as well as supplying London with the names of potential Fifth Columnists?" A broad grin appeared on his face. "You don't have to answer that."

Freeland smiled. "I wasn't going to. What I can tell you is that whoever killed the girl also cleared out the safe in his office. Any idea what it might have contained?"

"Money he's made on the side, stacks of it in US dollars." Matthews took another gulp of his neat whisky. "Mind you, that's pure guesswork but I'd bet a month's salary I'm right. One of the Chinese gangsters he rubs shoulders with probably did it, drilled the safe then killed the girl to shut her up."

"The safe hadn't been forced; someone who knew the combination opened it for the killer."

"Well, I suppose the girl might know the combination if Teale really trusted her but it would be out of character."

"Teale wasn't at home when I rang his house."

"When was this?"

"Roughly half an hour before the curfew," said Freeland.

"That doesn't sound too good. It could be your killer wasn't on his jack; maybe some of his friends kidnapped Teale and forced him to disclose the combination to the safe. Then the killer picked up his secretary because he needed the girl to get him into the Yangtze Insurance Building in broad daylight without arousing anyone's suspicion."

"I have to find Teale."

"Then you'd better look for him in the mortuaries, Harry, because if I'm right, that's where he'll be. Once they had that combination, he was of no further use to them."

"I think you're being a little pessimistic," Freeland told him. "I mean, if he is dead and his body had been found, surely you would have heard about it by now? Wouldn't the Chinese authorities notify every foreign consulate in Shanghai that they had an unidentified male Caucasian on their hands?"

"They might have done so a few months ago, now I'm not so sure. Chiang's administration was never noted for its efficiency at the best of times but with every senior official high-tailing it to Taiwan, it has reached a new low."

Matthews held his whisky up to the light, studied it thoughtfully as though he had just spotted some minute foreign body in the amber-coloured fluid. "On the other hand, Teale may have gone into hiding. He's not much to look at but the women seem to go for him. The latest girlfriend is Dominga Zaldivar, a Filipino hostess from the Orange Grove which is a taxi dance-hall cum knocking shop."

"Do you know where this Dominga girl lives?"

"She has a flat in Park Road near the North Station." Matthews swallowed the rest of his whisky and left the glass on top of the cabinet; Freeland assumed they were about to leave and did the same. "If the military police should stop us," Matthews continued, "we're on our way to dine with the Dwyers. He's a kingpin in the legal department of Butterfield and Swire."

From Broadway Mansions, Matthews drove towards Garden Bridge, then turned sharp right into a road that ran parallel with Soochow Creek. Although it was a warm, humid evening, he steadfastly refused to lower the car windows. The waterway was home for the boat people and the stench was apparently overpowering.

"Not so long ago, you could walk the best part of a mile from one boat to another without getting your feet wet but now, most of the vessels have gone. Give it a few more days and the Creek will be as deserted as the Whangpoo River. I can remember when there were freighters and tramp steamers moored bow to stern the entire length of The Bund and there was a whole army of coolies moving cargoes in and out of the godowns. Now there's hardly anything coming up river from the port of Woosung."

The jeep came out of a side road, cut in front of the Hillman and forced them to stop. There were four MPs; the officer in charge of the patrol was carrying an M3A1 sub-machine-gun while the two NCOs with him were armed with .30 calibre Garand semi-automatic rifles. The driver stayed in the vehicle where Freeland couldn't see him.

Matthews got out of the car and went forward to meet them. The officer was in a truculent mood and started to bawl him out before he had a chance to say a word in their defence. Somehow Matthews managed to remain unruffled even when one of the NCOs jabbed him in the ribs with his rifle after he had unintentionally turned his back on the officer to point out the CD plates on the Hillman. Gradually, the situation became less heated and finally cooled altogether when he persuaded the Chinese to accept a small gift. After that, it was smiles and handshakes all round.

"What did you give them?" Freeland asked when he returned to their vehicle after the jeep had driven off.

"Four silver dollars, which was a lot more than I wanted to hand over."

"I'd say that was cheap at the price. I certainly wouldn't care to cross swords with them; they're a mean looking bunch and well equipped too."

"Appearances are deceptive. The Yanks may have given Chiang Kai-shek billions of dollars in military aid but his army doesn't want to fight and the hardware's ending up in the hands of the PLA. Whole divisions have gone across to Mao with their weapons." Matthews took one hand off the steering wheel and rubbed the thumb across all four fingers. "All he had to do was find out how much it would take to buy the Commanding General."

The treachery had started at the very top with the Generalissimo himself. Towards the end of 1948, following a disastrous campaign in the north, it had dawned on Chiang Kai-shek that he was going to lose the war. Determined that no one should blame him, he had resigned from Head of State, appointed Vice-President Tsung-jen as his successor and had retired to his magnificent house at the seaside resort of Fenghwa. The transfer of power had been a complete sham; Chiang had retained his grip on the navy and air force and the best army divisions had been transferred to Taiwan together with their families. His one setback had been the defection of the captain and crew of the *Chungking*, flagship of the Nationalist navy. The air force however had restored face, sinking the 6-inch gun cruiser while she lay at anchor.

"Of course it takes a lot of money to keep an army, navy and air force sweet. So he did the only thing he could and robbed the Bank of China."

"That's one way of solving a financial crisis," Freeland said drily.

According to the story he had heard in London, the bullion had been carried off in a rusty old freighter that had been moored alongside The Bund directly opposite the Bank of China. With the connivance of the Board of Directors, the vaults had been emptied in the dead of night by scores of coolies. Each man had padded back and forth across the broad avenue of The Bund bowed down by the weight of the gold and silver ingots in the two panniers strung from a bamboo pole they carried over their shoulders. By the time they had finished their labours, China was broke.

"This is it," Matthews said and pulled up outside a small four-storey apartment house breasted in grey stone.

Dominga Zaldivar's flat was on the second floor overlooking the street. The building didn't run to a lift and the communal area looked in need of a face-lift.

Teale's latest girlfriend was under twenty-five, had a voluptuous figure and wore four-inch heels to make herself appear taller than she was. Her finger and toe nails were painted a deep purple to match the flamboyant silk dress which hugged her like an extra skin.

"Mind if we come in?" Matthews asked her.

"Yes."

Terse, cold, almost hostile. Freeland wondered if her apparent dislike of Matthews was reflected in her eyes but they were hidden behind a pair of dark sunglasses.

"All right," Matthews said affably, "just tell Howard I'm here and would like to have a word with him."

"You have come to the wrong place," Dominga said and started to close the door only to discover that he had his foot in the way.

"You don't mind if we take a look, do you?"

The flat consisted of one double bedroom, a kitchenette, living-room with dining area and a combined bathroom and lavatory. There was no sign of Teale.

"When did you last see Howard?" Matthews asked.

"Saturday . . . no, Sunday. He came to dinner."

"And stayed the night."

"Why not? He is my boyfriend, we marry soon, he tole me so." Her accent was thick and she couldn't get her tongue around the 'd'.

"If you believe that, little lady, you'll believe anything." Matthews reached out and removed her sunglasses and gave a low whistle. The left cheekbone was bruised and swollen, the eye closed to a slit. "Who did that?"

"Is no business of yours."

Dominga tried to grab the sunglasses from Matthews but only succeeded in knocking them out of his hand. She bent down to retrieve them, then groaned aloud as she straightened up, one arm hugging her stomach.

"Howard really gave you a beating, didn't he? I wonder what you'd done to deserve that? Could it be that you lied to him about the number of clients you've entertained since the curfew was imposed?"

"Go to hell."

"No, you're right. Howard wouldn't dream of hurting you, but some of the people he rubs shoulders with wouldn't give it a second thought. And at least one of them came here looking for him. Right?"

"Why ask if you already know the answer?"

"I'm only guessing," Matthews told her. "I'd like to hear it from you."

Dominga shrugged. "What is there to tell? They wanted to know where Howard had gone. I said I didn't know, so they beat me up."

"They?"

"Two Chinese. I never saw them before."

"When did this happen?"

39

"Day before yesterday in the morning. I phone Howard soon as they go but he not at home or in office."

"Did you phone his secretary?" Freeland asked.

"Wha . . a . . at?" Dominga turned to face him, her jaw sagging.

"The girl who worked for Mr Teale."

"I doan know her name."

"That would certainly make it difficult," Matthews said and caught Freeland's eye. "I don't think there's anything else we want to ask Miss Zaldivar, is there, Harry?"

The sudden use of his first name in front of the girl momentarily threw Freeland, but he caught the drift and shook his head. If they questioned Dominga all night she wouldn't admit to knowing what had happened to Teale.

"Of course she's lying about the secretary," Matthews said as they got into the Hillman. "Dominga shopped her out of jealousy because she suspected Howard was having a nibble on the side. The two Chinese caught Teale in bed with his secretary on Wednesday morning and persuaded him to give them the combination of the Chubb safe. Then first thing yesterday, one of them goes to the Yangtze Insurance Building with the girl while the other stays behind with Howard. They killed them both, the girl as soon as the safe had been cleaned out, Teale later on."

"Maybe."

Matthews started up, made a U-turn on Park Road and headed back the way they had come.

"Why only maybe?"

"We're still a body short."

"That may still be the case after I've checked the mortuaries tomorrow morning. This is a big city, they could have hidden Teale's body anywhere."

"I don't believe it happened quite the way you think," Freeland said. "Oh, Dominga told them where to find Teale's secretary all right but I've a hunch he'd already disappeared before they started looking for him. Suppose you were Teale's silent partner and one fine morning you heard on the grapevine that he had failed to show up at the office and then you discover he's not at home. Wouldn't you be worried in case he'd done a bunk with a lot of your money?"

"All right, Harry, you tell me where Teale is hiding himself."

"He isn't. I think he's under arrest."

"Never."

"Why not? When General Mao Sen was appointed Chief of

Police, he was instructed to clean up the city, and Teale is simply just another racketeer to him."

"There is that possibility." Matthews turned right, went over Garden Bridge and drove along The Bund. "Do you know where the British Consulate is?" he asked presently.

"Yes, we just passed it back there by the bridge."

"Well, I suggest you meet me there tomorrow morning around eight thirty and we'll brief Giles Caunter, the Assistant Consul General. If the Nationalists are holding Teale, he's the one man I know in Shanghai who can persuade Mao Sen to let him go. Thereafter, it's your problem to get him out of China."

It always had been, Freeland thought.

"Any idea how you're going to do it?"

By air, provided he could find a way to keep Joe Lander grounded at Lunghwa until he was ready to leave. Failing that, he would have to borrow a launch and make his way down river to the conflux with the Yangtze beyond Woosung where the cruiser *Belfast*, which had replaced the damaged *London*, was anchored with other British and American naval vessels.

"I haven't the faintest idea," he lied.

"You'd best give it some thought." Matthews pulled up outside the Cathay Hotel, then half turned to face him. "One other friendly word of advice, don't leave your passport with the desk clerk any longer than you have to. There are literally thousands of stateless people in Shanghai who would pay a small fortune to get hold of a British one."

But no one, it seemed, was interested in acquiring his. When Freeland went to collect his room key, the desk clerk returned his passport and informed him that the police had checked the registration cards while he was away.

*   *   *

Nina Burzova was forty-nine, but even those who knew her date of birth found it hard to believe. There wasn't an ounce of spare flesh on her trim figure, no varicose veins disfigured her legs and her bust was as firm as it had been when she was a young woman. She had never been to a plastic surgeon for a face-lift, nor had she any need to. What few lines there were on her neck were always concealed by a high collar or a silk scarf. It was this ageless quality and her exceptional good taste in clothes that had first attracted Claude Passy.

This evening, for instance, Nina was wearing Christian Dior's New Look, a simple mid-calf-length dress in black taffeta which

Han Son Loh in Yates Road had faithfully copied from a photo-graph in *Vogue* magazine. Chic, exciting, alluring were just three of the adjectives which sprang to mind as he sat there admiring her across the dinner table. Françoise and the children had made him an old man at the age of forty-three; installing Nina in the Villa Mer de la Chine after his wife and family had returned home to Lille on the advice of the French Consul General, was the best thing he had ever done. Nina made him feel young, vibrant and alive again. She flattered him, inflated his ego and gratified his sexual desires in a way that Françoise had never been able or willing to do. Moreover, like most civilised people, she was able to converse in French albeit with an unusual though engaging accent. There was, however, a price to pay; in return for her favours, Nina expected him to procure a passport and identity card for her. It was something she never allowed him to forget.

"Did you have any luck today, *chéri?*" she asked.

Passy guessed what was coming and tried to steer her off the subject. "Business is a little slack at the moment," he said obtusely, "but it's bound to pick up soon."

"That isn't what I meant, Claude, and you know it."

"The English have a saying – no news is good news."

"They are renowned for their platitudes," Nina retorted. "I, on the other hand, am only interested in facts."

Passy sighed. "The matter of your passport and identity card is being attended to in so far as the necessary papers have been sent to Paris. Of course, we're in the hands of the bureaucrats and they won't be rushed, but there is absolutely nothing to worry about."

It sounded glib, even to his ears, and he felt decidedly uncom-fortable under her steadfast gaze.

"I hope you are right, Claude. I certainly have no wish to be here when the PLA marches in."

"They are not ogres, Nina."

"Pah, you do not know the Reds as I do."

"I tell you they will not make trouble for us; they need our manufactured goods and machine tools if China is to recover from twelve years of continuous warfare."

The British were saying exactly the same thing, but they had four hundred million pounds worth of investments at stake in Shanghai and their optimism was largely based on wishful thinking.

"So why did you send Françoise and the children home?"

Because they did not work for the Compagnie Delacroix and, unlike him, they had not been ordered to stay on by head office.

Why else would anyone remain in Shanghai if they weren't obliged to do so? But he couldn't tell Nina that.

"Françoise's mother is seriously ill, so I encouraged her to return home." He smiled at Nina longingly, then lied in his teeth. "I wanted to make it possible for you and I to live together."

"I adore you, Claude."

"And I you."

She took a banana from the fruit bowl on the dinner table, peeled the tip slowly and licked the exposed portion; then, her eyes never leaving his, she took the banana into her mouth. It was, he knew, what she intended to do to him and he could feel himself growing erect.

The doorbell rang and presently he heard voices in the hall. Moments later, an officer and two soldiers stormed into the dining-room, driving his houseboy ahead of them at gun point. In a voice that was more muted than firm, Passy demanded to know what they thought they were doing.

"This woman is Burzova," the officer said, pointing to Nina. "And you are Major Fleeman, the English spy. You will come with us."

Passy was about to argue the point but then one of the soldiers pointed a rifle at his chest and fed a round into the breech and he thought better of it.

4

They had carried him down to the cellar, untied the ropes binding his wrists, elbows, knees and ankles and had then dumped him unceremoniously on to a horse-hair mattress on the floor. Some time later, a medic had reset his dislocated shoulders, inflicting so much pain on him in the process that Teale had passed out and damned nearly choked to death on his own vomit. The sour taste was still there in his mouth along with the mucus coating his tongue which he supposed was caused by dehydration. More than anything else, he wanted a drink of water but he couldn't raise his voice above a croak and the guards went out of their way to ignore him.

He was about to make one more attempt to attract their attention when the door opened and two men he'd never seen before walked into the room. No word was spoken; seizing Teale by the arms, they hauled him to his feet and took him upstairs to the same interrogation room where he had first encountered Colonel Li.

There was another prisoner waiting to be questioned, a woman in a black taffeta dress who stood facing the wall on the far side of the room opposite the door. Her wrists were handcuffed behind her back and they had blindfolded her with a shell dressing. She was mewling to herself like a frightened kitten and her whole body was trembling.

"Do you know who this is?" Li demanded.

Teale nodded; the auburn hair was unmistakable. "Nina Burzova," he mumbled.

"Louder."

"Nina Burzova."

"She spy for you. Right, Mr Teale?"

If Nina didn't know before who had betrayed her, she did now, Teale thought. "Only on the Communists," he said aloud.

"I am not understanding."

Well, of course Li didn't understand; he had deliberately misled the pint-size colonel in the hope that Claude Passy would raise Cain when the police attempted to arrest his mistress. Unfortunately, the Frenchman had obviously allowed them to detain Nina Burzova. He wondered why they had blindfolded her. Was it meant to frighten her or was it simply that Li didn't want Nina to know where she was being held? Teale hoped it was the latter; what she didn't know, she couldn't tell and therefore there was a chance that the police would eventually release her. But unless he gave Nina reason to be grateful, she would leave him to rot here.

"Why you no answer me?"

"Madame Burzova is on our side," Teale began. "She is not a Red . . ."

"You lie, this woman is Russian."

"And she hates Stalin . . ."

He never saw Li signal the guards to hit him, only felt an excruciating stab of pain when one of them punched him in the kidney.

"You speak only when I say," Li shouted. "You tell me I find woman at Villa Mer de la Chine where she meet other spy, Major Fleeman. You tell me now what he look like."

Teale hesitated. He could describe Passy and pretend he was the man Li wanted but that would be self-defeating. "I can't," he said, "I haven't met him."

"You make me believe he already in Shanghai but he only arrive yesterday and staying at Cathay Hotel. Only not calling himself Major. What you say now?"

"Nothing."

Of all the answers Teale could have given, he had unerringly picked the worst. A chopping blow felled him like a tree and almost broke his neck.

*   *   *

The large fan suspended from the ceiling whirred ineffectually, creating a warm, humid breeze that merely ruffled the papers on Giles Caunter's desk without lowering the temperature in the Assistant Consul General's office. Freeland was in shirtsleeves, so too was Matthews; Caunter, however, clearly felt that as an official representative of His Majesty King George VI, he would be letting the side down if he removed his tie and linen jacket. Instead, he was reduced to fanning himself with a Panama hat while gazing longingly at the telephone. So far, they had learned that Teale had not been admitted to hospital, nor was he lying in one of the city's mortuaries; now they waited to hear if he was being held in police custody.

45

"Do you think Mao Sen will admit it?" Matthews asked.

"I don't see why not," Caunter said. "After all, he won't lose any face by doing so; I've made sure of that."

When Caunter had rung General Mao Sen to report Teale's disappearance, he had practically invited the Chief of Police to search the Yangtze Insurance Building from top to bottom. He had, of course, taken steps beforehand to satisfy himself that there was no way the Consulate could be linked with the murder of the young Chinese girl. Although no one had been indelicate enough to mention the word bribery, Matthews had left him in no doubt that the night-watchman, Tara Singh, had not agreed to keep his mouth shut for purely altruistic reasons.

"If Mao Sen needs an excuse, he can always claim the police are holding Teale on suspicion of murder." Caunter dragged his eyes away from the telephone. "Don't you agree, Major?"

"Oh, absolutely."

Freeland was slightly taken aback. He had dropped the rank the day he had walked out of the Demob Centre in Woolwich dressed in the utility grey pinstripe a grateful nation had given him in exchange for his part-worn battledress. To MI6 and the Foreign Office he was plain Mister and a minor official like Giles Caunter wouldn't have access to his Army Record of Service. He wondered who had told Caunter about his background and why.

"You're a dark horse," Matthews said. "Fancy keeping that to yourself."

"I was strictly a wartime soldier; twenty-five-year-old majors like me were ten a penny."

SOE had given him the crown in 1944, shortly before he was sent into the Chartres area, under the mistaken impression that the French Forces of the Interior were more likely to take notice of a major than they would a junior captain. Nothing could have been farther from the truth. The French were divided amongst themselves, one faction looking to de Gaulle, the Communists to Moscow. The Almighty might have persuaded them to work in concert but unfortunately for Freeland, the Resistance did not believe that God was an Englishman even though his mother was French.

"Of course, if Mao Sen is holding Teale, it's by no means certain he will agree to release him." Caunter stopped fanning himself to gaze thoughtfully at Freeland. "In that event, will London bring pressure to bear on Chiang Kai-shek?"

"I don't know, it depends how badly they want to see him."

MI6, the Secret Intelligence Service, were definitely anxious to lay their hands on Teale; whether his superiors could carry the Foreign Office and the Labour Government with them was another matter.

"In that case," Caunter said grimly, "I doubt whether Mr Attlee will even clear his throat."

The phone rang in a half-hearted manner, making an intermittent burring noise as if there was a fault on the line. Caunter lifted the earpiece off the hook and drew the instrument nearer. He listened in silence, punctuating the one-sided conversation with the occasional grunt before eventually holding forth in fluent Mandarin. Freeland didn't understand a word he said, but his manner seemed amicable enough.

"That was General Mao Sen," Caunter said, replacing the receiver. "He is adamant that the police are not holding Teale; however, he is not so sure about Military Intelligence. Naturally the army denies they have detained any Europeans."

"So how does the General propose to resolve his doubts?" Freeland asked.

"By making enquiries. I suggest you contact me again between three and four o'clock this afternoon by which time I may have some news for you."

He thought Caunter was right to stress the word 'may'. The army wasn't answerable to Mao Sen and he would have to take whatever story they gave him on trust. Conversely, if the General was lying, Caunter could hardly go to Military Intelligence and ask them to investigate the Chief of Police. There was, however, no point in making an issue of it with Caunter. Instead, Freeland thanked him for all his help, said he would be in touch later on in the day and then left. Matthews followed him out into the compound.

"Tell me something, Harry," he said, "why do I have this feeling that you're not about to sit back and wait for enquiries to be made through the usual channels?"

"Because you know as well as I do that Caunter isn't going to achieve anything. Teale's either been kidnapped by one of his business associates or else he's being held in one of Mao Sen's interrogation centres. Broadway Mansions is home for practically every foreign correspondent in Shanghai; if I can't find someone who can tell me where to look for Howard Teale, they've no right to call themselves newspapermen."

"You should talk to Phil Ryan, assistant bureau chief of Associated Press. If anyone's got an ear to the ground, it's him."

"Where do I find Ryan?" Freeland asked.

"Give me five minutes and I'll run him to ground for you."

"Can you provide me with transport and an interpreter?"

"Not from the Consulate; we can't afford to be involved in any cloak and dagger work. But I know a cab driver who speaks pretty good English. His name's Henry Wang and he'll drive you around all day for half a dozen tins of strawberry jam."

"That's one item I forgot to pack," Freeland said drily.

"Be my guest," Matthews told him. "I'm up to my ears in tins of the stuff."

*   *   *

Until a few hours ago, all Passy had known about the Central Police Station was the fact that it was situated in Hankow Road which itself was midway between the racecourse and what was erroneously called The Country Club. In all the time he had lived in Shanghai, he'd never had any occasion to visit Police Headquarters and he wished he could have remained in ignorance of its precise location.

Ten years ago, no Chinese police officer would have dared to arrest a European. Ten years ago, the International Settlement had been an independent City State; until Pearl Harbour, even the Japanese forces occupying Shanghai had respected that Convention. But to please their ally, Chiang Kai-shek, Churchill and Roosevelt had signed away their Extra Territorial Rights in 1943 and France had been forced to follow suit shortly afterwards. When Passy, and other Europeans like him, had returned to Shanghai after the war, they had been shocked to discover they no longer owned the properties which had been theirs from time immemorial. The International Community no longer had their own police force and Courts of Justice; they were now subject to Chinese law administered by a corrupt police force and an equally corrupt judiciary. Now it was possible for Claude Passy to find himself incarcerated in a tiny cell with three coolies, a rickshaw boy, a waiter and an eighteen-year-old homosexual.

He hadn't the faintest idea of what had happened to Nina Burzova. The soldiers had bundled them into a prison van that had been parked outside his villa. A warder inside the vehicle had then put them into separate cells and thereafter he had neither seen nor heard her. The arresting officer had failed to put in an appearance since their arrival at the Central Police Station and, although Passy could speak the Shanghai dialect perfectly, the night-duty sergeant had pretended not to understand him when he'd demanded the right to telephone his lawyer.

He had spent a miserable night cooped up in a badly ventilated cell with six foul-smelling men, all of whom now looked as if they were getting ready to slit his throat from ear to ear. Their motives varied; the coolies and the rickshaw boy had already made it clear that they refused to believe he'd given them all the foreign currency there was, while the waiter probably hated him on principle. The eighteen-year-old homosexual might kill him out of pique, deeply angered that his friendly overtures had been rebuffed.

Deliverance came in the shape of a warder in plimsolls and a loose-fitting blue uniform who unlocked his cell and beckoned him to come out. Passy didn't ask him what he wanted nor where he was being taken. Anything was preferable to spending another minute in the company of drug addicts, thieves and perverts, his throat gagging from the foul smell of urine and excrement coming from the bucket which served as their latrine. Still holding a handkerchief to his nose and mouth, he followed the warder along a dark corridor leading to the charge room.

Pierre Weygand, the passport control officer at the French Consulate, was the last person he expected to see. Tears of relief welled in his eyes and it was some moments before he was able to find his voice.

"How did you know . . .?" he began.

"The authorities told me." Weygand indicated a military policeman whose khaki drill looked as though it had just been starched and pressed. "It seems they mistook you for someone else. The captain here was most apologetic that the error wasn't discovered sooner."

"Not as sorry as I am."

"I can understand your anger, Claude. I'd feel the same way in your position."

"Am I free to go now?" Passy asked impatiently.

"The captain would like you to sign a release note first."

"A what?"

"A mere formality." Weygand smiled nervously. "They simply want an undertaking from you that you will not seek redress for wrongful arrest. It's a small enough thing to ask."

"What do you take me for? A simpleton? Of course I'm not signing a disclaimer. These people entered my house without authority, manhandled one of my servants, held me up at gun point and then, without specifying any charges, took both of us into custody . . ." Passy broke off, it suddenly occurring to him that he was not the only aggrieved party. "What about Nina Burzova?" he demanded. "Has she been released yet?"

"I don't know, Claude." Weygand gesticulated helplessly, waving his hands as though they were flippers.

"Then it's about time we found out." Passy rounded on the military police captain and addressed the same question to him in both Mandarin and the local Shanghai dialect.

"Madame Nina Burzova is a Russian spy," the captain informed him solemnly. "She will be tried by a military tribunal."

"I've never heard anything quite so ridiculous in all my life."

"Claude!" Weygand plucked his sleeve and drew him aside. "Claude, listen to me," he murmured earnestly. "We live in difficult times and Nina Burzova is not our responsibility. She is not a French citizen."

"She is a very dear friend . . ."

"Be careful, Claude, we don't know what evidence they have against her. You don't want them to get the impression that you're an accomplice, do you?"

"Of course not."

"Then for heaven's sake sign the release note and let's get out of here before they change their minds. We can make enquiries about Madame Burzova after we've moved you into the Consulate where you will be under diplomatic protection."

Weygand was right, Passy decided. Borrowing a pen from the passport control officer, he signed the release note with a flourish. It wasn't until they were outside on the pavement that he realised one of his fellow prisoners must have relieved him of his own gold-plated fountain pen while he was dozing fitfully.

*   *   *

Phil Ryan was a small, chunky man with a monk's fringe of greying hair except for two long brown strands which he carefully trained across his bald scalp. He was sixty-three years old and his love affair with China had begun in 1923 when he'd arrived in Shanghai and had survived the death of his first wife from amoebic dysentery and the break up of his second marriage. He had not been back to Portland, Maine in twenty-six years and virtually no trace of his American accent remained. Home was now the Broadway Mansions and the Associated Press (AP) Office on Nanking Road.

"You must have known Howard Teale long before the war?" Freeland said.

"Not really. He arrived in '36; I moved to Chungking a year later to cover the Sino-Japanese conflict. The Bureau decided there was no point in my staying on in Shanghai after the Nipponese army had captured Nanking. Teale was just a lowly shipping clerk when I first met him; used to spend all his free time in the dance halls and night clubs on Bubbling Well Road. Towards the end of the month when he was waiting for the next pay cheque, he'd use the one dollar whores in the old Chinese city or the sampan girls who lived among the boat people on Soochow Creek. One thing you could say for Teale, he wasn't what you'd call fussy." Ryan left his desk and walked over to the bookcase next to the water cooler to help himself to a second cup of coffee from the percolator that was gently simmering on a two-ring hob. "Can I get you another?" he asked.

"No thanks."

"So where did you meet Teale?"

"I haven't, I only know of him."

Ryan glanced at him sideways. "They tell me your King George gave him a decoration of some kind."

"The British Empire Medal."

"Yeah, that's right. Back in '46, there was a story going the rounds in Shanghai that months in advance of Pearl Harbour, Teale had warned the British government that the Japanese were planning to invade Hong Kong and Malaya." Ryan returned to his desk and sat down. "Seems he was on first name terms with half the officers from the Jap army units occupying the Chinese Quarter and they tipped him off. For his part, Teale is supposed to have supplied the Nipponese with confidential information about the British-owned business corporations in the city. Of course it's probably a malicious rumour; all the same, there's no getting away from the fact that when the Imperial Army marched into the International Settlement in December '41, they were accompanied by a busload of Japanese businessmen. Ask anyone who was with the Hong Kong and Shanghai Bank in those days and they will tell you the Nips knew exactly what sort of operation they were taking over."

According to Ryan, not one of the old China hands had been interned with Teale. From this it had been inferred that he had been singled out for special treatment and had spent the war years in comparative luxury. The award of the BEM had put a stop to the slander even though the medal had been sent to him by registered post instead of the usual presentation ceremony.

"But you didn't come here to gossip about Teale, did you?" Ryan said.

"You know he's vanished?"

"Yeah, Matthews told me. He thinks Teale has been arrested by Mao Sen's people."

"And Frank told me that you might know the whereabouts of

the special interrogation centres General Mao Sen has established."

"How come the British Consulate doesn't have that information?"

"Presumably because you've got sources they haven't," Freeland said. "Local reporters, police informants and the like."

"You hear all kinds of rumours sitting at this desk and most of them turn out to be a pack of lies." Ryan helped himself to a cigarette from the half-empty packet of Camels he'd left in his pending tray. "Is Teale a Commie sympathiser?" he asked without any kind of preamble.

"Not that I'm aware of."

"Yeah, well, even if he is, I doubt he would find too many fellow-travellers to sympathise with amongst the indigenous population. Chiang Kai-shek slaughtered most of the Communists in this city when he moved against them in 1927. It was a bloody massacre; thousands upon thousands of people were shot and a fair percentage of them had never heard of the Manifesto. If the purge had been carried out by the Nazis, the Fascists or Stalin's NKVD, it would have been condemned in no uncertain terms by every newspaper in the Free World. But even in those far off days, Washington supported Chiang Kai-shek which is why all you heard was a deafening silence."

"So what are they doing with the survivors and the new blood?"

"For what it's worth, Communists and racketeers are taken to the interrogation centre on Hongkew Road West; that's about five blocks beyond the North Railroad station and adjoins Soochow Creek. The lesser fry are reputed to end up in the Municipal Jail on Ward Road."

"Thanks."

Freeland waited for the inevitable question, the one that had been on the tip of Ryan's tongue from the moment he had walked into the assistant bureau chief's office. Matthews had merely said that Teale was not to be found at his office, at home or in any of his usual haunts. He had not said why Freeland was looking for him.

"Are you a member of the diplomatic corps, Mr Freeland?" Ryan asked casually.

"No, I'm a civil servant attached to the War Crimes Commission."

The best and most believable lies were always the simple ones that needed very little embellishment. By repeating the allegation that Teale had received special treatment during the time he was interned by the Japanese, Ryan had shown just how receptive he already was to any further innuendoes.

"Is he a star witness, or what?"

"There are some questions we'd like him to answer," Freeland said carefully.

"Are you planning to visit these hot spots all by yourself?"

"I've got a driver outside who knows his way around and speaks pretty good English."

"Guys like Colonel Li will eat him for breakfast."

"Who's Colonel Li?"

"General Mao Sen's hatchet man, runs all the interrogation centres and is a real mean son of a bitch. He won't take any notice of you, or the Consul General or God Almighty himself."

"What about the Commander-in-Chief of the South China Front? I've got an open letter from him instructing whoever it may concern to afford me every assistance."

"Canton is a long way from here." Ryan scratched the prickly heat on his throat. "Your best bet is to try the letter out on General Chen Ta-chin, the Garrison Commander, before you go anywhere near Li. His tactical headquarters is on the Hungjao Road about four miles from the airfield. The way things are these days, it shouldn't take you above twenty minutes to get there."

Freeland knew what he meant. Six million people lived in Shanghai and it used to be said that you could bump into half the population in the time it took you to walk from one end of Nanking Road to the other. Now the street was practically deserted by Shanghai standards, the trucks, buses and ox carts requisitioned by the army, the hawkers, shopkeepers and clerks drafted in their thousands to dig the biggest anti-tank ditch in the world. Apparently, the Nationalist Generals had overlooked the fact that there were no armoured formations in the PLA.

*   *   *

The racecourse off Nanking Road had been the penultimate resting place for the dead before they were shipped back to the States ever since Chiang Kai-shek had decided that gambling was bad for the Chinese and had banned the sport of kings. Late yesterday afternoon, Lander had taken Berringer to one of the ornate grandstands which now served as the American mortuary. Although the melancholy task of recovering the bodies of 14th Air Force personnel killed in action during the Second World War had virtually been completed, a large stock of zinc-lined coffins remained. The paperwork was the one real problem Lander had encountered; knowing

53

only that Berringer's next-of-kin lived in Houston, he'd had to get their full address from the records held by the head office of Civil Air Transport in Shanghai. By the time he had sorted that out, the curfew was only twenty minutes off and it was too late to return to Lunghwa airfield.

He had spent the night in the Park Hotel and had risen late after holding a solitary wake for George C. Berringer. Aspirins washed down by several cups of coffee had cured his hangover and by mid morning Head Office had arranged for the grain to be unloaded and had located a spare compass at Kiangwin airfield north of the Whangpoo River. Head Office had also billed the British Consulate for the charter flight from Kweilin to Shanghai which was another thing that made him feel a little better about the whole lousy business.

His slow fuse began to burn again when he got back to Lunghwa. The Gooney Bird was still there on the dispersal apron but the army had parked two GMC trucks in the way, one slap in front of the nose, the other hard up against the tail of the aeroplane. Just for good measure, they had also deflated the tyres.

5

The Best Years of our Lives was showing at the Roxie movie theatre and several hundred men from the Nationalist garrison were at the head of the queue waiting for the doors to open at one thirty. If Freeland wanted any further evidence that the army would fold the moment the PLA moved on the city, he found it in abundance as they drove out to General Chen Ta-chin's tactical headquarters on the Hungjao Road. The Garrison Commander had decreed that all places of entertainment were to admit off-duty personnel free of charge, and the troops were also allowed to travel anywhere they liked on public transport without paying. The soldiers expected the brothel keepers and restaurant owners to do likewise, and it seemed to Freeland that half the army was out on the town.

To satisfy their desire for creature comforts, the staff had commandeered most of the better hotels and apartment houses. So far, they had left the Cathay Hotel alone but that happy state of affairs was unlikely to last much longer. The Shanghai Club, which was reputed to have the longest bar in the world and resembled a Roman temple with its marble floor and Delphic colonnades, had already been taken over as a rest and recuperation centre, as had the Country Club. The walking wounded had of course been left to fend for themselves.

"Maskee." Henry Wang shook his head. "Maskee," he repeated in the twangy drawl he'd picked up from the American missionaries who'd taught him to speak English. "You know what that means, sir?"

"No, I haven't heard the expression before."

"It's Shanghaiese for things can only get better."

"I doubt they can get any worse," Freeland said.

He was wrong there. As they made their way along the North Boundary Street of the old Chinese Quarter to pick up the Hungjao Road, they passed two elderly men, their hair plaited in traditional pigtails, kneeling by the kerbside in front of a group of soldiers.

Glancing back over his shoulder, Freeland saw a slovenly-dressed NCO shoot both men in the back with an automatic pistol while casually smoking a cigarette.

"Jesus Christ, what were they supposed to have done?"

"Search me." Henry Wang shrugged his shoulders. "Perhaps the man who shot them was settling an old score. I think they owned the tailor's shop back there and it could be they refused to make him a suit for nothing. Of course the army will claim they were spies or racketeers."

Freeland went through his pockets, found a packet of cigarettes and lit one. He rarely smoked but he needed to steady his nerves and he didn't possess a hip flask. It was no use telling himself that anyone who had spent the last fourteen months of the war in Flossenburg concentration camp had seen worse sights, the cold-blooded murder of one human being by another would always sicken him.

"Not much farther now," Henry Wang said as they left the old walled city behind them.

"Good."

Freeland noticed that the nearer they got to the front, the more businesslike the troops appeared. There was, however, more to fighting than building defence works and chopping down trees to provide overhead cover for the slit trenches and better fields of fire. The selection and maintenance of the aim, offensive action, and the maintenance of morale were the three most important principles of war; in neglecting all three, the Nationalist High Command had ensured they would be defeated.

"I reckon this must be the General's headquarters," Henry Wang said. "It looks a swell enough place."

The villa was set in about four acres and in happier days had obviously belonged to a middle-ranking Taipan from one of the big trading houses. Slit trenches had been dug in the lawns bordering the gravel drive leading to the imposing front entrance, while the camphor and flame trees had been felled so that their branches could be lopped and used to camouflage the command vehicles which were parked higgledy-piggledy in the grounds. The sentry guarding the front gates refused to let them enter and was not easily persuaded to use the field telephone to call one of the staff officers up at the house. Some considerable time later, a second lieutenant, who looked as though he belonged in a classroom with all the other schoolboys, finally condescended to put in an appearance.

Freeland showed him the letter from General Huang Chieh, Commander-in-Chief South China Front, waited patiently while he

56

read both the English and Chinese versions, then told Henry Wang to inform him that they wished to see the garrison commander. The letter got them past the gates and to the next ranking officer, a senior lieutenant, who listened to Freeland's request for assistance, then passed him on up the chain of command. By the time the Chief of Staff ushered them in to see Chen Ta-chin, the letter was beginning to look very much the worse for wear.

"The General asks what you want from him," Henry Wang said, translating.

"Tell him that I am looking for my friend, Mr Howard Teale, an English businessman who works in the Yangtze Insurance Building. Say that I believe he has been arrested by Colonel Li in mistake for someone else."

Freeland watched the General closely while Henry Wang struggled to translate his words into Mandarin. The scowl on Chen Ta-chin's face indicated that something had been lost in the process. When he spoke, his voice quivered with anger.

"The General says he will not listen to your lies," Henry Wang said, visibly shaken.

"Tell him that if Mr Teale is harmed, King George the Sixth and Mr Truman will be very angry. Make him understand that they will stop giving aid to Chiang Kai-shek and the Generalissimo will know who he has to thank for that."

"I can't," Henry Wang said nervously.

"Do it, then say all will be well if he phones Mao Sen and urges the Chief of Police to make sure my friend isn't being held for questioning at the interrogation centre on Hongkew Road West." Freeland gave the General a warm, friendly smile. "You can add that King George the Sixth will reward him for all his help."

Henry Wang took a deep breath, then launched himself into a long speech in which he fawned, cringed and flattered Chen Ta-chin outrageously. It was not Freeland's way of doing things, but it worked. Responding to Henry Wang's obsequious speech, he asked them to wait in the adjoining office and instructed one of his aides to bring them a cup of green tea. It was the first of many Freeland was to drink before the afternoon was over.

*   *   *

Teale was getting used to seeing a different set of faces every time Colonel Li sent for him. However, whether they were thin or fat, handsome or ugly, surly or cheerful, volatile or inscrutable, the one thing all the guards had in common was an infinite capacity for inflicting the maximum amount of pain short of actually killing the prisoner. And there was the same dreadful similarity about the termination of every question and answer session, since he had yet to leave the Colonel's presence on his own two feet. Except – he couldn't ever remember Li smiling at him before.

"Come in and sit down, Mr Teale." The welcoming smile extended to the corners of his mouth revealing a gold tooth on the left side. "A drink?"

Teale eyed the thimble-size glass of white spirit, then hesitating no longer, he reached for it and swallowed the measure in one go. The liquor burned his throat on the way down, warmed his stomach and subsequently made him splutter.

"You feel okay now?" Colonel Li enquired solicitously.

"On top of the world," Teale wheezed.

On top of the world when his face had been used as a punchbag? When his shoulders still ached and it was difficult to raise an arm above his head without groaning aloud? When his neck felt as if it was in a plaster cast? Teale stifled a derisive laugh.

"You help us again and everything will be A okay."

"Again? What do you mean by 'again'?"

"You told us about the Russian spy, now we are wanting the English one, Major Fleeman."

"Well, you know where to find him," Teale said. "You yourself told me that he is staying at the Cathay Hotel. All you've got to do is go there and pick him up."

"Is not so easy. Major Fleeman has powerful friends."

"Isn't he the lucky one?"

"You also could be fortunate. He is intending to take you to Hong Kong, then London."

"Who says so?"

"General Mao Sen; this is what he heard from British Consulate."

"Do you mean this Major Fleeman is actually looking for me?"

"Yes."

"How does he spell his name?" Teale asked.

Li picked up a hotel registration card from the pending tray on his desk and showed it to him. The surname printed in block capitals was easy enough to make out.

"Freeland."

"Yes, that is what I said. He is good friend, is he not?"

Teale nodded. The name still didn't ring any kind of bell with him but he valued his health too much to say so to Li. He didn't understand how London knew that his cover had been blown, but he was damned grateful for their prompt response. Of course, he would have had even more reason to be grateful had Freeland appeared on the scene before Li had sent his goons to arrest him.

"We would like Major Fleeman to find you . . ."

Teale stared at the diminutive Colonel, wondered if his ears had deceived him. "Why?"

"He will take you away from Shanghai; this will save trouble of deporting you. That make everybody very happy. Yes?"

"It does me."

"The British Consul will not complain."

Teale wasn't sure whether Li was asking for his opinion or was simply stating a fact. In the circumstances, it was safer to remain silent.

"If he asks, you will say the injuries were caused by your business friends."

"Of course, but will the Consul believe it?"

"I think so. When your office was searched this morning, the body of a young woman was found in one of the cupboards. Papers in her handbag say her name was Angelica Suyen, and she had been strangled."

Angelica Suyen, the half European, half Chinese girl, a graduate of St John's University in Shanghai whom he'd hired in September 1946. In less than a year she had learned all there was to learn about being a shipping agent and marine insurance broker. Indeed, she could run the business better than he could, which was one of the reasons he had trusted her so completely. And now she was dead, something Teale found hard to accept.

"The safe was locked," Li said, watching him closely. "How much money in it?"

Teale thought there was unlikely to be any. Whoever had taken Angelica to the office would have forced her to give him the combination; after he'd cleaned it out, for some reason he'd closed the safe again.

"Not a lot," he said, "the equivalent of no more than two hundred and fifty pounds sterling."

The income from the shadier enterprises was banked with Crédit Suisse International for immediate transfer to a numbered account in Zürich. Any money that was collected outside normal banking hours he kept overnight in a wall safe at home. Angelica had the combination to the office Chubb because there had been times in the past when she had been obliged to carry out certain transactions on his behalf while he was away on business in Nanking.

"You know who might have killed her?"

Teale looked up, peered at Li through eyes that were little more

59

than slits. "I could name half a dozen people who'd want to look inside my safe but you could try questioning Siao Chang."

Siao Chang was exactly thirty years old and the biggest gangster in Shanghai. He owned a piece of every dance hall, night club, gambling den and whorehouse in town. He had God knows how many concubines and a whole army of hired guns.

"I guess Siao Chang is too big for you to touch. I mean, he's got half the police force on his payroll and no judge is going to convict him."

"You are wrong, we will deal with Siao Chang."

"Good."

The bastard had it coming to him. Some informer at police headquarters must have told Siao Chang that he had been arrested and the opportunity to help himself to the contents of both safes had been too good to miss. He'd sent his people round to the house on Western Avenue to clean out the safe there, then had them pick up Angelica Suyen. Teale wondered who else they had called on.

"Is Dominga Zaldivar all right?" he asked.

"Who is she?"

"A friend, she has a flat at 224 Park Road."

"You not worry, we go there, see if she okay and tell you."

"Thanks."

"Very soon now you see her yourself. We take you to nice house later this afternoon, maybe tomorrow, and you call Major Fleeman on phone and he come and collect you. Then you both leave Shanghai for good."

In what?, Teale wondered. A couple of zinc-lined coffins? He couldn't think why London should have sent an agent all the way to Shanghai to bring him out, but it was good to know that his low level intelligence work in China since the end of the Second World War had been appreciated in the right quarters.

"You hear what I say?" Li demanded.

"I'm all ears."

"What?"

"I'm listening," Teale said hastily.

"Good. There is much I have to tell you."

As Li began to give him his instructions, his mind grappled with the problem of how he was going to save his own skin while warning Freeland that he could be walking into a death trap.

*   *   *

Although both cables carried an Op Immediate precedence, they had been given the low level classification of Restricted. The one

60

from the Foreign Office in London gave the bald outline of an emergency evacuation plan. The other had been originated by the Commander-in-Chief Royal Air Force Far East and was also addressed to RAF Kai Tak Hong Kong info Forward Element 215 Squadron Shanghai. It read:

OP FINAL CURTAIN (.) First (.) For RAF Kai Tak only (.) Contingency plan as promulgated in CAS/OPS/26 dated 10 May 1949 is to be implemented with effect from 0001 hours Greenwich Mean Time 23 May 1949 (.) Aircraft to be despatched at 45 minute intervals from H Hour (.) Turn round time SHANGHAI including embarkation and refuelling is one hour max (.)
Two (.) For British Consulate (.) Airlift comprises quantity 5 Sunderland Flying Boats with total capacity for 150 pax (.) Baggage allowance is one repeat one suitcase per person weight NOT to exceed 44 pounds (.) Request Liaison Officer from Consulate reports to Officer Commanding Forward Element 215 Squadron at 1100 hours your time (.) Liaison Officer will be required to furnish two copies of detailed flight manifest for each serial (.) Estimated Time of Arrival Shanghai of first serial is 1145 hours local (.)
Third (.) Acknowledge (.)

Matthews returned the cables to Caunter. "Seems clear enough to me," he said. "What's my job?"

"You're going to be the Liaison Officer. I'll be responsible for marshalling the evacuees at the reception centre here at the Consulate."

"Do you think there will be many takers?"

Less than a month ago, the Dutch had offered two thousand berths on the liner *Boissevain*. Despite extensive advertising in the local English-language newspapers, only one hundred and fifty people had applied. Of this number, sixty had changed their minds at the last moment.

"There are still four thousand ex-patriates in Shanghai; not all of them have been ordered to stay on by their companies. I hope many of the wives with young children can be persuaded to leave in addition to the sick and those who are nearing retirement." Caunter frowned. "This lull in the fighting won't last for ever and the sound of artillery fire in the distance could well make a lot of people face up to the reality of their situation."

Matthews thought it wasn't only the businessmen who had been wildly optimistic. It wasn't so very long ago that the Consul General himself had helped to foster the illusion that even if the Nationalists were defeated, it would still be business as usual under Chairman Mao Tse-tung.

"I won't pretend that we shan't have our work cut out to fill every plane, Frank. Details of the evacuation plan will appear in all the Sunday newspapers and I've been in touch with the Chamber of Commerce, the Press Club and the RAF Association. But that's not enough." Caunter opened the solitary file in the pending tray, extracted the top enclosure and handed it to Matthews. "This is a list of people who we believe are not obliged to remain in Shanghai. There are three hundred and eighty-one names there; the figure in brackets after each head of household indicates the number of dependant relatives. And we've also shown their home and office telephone numbers. The names are arranged in alphabetical order; I'll take A to N, you do O to Z."

"Right."

"If they're interested, say that we'll phone again on Sunday evening to tell them where and when to report for their flight. Any questions?"

Matthews skimmed through the list he was supposed to deal with and stopped at the letter 'T'. "Any word on Howard Teale?" he asked.

"I'm still waiting to hear from General Mao Sen."

"What about Freeland?"

"He's old enough to look after himself," said Caunter.

*   *   *

To the uninitiated like Henry Wang, the low rumble in the distance could easily be mistaken for thunder; Freeland, however, remembered a cold Spring morning in 1945 when the 3rd United States Army had been advancing on Flossenburg concentration camp and knew it was an incoming barrage from 155mm howitzers. So did the Nationalist staff officers at General Chen Ta-chin's tactical headquarters; suddenly no longer indolent, they looked wary and strung up, as though it wouldn't take much to make them cut and run.

"Sounds as though Hungjao is getting it," he murmured.

"What's that, sir?" Henry Wang asked.

"The phoney war is over, now they're starting in earnest again."

Back in London, an expert on China had told him that the civil war was more noise than action. Both sides went in for large-scale artillery bombardments but close-quarter combat was avoided whenever possible. More often than not, a battle was won by bribery and corruption and plain treachery rather than by hard and bitter fighting.

"You two come."

A bespectacled officer in an ill-fitting uniform pointed at Freeland and Henry Wang, then beckoned them to follow him into the General's office.

If his staff officers had looked ill at ease, General Chen Ta-chin was decidedly agitated. The way he spoke to his Chief of Staff and waved his arms about made this perfectly obvious. In the middle of the diatribe, he suddenly rounded on Henry Wang and in a few short sentences reduced the cab driver to a quivering jelly.

"The General says you have made him waste valuable time," Henry Wang said, translating nervously. "He says Colonel Li does not have your friend and that if we do not leave immediately, he will have us shot."

"Thank the General for all his assistance," Freeland said drily. "And be sure to tell him how much I appreciate it, then say that I know nothing bad can happen to Shanghai when there are brave men like him to defend the city." The smile on his lips belied the sarcastic words and although Freeland knew it was a futile, almost adolescent gesture, it made him feel better for saying it.

When they walked out of the house, the soldiers they'd seen earlier on were now in their slit trenches, their steel helmets no longer serving as a useful washbowl. It looked as though the sentry on the gate had followed their example but when Henry Wang instinctively turned left to head back into town, Freeland spotted him in the distance legging it as fast as he could.

"Should we stop and give him a lift?" Henry Wang asked, nearly choking with suppressed mirth.

"Not unless he's going to Lunghwa," Freeland said.

"Lunghwa?"

"There's nothing wrong with your hearing, Henry."

"Why you want to go there?"

"To see a man about a plane. Take the next turning on your right and go on down to Siccawei Creek."

Skirting the French Quarter, they picked up the outer ring road beyond the creek and crossed the railway track a couple of miles down the line from the South Station. Although Lunghwa was under military control, no one challenged Freeland's right to enter the administrative block. He found Lander on the south side of the terminal building, keeping an eye on the C46 from the comfort of a deck chair which he'd erected on the strip of grass that passed for a lawn. His vigil seemed a little unnecessary; with GMC 6×4 trucks parked in front of the nose and behind the tail, no one was likely to steal the plane.

"What's going on?" Freeland asked.

"The bastards have commandeered my ship," Lander said without looking round. "That's what's going on."

"Some bigwig planning to leave Shanghai?"

"Looks like it. The plane's all gassed up and ready to roll, my co-pilot is one of Chiang Kai-shek's flyboys and the ground staff have fitted the compass I picked up from Kiangwan airfield yesterday. My guess is that Chen Ta-chin, the Garrison Commander, is getting ready to bug out for Taiwan."

Freeland thought the American was probably right. Chen Ta-chin wouldn't be the first Nationalist General to desert the troops under his command, nor would he be the last.

"I don't think you will have long to wait. When I left his tactical headquarters fifteen minutes ago, the PLA were shelling Hungjao airfield."

"Yeah, well I shan't be sorry to leave, Shanghai's not the place it used to be." Lander reached for the beer can by his deck chair and raised it to his lips, then used a wrist to wipe the froth from his mouth. "You found your friend, Mr Teale, yet?"

"No, he seems to have vanished."

Freeland heard the rushing noise a split second before Lander and hit the ground first. The American rolled over to his left and landed on top of him, unintentionally shielding Freeland with his body. Each shell in the salvo of four impacted with the hollow boom associated with a 155mm or 5.5inch medium artillery piece. The ground quaked beneath him and he instinctively opened his mouth to equalise the pressure on his eardrums. Three shells landed between the runway and the dispersal apron, the fourth exploded somewhere in rear of the administrative block.

One of the GMC trucks was engulfed in flames and the C46 had lost most of the starboard undercarriage so that the plane was canted over, the wingtip brushing the ground. Fuel was spewing out of a ruptured gas tank.

"Run," Lander shouted.

Freeland didn't need to be told twice. His one thought was to put something solid between himself and the Gooney Bird before it blew up. Legs pumping, he raced through the administrative block, oblivious of the shards of glass beneath his feet as he attempted to keep up with Lander. Then, several hundred gallons of high octane fuel exploded like a bomb, reducing the C46 to scrap metal and scattering the wreckage as far as one hundred yards from the epicentre of the explosion.

When Freeland ventured back inside the building, the dust cloud from the shattered plaster ceiling had dispersed. A dozen or so spectre-like figures, many of whom were bleeding profusely from superficial wounds inflicted by flying glass, were wandering around in a daze, their clothing and hair covered with a fine white powder. As was often the case, those with the most serious wounds were the quietest, none more so than the young NCO sitting on the floor in front of the check-in counter, his left eyeball displaced from its socket, his right eye lacerated with glass splinters. Grabbing hold of the only medical orderly in the room, Freeland dragged him away from the major whose hand he was bandaging, and propelled him towards the wounded corporal.

The major followed him across the room, all fire and fury, his arms flailing like windmills. As they knelt in front of the corporal, Freeland heard the metallic click of a hammer being cocked, then felt the barrel of a hand gun boring into his neck. He sensed the finger on the trigger taking up the slack and flinched as the pistol boomed above his head and the bullet ploughed into what was left of the ceiling.

He owed his life to Lander. The American had charged in like an express train, had seized the major's wrist and raised his gun hand aloft just as he had been about to squeeze the trigger. Now the two men were doing a Viennese waltz as they struggled for the possession of the Colt .45 automatic. Freeland got up from the floor, dug a fist into the major's back, then pole-axed him with a forearm smash to the side of the head. The pistol slipped from his grasp and skidded across the floor; reacting swiftly, Lander pounced on the automatic before anyone else had a chance to get to it.

"I think we'd better get out of here," Freeland said quietly. "The natives don't seem at all friendly."

"You lead the way then," Lander told him.

Henry Wang had parked the cab on the verge just up the road from the administrative block. Now it was lying upside down in a dried-up paddy field more than twenty feet from a crater made by an eighty-pound shell. The roof had been crunched in and what remained of the side-panelling was pitted with jagged holes. A very dead Henry Wang was still behind the wheel.

"Your guy?" Lander asked.

"I'm afraid so."

"You know something, Mr Freeland? You're dangerous, people who meet up with you have a habit of dying violently."

65

Lander was referring to his friend, Berringer, but there had been many others before the pilot, in France and in the concentration camp at Flossenburg.

"I'm a survivor," Freeland said bleakly. "You should also take note of that."

Lander smiled. "All right, Mr Survivor, what do we do now?"

"We start walking back to town," Freeland told him.

6

Teale opened one eye as much as he was able to and stared at the dust motes swirling in the beam of light which entered the room through a small window near the ceiling. Sometime during the heat of the night, he had kicked off the thin grey sheet they'd provided, but it hadn't made him feel any cooler. Beads of sweat had collected in the hollow of his neck and the elastic waistband of the underpants he was wearing in lieu of pyjama bottoms was damp.

His body still aching from the battering it had taken, he pivoted on his right hip and gingerly raised himself up to sit on the edge of the bed. Teale had no idea where they were holding him since Li had taken the additional precaution of blindfolding his eyes before moving him from the interrogation centre under cover of darkness. The driver had taken a circuitous route, frequently doubling back in order to confuse him even further. At a rough guess, he reckoned they had spent almost half an hour driving aimlessly about before the guards had transferred him to a motor launch.

The boat journey hadn't lasted nearly as long and of the waterways they could have taken, he was inclined to rule out the Soochow and Siccawei Creeks. Both were extremely sluggish and, rightly or wrongly, it had been his impression that the launch had been swept along by a pretty strong current. That meant it had to be the Whangpoo River and they had obviously been heading downstream towards the port of Woosung. It was also logical to assume that Colonel Li would want to distance himself as far as possible from the ring of steel the PLA had thrown around the city, and east was the only direction open to him. They could therefore have taken him to a safe house either in the suburb of Hongkew or else they were holed up in the Pootung District on the south bank of the Whangpoo. To narrow it down any further was beyond him.

Some things, however, never changed no matter where they were, the sound of a key turning a lock, a door opening. Teale glanced to his left expecting to see the usual retinue with Li and was surprised when a plump Chinese woman in a black pyjama suit entered the room with him, carrying his lightweight suit in one hand, his brown leather shoes in the other. The shoes had been polished, the suit cleaned and pressed; the valet service also extended to the freshly-laundered shirt and new tie which Li was carrying. A second woman entered with a glass of weak tea and two cupcakes on a plate, a guard brought up the rear with a jug of hot water.

"Is good service, yes?" Li said, the gold tooth prominent in his smile.

"I couldn't do better if I were staying at the Cathay."

"Good. You sit here, please."

Teale got up from the bed and sat down on the raffia-bottomed chair by the washstand. The guard filled the metal bowl from the jug of hot water, then produced a stick of shaving soap and a brush.

"Last night we see your friend at number 224 Park Road – she okay."

"That's a relief," Teale said and winced. The guard who was lathering his face would have made a better window cleaner than a barber.

"Your other friends go there, give her black eye."

"Oh, shit."

"She popular lady. Two days ago Mr Mattu go see her."

"Mattu?" The penny dropped. "Frank Matthews?"

"Yes. You no hear me?"

"I'm a little deaf."

The guard opened a cut-throat razor and tested the blade on a strand of Teale's hair before starting to shave him.

"Other man with him, we think he Major Fleeman. They looking for you."

"That's nice."

The guard placed a finger under Teale's chin, raised his head and tilted it to the left, then scraped away at his beard. The blade rasped against the stubble and sounded as though he was being rubbed down with coarse sandpaper.

"I want you speak to lady, tell her you okay, ask she okay. Then you say other friends give you bad time and you in hiding."

"Right." Teale felt the razor at his throat and swallowed nervously. "Do I tell her where?" he croaked.

"Later, after you talk to Mr Mattu at Consulate. Everything in proper order, Mr Teale."

Everything in proper order was Li's oblique way of letting it be known that when he phoned Matthews he was to say that Dominga Zaldivar had told him that Frank had been round to her flat asking after him. It was dangerous to underestimate the Colonel, the little man was devious, cunning, ruthless. Teale wondered who had led him to believe that he and Freeland were Communists and for what reason.

"You wash now, get dressed, eat food, then we make phone calls – okay?"

"Sure."

The guard wiped the cut-throat razor on a scrap of newspaper and closed the blade. Teale stroked his chin and found he had blood on his fingers.

"You not take long," Li said and signalled the women to leave.

"I'll be ready in two shakes of a lamb's tail," Teale assured him.

*   *   *

Matthews lit a cigarette and leaned back in his chair. Considering how few names there were on his notepad, he didn't have much to show for all the hours of work he'd put in. So far, there had been very few takers among the O to Zs and by all accounts, Caunter had been no more successful. At the rate they were going, they would be hard pressed to fill even half the hundred and fifty seats the RAF were expecting. He had spent all Saturday phoning round like some bloody tout, now here he was on Sunday morning back at his desk hoping that some of the people who'd said 'maybe' would keep their word and phone in to let him know their final decision.

"Sure I can't persuade you to take up one of the seats?" he asked Freeland.

"Only if I find Teale between now and Monday afternoon."

"He's probably dead."

"Then I have to find his body. I was sent here to bring him out; I'm not abandoning the search until I have proof that he's no longer alive."

He had lost too many people over the years – Phillipe Arnaud from Montauban in the Garonne, René Emil Dussarat and Léon Gerson from Bouglainval and Chantal Kiffer – all of them put up against a wall and executed by a firing squad, some after being tortured by the Gestapo. He wished he had been allowed to stay on with the War Crimes Commission until they had found whoever had framed Chantal, but he had outstayed his welcome

69

in France and the men who ran the Secret Intelligence Service from the Georgian town house at 21 Queen Anne's Gate and 54 Broadway had wanted him back, doing the kind of work he was paid to do.

"In your shoes, I'd want to leave Shanghai well ahead of the PLA. They will be here any day now, you told me yourself that they shelled Lunghwa airfield yesterday afternoon."

"It was just four rounds harassing fire from a troop of medium guns some sixteen to eighteen thousand yards from the target. They got lucky and hit the only plane on the airfield. I don't see the PLA standing on Garden Bridge before next Tuesday or Wednesday."

"If you're wrong, Harry," Matthews warned him, "you could find yourself in serious trouble. The Consul-General, Caunter and the rest of us will be all right; we can claim diplomatic immunity. But you can't. You can't even give the Communists a convincing reason for being here. Even the most obstinate of our ex-patriates have an excuse of sorts."

"I don't intend to be caught."

"Oh yes?" Confidence was all very well, Matthews thought, but it ought to stem from something more solid than mere optimism.

"I intend to get hold of a two-man kayak."

"And then what are you planning to do – paddle your way back to Hong Kong?"

"No, just as far as Woosung and the cruiser *Belfast*. I'll travel by night, lie up during the day. If you can help me find a kayak, I shall then want to hide it somewhere downstream until it's needed."

Matthews studied the younger man, marvelled at his single-mindedness and admired him for it. Freeland wasn't bullshitting him, he was going to jeopardise his own safety because London wanted Teale, and if Howard was still alive, he was going to take the old sod down river. And no matter what the PLA did, they wouldn't be able to stop him. Caunter had already torn him off a strip for helping Freeland and had warned him that on no account was he to involve the Consulate in any more hare-brained ventures. But Caunter could go and wet himself.

"I'll introduce you to Jacob Stein, I know he's got a couple of boats. He's a forty-year-old German Jew who got out of Breslau in 1934 and but for Hitler, would have represented Germany in the '36 Olympics. As for hiding the canoe, your best bet is a mile or so beyond Tai Wan Po on the north bank. It's well clear of the city and there are innumerable inlets along the reed banks. Your only problem will be finding the boat again."

"Thanks, I'll bear that in mind. Now can you put me in touch with Jacob Stein?"

"You mean right now?"

"I'd like to take possession of the kayak today; it might be too late if I wait until the last Sunderland has departed."

Matthews glanced at his wrist watch. "Well, I doubt if he's left for the Country Club yet. Jacob likes to keep fit, most Sunday mornings you'll find him on the squash court."

The phone rang just as Matthews was about to reach for it. Teale was the last person he expected to hear on the line when he lifted the receiver.

"Dominga says you've been looking for me?" he said without preamble.

"Yes, where have you been hiding yourself?"

Matthews transferred the receiver to his left hand and kept on talking while he scribbled a note to Freeland, then motioned him to draw nearer and held out the phone so that he could hear their subsequent conversation.

"I've been conferring with one of my business partners," Teale said and forced a laugh which came out like a croak. "We had a difference of opinion and things got pretty heated for a time, but that's all behind us now.'

"Is it? The police found the body of Angelica Suyen in one of the cupboards at your office. She had been strangled."

"And they think I did it?"

"I wouldn't know," Matthews told him. "The Chief of Police hasn't confided in me, but obviously they're looking for you."

"They're not the only ones. Dominga tells me you weren't alone when you dropped in to see her the other evening. You had a friend in tow – a Mr Freeland who is also looking for me. Right?"

"Yes." Matthews paused, looked at Freeland and got an affirmative nod, then added, "As a matter of fact, he's sitting opposite me this very minute. You want to have a word with him?"

There was only a momentary hesitation before Teale told him to put Freeland on the line. "Do we know one another?" he asked.

"No, we haven't met."

"So why are you looking for me?"

"London thinks it's time you came home," Freeland said.

"I've no objection to that in principle. Unfortunately life's not exactly healthy right now. You understand me?"

"Yes."

"That's why I'm not at home."

"In other words, you're in hiding."

71

Teale gave another brittle laugh. "You're sharp, Mr Freeland, the thing is, are you sharp enough to make sure you're not being followed?"

"You can always run a check."

"I intend to. Where are you staying – the Cathay Hotel?"

"Didn't Dominga tell you?"

"I just wanted to make sure she'd heard you right." Teale paused, then said, "I'll arrange for a note to be delivered to the desk clerk telling you where and how to find me. You're to come alone, otherwise I won't show up. Clear?"

"Perfectly."

"I'll look forward to meeting you then," Teale said and put the phone down.

Much of what the older man had said didn't make sense to Freeland. He thought about the conversation Matthews had had with Dominga Zaldivar.

"You called me Harry," Freeland mused. "You never introduced me to Dominga, never said that I wanted to see her boyfriend, yet Teale knows my surname and where I am staying."

"He probably heard it on the grapevine, Harry. You'd be surprised at the amount of tittle-tattle that's passed around by word of mouth in this town. A woman gets up in the morning, puts on some fancy lingerie and before sundown, half the members of the Country Club know her black undergarments are trimmed with red lace. That's the way it is."

"Not in this case," said Freeland. "Only the police know my name, where I'm staying and the fact that I'm anxious to find Teale. And another thing, he didn't sound either shocked or surprised when you told him that Angelica Suyen had been murdered. In fact, Teale didn't ask you any questions at all."

"Of course he didn't, he already knows she's dead. You heard him say he'd had a difference of opinion with one of his business partners and how things had got a little heated. What Howard was really telling us is that he's lucky to be alive."

Matthews was playing the part of the devil's advocate but not very convincingly.

"I presume the man I spoke to was Teale?" Freeland asked.

"Of course it was, I'd know his voice anywhere."

"He sounded unnatural."

"So would you in his shoes; he's just had the fright of his life and has still got the shakes. Having seen what gangsters like Siao Chang can do to their victims, I've a pretty good idea of what Howard must have been through."

72

"He isn't out of the woods yet. He was being coached, I'm convinced of it. Someone was there at his elbow to make sure he didn't step out of line. If he had departed from the script, they would have broken the connection and persuaded him to try again."

"Who do you mean by 'they'?"

"Fifth Columnists, an undercover unit of the PLA or Nationalist police officers who want to curry favour with Chairman Mao Tse-tung – take your pick. Whoever they are, they've got Teale and now they want me to earn them a few bonus points. Maybe Howard sounded stilted because he was trying to warn me off?"

"Then you'd be wise to take the hint."

Freeland shook his head. "We don't abandon our people; it's an unwritten law and I'm not about to break it."

Nor did he want London to think he had failed yet again as he had on two previous occasions. Twice was more than enough for any man.

"I'd like to watch your back," Matthews said, "but I can't."

"I'm not asking you to."

"You don't understand; His Majesty's Government is determined that this Consulate will still be open for business when the Communists are in power. Therefore we are not, repeat not, to give them the slightest pretext for closing us down."

"It's all right, Frank. I already knew the score before I boarded the plane to Hong Kong."

Matthews got to his feet, unlocked the steel cabinet behind his desk and took out a large oilskin package tied up with string. "You may find this useful," he said.

Freeland undid the string and opened the packet to find that it contained a 7.63mm Mauser automatic of pre-First World War vintage.

"I know it's a museum piece," Matthews said, "but it can still drop a horse at thirty paces."

The weapon was in good condition, the working parts were rust free, had been regularly cleaned and were protected by a thin film of oil. There were also two eight-round clips of ammunition.

"Can this pistol be traced to you?" Freeland asked.

"Absolutely not."

"I hope you're right. I don't want you to stop any brickbats should it happen to fall into the wrong hands."

"There's no chance of that. Now, do you still want a kayak?"

"If all goes well, Teale and I will be on one of the Sunderlands, but a little insurance never hurt anyone."

73

Matthews lifted the receiver. "All right," he said, "let's see if we can put you in touch with Jacob Stein."

*   *   *

By Shanghai standards, Stein was only moderately well off. His villa on Great Western Avenue where he resided with his wife and twelve-year-old daughter, had been built on a quarter acre plot and resembled a doll's house when compared with the neighbouring properties. But then, as Stein frequently pointed out, he had arrived in Shanghai on board a tramp steamer with little more than the clothes he stood up in and the equivalent of twenty pounds sterling in his wallet. His only assets had been a good head for figures, an ear for languages, abundant common sense and considerable charm. Within two years he had learned to speak English and had qualified as a certified accountant. By 1938 he had his own practice and was a member of the Shanghai Club which had automatically made him a pillar of the community.

Stein had escaped internment during the war because the Imperial Japanese Army had failed to comprehend the racial policies of the Third Reich and had simply looked upon him as one of their German allies. For his part, he had taken it upon himself to look after the homes and valuables of those who had been interned, a selfless act which had earned him the undying gratitude of a considerable number of British and American expatriates.

About to depart for the Country Club when Matthews had telephoned, he was still dressed for the squash court when Freeland arrived on the bicycle he had borrowed from one of the clerks at the Consulate.

"Have you got a padlock and chain for that machine?" Stein asked.

"Afraid not."

"Well, I doubt if anyone will want to steal it but we won't take any chances."

Stein told his houseboy to keep an eye on the bike, then led Freeland into his study at the back of the house and poured him a glass of home-made lemonade.

"Frank tells me you're interested in buying a two-man kayak?" he said casually.

"Yes, he thought you might have one for sale."

"I could let you have a single but I'm not so sure about a two-man kayak. I've only got the one." Stein frowned at his glass of lemonade. "Of course, if it's important, I daresay my

74

wife wouldn't object. Hannah and I used to do a lot of canoeing, but I can't remember the last time we were out on the river."

"It's important," said Freeland.

"I'm afraid you will have to be a little more specific than that."

"Look, either you've got a kayak for sale or you haven't."

"I wish it were that simple, Mr Freeland. I come from Breslau which was once a German town; now it's a Polish one. However, that's really immaterial because neither Hannah nor I wish to see Germany again. Furthermore, I have no papers to prove who I am or what I am, so technically speaking my wife is married to a stateless person. Britain won't have us, America doesn't want to know. I suppose Israel would welcome us with open arms but we are not Zionists and Hannah would be dreadfully unhappy living in a kibbutz. Therefore, we shall stay here."

"I think I know what you are about to say."

"Do you?" Stein finished his lemonade and put the empty glass on the drinks trolley. "Perhaps I should make the point anyway. I shall probably lose most of my former clients within a year and I doubt the Communists will have much use for an accountant. Fortunately, my wife is a dentist and no matter who is running the country, teeth still have to be pulled. Clearly I can't afford to prejudice my future relations with the new régime by participating in some act before they come to power which they might subsequently regard as hostile."

"Would selling me one of your kayaks constitute a hostile act?"

"It depends on what you want it for and what you are doing here in Shanghai. You're a bit of a Johnny-come-lately, Mr Freeland, and you are not in the employ of Jardine Matheson or Butterfield and Swire. You are not Foreign Office either, yet a hardbitten security man like Frank Matthews seems only too willing to help you in any way he can." Stein smiled. "I think you must be an Intelligence Officer, Mr Freeland."

He could smile, pooh-pooh the suggestion, deny it vehemently or simply ignore it but whichever way he played it, Stein wouldn't believe him. Did he really need the kayak? If the answer was yes, he would have to pull the wool over his eyes somehow. Provided Teale kept his word and set a rendezvous, he had enough time in hand to make contact and whisk him out of Shanghai on one of the Sunderland flying boats. But what seemed perfectly feasible in theory often resulted in a complete cock-up when put to the test. The kayak was a fall-back in case things went wrong, and he couldn't afford to do without it.

"I'm not a spy, Mr Stein, but I am here to recover something of value, a symbol which we British can't afford to abandon."

Freeland hoped the older man would draw the conclusion he wanted and was not disappointed.

"Something of value and at the same time, symbolic." His eyes widened. "You are talking about a ship. The warship HMS *Amethyst* is going to make a dash for the open sea."

Freeland said nothing, knew his silence would encourage Stein to develop the idea he had planted in his mind. The Yangtze was treacherous to navigate, especially near the estuary where the depth under a ship's keel changed dramatically with the tide. To avoid beaching the *Amethyst*, her captain would have to cross the sandbars and mudbanks at high tide and preferably in daylight when he could see what he was doing. But then the shore batteries would blow him out of the water. The passage could only be made under cover of darkness and at low tide if someone marked the channel between the sandbars.

"I think I know why you need a kayak, Mr Freeland. Regretfully, I'm unable to sell you one of mine. It's too risky."

"I can understand that, I'll just have to look elsewhere."

"But I can show you the boatshed where they are kept, then you can steal one when you need it."

"Steal?"

"A figure of speech. I will give you a spare key but you will have to make it look as though the lock has been forced. Agreed?"

"Agreed."

"Good. It will take us roughly forty minutes to get there and back by car. You can pick up your bicycle on our return."

Freeland checked his wrist watch, saw that it was a quarter past eleven and calculated it would be close on one o'clock by the time he'd cycled back to the Consulate. Matthews would probably have gone to lunch by then and he wanted to collect the 7.63mm Mauser automatic he'd left with him for safe-keeping.

"Do you mind if I use your phone?" he asked.

"Help yourself," Stein told him.

That only left Teale, and there was no way he could let him know what was happening.

*   *   *

The man hunkered down under the low stone wall flanking The Bund opposite the Cathay Hotel was wearing a pair of sandals, frayed blue shorts, a matching shirt in the same state of disrepair and a large straw hat designed to keep the sun off his neck and shoulders. Too well fed to be a beggar, his calf muscles were also another sign that he was not what he appeared to be at first sight. His legs were neither bowed nor stringy like those of a dock worker who'd spent a lifetime carrying heavy loads on his back, but there were few Europeans about that morning and the other coolies knew better than to question him. He was, in fact, a member of Colonel Li's interrogation team and part of the reception committee who were lying in wait for Freeland. As of that moment, he was perplexed to know why the target had not yet appeared when the note from the other Englishman had been left with the desk clerk some considerable time ago.

7

The Foreign Correspondents Club of China was on the tenth floor of Broadway Mansions directly above the American Military Advisory Group. Although not officially a member, Joe Lander enjoyed the same privileges as those who were eligible to join and had paid the annual subscription. He owed his unique status to his long-standing friendship with Phil Ryan, the Associated Press (AP) assistant bureau chief whom he had first met in Chungking during the war when he'd been a fighter pilot with Chennault's Flying Tigers. As far as the other pressmen were concerned, Lander was a valuable source of information as well as being a genial companion. Genial, however, was the last epithet anyone would have used who saw him in earnest conversation with Phil Ryan on that particular Sunday.

"One lousy assault landing craft?" Lander stared at his beer, shook his head in disbelief. "Are you telling me that's all the Navy is planning to send up river? Hasn't anyone told them there are two thousand American citizens living in Shanghai?"

"The Navy already knows that. Furthermore, they've been told exactly how many people are to be evacuated and believe me, one assault landing craft is enough."

"So if space isn't a problem, why the hell won't they take Berringer home? Has the captain of this destroyer – whatever its name is . . . ?"

"The USS *Tucker*," Ryan said, interrupting him.

"Yeah, the *Tucker* – has he got some problem about having a coffin on board his ship?"

"I guess a body comes under the heading of freight. Every American who is leaving Shanghai courtesy of the US Navy has been limited to one suitcase."

"Freight." Lander spat the word out, then downed the rest of his beer and signalled the bartender to bring two more. "We're talking about a former captain in the United States Army Air

78

Corps who saw more action in the Second World War than nine guys out of ten who put on a uniform ever did. Every soldier's got a right to be buried in his own country; if that isn't written into the Constitution, it goddamn well ought to be."

Ryan lit a cigarette and waited for the storm to pass. Once Lander was on one of his hobby horses there was no stopping him. It was pointless trying to reason with him when he was deaf to every argument that was contrary to his opinion.

"What does the US Consulate have to say about it?" Ryan asked him when he eventually paused for breath.

"They said not to worry, there was a standard procedure for repatriating the dead and that the coffin would be sent by truck to Woosung and put on a US freighter going to Kobe, Japan. From there, it will then be flown back to the States."

"Then I don't see what you're worried about; everything seems to have been taken care of."

"I'd put the coffin on one of our CAT planes to Canton only head office here says that General Chennault has suspended all scheduled flights to Shanghai."

"Best thing you can do now, Joe, is get yourself down to The Bund tomorrow morning and hop aboard that landing craft."

Lander half turned to face the window on his left and gazed blankly at the British and American Consulates back to back the other side of Garden Bridge. Beyond them lay the broad sweep of The Bund, divided in two by the trees, shrubs and grassed area of the centre island.

"I was nosing around the North Depot earlier this morning," he said dreamily. "Saw a large column of troops on the move – foot soldiers, field artillery trucks, half tracks, jeeps. They were bugging out, heading east towards Woosung." Lander turned his back on the window, concentrated on his beer instead and swallowed half the stein in one draught. "You don't have to be a military genius to know they're aiming to join Chiang Kai-shek in Taiwan."

"So?"

"So what do you think the foot soldiers will do to any civilian truck driver who's stupid enough to try and force his way past them? Why, they'll haul him out of the cab and slit his throat before you can blink. And everything that's on the back of the truck will end up in a ditch because those foot soldiers are tired of marching. Now do you see why I'm unhappy about the arrangements the Consulate is making to ship Berringer home?"

"What about the railroad to Woosung?"

"The only freight going down that track is the personal effects of the Top Brass and the wealthy Chinese."

"I hear Kiangwin airfield to the north is still open," said Ryan. "I'm not saying you'll have any better luck with Chiang Kai-shek's China Airways but they're the only carrier still maintaining some kind of service, and you've got nothing to lose."

"I guess it's worth a shot."

"But whatever you do, don't miss that Navy boat. Life is going to be very unhealthy for guys like you and Freeland when the PLA are running Town Hall."

"Freeland? Are we talking about the same guy – dark hair, blue eyes, stands a little under six feet, weighs around a hundred and seventy to a hundred and eighty pounds, has the little finger missing from his left hand?"

"That's the man," Ryan said. "Where did you meet him?"

"He hitched a ride with us from Kweilin."

"Yeah? Well, he came to see me yesterday, asking if I had any idea where he might find an old reprobate called Howard Teale. Said he was with the War Crimes Commission and needed to get a deposition from him."

Lander grinned. "That's just so much hogwash."

Ryan sensed a story. "He told you different?"

"Nope. He just made small talk, gave the impression that he was confiding in us but when I thought about it afterwards, I realised he hadn't really told us a damned thing about himself. Even allowing for the famous British reserve, he was a very private person, almost secretive. Berringer asked him about his work with the War Crimes Commission and he implied it was classified, which is crazy. I mean, what's the big secret about Dachau, Auschwitz and Buchenwald? How many people do you know who haven't heard of those concentration camps?"

"I can't think of any offhand," Ryan said, "but then I only mix with newsmen. Maybe there's someone out there who only reads the comic section."

There had been other things which hadn't made sense to Lander. The Englishman claimed he had spent most of the war in London attached to the Free French as a liaison officer whereas most deskmen liked to give the impression they'd been in combat. He hadn't name-dropped either, which, in his experience, was another characteristic of the chairbound warrior. In fact, as far as Lander had been able to gather, he hadn't even come within hailing distance of de Gaulle.

"Something else. When Berringer asked him about his missing

finger, Freeland said he'd lost it as a result of a freak accident with his parachute when he was learning to jump. Neither of us doubted that he had earned his para wings but we didn't buy the bit about how his finger had been amputated by one of the rigging lines when his parachute began to candle on his eighth and last qualifying jump. The guy is just too modest and self-effacing to be real."

"What else was he secretive about?"

Lander frowned. "I don't think he ever lets anyone get really close to him, not even a woman. I can't recall how Berringer managed to drag them into the conversation, but girls were always a subject never far from George's mind. Anyway, Freeland made a brief reference to a girl called Chantal who was French and obviously pretty special, and for a while there it seemed like we'd unlocked a door, but it didn't last. Berringer asked him if it was serious and he said, 'not any more, she's dead'. Just like that, cold, flat, no emotion whatever."

"The British call it keeping a stiff upper lip," Ryan said.

"His must be petrified. The only other person Freeland was the slightest bit expansive about was somebody called Jenny. He said she was a sergeant in their air force and he made some joke that it paid to be nice to the girl who packed your parachute."

Ryan lit a cigarette. The AP bureau didn't object to him doing a bit of freelancing on the side and there was a feature story to be written around Freeland. It wouldn't be as good as the one on The Flying Tigers he'd called 'The Shoestring Air Force' which the *Saturday Evening Post* had printed; and it wouldn't make people angry the way 'Winter of '47' had done when he had written about the body carts that had gone round the streets of Shanghai collecting the paupers who had frozen to death during the night. But Freeland was the kind of enigma who would appeal to a certain features editor in New York if he could put a little more flesh on the bones. The Englishman would clam up in the presence of a reporter but he might loosen up in the company of Lander, especially if Joe wasn't aware that he was being used to gather raw material.

"I suppose Berringer was insured?" Ryan said. "I know money can't ease the sorrow but his next-of-kin might not be too well placed."

"They'll get the usual ten thousand dollars from his CAT policy but I guess that will only take care of the immediate expenses."

"George would be alive today if Freeland hadn't persuaded him to change the flight plan. Of course I'm not a lawyer but it seems to me that the next-of-kin would have a claim against the British Government if Freeland is in Shanghai on official business."

"Yeah." Lander looked thoughtful. "How are we going to prove it?" he asked.

"Someone would have to get close to him, win his confidence and discover just what he does to earn a living." Ryan paused, then said, "I think you're the man for the job."

"He's staying at the Cathay," Lander said, thinking aloud. "Maybe I can get a room on the same floor?"

"I think that could be arranged," Ryan said casually.

*   *   *

The letter was handed to Freeland by the desk clerk when he collected his room key. It had been delivered via the captain of bell boys who was unable to describe the man who had given it to him except in the most general terms. According to him, the 'postman' had been in his mid twenties to late thirties, had a full head of black hair, dressed like a Westerner and was roughly the same height and weight as most of the better-off Chinese. There were, Freeland thought, only two explanations why the bell boy was so vague; either he had been bribed to forget a face or else he had been too frightened to remember.

The envelope looked as though it had been written by an old man with the shakes. Freeland saw no reason to alter his opinion when he read the note in the privacy of his room. Teale's instructions were, however, extremely clear, proof that he was a long way from being senile. That aside, Freeland wasn't happy about the location of the rendezvous. But there wasn't anything he could do about it; Teale was calling the tune and he either obeyed his instructions or returned to London without him.

Freeland undid the brown paper parcel, took out the oilskin packet and removed the Mauser automatic. Wrapping it up in a parcel had been an effective way of concealing the firearm while he walked back to the hotel from the Consulate, but the time was coming when he might need to use it in a hurry.

He cocked the pistol by drawing the bolt to the rear, which in turn allowed the magazine spring to assert itself and raise the platform high enough to prevent the working parts from moving forward. Then he picked up a clip of eight rounds, inserted it in the guide rail and, as though loading a rifle, used his thumb to press down and feed the cartridges into the magazine. When he removed the empty clip from the guide rail, the bolt moved forward and pushed the topmost round into the breech. Finally, he applied the safety catch and laid the pistol down on the bed.

The overall length of the Mauser was a fraction over six inches which meant it was too big to fit comfortably into one of his pockets. The only thing he could do was tuck the barrel into the waistband of his slacks with the butt pointing forward so that he could draw the pistol quickly and cleanly. Since he was right-handed, Freeland positioned the automatic on his left hip. He wondered if he should carry the jacket over his left arm to conceal the firearm, then decided to wear it in case he needed to use both hands.

Before checking his appearance in the full-length mirror, Freeland removed his passport from the inside pocket and placed it under the sports shirts in the chest of drawers. The jacket didn't hang as well over the left side as he would have wished but only someone who was particularly observant would suspect he was carrying a gun. Finally, he looked round the bedroom to make sure he hadn't forgotten anything, then locked the door behind him and went on down to the lobby where he handed his room key to the desk clerk.

On the way out, he bumped into Lander on the way in. A bell boy carrying a travelling bag hovered in rear of the American.

"Hi," Lander said cheerfully. "Going some place?"

"Only for a stroll," Freeland told him. "I need the exercise."

"I'd join you but I haven't checked in yet. Had to get out of my hotel, been commandeered by the army."

"Tough."

"Yeah, war is hell." Lander grinned. "Why don't we meet in the bar for a drink before dinner? Say around six?"

"Make it six thirty." Accepting Lander's invitation seemed the quickest way to get rid of him.

"Sure. Mind you're back before curfew."

Freeland walked out into the street. He had been told to hire a sampan to take him across the river to Holt's Wharf where a guide would be waiting. Teale hadn't said how the man was going to recognise him but there were two possible explanations for that apparent oversight, neither of which was particularly comforting. For several days now, no European had ventured into the Pootung District because the area was said to be under Communist control; the other disquieting inference was the possibility that the guide already knew his face.

The Bund was quiet, virtually deserted. On Tuesday it would be different. Although the PLA were on the outskirts of the city and the Nationalists were beginning to desert in droves, the mayor had decreed there would be a Victory Parade. In a comic opera bid to lift morale, City Hall had ordered that every house and building would be decorated with flags and bunting. Massed bands were to lead the marching columns which the civilian spectators were invited to join in an expression of solidarity with Shanghai's gallant defenders.

There was the usual cluster of sampans moored alongside the landing stage. Freeland hired the oldest, most frail-looking owner, told him in pidgin English where he wanted to go, then positioned himself well forward in the bows and sat down facing the stern. As the boatman shoved off, a youngish-looking stevedore wearing a pair of ragged shorts and an equally frayed navy shirt jumped aboard. Opening his jacket, Freeland allowed him to see the Mauser automatic, then closed his hand around the butt.

"Just so as we understand one another," he said calmly.

The newcomer sat down, gazed at him impassively while the boatman battled against the current which threatened to sweep them down river. Ten back-breaking minutes later, he brought the sampan alongside a flight of concrete steps which led to the wharf above and held it there long enough for Freeland and the stevedore to scramble ashore. At the top of the steps, he motioned the Chinese to walk in front of him.

There were no cranes on Holt's Wharf and the warehouses were positioned lengthways on, some forty feet from the dockside. Between the sheds, an access road wide enough for two vehicles ran arrow-straight through the dockland area towards the jumbled chaos that was Pootung. There was no sign of life in the immediate vicinity.

"Are you the guide who's going to lead me to Mr Teale?" Freeland asked.

The question went unanswered and he tried again, resorting to pidgin English and sign language. "You savvy Mr Teale, white man like me? Send letter to Cathay Hotel?"

The stevedore continued to stare at him as though he had taken leave of his senses, then with a faint shrug, he turned his back on Freeland and walked away. When he reached the top of the access road, the man glanced over his shoulder as if to make sure he was following him.

Pootung itself was a rabbit warren of dilapidated houses hugger-mugger with back street workshops whose owners prospered on sweated labour. Most of the roads were unmade, which meant that they were still potholed and rutted from the last rainy season. No European lived in Pootung and as of that moment, it looked as though the Chinese population had cleared out of the immediate neighbourhood.

The stevedore was some fifteen to twenty yards ahead of him; rounding the next bend in the road, Freeland suddenly found that, having led him into a bottleneck, his guide had disappeared into one of the alleyways that hived off in all directions. It looked bad, it felt bad; he drew the Mauser, held it loosely by his side, barrel pointing downwards, then side-stepped across the road to put something solid behind his back. He scanned the houses opposite for a sniper in an upstairs room, heard a faint creaking sound somewhere off to his left and spun round.

End house, top of the cul-de-sac, a property of substance, enclosed courtyard, balcony first floor, nine dragons on ridge tiles of roof for good luck, and no prizes for guessing who was going to need it. He concentrated on the nail-studded oak door in the outer wall and saw the latch was now in a raised position. The door opened inwards and a roly-poly figure in a panama hat and a fawn coloured linen suit slowly emerged from the courtyard.

"Teale?" The European flinched and jerked his head as though someone had just slapped his face. "Is that you, Howard?" Freeland asked in a louder voice.

"Behind you."

The stevedore had made a wide flanking movement to take him in the back; he sensed the danger even as Teale croaked a feeble warning and turned about to face his attacker. Freeland didn't hesitate; holding the Mauser automatic in a double-handed grip, he fired twice, hitting the stevedore in the abdomen and left shoulder. The combined impact lifted him off his feet with such force that his skull cracked like an eggshell when he hit the ground.

Several high-velocity bullets struck the wall above Freeland's head at an oblique angle, gouging huge lumps out of the plaster façade before ricocheting. Almost in the same instant, he heard the unmistakable crack of a carbine, then a second man opened up with a heavy calibre submachine-gun. The noise was awesome and intimidating; fortunately, all SMGs were notoriously inaccurate above twenty-five yards and the gunman wasn't good enough to compensate for it. Freeland, however, didn't wait around to see if he improved; he set off on a jinking run for the alley down the street to his right. It was hardly any distance away but reaching it seemed to take for ever.

The alley didn't lead very far; within a matter of a few yards, it was sealed off by a high wall topped with shards of glass. Freeland tried the nearest dwelling, found the door unlocked and went inside. There were just two rooms, one where the family cooked, ate and sat, the other where they slept on bunk beds, head to toe. Out back in a small courtyard was an earth closet and a pile of logs for the stove. Using the woodpile as a step up, Freeland climbed over the wall and dropped down into a vegetable garden belonging to a much larger house.

Teale was the bait they had used to lure him into an ambush; that much was self-evident, but he hadn't the faintest idea who 'they' were or why they should want to kill him. And they weren't about to give up on him either, he could hear their voices in the alley. Two men with a lot more firepower than he had; it was also their territory, which meant that his chances of evading them were pretty slim.

He would have to lie low, wait until it was dark and then steal away. Breaking the curfew was the least of his worries; if he did manage to give them the slip, he couldn't return to Holt's Wharf because that would be the first place they would cover. He would have to go farther downstream, well below Broadway Mansions on the opposite bank, and hope he could find a boatman willing to ferry him across the river. If he couldn't find one or met with a blank refusal, he would just have to get his feet wet.

Their voices sounded louder, then he heard them in the courtyard and knew it was pointless to look any farther ahead than the next few minutes. The woodpile next door had merely been a convenient step up for him but they were undoubtedly much smaller and would have to use it. Freeland measured the distance to the wall with his eye; twelve, maybe fifteen feet, he couldn't miss.

The first man came over the wall faster than he anticipated. The gunman had slung his Springfield .30 calibre carbine bandolier fashion across his shoulders in order to give himself extra leverage. Once his chest and stomach were above the level of the wall, he retained a firm grip with his left hand and reached down as far as he could with the other. Then he rolled over, head and right shoulder first, while simultaneously pushing himself away from the wall with his lower hand to vault the obstacle and land upright on both feet. Freeland opened fire before he could unsling his carbine, hitting him in the leg, ribcage and head with three consecutive rounds.

Five expended, three to go and a spare clip of eight, but he couldn't afford to recharge the magazine out in the open when the second man was armed with a submachine-gun. Keeping his back to the far wall, Freeland side-stepped towards the house on his right. A forearm appeared over the wall, the hand clutching an M3, the barrel at an angle of forty-five degrees below the horizontal. Aiming blind, the gunman began to put down suppressive fire, swinging the SMG like a pendulum as he squeezed off bursts of four to five rounds at a time. It was a quick way to empty a magazine without achieving much in return. When the gunman was forced to reload, Freeland ran to the house, kicked the door in, making as much noise as he could, then changed direction and doubled silently forward to the facing wall where the first man lay dead.

The gunman ripped off a short burst with the fresh magazine for good measure before straddling the wall as though mounting a horse. He had been led to believe that Freeland was inside the house and the last place he had expected to see his quarry was by the wall directly in line with himself. His face registered total disbelief as the 7.63mm round hit him in the chest, then he dropped his SMG and toppled back into the courtyard.

Freeland moved towards the dead man lying at the foot of the wall. His legs felt as though they were made of cotton wool and he couldn't stop trembling. Functioning like a robot, he knelt beside the body, undid the web sling attached to the .30 calibre Springfield and removed the carbine. He searched the corpse, found a spare clip of ammunition in one of the jacket pockets, and changed magazines. The SMG was lying in a patch of maize a few feet away, its barrel clogged with earth. According to the manual, he should strip and clean it, but there wasn't time for that. The first .45 bullet down the spout would take care of the obstruction. The plug wasn't solid enough for the barrel to peel back like a banana; on the other hand, it wouldn't do the rifling a lot of good.

There was only the Mauser to attend to now and he could walk out of there armed to the teeth. He had just started to go through the reloading drill when a single rifle shot pierced the silence and he almost jumped out of his skin.

"Jesus Christ." Freeland licked his lips, looked round in every direction like a hunted animal. "Who's shooting at who?" he asked aloud, then told himself to get on with the job in hand.

Ejecting the remaining two rounds, he charged the magazine with a fresh clip of eight, then without thinking what he was doing, he squeezed the trigger after the working parts had gone forward. The automatic bucked in his hand and there was an angry whining sound as the bullet ricocheted off the wall in front of him. He took a deep breath, willed himself to calm down. Handle a loaded weapon carelessly and someone usually died; he'd got away with it this time but fate was unlikely to be so kind to him again.

Freeland applied the safety catch, tucked the Mauser into the waistband of his slacks and picked up the carbine with one hand, the SMG with the other. Both weapons were cocked and ready to fire. He walked through the house he had already broken into and found himself in yet another blind alley. He turned right because there was no other choice and began to make his way back to the lane where he had been ambushed. If it hadn't been for Teale, he would now be lying dead in the gutter with a bullet in his back. London had sent him to China to bring Howard home, now he had an even better reason for doing so.

The dead man was waiting for him around a bend in the alley. He was lying face down in a pool of blood, one arm outstretched as though in the moment before death, he had been pointing to something. He was dressed in Nationalist uniform and the badges of rank on the shoulder boards were those of a full colonel.

"Sniper."

Freeland voiced his conclusion aloud, backed up against the nearest wall and scanned the buildings on the opposite side of the alley from ground floor to roof. He could see no obvious fire position and was left with an itchy feeling that the sniper could be on his side of the alley. To check it out, he would have to cross the killing zone and that wasn't on. Moving sideways like a crab, he inched towards the lane where he had seen Teale.

The man London had ordered him to bring out was still by the courtyard gate, only now he was sitting down, his back resting against the wall, his legs splayed apart in a 'V'. His head was bowed and he was hugging himself with both arms. Drawing near, Freeland could see that he had been shot in the stomach.

"Water," Teale gasped and looked up at him, pleading with his eyes.

"I'll get you something better," Freeland promised him.

The bleeding had to be stopped and the wound dressed if Teale was to hold out while he got him to a doctor. He crossed the courtyard on the double, carbine in one hand, SMG in the other, and broke into the house, hitting the door with his left shoulder. Working his way up to the attic, he cleared each room in turn and found the place was deserted. In one of the rooms downstairs, he found an army-issue first aid haversack containing a shell dressing, three ampoules of morphine, a syringe, a pair of surgical scissors and enough aspirins to start a pharmacy. Leaving the carbine and SMG behind, he returned to the courtyard carrying the first aid pack.

Teale was no longer alone. Four men in plimsolls and ill-fitting green uniforms were clustered around him. Freeland didn't have to see the red star in their peaked caps to know whose army they belonged to. Smiling in what he hoped was a friendly and confident fashion, he slowly raised his hands.

8

Three of them were armed with bolt-operated rifles that had been obsolete before the Second World War began, the fourth had a Nambu pistol which vaguely resembled a Luger. All the firearms had been taken from the Japanese when the Imperial Army had surrendered in August 1945. It didn't make them any the less dangerous for that.

Freeland shook the haversack he was holding in his left hand and then pointed to Teale. "For him, okay?"

Four pairs of eyes zeroed in on his stomach and he suddenly remembered the Mauser automatic was still tucked inside the waistband of his slacks. He wondered if he should hand it to them butt first, then thought better of it. If there was a quicker way of getting himself killed, he couldn't think of one.

"Okay, you take it." He looked down at his waist and raised his head again with the warmest of smiles, a mime he had to repeat several times before the man with the Nambu pistol finally caught on. "Can I see to my friend now?" he asked.

Four inscrutable faces and total silence. Since no one seemed inclined to say anything, he assumed they had no objections and knelt down beside Teale. No specialist training was required to know that he was in a bad way. His face was like wax, smooth, shiny, colourless, which was hardly surprising considering the amount of blood he had lost. Although cold to the touch, he was perspiring freely and obviously running a fever.

The first thing Teale needed was something to kill the pain. Opening the haversack, Freeland took out a pair of surgical scissors and swiftly cut his right trouser leg to mid thigh. Then he filled the syringe with morphine from one of the ampoules, found an artery and gave him a shot. Once it had taken effect, he managed to make the soldiers understand that he needed their help to carry him into the house.

There was a couch of sorts in the living-room which was just long enough and wide enough for Teale. As soon as they had laid him down, Freeland went to work with the scissors again, cutting the clothing away so that he could examine the wound. There was a hole in Teale's stomach about the size of a coffee cup. Its irregular shape was consistent with an exit wound made by a heavy calibre, soft nose bullet that had been deflected from its original trajectory. He had been shot in the back and the bullet had probably clipped his spine and turned sideways on. If that should be the case, he would be paralysed from at least the waist down. Not that it would make a lot of difference to a man who was going to die anyway. Teale was practically busted in two and all that was holding him together was one lousy shell dressing.

"This man needs a doctor," Freeland said angrily. "A proper doctor, you understand, not one of your bloody acupuncturists."

He picked up the medical haversack, waved it in front of the Chinese, pointed to the red cross, then pretended to listen to Teale's heartbeat with a stethoscope. By the time they guessed what he was trying to convey to them in mime, Freeland had gone through the motions of performing a major piece of surgery on the older man.

It was shortly after one of their number had departed that he noticed the bruising on Teale's face. Until then, the stomach wound had commanded his whole attention. Frank Matthews and Ryan could give a dozen reasons why Howard had been beaten up and all of them would be wrong. The criminal fraternity with whom he rubbed shoulders were not responsible; the beating had been inflicted by Chiang Kai-shek's people.

Freeland couldn't think why the Nationalists should want to kill him but it was the only presumption that made any sense. They knew he was coming to Shanghai to bring Teale out and they had forced the old reprobate to lead him into an ambush.

"Freeland?" Teale's voice was low, yet petulant and fretful.

"I'm here," Freeland told him quietly, squeezing his hand.

"Where's Li?"

"You mean Colonel Li?" he asked, recalling the army officer he'd seen lying face down in the cobblestoned alley.

"Yes."

Freeland smiled grimly. At least he could now put a face to a name he knew only by reputation. "He's dead."

"Good riddance. Are . . . you . . . a . . . Communist . . . Major Freeland?" Every word was a tremendous effort for Teale and taxed to the limit what little strength he had left.

"No. Who said I was?"

"Li did . . . he hates the Reds . . . made me say . . . Nina Burzova was one . . . I think . . . they are holding her . . . in Ward Road Jail . . ."

"Yeah?"

"Get her out . . . Major Freeland . . . she hasn't done anything."

"I'll do what I can."

"Promise?"

"You have my word on it."

"Thanks."

Teale closed his eyes, exhausted. His skin was the colour and texture of waxed paper and there was a bluish tinge to both lips. Freeland felt his pulse and wasn't surprised to find that it was faint and irregular. By the time the doctor arrived accompanied by a political commissar, he was unconscious and fading rapidly.

The commissar wore no badges of rank on his olive green uniform and was identified only by the red star surmounting a hammer and sickle on the lapels and sleeves of his tunic. He was a slightly-built man in his mid forties with iron grey hair. He wasn't wearing spectacles but the pinch marks either side of his nose showed that he needed them for close work. His name was Tu Yush-sen. Until 1948 he had been a professor of Agrarian Economics at the American-funded University of St John's and was therefore fluent in English.

"Our doctor will do all that he can for your friend, Mr Teale."

"I'm sure he will," Freeland said.

"In the meantime, I think you and I should leave him to get on with it while we have a quiet talk upstairs."

It was the kind of suggestion that was impossible to ignore, especially as Tu Yush-sen had four armed men to back him. Two of the soldiers accompanied them up to a north-facing room on the floor above, where one remained outside on the landing. The other took post by the window, presumably in case Freeland took it into his head to shin down the drainpipe. The furniture consisted of two upright chairs and a heavy table, all of which looked crude enough to be home made.

"Please sit down, Mr Freeland."

"Thanks. Mind if I smoke?"

"Please do."

Freeland took out a packet of Goldflake and offered them round. Both Tu Yush-sen and the soldier declined politely.

"Why did the Nationalist police try to kill you?" Tu Yush-sen asked.

"You mean those were Chiang Kai-shek's people?" Freeland put on an astonished expression. "I thought they were gangsters."

91

"You're evading the question, Mr Freeland."

"Not at all. I assumed the men who ambushed me were criminals because Teale put them up to it, and if you know anything at all about him, you'll have learned that many of his business acquaintances were in the underworld."

"I thought he was supposed to be your friend."

"Where did you get that idea? I never said he was. As a matter of fact, I'd never laid eyes on him before this afternoon. If you must know, I'm a civil servant attached to the War Crimes Commission. I was sent out here because a former sergeant in the Royal Air Force made a statement saying that Teale actively collaborated with the Japanese guards when they were in a prisoner-of-war camp at Kobe. He heard I was looking for him and decided I had to be stopped one way or another."

The story was a pack of lies from beginning to end, but he had to protect himself and nothing he said could possibly hurt Teale now.

"One thing puzzles me, Mr Freeland. How did he know you were looking for him?"

"His Filipino mistress, Dominga Zaldivar, must have told him. I called on her when I didn't find Teale at home. Of course, I didn't tell Miss Zaldivar exactly why I wanted to see her boyfriend, but war crimes were mentioned and he obviously drew his own conclusion."

"There are bruises on Mr Teale's face. How do you account for that?"

"I can't." Freeland shrugged. "Maybe he tried to double-cross some of his shadier business associates and they took it out on his hide?"

Tu Yush-sen nodded sagely, then turned away to question the soldier in Shanghaiese. The exchange, which started slowly, accelerated to machine-gun speed, both men becoming excited in the process.

"Comrade Tsun here claims you were armed," he said, switching back to Freeland. "Do you deny it?"

"I saw all kinds of people while I was trying to run Teale to ground, many of whom didn't have a good word to say for him. When I heard about the sort of company he was keeping, I went out and bought myself a firearm."

"From whom?"

"It didn't seem politic to ask his name." Freeland pinched his cigarette out between finger and thumb and pocketed the stub. "Anyway, he wouldn't have told me if I had."

Tu Yush-sen stared at him blankly. Although his face gave

nothing away, it wasn't difficult to guess what he was thinking. By definition, all Intelligence officers are natural born sceptics and the former professor of Agrarian Economics at St John's University was no exception.

"I think you are lying, Mr Freeland," he said quietly. "You didn't buy that pistol from a crooked arms dealer; it was issued to you by your Foreign Office superiors here in Shanghai."

"A 1910 Mauser 7.63mm automatic? You've got to be joking."

"Comrade Tsun says that you also had an American carbine and submachine-gun."

"Weapons I took from the two men I killed."

"My comrades found a third man in the lane outside the house." Tu Yush-sen paused, then said, "You're not exactly a novice with a hand gun, are you, Mr Freeland?"

"One can't help acquiring certain skills. I was a soldier in the last war; so, I imagine, were you."

"You have no papers to prove who you say you are. I think you are a member of the British Secret Service and your mission is to spy on the People's Liberation Army . . ."

"And that's why the Nationalists tried to kill me, is it?" Freeland demanded angrily, and immediately regretted losing his temper; it could only make an already tricky situation even more fraught. "Look, the British Government has no quarrel with Chairman Mao and the PLA; the Yangtze incident was a mistake that should never have happened."

"A mistake? Not only has your Mr Attlee refused to apologise for an act of unprovoked aggression by the British Navy, he has also declined to compensate the relatives of those unfortunate peasants who were killed when HMS *Amethyst* recklessly opened fire."

Tu Yush-sen was far too intelligent a man to believe half of what he was saying, but this was the Party line and he had learned it by rote. Sensing it was pointless to interrupt him, Freeland waited patiently until he had finished the diatribe and appeared to be in a more receptive mood.

"Mistakes have been made," he said diplomatically, "and you're making one about me. I came here to obtain a statement from Mr Teale, now all I want to do is get him to a hospital across the river. May I do that?"

"He is dying, Mr Freeland, you know that as well as I do. Move him, and you will kill him just that little bit sooner. In any case, we couldn't guarantee your safety if you left this house; Pootung is still held by Chiang Kai-shek's gangsters."

"I thought it had already been liberated."

"Oh no, we merely belong to the local resistance group; the regular forces of the People's Liberation Army won't enter the city until Wednesday morning. This will give the mayor time to hold his Victory Parade and allow many more thousands of Nationalist soldiers to desert. I am sure you will agree that there is method in our apparent madness."

"You'll save a lot of unnecessary bloodshed," Freeland said.

"Quite so." Tu Yush-sen got to his feet and moved towards the door, then turned about and gave him the bad news. "I'm afraid you will have to remain here until things return to normal. I'll arrange for some hot food to be brought in and one of the women hereabouts will make you up a bed on the floor."

"Thanks. In the meantime, may I sit with Mr Teale?"

"I will ask the doctor and let you know before I report to the Pootung District Committee. After seeing them, I shall probably have some further questions for you to answer tomorrow, Mr Freeland."

There were always more questions and the interrogators would inevitably take a much harsher line with him as time wore on. He remembered how it had been in February 1944 when Feldwebel Karl Heinz Grothmann of the Abwehr's Field Security Police had urged him to co-operate. What was it he'd said? – 'I have no wish to hand you over to Sturmbannführer Hausser of the SS but unless I am seen to be making progress, I'll have no say in the matter.' Agents who were arrested were required by the Special Operations Executive to hold out for seventy-two hours so that the rest of the affected cell would have time to disperse and go underground. After three days, the captured agent was then free to talk his head off, provided he'd reached the limit of his endurance. However, by 1944, German Intelligence had been well aware of this standard operating procedure and consequently their aim was to break a prisoner before the remainder of the resistance cell could disband and reorganise elsewhere. And when it came to applying force to extract the information they wanted, the SS had few equals.

Freeland sat there in the gathering darkness looking at the misshapen stump on his left hand where the little finger had been crudely amputated and wondered if he would have to suffer the same kind of agony again tomorrow, wondered too if anyone would notice his absence before then.

*　　　*　　　*

Lander glanced at his wrist watch and frowned. Freeland had said he would meet him for drinks in the bar at half past six and here it was almost twenty-five after seven and there was still no sign of him. Leaving his glass on the bar, Lander walked through the lobby and approached the desk clerk. The guy who'd given him Freeland's room number twenty minutes ago was still on duty, but that was no sweat, there was hardly a Chinaman in Shanghai these days who couldn't be bought. Slowly and very deliberately, he removed his class ring and placed it on the counter in full view of the clerk. It wasn't the most aesthetic piece of jewellery in the world and the Prussian blue bauble wasn't even semi-precious but the gold in which it was set was twenty-two carat and would fetch an even hundred.

"Room 911," he said crisply. "I'm afraid I've lost my key – you got a duplicate?"

The key to 911 was where it was supposed to be, tucked inside its allotted pigeon hole in the rack on the far wall in rear of the counter. The desk clerk knew it was there, knew also what was expected of him. Reaching under the counter, he produced a pass key and gave it to Lander, then swiftly palmed the gold class ring.

"Thanks."

"You're welcome, sir."

"Yeah, well, give me a call if the real key should turn up," Lander told him.

The curfew had been in force for well over an hour and although Freeland was now unlikely to return before morning, Lander believed in playing it safe. If by chance the Englishman should return while he was searching his room, the desk clerk would ring 911 to warn him. Entering one of the elevators, he went on up to the ninth floor.

Lander wanted to satisfy himself that Freeland hadn't simply walked out of the hotel and vanished into thin air. He also hoped to find something which would substantiate his conviction than Harry was a British Intelligence Officer, though whether a professional undercover man would be that careless was a mite optimistic.

There were two pairs of light grey slacks hanging in the wardrobe, socks, underpants and a couple of sports shirts in the chest of drawers, the latter coyly hiding a British passport. There was also a distinctive tie, the kind the British were fond of because it demonstrated that the wearer was a member of some exclusive club. A freshly laundered shirt, which had obviously been sent up to the room shortly after Freeland had left the hotel, lay on the small coffee table between the two easy chairs in the right-hand corner of the room. Lander had never heard of St Michael but he guessed it was some kind of mass retail outlet. Only the tie was exclusive and he thought it significant that the maker's label had been removed.

He returned to the wardrobe and took down the travelling bag which Freeland had placed on the flat top. It was just an ordinary piece of luggage though its condition suggested that either it had been purchased long before the war or else it had received some pretty harsh treatment along the way. There was a solitary tie-on label; examining it, he saw that Freeland's home address was Dolphin House, Chatham Place, London, SW1.

On the escritoire positioned near the window overlooking The Bund, he found a cheap writing pad containing an unfinished letter to a girl whom Freeland called Jen. Recalling the conversation with Berringer, he assumed this was his private nickname for the one-time sergeant in the Women's Auxiliary Air Force. The content was all very restrained with few terms of endearment and, aside from the occasional personal note, it read like a travelogue from the *National Geographic*.

Lander closed the writing pad, suddenly disgusted with himself for behaving like a Peeping Tom. The letter didn't tell him a damned thing he didn't already know about Freeland. When you came right down to it, he thought, Phil Ryan was just using him to sniff out a story and all that concern for George's kith and kin was just so much horse feathers.

Lander left the room, went down to the lobby and returned the pass key to the desk clerk. His unfinished drink was still there on the bar but the crushed ice had melted, diluting the whisky to the point where it resembled urine. He ordered another Jack Daniels on the rocks and drank it slowly. Smooth as the liquor was, it didn't wash away the sour taste in his mouth.

*   *   *

A grey morning in December, a thin covering of snow hiding the cobblestones. Some of the cobblestones at the far end of the courtyard have been removed and there are four wooden posts embedded in the ground. Each one is over six feet high and they are evenly spaced apart. To a certain extent, the wall behind is protected by a sandbank but at chest height some of the bricks are pockmarked.

A door opens to his right and a priest in a black cassock appears, followed by a young woman in a shapeless prison uniform who is escorted by two warders. Her head is bowed and she is clutching a rosary. The procession halts opposite the second post from the right and the young woman turns to face him. Her name is Chantal Kiffer, she has ash-blonde hair, green eyes and an astonishingly beautiful face that is marred only by an old scar on her chin, the result of a riding accident when she was a child. She is thirty-one years old, a doctor of medicine, and since 1938 has been living in the village of St Aubin des Bois near Chartres where she is the local GP. There is a Monsieur Emil Kiffer who was called up for military service in August 1939, but he has not been seen or heard of since the following June when his regiment was decimated by the 7th Panzer Division in the breakthrough at Sedan. She and Freeland are lovers.

The priest recovers the rosary and makes a sign of the cross while giving her absolution for whatever it is she is supposed to have done. The two warders tie her wrists together behind the stake and bind her ankles; a rope is then passed round Chantal's waist in order to hold her upright because she is trembling so much that she is unable to do so without assistance. One of the warders blindfolds her with a silk scarf, the other pins an aiming mark over her heart.

The priest and warders move away to one flank; off stage, the officer in charge of the firing squad gives the orders to load, aim and fire in her native language. The volley is ragged with at least three of the soldiers shooting late. Most of the squad hit the white aiming mark; behind her, the post splinters and small puff clouds of brick dust rise from the far wall. Chantal rears back at the moment of impact, then folds in half and is only held upright by the rope around her waist. There is no need for the Provost Marshal to administer the coup de grâce *but he does so nonetheless.*

The pain is excruciating and there is a limit to the amount anyone can stand. London knows this, so does Sturmbannführer Hausser into whose hands he has been delivered by Feldwebel Karl Heinz Grothmann. The SS have tried shoving an electrode up his anus and his penis and testicles have been wired to a 12-volt battery, which the harpies from the typing pool who had been allowed to witness this phase of his interrogation, had found vastly amusing. They have also given him the water treatment but that too has failed even though he came close to drowning on several occasions. Now, with time running out, Sturmbannführer Hausser is becoming desperate; Berlin wants results and he is not getting them.

Freeland cannot move. They have tied him down on the operating table and the surgeon used to be a butcher in Wuppertal before he put on an SS uniform. His surgical instruments belong in a carpenter's tool box and he does not see the need for anaesthetics. A carpenter would have used the pincers to draw a nail; in the butcher's hands they are a cutting instrument. The amputation of the little finger on his left hand is done slowly, a joint at a time, the bone crunching between the jaws of the pincers, and whenever he slips into merciful unconsciousness they bring him round with smelling salts or use a lighted cigarette on his chest. And when they have butchered the little finger to a bloody stump, Sturmbannführer Hausser tells him they propose to do the same with his thumb, and so he talks, giving them everything they want

97

*to know, names, places, frequencies, call signs . . . But it is Chantal Kiffer
who pays the ultimate price for his treachery, tried and executed by the French
Forces of the Interior while he is incarcerated in Flossenburg.*

A hand gripped his shoulder and shook it urgently, a flashlight
played on his eyes and Freeland woke up screaming.

"You come, you come."

Freeland got up off the floor, his heart still thumping. One
recurring nightmare had ended, a new one looked as though
it was about to begin. Guided by the torch, he followed the
soldier downstairs into a room lit by a single hurricane lamp.
Teale was still lying on the couch; no one had to tell Freeland
that he was dead.

9

Unlike Freeland, it was evident that Tu Yush-sen had enjoyed a good night's sleep. There were no tell-tale smudges under his eyes, his face was clean-shaven and although his uniform was still a bad fit, the olive-green tunic and slacks had been recently laundered.

"I'm sorry about your friend, Mr Teale," he said, then sat down at the table and motioned Freeland to do likewise. "However, I think you'll agree that the doctor did everything he could to save him."

"I'm sure he received the very best of attention," Freeland said carefully.

"I'm glad to hear you say so. Unfortunately, he wasn't able to stop the internal haemorrhaging."

"I see. Have you notified the British Consulate of his death?"

"Not yet. It is too dangerous to send anyone across the river while the Nationalists still control the city."

"You could telephone Mr Caunter."

"Telephones can be tapped."

"So what have you done with his body?" Freeland asked.

"We were able to obtain a plywood coffin for the corpse and then we put it in the cold store belonging to Butterfield and Swire."

Tu Yush-sen had an answer for everything. Under no circumstances would he let the Consulate know what had happened to Teale before he had finished interrogating him. If he did, both Caunter and Matthews would ask what had happened to him, and Tu Yush-sen wouldn't like to be caught out in a lie. For all that he had been a professor of Agrarian Economics at the University of St John's, he was still Chinese enough not to want to lose face.

"Will Mr Teale be buried here in Shanghai or will the British Consulate arrange for his body to be sent home?"

"That's up to the next-of-kin, assuming there are any." Freeland sensed another question and answer session was about to begin and

99

immediately seized the initiative, one of the techniques of resistance to interrogation the Special Operations Executive had taught him during the war. "Did you find any papers on him?" he asked.

"His pockets were empty."

"I guess they would be. According to his girlfriend, Dominga Zaldivar, more than a week has gone by since the police arrested him. What puzzles me is why they should have thought Teale was a Communist agent."

"You disappoint me, Mr Freeland. I thought you were far too intelligent a man to invent such a childish story."

"It happens to be the truth."

"Or your version of it. I am willing to concede however that, like you, he was certainly a British spy."

"Forget about me for the moment, let's concentrate on Howard Teale. When you saw those bruises on his face, you must have noticed that only one or two were purple while the rest were yellowish, like over-ripe bananas."

"I am not blind, Mr Freeland."

"Then you agree that he was repeatedly beaten up over a period of several days?"

"Perhaps."

"There's no perhaps about it. Colonel Li believed he was a Communist and had his people torture him until he gave them some names. I think he gave them mine."

"I'm beginning to appreciate what a fertile imagination you have."

"Teale spoke to me while one of the comrades was looking for a doctor. He was still conscious then; ask the other soldiers if you don't believe me."

Every piece of disinformation should contain a grain of truth which the interrogator can verify; that was guideline number two the SOE had drummed into him. The soldiers might not understand a word of English but they could tell Comrade Political Commissar Tu Yush-sen that, badly wounded though he'd been, Teale had managed to have a few words with him.

"You're an Intelligence Officer, Mr Freeland . . ."

"What about Nina Burzova? Is she also a spy?"

"I've never heard of her."

"Neither had I until Teale mentioned her name. He told Li she was a Communist and the Colonel had her arrested. She's being held in Ward Road jail."

"You must think I am a fool . . ."

"Check it out," Freeland said, cutting him short.

"Impossible . . ."

"Don't tell me that, the whole of Shanghai is riddled with your Fifth Columnists. You've got informants in every department; I bet you even know what colour socks the mayor is wearing today."

"I'm flattered that you should think so highly of our network but you exaggerate our capabilities. However, one does hear rumours; for instance, it is said that your Air Force is sending five flying boats to evacuate those British residents who wish to leave Shanghai. I've also heard that the flying boats will land on the Whangpoo near Lunghwa."

"Will you fire on them if they do?"

"There are no war criminals in the PLA; we do not kill innocent people like the Anglo-American Imperialists."

"The day before yesterday your artillery bombarded Lunghwa, destroying a civil airliner, the only plane on the airfield. There were a number of civilian casualties, some of them fatal. I was there, I saw it happen."

"The plane you speak of was a C46 belonging to Civil Air Transport." Tu Yush-sen allowed himself a brief smile. "We do not like Major-General Claire Chennault, so the District Committee decided to teach him a lesson."

"You were glad of his help during the war."

"Indeed we were; his mistake was in coming back to China after it was over. Rest assured, Mr Freeland, we have no desire to prevent any foreigner leaving Shanghai who wants to do so."

"Including me?"

"I regret you are the one exception. My comrades on the District Committee aren't satisfied that you are what you say you are. We have therefore decided that you should remain a guest of the People's Liberation Army until all China has been liberated when it will then be safe to deport you."

To be told that you were a guest of the PLA sounded much cosier than being a prisoner-of-war, but it amounted to the same thing. And how long would it take Lin Pao and the other Communist generals to drive the last Nationalist soldier from mainland China – six months? – a year? Freeland was damned if he was going to wait that long.

"Are you being looked after?" Tu Yush-sen asked.

"I've no complaints."

The elderly woman who had made him up a bed on the floor had reappeared early that morning to tidy up the room. She had also brought him breakfast, a bowl of lukewarm rice, bamboo shoots, beans, soy sauce and meat. The meat was like nothing Freeland had ever tasted before and he'd wondered if one of the neighbourhood dogs had ended up in the cooking pot.

"Good. For the time being, you'll have to stay here. Later on, we shall be able to find more suitable accommodation for you."

Suitable accommodation probably meant a cell in Ward Road jail. "When's that likely to be?" Freeland asked.

"Two, three days, perhaps longer."

"And in the meantime, I'm to stay here, cooped up in this room?"

"Except for exercise periods."

"What's that mean, a gentle stroll round the courtyard twice a day?"

If he was going to escape, it was important to establish what sort of prison routine he would have to contend with.

"I think I can agree to one hour in the morning and afternoon. And yes, you will be restricted to the courtyard. This is for your own protection."

"Naturally." Freeland pointed to the guard who was standing in his customary position in front of the window. "Does he know that I'm allowed out twice a day?'

"He will be informed."

"Well, while you're at it, tell him that when I ask to go to the lavatory, I don't expect to be told that I must wait for the next exercise period. There are no toilet facilities in this room and I'm not pissing in a bucket for anyone."

There was a momentary and very uncomfortable silence before Tu Yush-sen threw back his head and laughed. There was nothing spontaneous about his mirth. Freeland had touched a raw nerve but he hadn't wanted to show his anger in front of a subordinate and so he'd acted as though they were enjoying a private joke. It was yet another example of Tu Yush-sen's horror of losing face.

"You are a very funny man, Mr Freeland."

"Good of you to say so; for a moment, I thought I'd gone too far."

"I think there is very little danger of you doing that."

It was a subtle way of letting him know that they were determined he shouldn't escape. When they left the room, Freeland waited to see if Tu Yush-sen would order the soldier to lock him in but it seemed the political commissar considered an armed guard on the landing was sufficient. From the north-facing window, Freeland saw that another sentry had been posted in the alleyway behind the house.

*　　*　　*

Matthews scanned the horizon looking for a silver speck in the sky, visual confirmation that the first of the Sunderland flying boats was only minutes away from touch-down. The pilot had called the control tower a good twenty minutes ago to confirm his estimated time of arrival and, on learning this, Caunter had immediately despatched the initial plane-load of evacuees from the Consulate where they had foregathered.

There were twenty-nine evacuees, one less than the planned total. Most of them had arrived in trucks which the Consulate had hired from the Public Works Department, a few had rolled up in their own vehicles. Two of these had now been abandoned near the operations shack to the undisguised annoyance of the officer commanding the forward element of 215 Squadron RAF who'd made his displeasure known to Matthews.

"If this keeps up," he'd said, pointing to a Jowett Javelin and a 1939 model Pontiac, "people will think I'm either in the second-hand car trade or running a junk yard."

It was, Matthews thought, all very well for him to say that he wanted them moved but who was going to do it? The Jowett Javelin belonged to a seventy-year-old lawyer and his wife whose Chinese chauffeur had mysteriously disappeared shortly before they were due to leave their house, and the owner of the Pontiac claimed that the man he'd sold it to would be along to collect it at any moment. Both offenders had reasonable excuses and the Consulate certainly didn't have any drivers to spare, and much as Matthews also liked things to be neat and tidy, his mind was preoccupied with more pressing matters.

The seaplane base was located almost cheek by jowl with Lunghwa airfield and he couldn't forget that less than forty-eight hours ago, Communist artillery fire had destroyed Lander's plane. Caunter had provided him with the biggest Union Jack the Consulate possessed and he had run that up on the flagstaff outside the headquarters of 215 Squadron where it hung limply in the still air. He had also pegged out a smaller version on the corrugated iron roof of the single-storey building, but he doubted if either could be seen from observation posts established within Pootung itself.

The suburb of Pootung lay north-east of the seaplane base and the nearest house was a good two miles from their position. At that distance, the suburb across the river looked peaceful enough, but

103

appearances were deceptive. Although the Nationalists still held most of Pootung, local Communist guerilla units had established a number of enclaves and it could only be a question of time before the skirmishing developed into a full-scale battle. Matthews just hoped the unofficial cease-fire would hold until after the last Sunderland had taken off. Certainly, Caunter and the other consular officials had done their best to ensure that both sides knew about the airlift. Details of the evacuation plan had appeared in all the English and Chinese newspapers and had been repeated on local radio.

He had one other worry nagging at the back of his mind. Earlier on, he had phoned the Cathay Hotel and had been informed by the desk clerk that Freeland had not been seen since leaving the hotel at four o'clock the previous afternoon. Teale was hiding somewhere in Pootung and Freeland must have run into trouble after he had gone across the river to collect him. Much as he was reluctant to accept this premise, it was the only logical explanation to account for his disappearance. With the Foreign Office making it clear that the Consulate was not to get involved with any Secret Intelligence Service operation, it was pointless passing on his worry to Caunter. And even if Freeland hadn't been virtually *persona non grata*, there was nothing they could do to help him. In the circumstances, Matthews could only keep his fingers crossed and hope for the best.

"Here she comes . . . at last."

Matthews swept the horizon with his binoculars but could see no sign of the flying boat. "You've got better eyes than I have," he told the flight-sergeant standing next to him.

"Behind you – the missing evacuee from the first serial."

Matthews turned about, gaped at the open truck which had just pulled up outside the headquarters building. The baggage allowance was one suitcase per person; the movement instructions issued by the Consulate had been very specific about that and there was really no excuse for anyone to plead ignorance. There were, however, people who went through life convinced that they were exempt from irksome regulations. The Honourable Mrs Alma Hughes-Murchison was clearly one of them; loaded on the back of the truck were the most valuable items of her household possessions which included a grand piano.

"Someone will have to put her straight," the flight-sergeant said, looking at him.

"And guess who's elected," Matthews said with a sigh.

He only knew the Honourable Mrs Alma Hughes-Murchison by reputation which was why he had no desire to make her acquaintance. Queen Victoria had been on the throne when she had arrived in Shanghai as the nineteen-year-old bride of the International Settlement's most prominent businessman and heir apparent of Murchison and Cranley, Tea Planters. It was said of the Hughes-Murchisons that Alma supplied the class, husband Nigel the wherewithal to establish their social pre-eminence. They had lived in style in a ten-bedroom mansion on Yu Yuen Road with a small army of servants to tend to their every need, and an invitation to dinner from Alma had been the equivalent of a royal command.

Imperious, autocratic and completely single-minded in the pursuit of her own interests, Alma had been such a thorn in the side of Chiang Kai-shek throughout the five years she had been forced to spend in Chungking during the war that the Generalissimo couldn't wait to see her re-established in Shanghai. Of all the expatriates who had returned to the city in 1945, she was the only one whose property was restored to its former glory by Japanese prisoners-of-war. It was a measure of Alma's dominant personality that few people could now recall Nigel or even remember when it was that he'd died. At the age of seventy-eight, she had not mellowed one bit, as Matthews quickly discovered when he tried to explain that the baggage allowance was one suitcase per person.

"One miserable suitcase?" Her eyes flashed angrily. "Do you really think I am going to bequeath my Chippendale furniture and Meissen ornaments to that ignorant upstart, Chairman Mao?"

"I'm afraid there's no room for them on the flying boat," Matthews told her politely.

"Young man, I don't think you quite understand the situation." Alma was only an inch over five feet, yet when she drew herself up, Matthews felt as though she was towering over him. "I have no desire to leave Shanghai; it was your Consul General who begged me to go, he said it was my duty to set an example to the others. Now, how he could really imagine that I was going to leave behind all my most precious possessions is simply beyond me."

"Nevertheless, he does."

"In that case," said Alma, "we have nothing further to say to one another and I bid you good day."

The Ford truck was on its last legs, but the Chinese driver was dressed in a chauffeur's livery and he placed a footstool on the ground to enable her to climb up on to the running board. Watching the Honourable Mrs Alma Hughes-Murchison as she drove away, Matthews reflected that he would probably never see her like again.

105

Right on schedule and some twenty minutes after she had departed, the first Sunderland landed on the Whangpoo River at 1145 hours and the evacuation began.

*   *   *

Of the three airfields in use, Kiangwin to the north of Shanghai was far and away the best equipped. While under their control, the United States Air Force had lengthened the runways and installed the most up-to-date radar equipment. Protected by the guns of the Woosung forts at the conflux of the Yangtze and Whangpoo rivers as well as a flotilla of destroyers, Kiangwin was regarded by the Nationalists as their most secure airbase. Then the PLA began to move on the city and suddenly it was no longer the desirable piece of real estate it had once seemed. When Lander had gone there on Thursday to collect a replacement compass there hadn't been a single plane on the runway; today, however, things were different; today there was a solitary DC3 guarded by a ring of a dozen armed sentries.

The Dakota was the reason why he was there. The manager of the Civil Air Transport office in Shanghai had rung him at the Cathay Hotel to relay a message from General Chennault. A C46 belonging to CAT had somehow been stranded in Taiwan and the General wished him to recover this valuable piece of property. The fact that he knew a Dakota was leaving Kiangwin for Taiwan didn't surprise Lander; the General had always been on the friendliest of terms with Madame Chiang Kai-shek and he assumed that she had told him. He had also assumed that this cosy relationship automatically guaranteed him a seat on the plane until the little blowhard of a Colonel who was running the show had disabused him of the notion. Chennault could have two fingers up Madame Chiang Kai-shek for all the Colonel cared; he had his orders and there was a long queue of VIPs ahead of Lander. If Lander was lucky, he might just be able to squeeze him aboard for a consideration.

Lander had kept a 'C' note in his billfold for just such an emergency but it seemed the Colonel merely regarded this as a retainer. He had been sitting on the grass outside the ring of soldiers watching the VIPs arrive in dribs and drabs for more than two hours now and the plane was damned nearly filled to capacity. If the order to retrieve the stranded C46 had come from anyone else, he would have called it a day, but you didn't give up on General Chennault.

A black Rolls Royce glided towards the Dakota and stopped just short of the armed sentries. A liveried chauffeur got out and

106

opened the rear offside door of the limousine. A dumpy Chinese lady alighted and was followed by a glamorous young woman in an oyster-coloured cheongsam and four inch heels. Lander gave a low whistle, eyeballed her all the way to the plane. Legs like Betty Grable and a cute little ass; searching for an apt phrase to describe her, he decided she had style and class. He watched her ascend the flight of steps to the cabin and experienced a sense of loss when she finally disappeared from view.

Someone else rapidly disappeared from view. Before Lander realised what was happening, the blowhard little Colonel raced up the steps and with assistance from one of the cabin staff, closed the door behind him. Then one of the soldiers wheeled the steps away and the ring of soldiers dispersed.

"You son of a bitch." Lander scrambled to his feet, shook his fist at the aircraft and everyone aboard. No seat on the plane and the 'C' note gone for good.

"You goddamned lousy son of a bitch," he roared.

The port engine whined on the self-starter, spluttered into life, then the starboard caught first time. The pilot ran both Pratt and Whitneys up to full power and held the plane at the end of the runway. A green Very light soared into the sky from the direction of the control tower, then the brakes came off and the Dakota started rolling.

It was a perfect take-off, and it wasn't until the plane had reached an altitude of roughly a thousand feet that the passengers and crew ran out of luck. Units of the PLA were no more than five miles due west of the airfield and the pilot had drifted dangerously near the front line as he climbed in a spiral. Half a dozen black puff balls appeared above and below the Dakota, bracketing the aircraft close enough to rock it visibly. The plane began to seesaw and Avgas from a ruptured fuel line streamed from the port engine. The tip ignited, flared like a child's sparkler, then became a fiery comet chasing its own tail. The slipstream held the fire momentarily in check while the pilot struggled to regain control and take what evasive action he could to avoid the heavy concentration of flak. Then suddenly the tongue of flame lanced forward to engulf the entire port wing and the plane exploded like a bomb.

"Jesus."

Lander stared at the incandescent fireball in the sky, then turned away, numbed by the sight. It wasn't a new experience for him, he'd seen other planes go the same way, had even burned a Zero over Kunming himself, but this was on a much bigger scale and therefore somehow more shocking.

It was a long walk back to town. By the time Lander reached the outskirts, the sun was well down on the horizon and the uneasy truce which had existed while the British and American civilians were being evacuated no longer pertained. Across the Whangpoo River, Communist artillery batteries were shelling the Nationalist enclaves in Pootung.

* * *

The last Sunderland had departed at 1740 hours while Freeland was pacing up and down the courtyard under the watchful eye of one of the guards. He had heard it take off and had tried to catch a glimpse of the flying boat as it passed overhead, but the guard had decided that only physical activity was allowed during exercise periods and had forbidden him to look up at the sky. The incident was, Freeland thought, a foretaste of things to come if he failed to escape.

The exercise period was cut short by the artillery bombardment. Although they had never been in danger, the guards had hustled him inside the house, possibly because they were afraid he would take advantage of the noise and confusion and try to escape. From his room at the back of the house, he could see that the fire was being directed against a number of pinpoint targets, the nearest of which was about a quarter of a mile away. Each Nationalist strong point was engaged by a battery of six to eight guns but there was no set pattern to the bombardment. Individual batteries lifted from one target to the next, fired an indeterminate number of rounds, then switched back to the first.

Sometimes the guns would fall silent and the lull would last for anything up to twenty minutes, then suddenly all hell would break loose again. The cat and mouse tactics were intended to harass the Nationalist defenders, inflict the maximum number of casualties and thereby undermine their morale. The preparatory bombardment also gave Freeland an indication of what ground was held by the PLA north of the house. Judging by the noise, the Nationalist positions to the south were taking a hammering too but since there was no window facing in that direction, he had no idea where the Communist lines ended and Chiang Kai-shek's began.

Not all the shells were on target. Every now and then a stray landed uncomfortably close and those civilians who hadn't moved out of the immediate neighbourhood were obviously keeping their heads well down. There was also a certain amount of incoming counter battery fire from across the Whangpoo and the sentry who was normally on duty in the alleyway had been withdrawn. The

108

window was roughly eighteen to twenty feet above the a̶
though smaller than the table in his room, was large eno̶
Freeland to squeeze through. Realising this, the guards had ̶
the window to the frame so that he couldn't open it. Kno̶
together, the pair of cotton sheets would cut the drop by so̶me
eight feet and reduce the risk of breaking an ankle when he landed
on the cobblestones. Whether the threadbare sheets would take his
weight would be answered soon enough. Although no one could
prevent him smashing the glass, the timing was all important and
that was something he was powerless to regulate.

Freeland checked his wristwatch again. This particular lull
seemed to be going on for ever but the minute hand had scarcely
moved since the last time he'd looked. But what if the bombardment
had finished? How long before the old woman who brought him
his meals judged it safe to leave the shelter where she had taken
cover? When the guard opened the door for her, he would see the
knotted bedsheets and then it would be infinitely more difficult for
him to escape. For peace to break out now was the last thing he
wanted.

The next phase of the artillery fire programme began just as
Freeland had decided to dismantle the makeshift rope ladder. The
nearest target for the Communist guns was about half a mile away
and he waited, keyed up to fever pitch, to see what happened when
that particular battery switched to the next fire mission.

A battery of 105s opened up on what Freeland assumed was
a Nationalist position four or five streets due north of the house.
Whatever its precise location, the target was close enough for the
blast from the incoming shells to rattle the window. Then a salvo
fell wide and he decided it was now or never. Lifting one of the
heavy wooden chairs with both hands, he swung it at the window,
smashing the pane into hundreds of fragments. At the same time,
he began screaming at the top of his voice as though he had been
badly cut by flying glass. Then he moved swiftly and silently across
the room to stand with his back against the inner wall.

The sentry out on the landing opened the door and charged
headlong into the room. Timing it to perfection, Freeland tossed
the chair into his path, cutting his legs from under him so that he
went sprawling. The ancient Japanese rifle slipped from his grasp
and skittered across the floor. Pouncing on the weapon, Freeland
grabbed hold of the barrel and clubbed the guard across the head
with the butt.

He dropped the rifle, moved the table up to the window and,
doing his best to steer clear of the shards of glass embedded in

the frame, climbed out and used the bed sheets to walk down the wall. There was a loud rending sound as the bottom sheet ripped in half and he landed heavily on the cobblestones below, twisting his left ankle. The moment Freeland picked himself up and started running, he knew he'd sprained it badly.

10

The ankle held Freeland back, making it impossible for him to do more than lope along like a man with a wooden leg. Up ahead, the alleyway curved to the right and the marksman had yet to be conceived who could bend a bullet round a corner. Although he could hear nothing above the noise of the artillery bombardment, he assumed the other guards would have raised the alarm by now and at any second, they would be using him for target practice. They wouldn't give him an opportunity to surrender; he had probably killed their comrade and, whatever their nationality, soldiers didn't take kindly to that sort of thing. As if to confirm his prognosis, a bullet thumped into the wall above his head and careened off into the night, the first shot of a ragged volley.

The guards were equipped with obsolete rifles. To eject the spent cartridge case from the breech and reload, it was necessary to open and close the bolt manually. A trained soldier could empty a ten-round magazine in as many seconds but these men were part-time irregulars and had probably received the minimum amount of weapon training. They were also excited and their aim would suffer as a result. Freeland clung to those comforting thoughts as he struggled to reach the bend in the alleyway before their marksmanship improved. Five more paces . . . four . . . three . . . two . . . one; he turned the corner and gasped with relief.

As long as he continued to head north, they were unlikely to follow him. If they did, they would be walking into their own artillery fire and would inevitably come up against the forward defended localities of the Nationalists. They had a choice, Freeland didn't. There was no neutral ground in Pootung and no matter which direction he took, someone was going to shoot at him.

The alley jinked to the right again, taking him farther away from the river. A lane on the opposite side of the street appeared to lead in the right direction but it petered out after twenty yards or so and he found himself confronted with a choice of footpaths

111

meandering through a shanty town of wooden shacks, all of which seemed to have been abandoned by their occupants. There was nothing of military significance in the area but like most of the other inhabitants of Pootung, they evidently weren't taking any chances and had moved out into the countryside.

The preparatory bombardment began to ease off once more, the batteries coming out of action one by one. Somewhere over to the north-east, a stores depot was on fire and he could smell the acrid tang of burning rubber. The dense pall of black smoke rising into the night sky added to the overcast and blanked out the stars. Lacking any kind of navigational aid to guide him, Freeland relied on an ingrained sense of direction when it came to choosing which footpath to follow.

The left ankle was really swollen now and the top of his head felt as though it was about to lift off every time he put any weight on that leg. Both palms felt slippery, the right more so than the other which struck him as an odd way for nervous tension to manifest itself. Then his thumb encountered a jagged wound and he realised that he must have cut his hand on a shard of glass when climbing out of the window. He limped on, stopping frequently to listen. Once he heard a sentry cough, another time it was the sound of a man urinating. On both occasions he backtracked and made a wide detour to avoid what he assumed was a Nationalist outpost.

It took him more than two hours to reach the Whangpoo. None of the landmarks were familiar; however, the paucity of lights on the far bank suggested that he was roughly in line with Hongkew. There were no heavy duty cranes on the dockside and the general run-down appearance of the wharf led Freeland to believe it was no longer in use. There were no lighters or sampans moored alongside, nor were there any within hailing distance that he could see. Things might be different in the morning but he couldn't afford to wait until then.

Freeland searched the wharf from one end to the other looking for materials which he could use to build a raft. Other scavengers had evidently been there before him but he did manage to find several hanks of rope, a couple of used tyres that had served as fenders and a length of four-by-two timber. The pair of outsized waterwings he ended up with were a far cry from what he'd originally had in mind, but it was the best he could do in the circumstances. He removed his jacket, eased off his shoes and socks and, bundling them all together, hurled the lot into the river. Then, dragging the waterwings behind him, he scrambled down the flight of steps leading to the water's edge and dropped in.

Even close to the east bank, the current was a lot stronger than he'd anticipated. The Whangpoo was about eight hundred yards wide where he had chosen to cross, but long before he reached midstream, it was already beginning to seem twice as far. Hanging on to the makeshift life raft with one hand, he kicked and clawed his way towards calmer waters. At times he wondered if the current would carry him down river to the conflux with the Yangtze and the open sea beyond. Then suddenly, just when Freeland thought he wasn't going to make it, his feet touched bottom and he fetched up on a mudbank some distance from Hongkew. Totally spent, he lay there flat on his stomach, the right side of his face pressed into the mud. Once his chest had stopped heaving, sheer willpower got him up on to his feet again. Drunk with fatigue, he started walking towards the lights of Hongkew, oblivious of the pain from his swollen ankle and the fact that he was barefoot.

Although the curfew had been in force for several hours, he didn't expect to be troubled by the military police. According to Matthews, Chiang Kai-shek's 'Snowdrops' only made their presence felt during the first hour; thereafter, they were normally conspicuous by their absence. There were, of course, always exceptions to every rule and it would be just his luck to bump into a mobile patrol led by a military fanatic. But he was too damned tired to dwell on that possibility.

Freeland trudged on through the outskirts of Hongkew, taking care never to stray very far from the river in case he lost his bearings. If ever he needed a reason to explain why so few Chinese were prepared to die in the last ditch for the Nationalists, he had only to look at the thousands of down-and-outs sleeping rough on the pavements. And no exhortation from the mayor of Shanghai could compete with Chairman Mao's promise of an acre of land for every peasant.

Almost two hours after struggling ashore, he turned into Broadway Mansions and took the lift up to the twelfth floor. He rang the bell to Matthews' apartment and kept his finger on the button until a very bleary-eyed security man opened the door to him.

"Bloody hell." Matthews looked him over from head to toe, noted his mud-splattered features and sodden clothing and gave a low whistle. "What in God's name have you been doing to yourself, Harry?" he said, and opened the door wider.

"Been for a midnight swim." All at once, the coldness of his body temperature got to Freeland and he began to shiver. "I fouled up."

"Tell me about it later; what you need right now is a good stiff

113

drink. Then you can strip off and take a bath while I make you up a bed on the couch."

"Teale is dead . . ."

"I'm sorry to hear that." Matthews crouched in front of the teak cabinet, took out a bottle of whisky and two glasses. "How did it happen?"

"One of Colonel Li's henchmen shot him. I'd have walked into an ambush if he hadn't warned me."

"Why should the police want to ambush you?"

"Li thought I was a Communist agent. Can you believe that?" Freeland took the glass of whisky with his left hand. "I mean, who on earth gave him that idea? It sure as hell wasn't Teale."

"How did you get that nasty gash on your hand, Harry?"

"I cut it on a shard of glass."

"Before or after the ambush?"

"After. I killed three of them – Nationalists I mean. Then, when I was working my way back to the house where Teale was being held, I came across the body of Colonel Li. A PLA sniper must have got him; anyway, one of their guerilla units had taken over the neighbourhood by the time I arrived to collect Teale and they insisted on putting me up for the night. Then it turned out they didn't want me to leave at all, so I went out through the window." Freeland took another large sip of whisky, felt the warm glow spread outwards from his stomach. "I lost the Mauser automatic you lent me."

"I had noticed," Matthews said drily.

"You did say that the weapon couldn't be traced to you?"

"Yes, it's never been registered."

"Thank God for that. I clubbed one of the guards over the head with his rifle; it could be I hit him too hard." His voice sounded a long way off and couldn't match the speed of his thoughts.

"We'll talk about it in the morning, Harry."

"I can't stay here."

"Of course you can."

"No, I meant Shanghai – got to escape. Can't have Salusbury thinking I've let him down again."

"Who the hell is Salusbury?"

"One of the colleagues in London. Guy Salusbury was in France with me, ended up in a concentration camp because I blew the whistle too soon."

"I see," Matthews said, but his frown told Freeland that he didn't.

"I'm sorry to have got you up in the middle of the night but I could hardly walk into the Cathay Hotel looking like a drowned rat. It would have provoked too many awkward questions."

"I don't think you should ever go back there, Harry. I'll collect your gear from the hotel."

"Caunter won't like that."

"You let me worry about him."

"Could you find out if Joe Lander is still registered at the Cathay?"

"Sure. Any reason?"

"Jacob Stein has lent me a two-man kayak and I'm looking for someone who wants to go down river as much as I do. Lander seems the most likely candidate."

"I'll see that he gets your message. Meantime, the sooner you have a bath, the sooner you get your head down."

"Right."

"On second thoughts," said Matthews, "make it a shower. I don't want you falling asleep in the tub."

Barely ten minutes later, having showered in record time, Freeland crawled into the makeshift bed on the couch and went out like a light. The intermittent rumble of artillery fire did not disturb him.

*   *   *

The flags and bunting appeared soon after daybreak; by a quarter to nine, two separate processions had formed up in Hongkew and the Old City. Each consisted of a marching column and several bands, both Western and traditional Chinese. There were nine dragons to bring good luck and truckloads of schoolchildren who had been provided with red, white and blue streamers to throw at the crowds lining the processional routes in order to encourage spontaneous gaiety. The population of Shanghai had of course been ordered to attend but even if the city hadn't been under martial law, the turn-out would still have been more than adequate for propaganda purposes.

At nine fifteen, both processions moved off to follow a circuitous route from their respective start points to the racecourse on Nanking Road where they would eventually disperse after the Mayor and Garrison Commander had made their victory speeches. The plan called for the parade which had formed up in the Old City to march down The Bund and wheel into Nanking Road while the column from Hongkew was to cross over Garden Bridge and arrive at the junction point in time to tag on to the rear of the first procession. Like most things planned by the Nationalists, it looked better on

115

paper than it turned out to be in practice. A failure to synchronise watches meant that the column from Hongkew approached the rendezvous ahead of schedule and had to be stopped at Garden Bridge. The bands continued playing and the cymbals were now accompanied by a cacophony of horns from the trucks. The din was appalling, yet Freeland would have slept through it had it not been for the persistent burring of the telephone. Still not fully awake, he rolled off the couch, peered round the living-room to see where the phone was located, and moved stiffly to answer it.

"I'm glad you're back in the land of the living," Matthews told him. "You were dead to the world when I looked in earlier on. In case you haven't noticed it, your travelling bag is on the floor by the couch."

"I see it."

"Your passport is inside, under the shirt you had laundered, and I've settled your hotel bill."

"Thanks, Frank. How much do I owe you?"

"Forty-five million Chinese dollars or fifteen pounds sterling in real money."

"I'll have to wire it to you from London; the PLA confiscated my money belt."

"Better send it through the diplomatic bag. I don't think the bank in Shanghai will be able to handle that kind of transaction in future."

"Right – and thanks again for everything."

"No sweat. By the way, I bumped into Lander in the hotel lobby. He said to tell you he would be in the Correspondents Club around eleven thirty."

It seemed to Freeland that Joe Lander hadn't suggested the Press Club just because it was convenient; he wanted something, and Phil Ryan, the AP assistant bureau chief, would be there to help him get it.

"I'll have to get a move on then." Freeland paused, then said, "I'm not going to forget what you've done for me, Frank. I only hope you can keep your nose clean."

"I'll be okay, but you ought to get that hand of yours seen to. Go and see Dr Waters, he's a good man with a needle. His surgery is on Nanking Road just before you come to the Country Club."

Freeland said he would do that, then put the phone down. He unzipped his travelling bag, took out his shaving tackle and limped into the bathroom. He wouldn't have time to see Dr Waters; opening the medicine cabinet above the wash basin, Freeland found a bottle of iodine, a roll of lint and a bandaid. The iodine stung like hell and he hurriedly covered the wound with a square of lint and taped it up with the sticking plaster. Then he dressed, packed his shaving tackle and carried his travelling bag down to the Foreign Correspondents Club on the tenth floor.

Lander was already there, perched on a bar stool near the window. As he had anticipated, Ryan was keeping him company.

"Going some place?" Lander said, eyeing the bag.

"Yes, home. I thought you'd want to leave Shanghai too."

"Me? Why should I want to go? I like it here."

"I hear Pootung is not exactly a healthy place these days," Ryan said casually. "Matter of fact, I'm told you ran into a mess of trouble over there."

There was no point in playing the innocent. Lander had seen him cross the river in a sampan on Sunday afternoon and had probably been keeping a look-out for him ever since. Better to give the Americans a laundered version of the truth than a downright lie.

"The natives were none too friendly," Freeland admitted, "and the artillery bombardment didn't help matters."

"There's a story going the rounds that Howard Teale is dead. Anything in it?"

"He got caught in the crossfire."

"I've said it before," Lander told him, "people around you have a habit of dying. No one could attract so much shit unless they were high on someone's death list."

"You're not doing too well in the popularity stakes either. A certain Tu Yush-sen is going to make life very unpleasant for you if you're still here when the PLA takes over."

"Never heard of the guy."

"Mr Ryan has." Freeland raised a questioning eyebrow at the assistant bureau chief. "Tu Yush-sen used to be a professor of Agrarian Economics at St John's University; nowadays, he's a political commissar."

"Is that right, Phil?" Lander asked.

"There was a Professor Tu Yush-sen at the university," Ryan said cautiously, "and he did disappear in 1948."

"Yeah?" Lander frowned. "So what's he got against me for Chrissakes? I haven't done him any harm."

"Your General Chennault is one of his pet hates, so I guess it's guilt by association. Of course, I could be wrong but in your shoes, I wouldn't hang around to find out."

"How do you propose we get out of Shanghai?"

Freeland liked the 'we' part; it told him that Lander was more than open to persuasion.

117

"I've got the key to Jacob Stein's boathouse in my bag. We'll go there, help ourselves to a two-man kayak and paddle the ten miles down river to Woosung and rendezvous with HMS *Belfast*."

"What makes you think she's still there? All the civilians who wanted to leave were evacuated yesterday."

"You forget the *Amethyst* is trapped ninety miles up the Yangtze. The British Government may wish they'd never heard of that frigate but the Navy isn't going to leave before she rejoins the fleet."

"And it's only ten miles to Woosung?"

Freeland nodded. He didn't think it politic to mention that the open sea was a good seventy-five miles beyond the port. He also glossed over the fact that the cruiser would be anchored well out of range of the forts guarding the conflux of the Whangpoo and Yangtze rivers. Nobody ever got anything done by emphasising the difficulties.

"You think I should go, Phil?" Lander asked.

"I can think of a dozen good reasons why you shouldn't stay," Ryan told him.

"Okay, when do we leave?"

"Now," said Freeland. He picked up his bag and started to leave the bar, then turned about to face the assistant bureau chief. "One piece of advice – don't do a story on Tu Yush-sen before you're ready to leave China for good. I got the impression he doesn't like publicity."

"How about you?"

"It won't bother me," said Freeland. "A couple of weeks from now I may have a different name."

The parade had finished but the crowds lining the route had not yet dispersed. Faced with a milling throng which ruled out any hope of getting a pedicab, they crossed Garden Bridge on foot and immediately turned right into the relatively quiet Hangchow Road. Stein's boatshed was roughly half a mile beyond the American Consulate and no one paid much attention to them when they went down on to the quay and unlocked the door. Stacked inside the shed on racks were a double and four single kayaks.

"Does this guy build boats for a living, or what?" Lander asked.

"Stein would have represented Germany in the '36 Olympics had he not been a Jew, which is why he chose to leave the country before Himmler could put him in a concentration camp." Freeland opened the large wooden chest at the back of the shed, took out a couple of life-jackets and gave one to Lander. "Roll up your sleeves so that people will think you're wearing a sports shirt, then put this on."

"We're going in broad daylight?"

"I aim to be well clear of Shanghai before sundown. I want the Nationalists to think we're just a couple of crazy Europeans enjoying an afternoon on the river. If we go at dusk, we'll be breaking the curfew and they won't take kindly to that. On the other hand, I would prefer to steal past Woosung before it gets light. From what I hear, there's been a complete breakdown of discipline among the army units awaiting evacuation to Taiwan."

"Okay, let's find somewhere between Shanghai and Woosung where we can lie up."

"My thoughts exactly."

Freeland also thought the *Belfast* would be vulnerable to an underwater attack by frogmen during the hours of darkness. To guard against that, her captain would undoubtedly up anchor at dusk and patrol the estuary until dawn. It was therefore essential to rendezvous with the cruiser soon after first light when she was on a reciprocal course for Woosung. And that called for fine judgment, perfect timing and a large slice of luck.

"I'm ready when you are," Lander said.

"I won't be a minute." Freeland looked round the shed, found an old tyre lever and splintered the wood around the lock to make it look as though the door had been forced. "Got to think of Jacob Stein," he said. "I don't want him in trouble on our account."

"Right."

They carried the kayak out of the shed and put it in the water, then got in gingerly. Neither man had much practical experience of canoeing but they managed to get themselves settled without capsizing the boat. Gradually becoming more proficient, they paddled down Soochow Creek, joined the Whangpoo and then headed downstream. Across the river on the north-eastern outskirts of Pootung, a column of black smoke was still rising from the stores depot which had been burning since early on Monday evening.

Approximately three miles south of Woosung, Freeland spotted an inlet amongst the mudbanks where they could lie up for the night. He needn't have bothered; throughout the hours of darkness, the horizon was lit up by the reflected glow of numerous fires on the dockside which were raging out of control. To add to the confusion, tracer bullets from a burning ammunition dump arced into the night sky in a gigantic firework display that was augmented by the crump of artillery shells. In the circumstances, it was hardly surprising that no one paid the slightest attention to them when they made their way past the port at first light.

At precisely 0548 hours they were picked up by HMS *Belfast* some eight miles north-east of Woosung. That their small craft was spotted by the officer of the watch was something of a miracle, but as Lander pointed out, it was their lucky day.

It was not a lucky day for the mayor of Shanghai. He awoke that morning to find City Hall in the hands of the PLA.

1952

MÜNSTER – WEST GERMANY

Monday 1 December
to
Friday 12 December

11

The Brigadier was the only man Freeland had met who looked debonair in battledress, but then the blouse and slacks had been made to measure out of the finest barathea by a Savile Row tailor. The fact that he had a trim athletic figure also helped. He was forty-three years old and, except for the sleek black hair, bore more than a passing resemblance to Field Marshal Montgomery, which did him no harm at all. Above the left breast pocket he sported the medal ribbons of a Military Cross, the 1939–1945 Star, the Italy Star, the France and Germany Star as well as the Defence and War Medals. The Americans had also decorated him with the Silver Star when the Division he had been serving with had landed at Salerno under command of General Mark Clark's 5th Army. Now, some nine years later, he was Rhine Army's Chief Intelligence Officer and a key member of the General Staff. In military parlance, he was therefore known as the BGS(I).

Twice a month, Freeland drove all the way from Cologne to Bad Oeyenhausen where the headquarters of the British Army of the Rhine was housed in the former Kaiserhof Hotel; twice a month, Freeland listened to the BGS(I) describe the disposition, state of readiness and order of battle of the Soviet forces stationed in East Germany. Nothing varied very much from one month to the next; the Brigadier, however, had a special talent for making each threat assessment sound as though it was the hottest news since the A-bomb was dropped on Hiroshima.

The meeting was always chaired by the Chief of Staff and was attended by the senior Operations, Intelligence and Administrative officers of Headquarters 1st (British) Corps, 2nd Infantry and 6, 7 and 11 Armoured Divisions. The format never varied; after the threat assessment, the senior staff officer (Operations) gave a progress report of the measures in hand to counter the Soviet threat. Since the sappers were busy chambering every road, bridge and railway line for demolition, he was inevitably assisted in this

123

task by the chief engineer. Corps and Divisions then had their say, leaving Freeland to round things off, rather, he thought, like the corporation dust cart after the Lord Mayor's Show. Freeland, who had heard it all before, found it difficult to stay awake during this latter stage, especially in the oppressively warm atmosphere of the briefing room.

"Mr Northover." The voice sounded very hazy.

"Mr Northover." The voice was sharper this time which was why Freeland opened his eyes and sat up straight.

"May we hear from you, please?" the Chief of Staff asked, his accompanying smile a trifle glacial.

"Yes, certainly."

Freeland got to his feet and walked towards the podium. Back in 1949 he had told Phil Ryan, the AP assistant bureau chief in Shanghai, that he wasn't worried about publicity because he would probably have a different name within a fortnight. He had said it jokingly, never dreaming the SIS would give him a new identity, but they had, and very confusing it was too at times.

He glanced at the map of North West Europe on the wall behind the podium, then turned to face his audience, all of whom were familiar faces with the exception of the newly-appointed Assistant Adjutant and Quartermaster General of 2nd Infantry Division. Although he would have been briefed by his predecessor, Freeland decided it would do no harm to introduce himself.

"I'm responsible for the recruitment, training and organisation of clandestine forces in the British Zone. These units are, of course, dormant in peacetime."

So much for the job description, he thought, and picked up a pointer staff to indicate on the map the area bounded by Hamburg in the north, Braunschweig to the south and as far west as the general line Wilhelmshaven, Münster and Dortmund. Since the last meeting, he had appointed only two new cell leaders, but it sounded a whole lot better if he reminded his audience of the other sixty units which already existed within the area he had just described. The art of window-dressing was one of the things the SIS had taught him before he was posted to Germany.

"What about Schleswig Holstein?" the Chief of Staff asked. "How's recruitment going up there?"

"Not as well as I should like," Freeland admitted.

"Still only a dozen cells?"

"Yes, sir. Finding volunteers of the right calibre isn't easy."

"We've got to try harder, Mr Northover."

Unable to contribute any practical suggestions for overcoming the difficulties, the Chief of Staff had resorted to exhorting the underlings to try harder, a tactic which Freeland had noticed was very popular with senior officers. The Chief of Staff, however, had every right to be worried about Schleswig Holstein. The army was thin on the ground up there and while the Soviet main thrust would almost certainly be directed against the Rhine, they would also hook into Denmark with the aim of opening up the Kattegat and Skagerrak to their submarines. The armchair strategists believed the next conflict would be over within a matter of days but as of the first of January, the Russians had approximately fifty A-bombs to the Americans' five hundred. There was, therefore, a long way to go before the era of push-button warfare became an established fact.

"May one ask what sort of men you are looking for, Mr Northover?"

A silky question from the new boy. Freeland wondered if he was genuinely interested or had some axe to grind.

"Former soldiers with plenty of combat experience on the Eastern Front. I would prefer them to be under the age of forty but primarily, they should be well motivated."

"Well motivated? Could you be a little more specific?"

"Dedicated anti-Communists," Freeland told him. "Men who have good reason to both hate and fear the Russians."

"I hope that doesn't mean that we are recruiting former members of the Waffen SS?"

The disapproving, almost censorial tone of voice stung Freeland. More than anyone else in the room he had cause to hate the SS and it was bitterly ironic that in his present job he was required to rub shoulders with former members of Himmler's private army. Worse still, in some cases, he was actually obliged to cultivate them.

"Every volunteer is screened," Freeland said tersely. "Only those individuals with an unblemished record are accepted."

"In other words, we are recruiting former SS men."

"Everyone is – the French, the Americans and the Russians. They're with the Foreign Legion Regiments fighting in French Indo-China, the CIA wouldn't have an East Zone network without them and the NKVD are receiving tuition in the methods of interrogation employed by the SS."

"I can't believe Her Majesty's Government is happy about this."

"They would be a damned sight unhappier if the Red Army achieved a major breakthrough and no one was harassing their second and third echelons as they made for the Channel ports."

"Quite so." The Chief of Staff stood up and glared at the

assembled company. "I take it you have no further questions, gentlemen?"

No one felt inclined to disagree with his assumption. After a few, mercifully brief closing remarks, the date and time of the next meeting was confirmed and the conference dispersed.

Leaving the headquarters building, Freeland made his way to the Visitors' Car Park, collected the black Mercedes which the West German Government had been obliged to provide out of Reparations and headed for the autobahn. The meeting had started at two o'clock sharp and it was now after four. In another quarter of an hour it would be dark and there was every likelihood of running into sleet or snow showers on the way back to Cologne. He would have preferred to have gone straight home but he had a date with Gunther Altmüller in a little village called Wolbeck near Münster, and the German had asked to see him urgently.

At the Rheda exit, he left the autobahn and followed Route 64 to Münster, branching off at Warendorf to take the minor road through Freckenhorst and Everswinkel to Wolbeck. A couple of miles from the village, he pulled on to the grass verge, unlocked the glove compartment and took out a .38 Colt revolver with a three-inch barrel. Although Freeland had checked the weapon before leaving the house that morning, he nevertheless released the cylinder, pushed it clear of the frame and checked the rounds under the courtesy light to make sure none had been substituted with blanks. Despite the fact that his Mercedes didn't look as if it had been tampered with when he'd collected it from the car park, the NKVD were believed to have put a price tag on the head of Mr Northover, and he worked on the premise that you couldn't be too careful. Closing the cylinder, he tucked the revolver into the shoulder holster he was wearing under his jacket and drove on.

Gunther Altmüller was thirty-four but looked much older. A short, stocky man with receding light brown hair that matched the colour of his eyes, he had left bits and pieces of his anatomy on the Eastern Front. Frostbite had claimed a couple of toes on his left foot in the winter of '41, a grenade had removed part of the heel on the same foot the following autumn leaving him with a permanent limp, and a shell had destroyed his right arm in the spring of '44. He was one of the very few survivors from the old 6th Infantry Division which had been raised in the Bielefeld area. A corporal in September 1939, he had ended the war as a captain. In between, he had fought in France and had marched all the way to the gates of Moscow.

Altmüller considered himself a fortunate man on two counts: he had been recuperating in a Reserve Army Convalescent Depot when his Division had been encircled at Stalingrad with the rest of the 6th Army, and in 1944 he had been lying in a base hospital when the reconstituted Division had been annihilated on the River Vistula.

Freeland parked the Mercedes in the small lot adjoining the Gasthof Richter in the centre of Wolbeck, then locked the car doors and walked into the bar. Gunther Altmüller was already there, seated at a corner table at the far end of the room. There were only two other customers – farm-labourers who had obviously stopped off for a drink on their way home.

"They're not for us, Herr Northover," Altmüller said, before he had a chance to ask who they were.

"Pity." Freeland unbuttoned his duffel coat. Like the conference room at Rhine Army Headquarters, the Gasthof was uncomfortably warm.

"That is, unless things are really desperate . . ."

The army was definitely overstretched; it was fighting a conventional war in Korea, the Chinese Communists in Malaya, the Mau Mau in Kenya and the Egyptian Fedayeen in the Canal Zone. Excluding the Guards Regiments on Palace duties, there were only three infantry battalions in the whole of the United Kingdom and, shades of 1940, Churchill had been moved to re-form the Home Guard.

"You see the small one on the left?" Altmüller continued. "He has two convictions for theft and his friend only became a farm-worker during the war to avoid being conscripted into the army."

"You seem to know a lot about them."

"Keeping my eyes and ears open is part of the job, isn't it?" Altmüller signalled the barman to bring Freeland a small beer and a schnapps to chase it down. "Their names are Dieter Frick and Hermann Macher if you're interested."

"You were right the first time, Gunther, we don't need them."

"The same goes for Karl Heinz Grothmann, but he badly wants to see you."

The Feldwebel. What was it that Grothmann had said to him? 'I have no wish to hand you over to Sturmbannführer Hausser of the SS but unless I am seen to be making progress, I'll have no say in the matter.'

"He claims he knows you, Herr Northover."

A dozen questions sprang to mind, all of them full of disturbing implications. With an effort, Freeland kept his face impassive and his voice calm.

127

"His name doesn't ring a bell with me. What does Grossmann look like?"

"Grothmann," Altmüller corrected him. "He's about my height, a good twenty kilos lighter, grey-haired, doesn't look at all well – pasty complexion, sunken cheeks, dark shadows under his eyes – coughs a lot."

"I don't recognise the man," Freeland said with some truthfulness. The Grothmann he had known had been plump and sleek, like a pampered cat.

"He was a detective in the Kriminalpolizei of Hamburg before the war; the Abwehr got their hooks into him in 1940 and stuck him in Field Security. The way he tells it, he was the scourge of the French Resistance."

"And now he's on his last legs." Freeland drank his beer, took a sip from the glass of schnapps. "You're right again, he's no good to us."

"I don't think he wants to join us anyway, Herr Northover. He only claims to have some information for you."

"Yes? What does Grothmann do for a living?"

"He works for the British Army in Münster as a labourer in 87 Supply Depot." Altmüller paused, then said, "Why do you ask? Are you going to run a check on him?"

Freeland didn't answer, looked straight ahead as if deep in thought. "How did Grothmann come to approach you, Gunther?" he asked finally.

"We're members of the same ex-servicemen's club. We have a get-together once a fortnight in the Bierkeller on Prinzipalmarkt," Altmüller said and launched into a lengthy explanation.

Freeland listened to him with half an ear, his mind preoccupied with related thoughts. Grothmann belonged to the past and he did not want to be reminded of Chantal Kiffer. She had been dead for eight long years and since leaving Shanghai, he had made a determined effort to forget her. He had a wife and child back in Cologne and Jenny shouldn't have to contend with Chantal's ghost ever again. God knows he owed her that much.

"Are you going to see him, Herr Northover?"

"Who?"

"Grothmann. Who else have we been talking about?"

"Any idea what sort of information he's offering?"

Altmüller shook his head. "He refused to tell me, said it was highly secret and for your ears only."

"All right, fix it."

"When for?"

"Tomorrow night," said Freeland. "The Kaufhaus in Rothenburg Strasse, five thirty sharp, Menswear department, shirt counter."

"Very good."

"Can I get you another drink, Gunther?"

"Thank you, Herr Northover, but no; I think I have had enough for today."

"So have I."

Freeland buttoned his duffel coat, said goodnight to Altmüller and left the Gasthof. It started sleeting long before he reached the autobahn.

*   *   *

Grothmann stared at his cup of weak coffee and wondered how much longer he could make it last. Much as he would like to oblige the proprietor by ordering another, he simply couldn't afford it. There were still three days to go before payday and he had just two Marks eighteen in his pocket. Altmüller had said he would meet him in the Café Diercksen at the Hauptbahnhof no later than six thirty but the 1910 to Osnabrück had left some five minutes ago and it was beginning to look as though he wouldn't show up.

The thought made him feel sick. The foreman in charge of his shift at the Supply Depot was a sadistic bastard and was threatening him with dismissal because he wasn't physically capable of doing the work, and then what would he and Anna do? They couldn't manage on the pittance she earned as a cleaner working part-time for the wife of a British Army Officer. The Englishman whom the Abwehr had known as 'Felix' was his only hope. However much Herr Northover might dislike him, he must really hate Joachim Hausser. Revenge, they said, was sweet; if that was true, then he, Karl Heinz Grothmann, could deliver the former Sturmbannführer on a plate.

That ought to be worth more than a pat on the back. He wasn't looking for the usual reward, though a fifty Mark hand-out wasn't to be sniffed at. What he wanted was a good steady job as a driver for the Field Security Section in Münster. This would afford him the opportunity to show the British just how good a policeman he had been, and that would lead to even better things. To hell with the café proprietor, he would linger over his coffee until the down-stopping train to Hamm, Dortmund, Düsseldorf and Cologne pulled into the station. If there was still no sign of Altmüller, he would wait for him in the concourse. Anxious to avoid the scornful gaze of the owner, he picked up a copy of the *Münstersche Zeitung* which had been left behind by another customer and retreated behind the pages of the daily paper. He therefore did not see Altmüller enter the café and was unaware of his presence until he plucked the newspaper from his grasp.

"Who are you hiding from, Karl Heinz?" he asked genially.

"The owner; he'd like me to spend more money than I've got in my pocket."

"It's a cold night," Altmüller observed. "You want a schnapps to warm you up?"

"Only if you're paying."

"You're beginning to sound like a Münsterlander," Altmüller said, then told one of the waiters to bring a large schnapps and a glass of wine for himself.

"What are we celebrating?"

"Nothing in particular; I'm just feeling good."

"I was hoping you would have some news for me," Grothmann said, trying unsuccessfully to hide his disappointment.

"Oh, but I have. Herr Northover will see you tomorrow – the Kaufhaus in Rothenburg Strasse, Menswear department, shirt counter, five thirty sharp." Altmüller reached into his jacket pocket with his left hand and brought out three ten-Mark notes and slipped them to Grothmann. "Smarten yourself up," he said.

"I can't take this money."

"It's an investment, Karl Heinz. I know what you're hoping for and if you do get taken on by the Field Security people here in Münster, I want you to keep me fully informed of what's going on. You know what I mean?"

"I understand you perfectly," Grothmann said, pocketing the notes.

*   *   *

On the night of the thirtieth of May 1942, the RAF had launched the first ever thousand bomber raid. Between 0047 and 0225 hours, one thousand and forty-seven aircraft drawn from front line squadrons and operational training units had dropped two thousand tons of bombs on Cologne, destroying nearly three thousand five hundred houses and damaging a further nine thousand. Of the factories in the city, thirty were totally destroyed, seventy were badly damaged and another two hundred required minor structural repairs. The docks and railways were severely hit and the tram service was out of action for months.

It was not the only visit Bomber Command had paid to Cologne; by the end of the war, ninety per cent of the central district was uninhabitable. Miraculously, the cathedral was untouched; the same applied to Gartenstrasse, four miles due north of the

Dom Platz, where Freeland now lived. Ten years back, the leafy, suburban avenue near the river had been home for many of the city's wealthy industrialists; now it was a small piece of Britain, populated by Civil Affairs officers, broadcasters and journalists from the British Forces Network and officials from the British Consulate in Düsseldorf.

Freeland turned into the driveway of number 39 Gartenstrasse and ran the car straight into the open garage. Crime was practically unknown in this part of the city; none of his neighbours had been burgled, nor had their cars stolen nor returned home late at night to find that their properties had been vandalised while they were out. When Freeland closed and locked the garage door, it was to protect the Mercedes against the elements rather than to deter some would-be car thief. Picking his way through the slush lying on the drive, he let himself into the house.

Jenny was curled up on the sofa in the living-room, both feet tucked under her rump. The radio was tuned to BFN and Mantovani and his Cascading Strings were playing Bali Hai from *South Pacific*. There was a flat-looking gin and tonic on the sofa table and *The Young Lions* was balanced precariously on the edge of the couch, her left thumb marking the page she had reached before dozing off. When Freeland gently removed the book from her grasp, she did not jump but merely opened her eyes and smiled lazily up at him.

"Hullo, Harry," she said in the slightly husky voice that had attracted him when he'd first met her during the war up at Ringway. "What time is it?"

"Twenty past nine. There was a pile-up on the autobahn about five kilometres the other side of Essen. A truck towing the usual two trailers jack-knifed on an icy patch as it was being overtaken by an Opel Kapitan. The car was side-swiped into the central crash barrier and then rammed up the backside by a delivery van that was travelling much too fast and much too close. As a result, both lanes were blocked and I only just managed to stop in time."

"Thank God you're okay." One arm went around his neck and she kissed him on the mouth. "You are okay, aren't you?"

"I'm fine."

He straightened up and Jenny came with him, uncurling her legs and pressing herself against him, her lips parted, her tongue probing. He pulled her closer still, his arms around the small of her back, one hand moving lower to caress the soft roundness of her buttocks. The muscles contracted under his touch and she trembled expectantly. She leaned away, her thighs thrust against his, arousing him.

131

"Hungry?"

"Can't you tell?"

"Idiot." She raised her head, looked up at him smiling, rounded chin, perfect teeth, small upturned nose, dark curly hair, affection in her blue eyes; so very different, he thought, to Chantal Kiffer.

"Have you had anything to eat?"

"Not since lunch."

"I'll make you some scrambled eggs – okay?"

"Why can't Hildegarde do it?" Hildegarde was their middle-aged, live-in housekeeper who'd left Königsberg in 1944 to move west ahead of the advancing Red Army.

"It's her night off, Harry. She's gone to the cinema in town."

"That's nice," Freeland said vaguely and followed Jenny into the tiled kitchen overlooking the small garden at the back of the house. Picture of domestic bliss, he supposed, watching her as she crouched in front of the fridge – the devoted wife, and mother of their eleven-month-old son fast asleep upstairs, except that the ghost of Chantal Kiffer kept intruding. "What sort of day have you had?" he asked automatically.

"Mark's been a bit fretful, I think he must be cutting another tooth."

"Does that mean we're going to have a restless night?"

"I got the impression that was already on the cards," Jenny said, winking broadly.

"Yes."

Her smile froze, then slowly disappeared as she sensed something was wrong. "What's the matter?" she asked sharply.

There was no point telling her that there was nothing. Jenny had an uncanny knack of reading his thoughts and although he could lie convincingly when necessary, he had never been able to deceive her. Work was something he left at the office and never discussed at home because those were the rules. But there was no security classification on Karl Heinz Grothmann and he had told Jenny all about the former Abwehr Feldwebel soon after he had been released from Flossenburg concentration camp.

"Are you going to see Grothmann?" she asked when he had finished telling her about his meeting with Altmüller.

"I think so."

"Why? Because you fancy a trip down memory lane and want to talk about Chantal Kiffer?"

"He told Altmüller that he has some information for me."

"What about – the last war? It's over, Harry – didn't anyone tell you that?"

132

"I have to do my job the way I see it."

Jenny buttered the two slices of bread she had toasted under the grill, then spooned the scrambled eggs out of the saucepan. "You'll find a knife and fork in the kitchen drawer, tablecloth in the dresser," she told him in a cold, neutral voice.

"You're angry with me."

"The subject's closed, Harry. I don't want to discuss it any further." Jenny sat down at the kitchen table. "I had a letter from Ma this afternoon," she said before he had a chance to come back at her.

"Oh yes, how are they keeping?"

"Pa's angina is playing him up. Trouble is, he won't do as the doctor tells him."

Freeland thought that was typical of his father-in-law. Sidney Vail had never taken anyone's advice, had always believed he knew best. One day his pig-headed obstinacy was going to kill him.

"Of course, he's worried about the business, who'll run it in his absence."

Vail and Son, Estate Agents, with offices in Tamworth, Lichfield, Cannock and Walsall. Only the son was dead, killed in a flying accident during the war when he'd flown the plane he was piloting into the Brecon Beacons.

"I thought I'd go home, Harry, to sort things out. We either find someone to run the business or sell it to one of our larger rivals. I'm pretty sure I can get a good price for it."

"When are you thinking of going?" he asked quietly.

"Tomorrow. I'll catch the boat train to the Hook of Holland."

"I see." And he did too, in more ways than one. Jenny was acting on the spur of the moment; much as she worried about her father, she would never have upped sticks at the drop of a hat if he hadn't mentioned Grothmann.

"How long will you be gone?"

"Two, three weeks – who knows?" She shrugged her shoulders, then said, "Come and fetch us when you've finally got Chantal Kiffer out of your system."

And how long was that going to take, Freeland wondered, another month, another year? God knows he had tried to forget Chantal, but he had helped to kill her and that was something that would stay with him for ever.

133

12

Freeland left the Mercedes on the piece of waste ground that
had once been 87 Magnus Strasse and walked the rest of the
way to the British Council offices at the top of the street near the
Roman tower which, like the cathedral, had survived the thousand
bomber raid intact. The dock area was still largely devastated but
the city centre had been almost completely rebuilt, and pretty soon
now he would have to find himself another parking lot.

The British Council occupied what had formerly been a substan-
tial private residence. The ground floor was now in use as a library
and meeting room, the Council offices and administrative staff were
on the second, with the Anglo-German Society above them in the
attic. The President of the Anglo-German Society was a retired
doctor who had been banned from practising medicine under the
Nazis because of his outspoken opposition to the National Socialist
Party. Freeland was the Executive Vice-President who provided the
guest speakers and generally encouraged the army units in his area
to establish cordial relations with the local population. The real
work was done by Anthea Clowes, a middle-ranking SIS officer
who, before the war, had been employed as a secretary by one
of I.G. Farben's subsidiaries. Her primary task was to sustain
the illusion that the Anglo-German Society was simply that and
nothing more.

The nature of their real function was disguised by a number of
routine security measures. His alias did not appear on anyone's
staff list and all correspondence for Mr Northover was addressed
to the box number of the British Consulate in Düsseldorf. The
Northovers did not exist outside Germany; personal letters from
friends and relatives at home were addressed to the Freelands
care of the Foreign Office in London where they were then
double-enveloped and sent on in the Diplomatic Bag. His office
number appeared in the Rhine Army telephone directory under
the training branch where his appointment was described as

Civilian Liaison Officer (Army Manoeuvres), otherwise it was not listed.

Usually, Anthea Clowes had opened and filed all the incoming mail by the time Freeland showed up at the office, but this morning he arrived early. The atmosphere had been decidedly chilly over breakfast and Jenny had made it clear that she could manage to pack a couple of suitcases without any help from him. Wanting a chance to patch things up between them, he had tried to persuade her to catch the 1500 hours BEA flight to Northolt. It was likely that Düsseldorf would be fogged in by then and she wouldn't be able to leave, but she had heard the weather forecast on the British Forces Network and had rejected the suggestion.

"I woke up in the early hours and couldn't get back to sleep again," he told Anthea Clowes. "Thought I might as well come into the office."

"I'll make you a cup of coffee, Mr Northover."

Anthea Clowes was a professional to her fingertips. Even when they were alone, she always addressed him by his alias. His real name was in the Foreign Office Blue Book but as far as Anthea was concerned, she had never met Harry Freeland.

He went on through to his own office, walked over to the window and stood there gazing at the twin spires of the cathedral rising above the skeletal remains of those tenements, government office blocks and department stores which still awaited demolition. A cold overcast day with the prospect of freezing fog before nightfall, a depressing outlook which mirrored his own feelings. After all that Jenny had said to him last night, did he really want to meet Grothmann? Did he have to? If the first question had him vacillating between yes and no, the second produced an unequivocal response. Grothmann had recognised him from the past; his cover was therefore in jeopardy and it was essential to discover just how much damage the former Abwehr Warrant Officer could inflict.

He turned away from the window, moved to the desk and picked up the phone. All German civilians were screened by Field Security before the army employed them and the detachment at Münster would have a dirt card on Grothmann. He rang Rhine Army Headquarters at Bad Oeyenhausen, asked for the officer commanding the Intelligence and Security Group and told him what he wanted to know.

Freeland had finished the cup of coffee Anthea Clowes had made for him and was on his second cigarette of the day when the Intelligence Corps officer at Rhine Army returned his call. The information on the dirt card was hardly illuminating: Karl Heinz

135

Grothmann was forty-two years old, had no previous convictions and had never been a member of the National Socialist Party.

* * *

Thomas Egan was rising fifty-three. Born on the first day of the twentieth century, he had been sent to Dartmouth at the age of twelve and had been a midshipman serving on the battle cruiser HMS *Lion* at Scapa Flow when the Kaiser had fled to Holland. By 1932 he was still only a lieutenant and unlikely to go any further despite being one of the best signal officers in the Navy. The stringent economies imposed by the National Government had created a promotion block with too many officers chasing too few sea-going appointments. The invitation to join the Secret Intelligence Service could not therefore have come at a more opportune moment.

With little or no training, Egan had been sent into the field as a passport control officer at the British Embassy in Budapest. On the principle of never fouling one's own doorstep, his Intelligence activities had been directed against the neighbouring countries of Austria and Czechoslovakia. Three years later he had been transferred to Warsaw, and Austria had been dropped in favour of Nazi Germany which, of course, included East Prussia. Chased out of Poland by the Wehrmacht, he had been forced to make a similar undignified exit from the Low Countries in May 1940, having been sent there to rebuild the SIS network after Best and Stevens had been lured to Venlo and kidnapped by Schellenberg. Thereafter, he had been assigned to Section V at 54 Broadway who were responsible for counter-espionage. His immediate superior was Major Neville Acland, a former regular army officer of impeccable breeding, great charm and *savoir faire* but limited intellect.

Neville Acland rarely appeared before nine thirty; the last time he had done so had been that never-to-be-forgotten morning back in May 1951 when the SIS learned that Burgess and Maclean had skipped to Moscow. When Neville Acland sent for him shortly after ten minutes past nine that morning, Egan assumed they were faced with a crisis of equal magnitude. The former Guards officer was standing in front of the window gazing down at the passers-by in the street six floors below, hands clasped loosely behind his back and holding a large page which looked as though it had been torn from a magazine. Aware of Egan's presence, he turned slowly about.

"Morning, Tom," he said, handing him the page. "What are we to make of this?"

The Director-General had asked the same question in green ink on a compliment slip attached to the page with a staple. The page came from *Esquire* magazine and formed part of an article entitled 'Latter Days in Shanghai' written by someone called Phil Ryan. The paragraphs which merited special attention had been sidelined with a red biro and gave a graphic account of a British Intelligence officer who'd escaped from Pootung after being taken prisoner by the People's Liberation Army.

"I presume this Harry Freeland is one of ours?"

"Ex-SOE, joined us after the war." Acland waved him to a chair, then sat down behind his desk. "Comes from Lichfield, father's headmaster of some local prep school, might even own it."

"Well, he's certainly committed a major breach of security in allowing Ryan to identify him."

"But is that all he's done? The fellow's captured by the Communists and less than twenty-four hours later he's back with us? Doesn't make sense – look how long the *Amethyst* was bottled up in the Yangtze by the PLA before Lieutenant-Commander Kerens was able to give them the slip and take the frigate down river to rejoin the fleet."

"Are you implying that Freeland is a traitor, Neville?"

Acland winced as though Egan had struck him. "I don't know what to think any more; the fellow comes from good stock, father got a Military Cross in the First War, and he went to Shrewsbury . . ."

The defection of Burgess and Maclean had called into question all the age-old assumptions. Nowadays, a man was not necessarily a patriot because he had been born into a middle-class family and had been educated at a good public school where he had been taught the virtues of loyalty, honour and service to one's country.

"Of course his mother is French," Acland continued, as if that explained everything.

"Really?"

"Made a nuisance of himself over a woman called Chantal Kiffer whom he claimed had been unlawfully executed by the French Forces of the Interior. Got so bad, the Frogs kicked him out of their country. It's all there in his file, took it home and read it last night after the Director-General had dropped this little bombshell on me."

The file was lying in the pending tray, the only one of three on Acland's desk that had anything in it. Egan wondered if he was meant to examine it.

"Who sent us the clipping?" he asked.

"Guy Salusbury. Joined the Service some years before the war.

Came to us from the Foreign Office on transfer. Went to Oxford. A good man."

Egan nodded. He had met Salusbury in 1947 when the latter had been looking after the Far East Desk as a stop-gap.

"Volunteered for SOE in 1942, thought it was his duty since he could speak French. Anyway, we're interested in Freeland, not Guy. Take his file away, read it from cover to cover and let me know what you think. The Director-General wants to know if we can still trust him after what apparently happened in Shanghai."

"How long have I got?"

"As long as it takes to interview the referees he nominated when he joined us," Acland told him.

*   *   *

Freeland had to look twice before he recognised Grothmann. The German had aged twenty years or more since Chartres and was now an old man. Had Grothmann not been in the right place at the right time, had the ex-Abwehr man not smiled hesitantly, he wouldn't have spared him a second glance. He looked at the shirts on display, caught Grothmann's eye and moved on, gradually working his way back to the entrance. The Kaufhaus was crowded with people shopping early for Christmas; no one was interested in Freeland or the old man tagging along behind who was determined not to lose sight of him. Turning left outside the store, he walked down Rothenburg Strasse to the more dimly lit Pferdegasse where he had left the Mercedes. Behind him, he could hear the German coughing and spluttering in the cold night air, his weak chest affected by the sudden change of temperature.

Freeland unlocked the offside door, got in behind the wheel and, leaning across the passenger's seat, raised the catch on the opposite door. Grothmann materialised from the shadows and slipped into the car.

"Good evening, Herr Felix," he said nervously as they drove off. "It is good to see you looking so well after all these years."

Freeland had attended a year long course in German on his return from Shanghai and had acquired a wide-ranging vocabulary which enabled him to tell Grothmann in no uncertain terms what he could do to himself.

"Verstehen Sie?"

"Jawohl, Herr Major," Grothmann said woodenly.

"Good. From now on we speak English."

"Whatever Herr Northover desires."

138

"What I desire is for you to tell me how you found me again."

"Gunther Altmüller was a good soldier, few men have a better combat record, but he is not discreet. He gets a few schnapps inside him and his tongue loosens up. Names were never mentioned, you understand, but it was common knowledge amongst the regulars of the Bierkeller in the Prinzipalmarkt that he was recruiting former members of the Wehrmacht on behalf of the British."

Clandestine forces were dependent on secrecy for their survival. Good as he was at talent spotting, Freeland resolved that Altmüller would have to go.

"Gunther told me I wasn't fit enough to join," Grothmann continued. "I said that was difficult to understand, coming from a one-armed man with part of one heel missing. I thought Gunther had had too much to drink when he started laughing, but then he told me he was in good company because the Englishman he worked for was missing a little finger."

Grothmann had already deduced that at least two men were involved in organising a resistance movement throughout West-phalia, a task which he believed could only be undertaken by someone with previous experience in this field. It was therefore too much of a coincidence to suppose there were two former SOE officers with identical mutilations.

"What brought you to Münster?" Freeland asked. "I thought Hamburg was your home town."

"So it was, but there was nothing to keep me there when I returned in 1949 – no home, no wife, no surviving relatives. I went to Munich because a cousin of mine lived there and I needed a roof over my head. I also thought she might know where I could find employment."

Freeland could think of yet another factor. Munich happened to be in the American Zone and they paid better than either the British or the French. However, whatever his reasons, Grothmann had eventually found employment as a boilerman in Patton Barracks which was then occupied by V Corps Headquarters.

"The Americans fired me just over a year ago – for making a nuisance of myself, they said."

"And were you?"

"I was only trying to be helpful."

"I bet you were," Freeland said acidly.

They were out in the country now, heading towards a hamlet called Ostbevern. Looking for somewhere to park, he turned off the main road into a lane that led to an abandoned refugee camp set in a small copse, where the former inmates had been hidden from the local inhabitants, presumably in case they made the indigenous population feel guilty.

"The Americans have a secret Intelligence base near Pullach which is about ten kilometres west of Munich. It is run by a former general called Reinhard Gehlen. You have perhaps heard of him?"

Freeland nodded. Gehlen had risen to Chief of Intelligence at OKW, the Supreme Headquarters of the German Armed Forces in the Second World War. He had helped to plan Barbarossa, the invasion of Russia, and had played a major part in raising General Vlassov's Army of Liberation from disaffected prisoners-of-war. He had recruited Cossacks, Ukrainians, Crimean Tartars, Georgians, Lithuanians, Estonians and Latvians to hunt down Soviet partisans operating behind the German lines. His exploits on the Eastern Front were legion, he was said to have infiltrated agents into Marshal Zhukov's headquarters and had sent in a Russo-German Commando force to seize the Maikop oil refinery in the Caucasus before it could be destroyed by the Red Army. After the war, he had been the man the Central Intelligence Agency had turned to when they had sought to establish an Intelligence network behind the Iron Curtain.

"I hoped Gehlen might be able to use me," Grothmann went on. "After all, I had a lot to offer and I didn't want to be a boilerman for the rest of my working life. Anyway, I took a day off, put on my only suit, and went out to Pullach to ask for an interview. The sentry on the main gate wouldn't even let me into the Guard Room. It was while we were arguing that an Opel Kapitan drew up and the driver sounded the horn for the sentry to raise the barrier. You'll never guess who was sitting behind the wheel."

"Sturmbannführer Hausser."

"How did you know?" Grothmann said, unable to disguise his disappointment.

"I didn't, it was just a shot in the dark."

The headlights picked out a wooden barrack hut on the fringe of the copse. Every windowpane had been broken and the door hung open, sagging on its hinges. Freeland put the wheel hard over to the right, turned off the lane and stopped. Then, shifting into reverse, he backed the Mercedes on to a patch of grass next to the hut and switched off the lights and ignition.

"I think you must be psychic, Herr Northover."

"Not at all. What other mutual acquaintances do we have?"

"Chantal Kiffer?"

"Bastard."

140

Freeland lashed out with his right hand, hitting the left side of Grothmann's face with the heel of his palm. Then grabbing what little remained of Grothmann's hair, he smashed his head against the nearside door pillar.

"I ought to kill you for what you did to her."

"It was the war," Grothmann whimpered and was immediately racked by a paroxysm of coughing.

"First you turned Chantal round, then you deliberately betrayed her. You, you bloody animal, you set her up for a firing squad."

"Please . . ." Grothmann fought for breath and, at the same time, tried to stop coughing. He touched the right side of his head and showed Freeland the blood on his fingers. "Please don't hit me again," he pleaded.

"I ought to squash you like a bug."

"I never turned Chantal Kiffer."

"Say that again."

"She was never a double-agent, Herr Northover. St Aubin des Bois is a very small village and some of the malicious gossip about the number of lovers Chantal Kiffer was supposed to have entertained in her cottage reached my ears. That's how we got on to you; I must have had you under surveillance a week or so after you arrived in the Chartres area. I wasn't the only one."

According to Grothmann, the Gestapo, backed up by a special action group led by Sturmbannführer Hausser, had also been keeping an eye on Freeland. The Abwehr hadn't been warned off; on the contrary, both Intelligence departments had continued their operations independently of one another. Then one day, Abwehr Headquarters in Paris had ordered Grothmann to arrest 'Felix', the codename of the SOE agent operating in his area.

"Only you were to be arrested, Herr Northover, not any of the suspects who had come to our notice as a result of your activities. Abwehr Headquarters were very specific about that; they were also very specific concerning my task. I was to disorientate you, to make each day seem like two."

"And you were successful; too bad the SS stole your thunder."

"I didn't want to turn you over to Hausser; I could guess what his thugs would do to you."

But an order is an order. Freeland had lost count of the number of times he had heard that hoary old defence even though the premise had been destroyed at the Nuremberg Trial when Goering, Jodl and Keitel had been found guilty of war crimes.

"I made a nuisance of myself, Herr Northover, so they sent me to the Eastern Front where I was taken prisoner when the Red

Army crossed the Vistula. When the Russians discovered I was in the Abwehr, they shipped me back in a cattle truck to some God-awful camp in the Urals."

"My heart bleeds for you," Freeland told him curtly.

"Quite so. Anyway, that's where I ran into Sturmbannführer Hausser again."

"I'm glad to hear there is some justice in this world."

"But not as much as you would like, Herr Northover. Hausser was treated like an honoured guest."

"Did he recognise you?"

"He didn't even know I existed. We were in different compounds; I only saw him in the distance a couple of times. Hausser was living at the 'Adlon Hotel'; that's what the NKVD guards called his compound. It was like a luxury hotel compared to our hovel, all the comforts of home, plenty of food, liquor on tap and an endless supply of women available from the other camps in the area, young men too if Hausser wanted them. The last time I saw him in the Soviet Union was in the late spring of 1948. The Russians let me go in July 1949."

"And the next time you bumped into Hausser was just over a year ago in Pullach?"

Grothmann nodded eagerly. "The twenty-third of September; the date is engraved on my memory because the Americans wouldn't listen to me when I tried to open their eyes to what was going on down in Pullach."

The Americans had fired Grothmann on the spot, they had also dealt with his second wife in like fashion. A widow, who he'd married within six months of arriving in Munich, she had been employed as a wages clerk in the German Civil Labour Office.

"You understand what I am saying?" Grothmann asked.

"Of course."

Only someone with space to rent between his ears could fail to see what Grothmann was getting at. Hausser's case officer worked in Dzerzhinsky Square and Gehlen's Bureau had hired an NKVD agent. It was as simple as that, but who was going to believe it? Freeland touched the mutilated stump of the little finger on his left hand; the Americans would say he was prejudiced against Hausser and was looking for revenge because of what the SS man had done to him during the war. And how credible a witness would Grothmann make? He was the kind of man with an eye to the main chance who would have denounced his own mother to the Gestapo to earn himself a few Brownie points.

"What was the name of this PW camp in the Urals?"

"Number 129 Special Punishment," Grothmann said and shuddered.

"Who else among the inmates might have seen Hausser?"

"You mean my testimony isn't good enough?"

"It helps to have corroborating evidence."

"There are no other survivors."

"How very convenient," Freeland said acidly.

"You think the Geneva Convention was observed by the NKVD? Listen, the guards out there hadn't even heard of it. They worked us to death on a starvation diet and we died in our thousands, like flies in the winter. There are statistics to prove it; of the ninety-one thousand men of the 6th Army who surrendered at Stalingrad, only one in eighteen has returned to Germany." Grothmann pounded his chest. "I am lucky to be alive," he said and started coughing again.

Freeland switched on the ignition and started the engine, then put on the lights. The freezing fog which the weathermen had promised for earlier in the day had finally closed in while they had been sitting there, and he had to feel his way back to the main road.

"What are you going to do about Hausser?" Grothmann asked him presently.

"I'm not sure . . ."

"You are thinking that perhaps the Americans know all this and are playing some great game?"

"It's possible."

"Yes, anything is possible with Sturmbannführer Hausser. One day I must ask him why he ordered me to be so nice to Chantal Kiffer after you had all been arrested."

Freeland had heard about the kid glove treatment from the French authorities in 1946. He had also read the transcript of the trial and had noted that the advocate who had prosecuted Chantal Kiffer for high treason had called several witnesses to testify to the various favours she had received from the Wehrmacht. Now, however, Grothmann was implying that the SS had deliberately set out to smear Chantal and he wondered why they should have gone to such lengths to frame her.

"It's also one of the questions I'll be asking Hausser," he said grimly.

"Then you are going to use my information after all?" Grothmann said and gave a sigh that was half relieved, half triumphant.

"I can't ignore the allegations you've made about Hausser."

"Good. One does not look for reward of course . . ."

Freeland laughed. "Don't worry," he said, "you'll get yours."

13

Of all the referees Freeland had nominated, Cyril Upham had been the easiest to trace and the most readily available. A well-built, pugnacious-looking man with jet black hair and dark eyes, he looked as though he would be more at home in a boxing ring than as a buyer specialising in ladies fashions. He had learned his trade with Galeries Lafayette in Paris before the war; now aged fifty-one, he was the sales director of Bond and Hales in Regent Street. His office was on the fifth floor and looked out on to Liberty's across the road. From 1941 to 1945 he had been the Chief of Staff for SOE's French Section.

After their brief conversation the previous day when he'd telephoned Upham to make an appointment to see him, Egan had been of the opinion that the former SOE man was unlikely to be very forthcoming unless he satisfied his natural curiosity to some extent.

"This is just a routine follow-up," Egan informed him after they'd shaken hands. "We've had to re-examine our security procedures with a cold, hard eye in the light of the Burgess and Maclean affair. Hence, our Director-General has decided we should look at all our personnel again to make sure there are no other bad eggs amongst them."

"Seems a reasonable precaution." An amused smile made a brief appearance. "What did I say about Freeland the last time you people interviewed me?"

"You told us he was a good young officer – brave, dependable, had a good head on his shoulders and that there was no reason to doubt his loyalty to king and country."

"Then you know as much about him as I do. I can't think of anything else I'd want to add except that today I'd have to substitute queen and country for king and country. Of course our paths haven't crossed since 1946."

"Quite." Egan paused, then posed the first of several questions he and Neville Acland had compiled between them. "Did Freeland ever say anything which led you or any of his instructors at the Training School to think he had left wing views?"

"We never had time for politics," Upham said briskly, "we were too busy trying to win the war."

Egan ran his eye over the remaining questions and thought most of them would elicit the same kind of response, which left him groping for a different approach. Although V Section had always been charged with counter-espionage, their charter had been redefined six months ago and they were still feeling their way in what was an entirely new area. Hitherto, they had dealt with the external threat posed by men like 'Cicero', the Albanian valet to the British Ambassador in Ankara who, having taken wax impressions of the keys to the black despatch box, had photographed the Top Secret cables addressed to His Excellency from the Foreign Office in London. Now they were being asked to look inwards and question all the old values whereby it was assumed that a man was bound to be all right if he came from a certain background, had been educated at a good public school and was a member of a prestigious London Club.

"Would you say Freeland was a stable personality?" Egan asked, casting round for an opening.

"He was when I knew him."

"He wasn't emotional?"

"You've just confirmed that I said Freeland had a good head on his shoulders."

"What about the way he behaved over Chantal Kiffer?"

Upham frowned. "Yes, he did go slightly overboard about her, couldn't accept that she had betrayed so many people."

"But you could?"

"Oh yes, all the evidence pointed to her. Of course, the Loiret Bleu network was badly organised; it had been rapidly expanded to meet the needs of D-Day and she was in contact with too many other cells, but that doesn't alter the fact that she was a double-agent. The SS gave Freeland a very hard time and they broke him in the end, but not before the seventy-two hours were up. In any event, he'd never heard of half of those who were rounded up, so how could he have betrayed them? Guy Salusbury made the same point over and over again when we debriefed him."

"Let's talk about Guy for a moment," Egan said. "How did he measure up in the field?"

"Pretty well, all things considered. And I don't mean that disparagingly I hasten to add."

145

Cyril Upham evidently recalled the bitter rivalry that had existed between the Secret Intelligence Service and SOE and had no desire to reopen old wounds. SOE had been raised to set Europe ablaze; their operatives were supposed to kill Germans, blow things up and create mayhem. But all too often it had seemed to the mandarins of the SIS that the so-called Baker Street Irregulars were encroaching upon their territory and would take them over if they weren't careful.

"I'd appreciate your frank opinion," Egan said quietly. "Salusbury was Freeland's superior officer in war and peace; he gave him a tremendous write-up and I'd like to know how much reliance we can place on his judgment."

Upham gazed at him quizzically as though wondering just how much trust could be put in his discretion, then shrugged his shoulders as if to say, what the hell.

"Guy was thirty-seven when he joined us in 1942 and was the oldest volunteer we had. He was also the least physically fit and I doubted if he would stay the course. I told him so at the selection interview and he begged me to give him a chance, said he wanted to do something worthwhile for a change instead of evaluating the efficiency of de Gaulle's Intelligence Service."

Egan could understand Salusbury's point of view. By 1942, the Wehrmacht had chased the SIS out of every country in Europe with the exception of Sweden, Switzerland, Spain, Portugal and Turkey. Every Intelligence network lay in ruins and Whitehall had regarded the Service as a spent force.

"Anyway, to cut a long story short, Guy proved me utterly wrong. He had a great deal more physical and mental resilience than I had credited him with."

The kind of resilience Upham had in mind was best illustrated by the manner in which Salusbury had succeeded in totally dominating his captors. Although the SS had given him a real beating when he was taken to their headquarters in Paris, he hadn't been systematically tortured the way Freeland had. Salusbury had played on his family name, claiming he was related to the Marquis of Salisbury and that Winston Churchill had been a frequent house-guest at his parents' home in Gloucestershire. By 1944, even the most ardent Nazi was having doubts about the outcome of the war and Salusbury had exploited this uncertainty, offering his protection to all and sundry.

"His message to them was brutally simple," Upham continued. "They were given to understand that so long as they didn't harm him, he would ensure they never stood trial for war crimes. When he learned that Freeland had also been arrested, he made it a condition that no harm should come to him either. The ruse would never have worked if Guy hadn't been such a good judge of character. Sheer force of personality; that's how he carried it off and I don't know any other SOE agent who could have done it. So, if he says Freeland is okay, I reckon you haven't got much to worry about."

"Quite."

"Is there anything else I can tell you?"

Egan recognised the question for what it was, a subtle hint that he was beginning to outstay his welcome.

"I don't think so. I've found our talk most helpful and I'd like to thank you again for seeing me at such short notice." Egan paused, then said, "Of course, our little *tête-à-tête* must remain strictly confidential."

"What *tête-à-tête*?" Upham asked, and showed him to the door.

But a few minutes after Egan had left Bond and Hales, he wrote a brief letter to Freeland and addressed it care of the Foreign Office, King Charles Street.

*   *   *

The Gehlen Bureau at Pullach was funded by Washington and worked to the Central Intelligence Agency. This being the case, it could be said that ex-Sturmbannführer Hausser belonged to the Americans who, of course, could be relied upon to look after their property. In deciding to go after him without official backing, Freeland knew he would be chancing his arm in much the same way as would a blind man foolish enough to pick his way through a minefield without the benefit of either a metal detector or a probe. To avoid getting himself blown up, he needed someone to point him towards the safe lane through the obstacle, and Steve Johansen was the only person he knew who could do that.

Steve Johansen was roughly the same age and their careers had followed a broadly similar pattern. The American had served with the Office of Strategic Services during the war and, like Freeland, he was now responsible for organising special sabotage groups to attack the rear echelons of the Red Army in the event of a showdown with the Soviet Union. He also was married and had one child, a girl aged two. They had met at the regular six-monthly conference held in June and December at SHAPE Headquarters, Fontainebleau, and had known one another professionally for some eighteen months. With Freeland living in Cologne and Johansen in Wiesbaden, there was little opportunity for socialising, but they had spent the

147

occasional family weekend together and if they weren't the closest of friends, they were at least more than casual acquaintances.

Johansen ran his operation from a large house set in the woods above the town, roughly three-quarters of a mile beyond the last tram stop. Before leaving Cologne, Freeland had telephoned his office asking him to check Grothmann's record with his former employers.

"We're talking about Karl Heinz Grothmann, right?" Johansen said after pouring him a cup of coffee from the pot simmering on an electric ring in his office. "Born Hamburg April twenty-seventh 1910, ex-detective Kriminalpolizei, ex-Abwehr Feldwebel, former Russian POW?"

"That's the man."

"Yeah? So what's he doing in your neck of the woods?"

"Working as a labourer in 87 Supply Depot at Münster. One of my talent spotters thought we could use him."

"And can you?"

"No, he's not up to it physically. But he said something during the interview which made me wonder if Field Security hadn't slipped up when they screened him. For instance, he made no mention of his previous employment with your V Corps Headquarters in Munich when he filled out the job application form. That fact only came to light when I was interviewing him. I asked Grothmann why he had left the American Zone to come and work for us and he gave me a cock and bull story about his face not fitting." Freeland laughed. "You wouldn't have palmed a dyed-in-the-wool old Nazi off on us, would you, Steve?"

Johansen glanced at his scratchboard as if to refresh his memory. "According to the Civil Labour Unit, V Corps sacked him because of his poor work record; the guy was continually off sick."

"Then there's nothing in his papers that says V Corps fired Grothmann because he was making a nuisance of himself?"

"Absolutely not." Johansen leaned back in his chair, elbows on the arm rest, his hands pressed together as though in prayer. "What exactly did he tell you, Harry?"

"Grothmann wanted to get back into the Intelligence game and he started hanging around the Gehlen Bureau down at Pullach on his days off, hoping he could persuade someone to at least give him an interview. That's when he saw this former Sturmbannführer driving around in an official car. Now, there's nothing wrong with employing former SS men, we all do it, but this guy happens to be wanted for war crimes."

"Does he have a name?"

"Joachim Hausser."

Freeland didn't bother with the detail of the Sturmbannführer's date and place of birth; instead, he described his features so minutely that even a novice could have produced a likeness as good as any photograph. Although it was more than eight years since he had seen Hausser, he would never forget his face – the pointed chin, his thin bloodless lips, the long straight nose with pinched nostrils, the deep-set grey eyes, the sloping forehead and the receding blond hair.

"Why are you giving me such a detailed description of the guy, Harry?"

"Because he may have changed his name."

"But he hasn't altered one bit?"

"Not unless they had plastic surgeons in Camp 129."

"Where's that?"

"In the Urals," said Freeland. "According to Grothmann, he was on buddy-boy terms with the NKVD guards and living the life of Riley while the other inmates starved. Grothmann was released from the prison camp in July 1949; Hausser may have got out earlier because he wasn't seen around the camp after the late spring of '48."

"Are you saying he's a plant?"

"I'd bet a month's salary on it." Freeland smiled lopsidedly and held up his left hand. "Of course, some people would claim I'm prejudiced."

"He removed your little finger?" Johansen said in an awed tone of voice.

"With a pair of pincers, a joint at a time."

"Jesus." The American gave a low whistle, then looked at him through eyes narrowing with suspicion. "Now hold on a minute," he said, "I remember you telling me that you'd lost your little finger as a result of an accident, something to do with the rigging lines of your parachute."

"That's the usual explanation I give when I'm asked."

"Yeah? Well, maybe there are a number of explanations for what Hausser is supposed to have done in Russia, assuming he was even there."

"Yes, Grothmann could have made it up," Freeland said calmly. "Though what he hoped to gain by that isn't exactly clear to me. Then again, he might be telling the truth and Hausser simply buttered up to the guards in order to get out of the camp as soon as he could. Or there is the possibility that Hausser is indeed a NKVD plant but your people have tumbled to it and are using

149

him as a double-agent. You can take your pick, but it might be wiser to check with the Gehlen Bureau to see what they know about him."

Johansen thought about it for several moments, then said, "I guess it would do no harm to check Hausser out on the teleprinter link to Pullach."

"Right."

"Do you mind giving me his physical description again in case they have him logged under a different name?"

Freeland reached inside his jacket and took out a slip of paper. "Here," he said, "I wrote it out last night just in case you asked."

It took Johansen slightly over twenty minutes to draft and encrypt the signal; one hour after they acknowledged receiving it, Pullach came back to say that no one called Hausser was serving with the Bureau, nor did they have anyone who matched his description.

*   *   *

Neville Acland enjoyed a reputation for being a good listener. Any subordinate who had to brief him knew that he would not be interrupted by a spate of questions, most of which would have been quite superfluous had the person concerned been content to wait until the end before opening his mouth. Egan counted himself fortunate to have such a man as his superior officer; he could name at least two directors he had worked for who would have started to cross-examine him long before he had finished recounting the ins and outs of his interview with Cyril Upham, late of the SOE's French Section.

"So Upham stands by what he originally said about Freeland?" Acland said, encapsulating the briefing in a sentence.

"Yes." Egan paused, then said, "Of course, he has no reason not to; by his own admission, he hasn't seen Freeland since 1946. I have a feeling that the same applies to all the other referees. Within the Service, Salusbury knows him best, but he's in America and I doubt the Paymaster will agree to pay my air fare to New York."

"Not unless we put up a very good case."

"Quite. That's why I spent the rest of the morning and most of this afternoon going through the dead files in Central Registry. I wanted to read Freeland's account of what happened in Shanghai and found myself instead doing a lot of background research on Howard Teale, the man he was supposed to bring out."

Howard Teale's name had never appeared in any edition of the

Diplomatic Service List and, unlike the career officers, he had never appeared before a selection board. Had he been moved to join the Service officially, his poor academic qualifications would have stood out on the application form and led to his instant rejection at the first hurdle. As an *ex officio* member of the SIS, he was, however, the best Intelligence officer in the Far East.

"Teale gave us the complete Order of Battle of the Japanese Army in China and the names of all the Divisional commanders," Egan continued. "Three months before Pearl Harbour, we knew where, when and how Lieutenant-General Tomoyuki Yamashita proposed to invade Malaya; had we given Teale's information the credence it deserved, the Japanese would have received a very bloody nose when they came ashore at Kota Bharu. But it seems Teale had always been coy about his sources and one gathers he was a rather unsavoury character."

"Most spies are," Acland said with unconscious irony.

"Really? Well, the information he provided after the war wasn't up to the same high quality, but even when Mao was still bottled up in the north, he couldn't see Chiang Kai-shek and the Nationalists coming out on top. However, his wasn't a lone voice crying in the wilderness; the SIS Residents in Nanking and Shanghai had reached the same conclusion some time before he did."

Both officers had also submitted adverse reports on Teale. They hadn't liked his business activities and considered he was too well known by the Chinese which made him a security risk.

"They believed he was a menace; too careless and too fond of the sound of his own voice to be trusted. He was a difficult man to exclude because he had so many contacts amongst the Chinese community and knew who we were trying to recruit in Shanghai. The SIS Resident expressed the fear that Teale would accidentally blow the network he was trying to establish against the day the Communists seized power. That's why he wanted London to persuade Teale it was time to come home. Unfortunately, he was making too much money in Shanghai and he refused to leave. The Consul General tried to have him deported but Teale had greased the right palms and couldn't be shifted. When we couldn't get our way through diplomatic channels, the Service began to consider other means. Guy Salusbury was running the Far East Desk in those days and he decided to get Teale out with or without his consent."

"And he sent Harry Freeland in to do it?"

Egan nodded. "They had served together in the same resistance group in France and he had a high opinion of him. Freeland's post-action report is on the HARVESTER file, the codename given to the operation Salusbury mounted to recover Teale. I'd like to read it to see what orders Freeland thinks he was given. You never know, it may give us another lead to follow."

"Right, do it."

"I need your signature," Egan informed him. "The HARVESTER file is in the archives and the custodian won't release it to anyone under the rank of Assistant Director."

There was just the briefest pause before Acland told him to prepare the necessary docket.

*   *   *

Anna and Karl Heinz Grothmann had two rooms on the ground floor of 64 Lippstädter Strasse, one of the few pre-war tenements near the railway to have survived the destruction of Münster in October 1944. Beyond number 64, the wasteland stretched as far as Route 51 to Dulmen. Where houses had once stood, there were now uneven mounds of grass-covered bricks fenced in by overgrown bushes interlaced with brambles. The potholed sidewalk was dimly lit by the few remaining streetlamps which still worked.

Freeland turned off Route 51 into Lippstädter Strasse, pulled across on to the wrong side of the road and stopped just short of number 64. The woman appeared from the deep shadows and picked her way towards the Mercedes, taking care to avoid the potholes in her four-inch high heels. Halting a few paces from the car, she undid the bottom three buttons on the black, military-style swagger coat she was wearing and flipped the skirt aside to let him see that apart from the garter belt and rayon stockings, she was naked from the waist down. Then she rapped on the window until eventually he was forced to lower it.

"Looking for a good time?" With her face camouflaged by layer upon layer of make-up, she could have been any age between twenty and forty.

"Save your breath," Freeland told her, "I'm waiting for a friend."

He closed the window, took out a packet of cigarettes and lit one. Grothmann cycled to and from work on the other side of town and would approach Lippstädter Strasse from the direction of the Halle Münsterland, the large concert hall on Albersloher Weg which resembled the Wembley Ice Stadium and could seat six thousand people. Another Mercedes turned off the main road directly ahead and kerb-crawled past him. Watching the vehicle in the rear view mirror, he saw the brake lights come on as the driver stopped briefly to pick up the whore. It was followed in short order by a convoy comprising a Borgward, two Opel Kapitans and a DKW. Lippstädter Strasse was the sort of thoroughfare that was automatically out of bounds to all servicemen, a restriction diligently enforced by the military police. Tonight was no exception even though it was Wednesday, a time when most soldiers were flat broke.

The clock in the dashboard showed nine minutes to six. Freeland was beginning to wonder where Grothmann had got to when he saw the blurred figure of a cyclist pedalling slowly towards him. Recognising the former warrant officer, Freeland stubbed his cigarette into the ashtray and got out of the car in time to intercept him by the front gate.

"Herr Northover." Grothmann tried to catch his breath. "What are you doing here?" he wheezed.

"Waiting for you." Freeland grabbed hold of an arm and steered the German round to the side of the house where they wouldn't be seen from the road. "I've been talking to a friend in Wiesbaden about you. I asked him to run a few checks for me, and you know what? The Gehlen Bureau has never heard of Joachim Hausser. As a matter of fact, they don't have anyone who even remotely resembles his description."

"Well, they would say that, wouldn't they?"

"Furthermore, the Americans didn't fire you because you had a bee in your bonnet about Hausser. They sacked you because you were always sick."

"That's not true, Herr Northover," Grothmann said with quiet dignity.

"They're going to send me photostats of your worksheets."

"They can be faked."

"Prove it."

"How can I possibly do that?"

Freeland reached inside his duffel coat and took out a sealed envelope. "There's five hundred Marks in there, more than what you earn in a month. Take it, go down to Munich first thing tomorrow and move in with your cousin for a few days."

From Wiesbaden, Freeland had driven straight back to Cologne and drawn the money out of the contingency fund, something which had caused Anthea Clowes to raise her eyebrows. She had looked even more askance when he'd told her he would be staying the night in Münster.

"I don't understand," Grothmann said, staring at the envelope in his hand.

153

"You told me you had seen Hausser driving around in an Opel Kapitan, so you can bet your shirt he isn't living in Pullach. Borrow a motorbike and try following one of the bigwigs home from work; people in the Intelligence world usually live cheek by jowl with one another, and he may lead you to Hausser."

"What am I going to tell Anna?"

"You'll think of something. Give it a week; if you haven't found him by then, come on back. There's a phone number on the inside flap of the envelope; use it to leave a message for me if you get lucky."

"What about my job at the supply depot?"

"Don't give it another thought," Freeland told him. "I know a friendly doctor who'll be only too happy to give you an authentic sick note."

14

Freeland couldn't make up his mind whether it was the chink of grey light he could see in the gap between the curtains that had woken him or the fact that his feet were cold because the duvet had ended up on the floor. He turned over on to his left side to retrieve it and found himself gazing at an unfamiliar table lamp. For a panic-stricken moment he wondered where he was, then the voice of reason told him not to be such a damned fool. This was a single room on the third floor of the Hotel Movenpeck in Münster which the ever-efficient Anthea Clowes had booked for him. A calm, practical and eminently sensible woman, maybe she could advise him how to square things with Jenny?

He had booked a call to Lichfield within minutes of checking into the hotel the previous evening. Considering how many telephone exchanges were involved, it had come through very quickly and the line had been passably good too. He had asked after his father-in-law and had learned that Sidney Vail's latest attack of angina had not been nearly as bad as Jenny's mother had made out. On the other hand, his eleven-month-old son had developed a bit of a sniffle, which was hardly surprising. Like most houses in England, number 32 Chestnut Close was as cold as charity in winter and Mark was used to central heating.

He had told Jenny how much he missed her and how empty the house seemed when she wasn't around, and he had meant every word. But Jenny had been sceptical and had asked him about Grothmann, and he hadn't known how to answer that question. If he said he hadn't bothered to see the former Feldwebel, she would know he was lying; if he told her the truth, she would be even more convinced that he was obsessed with the ghost of Chantal Kiffer. He had still been groping for the right answer when the line went dead; when he had tried to re-establish the connection, the international operator in England had told him the Lichfield number was engaged.

Freeland got out of bed, walked over to the window and drew back the curtains. Seven twenty-five: a cold grey dawn, the street lights still on, the waters of Aasee lake dark and forbidding, a thin covering of snow with a lot more to come if he was any judge of the weather. Jenny was right of course; he was obsessed with Chantal Kiffer, though not in the way she imagined.

There had been a time when he had been in love with Chantal and had thought she was in love with him, but with hindsight, he could now see that there had never been any commitment on her part; every time he had been invited to her bed, it had simply been to satisfy her needs. Had her husband, Emil, not been taken prisoner in 1940, she would not have spared him a second glance. Chantal Kiffer continued to obsess him because, in spite of all the evidence, he could not bring himself to believe that she had betrayed the entire Loiret Bleu network. If she had done that, why had the SS tortured him to get a lot of names they already had? He had talked, so had a lot of other cell leaders and the survivors had been only too happy to testify against Chantal Kiffer. They had wanted to save their own skins and she had been the ideal scapegoat. But Hausser was the one who had really set her up and he was determined to learn the reason why.

Freeland turned away from the window and went into the bathroom to wash and shave. Gunther Altmüller started work at eight o'clock and Hiltrup was approximately five miles from the city centre. Half an hour later, having breakfasted off coffee, rolls, cheese, hard boiled eggs and cold sausage, Freeland collected his travelling bag from the bedroom and checked out of the hotel.

*   *   *

The timber yard where Altmüller was employed as the office manager was located on the outskirts of Hiltrup between the railway and the Dortmund-Ems canal. When Freeland drove through the gates, one truck had just arrived with a load from the sawmill while two others were collecting chipboarding and four-by-two joists for a local builder. Although it was the first time that Freeland had been to the yard, Altmüller greeted him as though he was an old and valued customer.

"Good morning, Herr Northover," he said cheerfully. "If you would like to wait in the office, I'll be with you as soon as I can."

The office was a wooden hut that was just large enough to accommodate a three-drawer filing cabinet, a stationery cupboard and two desks, one of which was occupied by a clerk typist. Heating was provided by a small electric fire which Freeland thought was probably why the middle-aged woman who was busy putting invoices into envelopes hadn't bothered to remove her coat.

"Herr Altmüller said I should wait for him in here," Freeland explained.

The woman nodded and went on with her task, carefully addressing the envelopes in long hand. Presently it started to snow again in the way small children usually depict it with large lumps of cotton wool falling straight to earth from a leaden sky. A truck lumbered out of the yard, turned left outside the entrance and headed towards Münster. A few minutes later, Altmüller entered the hut.

"I reckon we're in for a heavy fall," he said.

"Looks like it," Freeland agreed.

Altmüller nodded sagely, then faced the woman. "I think we'll have a little something with our coffee, Gertrud." He dug into his pocket with his left hand and counted out three one-Mark coins. "A florentine for Herr Northover and myself and whatever you fancy. Also a small carton of cream to go with the coffee."

Gertrud put on the pudding-bowl hat that she had hung from a hook on the wall behind her desk and wrapped a scarf around her neck, pulling on thick woollen gloves before leaving the office.

"The Konditorei is the other side of the railway," Altmüller said as soon as they were alone, "so we have approximately fifteen minutes to ourselves."

"Joachim Hausser," Freeland said abruptly, "does the name mean anything to you?"

"No, I've never heard of him."

"You have now. He was born in Nuremberg on the sixteenth of May 1914 and was a Sturmbannführer in the SS. A haughty looking bastard, grey eyes, blond hair, the true Aryan type Hitler was always on about."

"He still doesn't ring a bell with me . . ."

"Hausser married a girl from Osnabrück, a Fraulein Elisabeth von Nebe. Her father was a judge."

"And a member of the Nazi Party?"

"What else?" Freeland took out a packet of cigarettes, offered one to Altmüller and lit up. "In early 1944, Hausser was commanding a special Amt VI action group based in Paris; his most successful operation was the destruction of the Loiret Bleu network. We know Schellenberg recalled him to Berlin in January '45 but that's the last trace we have on him. Grothmann claims to have seen him in a special NKVD punishment camp for Intelligence Officers

157

somewhere in the Urals and says he is now working for the Gehlen Bureau in Pullach."

"Which the Americans deny?"

"Yes."

"This is all very interesting, Herr Northover, but what's it got to do with me?"

"I want you to find out what happened to the von Nebes, father, mother and daughter Elisabeth. If any of them are still alive, I want to know where they are now living."

"With all due respect, that's a job for the police, isn't it?"

"This is unofficial business," Freeland told him, "that's why it's got to be done on the quiet. We've got a cell in Osnabrück, put them on to it. I seem to recall you telling me that one of their brethren served in the SS on the Eastern Front?"

"Waffen SS," Altmüller said quickly. "They were soldiers first, and anyway he was a conscript. He wouldn't have had any dealings with the likes of Hausser."

"You're wrong, Gunther. They're a fraternity like the Freemasons, every city has its own Lodge. Tap into their grapevine and you never know what you may come up with."

"I'll do the best I can, Herr Northover. I can't say more than that."

A wind had got up, driving the snow before it so that visibility was reduced to about twenty yards. A horse and cart turned into the yard and went slowly past the window, the driver sitting bolt upright on the buckboard.

"That's old man Ohlendorf's son," Altmüller informed him. "They've got a farm on the outskirts of Hiltrup. He's here to collect a load of timber to rebuild the barn your soldiers burned down in early October. The old man let them sleep in it when they were on manoeuvres and someone didn't stub his cigarette out properly. Soon after they left, the whole place went up in flames. Of course, the British paid him compensation, but how's he going to replace the hay he lost?"

"Are you a heavy drinker, Gunther?"

"What?"

"Grothmann says your tongue begins to wag after you've had a few."

"That's a damned lie."

"He says you told him about our organisation one evening when you were in your cups."

"I didn't have to tell him anything; he already knew the Americans were raising similar 'stay behind parties' in their zone and guessed

158

the British were doing the same. I walked into the Bierkeller a week ago last Tuesday and one of my men points Grothmann out and says I ought to have a word with him because he's too damned nosy for his own good. And so I hear all there is to hear concerning Grothmann's war against your SOE and the American Office of Strategic Services, and then he calmly informs me that both wartime organisations are back in business, only this time they are operating on German soil. He also has a fund of stories about the political squabbles inside the French Resistance and how the Communists and Socialists weren't above betraying each other to the Gestapo. And I gathered that was how the SS got a lead on the Englishman whose codename was 'Felix' and whose little finger they chopped off . . ." Altmüller paused, then said, "I should have kept my mouth shut, I know, but it was such a coincidence that I couldn't help mentioning that I knew someone who had also lost his little finger in the war."

Freeland was inclined to believe there was more than a grain of truth in Altmüller's version but the post-mortem could wait. Two days ago he had decided that Altmüller would have to go; forty-eight hours later, it was a different story.

"You think Grothmann heard about these 'stay behind parties' when he was working at V Corps Headquarters?"

"He was a boilerman, Gunther."

"Precisely. And perhaps the Americans were careless when they consigned some of their old Top Secret files to the furnace? Maybe the officer who was in charge of destroying the papers didn't wait to see them consumed in the flames? Maybe Grothmann found some charred remains when he raked the boiler?"

"You're trying too hard," Freeland said tersely. "The fact is there has been a leakage of information and it's down to you. Fortunately, it looks as though the damage has been limited to the cell in Münster and I can live with that, but my faith in you has taken a knock. Trace the von Nebes for me and you'll go a long way towards restoring it."

Altmüller looked as if he was about to explode, the colour drained from his face and his eyes narrowed venomously. Then the door opened and Gertrud walked into the office clutching a paper bag in one hand, a small carton of cream in the other, her hat transformed into a wedding cake by the snow.

"What the hell kept you?" Altmüller snarled, venting his anger on her instead of Freeland.

Gertrud made some excuse in a low voice that neither man was intended to hear, then filled the electric kettle with water from a

plastic container she kept in the stationery cupboard. The coffee
was made from something dark and liquid that came out of a bottle
and tasted vaguely like chicory. There was nothing wrong with the
florentines but Altmüller was in a mood to find fault with everything.
He thought the chocolate was too bitter, there were too many nuts
and not enough cherries. Gertrud became even more tight-lipped
and the atmosphere progressively more sullen. It was not the best
start to the day; Freeland just hoped it wasn't a portent of things
to come.

*　　*　　*

It wasn't snowing in London; the capital was shrouded in fog.
Although not yet thick enough to constitute a real pea-souper, the
smog obscured the outlines of familiar landmarks. Egan reckoned
the HARVESTER file did much the same thing for the Teale affair.
He had spent the whole morning and most of the afternoon reading
the After Action Report submitted by Freeland and was now more
perplexed than ever.

"And what conclusions have you come to?" Acland asked him.

"None," said Egan. "But there are a number of things which
puzzle me. For instance, I don't understand where Freeland could
have got the idea that Teale had refused to leave Shanghai after
being ordered to do so. Teale was not a member of the SIS and
there is a pencil notation in the margin by Guy Salusbury pointing
out that in view of this, London had no authority to order him to
come home."

"What did Freeland have to say about that?"

"Nothing. It appears he never saw the report again after he
submitted it to Salusbury. Guy commented on it in order to clarify
certain matters for the Director-General."

"And to protect himself?" Acland suggested.

"Possibly – though by and large he defended Freeland against the
Foreign Office who accused him of impairing diplomatic relations
with Peking."

The illusion nurtured by the British Community that somehow
it would be business as usual under the Communists had rapidly
gone the way of all mirages. Within a matter of a few weeks, taxes
had been raised to astronomical heights and the man responsible
for imposing them had been Tu Yush-sen, the former professor of
Agrarian Economics at St John's University.

"Tu Yush-sen went underground in 1948," Egan continued.
"When he surfaced again, he was the political commissar of the local
guerilla unit in Pootung. Freeland was interrogated by him while he

160

was being held prisoner. He escaped from custody, killing one of the PLA guards in the process; because of that, the Foreign Office holds him responsible for the initial crackdown by Peking."

"How long was he in Communist hands?"

"A little over twenty-four hours, and there are several independent witnesses to corroborate this. I doubt if they managed to convert him to their way of thinking in that time."

"Long enough for him to have had quite a *tête-à-tête* with his political masters," Acland observed, then added, "assuming he already belonged to Moscow."

"Freeland alleged the Nationalists claimed he did – or to be more accurate, a certain Colonel Li accused him of being a Communist spy. He is also supposed to have tortured Teale and then used him to lure Freeland into an ambush."

"Is there any evidence to support this allegation?"

Egan shook his head. Although Teale's body had been kept in the cold store belonging to Butterfield and Swire, a number of power cuts had occurred between the estimated time of death and Wednesday the first of June when his body had been handed over to the British Consulate. Since the cadaver was badly decomposed, no autopsy had been carried out prior to burial in the local British cemetery.

"One is almost inclined to believe that Freeland's account is simply a very good cover story to explain his meeting with the PLA."

"Except the Nationalists arrested Teale before he arrived in Shanghai."

"A good cover story is always based on a measure of truth, Tom."

"I think you should read the report," Egan said quietly. "The cover story theory doesn't hold up because Frank Matthews, the Consulate security officer, was present when Teale phoned Freeland and gave him a RV in Pootung."

"Where is Matthews now?"

Egan smiled. When you had worked for Acland as long as he had, you learned to anticipate such questions and prepared yourself accordingly. "Doing the same job for the Embassy in Bonn."

"How very convenient," Acland murmured. "We may need to borrow him, but that's something I can arrange. Is there anything else I should know?"

"Yes. Freeland says this Colonel Li knew in advance that he was coming to Shanghai. A Top Secret cable was sent to the Consulate and the SIS Resident in Hong Kong briefing them about Operation HARVESTER. In accordance with normal procedure, it

161

was encrypted and transmitted by 804 Signal Troop at Bracknell. When asked to account for the leak, the army maintained that the Nationalists did not have the capability to either intercept or decode the message."

"What about the Americans?"

"They could certainly have intercepted the transmission; they could probably have broken it too, given the time and inclination. But they had already written the Nationalists off as a dead loss so far as mainland China was concerned. Besides, they were working hand in glove with us; their Consul in Hong Kong wrote an open letter to the management of Chennault's private airline asking them to provide Freeland with every assistance. Everyone agrees the leak didn't occur in Hong Kong, which leaves Shanghai. The signal was addressed 'Exclusive for Head of Station'; in his absence on duty in Nanking, Giles Caunter took it upon himself to open it."

"We'd better have a word with him," said Acland. "Where is he now?"

"In St Mary's churchyard at Berkhampstead."

"He's dead?"

"I'm afraid so, he was killed in the train crash at Harrow and Wealdstone this October."

Giles Caunter had returned from the Far East in September 1951 and had been given a desk job in Matthew Parker Street. On the eighth of October, he had caught his usual commuter train to Euston. Despite patchy fog, the stopping train had arrived at Harrow and Wealdstone more or less on time. The driver of the Perth to London Express, who had encountered far worse conditions, was running ninety minutes late and was just beginning to work up speed. For some unknown reason, he had gone through two stop signals before cannoning into the back of Caunter's train at an estimated speed of fifty-five miles an hour. At the precise moment of impact, the Euston to Manchester Express passed the last signal before Harrow and Wealdstone which was set at green. Still travelling at maximum speed, the express had ploughed into the wreckage from the other two trains which were blocking the down line. Caunter was just one of a hundred and twelve people who had died that morning.

*   *   *

It was Theatre Hour on AFN and the network was serialising *Captain Horatio Hornblower* with Gregory Peck starring in the same role he'd played in the movie. Freeland relaxed in an armchair with a whisky and soda, closed his eyes and listened to the creak of ship's timbers, the rattle of the anchor chain and the gentle lapping of the sea. He had read the books and seen the film but it had been one hell of a day and he was too bushed to search the dial for something else.

From Hiltrup he had gone on to Paderborn to look at a possible site for a clandestine radio station on the Eggegeb ridge, and had then doubled back to Iserlohn. The operational hide for the local resistance cell, which had been selected with such care eighteen months ago, was now threatened by a proposed housing development. He had hoped to find one or more other locations in the wooded slopes above the small market town, but the weather had defeated him. Although it had stopped snowing by the time he'd reached Iserlohn, drifts had blocked the minor roads leading into the hills and he had been forced to turn back. In the process, he'd managed to put the rear wheels of the Mercedes into a ditch and it had taken the combined efforts of three farm-labourers and a tractor to get the vehicle back on to the road again.

Moments after his head began to droop, the telephone suddenly brought him wide awake. Freeland put the glass of whisky down and walked over to the desk by the window; lifting the receiver, he switched off the radio with his free hand.

"Harry?"

"Yes, Innes, what can I do for you?"

Every town of any consequence in the Federal Republic had a British Resident who acted as a sort of honest broker between the local German authorities and the British garrison. Innes Dalwood presided over Cologne even though the military presence was virtually non-existent.

"I've just had a phone call from the Feuerwehrmeister. I'm sorry to tell you this but it seems your offices are on fire."

"Christ."

"Fortunately, none of the staff was on the premises."

Nine thirty-five and this was a Thursday which was a stroke of luck. Twenty-four hours earlier and the fortnightly meeting of the Anglo-German Society would have been drawing to a close.

"Who else have you told?" Freeland asked.

"No one. I tried to contact the resident British Council Officer but he's not at home."

"Do me a favour, Innes, keep on ringing him until I get back."

Freeland hung up, grabbed his duffel coat from the cloakroom and left the house. Nightfall had brought a sharp drop in the temperature and the snow in the driveway had frozen so that opening the garage doors proved a damned sight more difficult

163

than when he'd closed them on his return from Iserlohn. He started the Mercedes and backed out into the road. Under normal conditions, Magnus Strasse was a ten-minute drive from his home in Gartenstrasse but the impacted snow had turned to ice in places and he took it carefully.

Magnus Strasse was sealed off by police road blocks and Freeland had to call the Inspector over before the officers manning the barrier would allow him through on foot. Six engines were fighting the fire and their hoses criss-crossed the street like so many grey-coloured pythons. Even to his unprofessional eye, it was obvious that the firemen were simply endeavouring to contain the blaze rather than put it out. The whole building was engulfed in flames; the second floor had already collapsed and the roof tiles were exploding like small mortar bombs. The heat was so intense that the snow within the vicinity of the conflagration had melted; avoiding the larger puddles, Freeland walked up to the Fire Chief and introduced himself.

The alarm, he was informed, had been received at 2051 hours and the first engine had arrived at the scene eight minutes later. The Fire Chief was less certain how it had started.

"Somewhere on the ground floor, Herr Northover, probably behind one of the bookshelves where the flames couldn't be seen from the road until the fire had really taken hold. The buildings in this neighbourhood are more than fifty years old; who knows, maybe the wiring was at fault." He shrugged his shoulders, then said, "Of course we shan't know the answer until we can examine the interior."

Freeland thanked him, picked his way back to the car and drove slowly home. Just beyond the Stadt Museum in Zeughauptstrasse, he pulled into the kerb and rang Anthea Clowes from a public call box. An age seemed to pass before she answered the phone.

"Hi," he said, "it's me, Harry. Listen, I'm sorry if I've disturbed you but I wanted to make sure you were okay."

"It's very kind of you to ask but it's only a head cold."

"You haven't heard the news then?"

"What news?"

"Our office is on fire. As a matter of fact, the whole building is in flames."

"My God."

"Better not open the door of your apartment tonight unless you know who it is."

"Are you saying the fire was started deliberately, Harry?"

"I don't think it was an accident," Freeland told her.

15

Freeland ate the last slice of toast and marmalade, then reached for the strong cup of tea. If a week was a long time in politics, it was an eternity without Jenny. The time might pass quickly enough during the day but the evenings were long, slow and empty without her. And the telephone was no help; somehow it made Jenny seem even farther away rather than nearer. She would be home for Christmas, he had her word on that, but this was only the ninth of December and he didn't know how he was going to get through the next fortnight.

He wanted to drop everything, go back to England and collect her. Unfortunately, he couldn't walk out and leave Anthea Clowes to mind the shop, especially when they were still in the process of re-establishing themselves in the new premises. In any event, London paid his salary and London wanted to know what the hell was going on.

Freeland gulped down the rest of the tea, folded his napkin into its ring and left the breakfast room. Hildegarde, their live-in housekeeper, was busy in the kitchen and he called out to tell her he would be home at the usual time, then grabbing his duffel coat from the cloakroom, he let himself out of the house.

The new offices of the British Council were in Hohe Strasse within easy walking distance of the town centre. It was a prime location, one that would have made the English Language Officer very happy had he been able to restock the library. From Freeland's point of view, the property was less than desirable because it shared a dividing wall with the Reisebüro next door. Innes Dalwood, who had used his not inconsiderable influence as the British Resident to get them in at short notice, thought it was an absolutely ideal place but of course he had no idea just how much highly sensitive material was handled by Freeland and Anthea Clowes.

Freeland left the Mercedes in the reserved parking space at the back of the building and walked inside. Anthea Clowes had already collected the mail from the British Consulate in Düsseldorf and had filed the letters in the temporary jackets they'd opened in the aftermath of the fire. There was a Secret letter from London covering a Foreign Office memorandum which listed six former SS men who were wanted for questioning in connection with war crimes committed in the Ukraine. They had been identified by the Israelis whose sources indicated that all six were living in West Germany under various aliases. The memorandum was accompanied by the appropriate number of Wanted posters complete with a grainy photograph and physical description of each suspect. London wanted to be assured that none of them were on the SIS payroll, which was asking a lot in the circumstances.

He was still going through the mail when Anthea Clowes announced that he had a visitor and Frank Matthews walked into the room. He had aged a lot and lost considerable weight since Freeland had last seen him more than three years ago in Shanghai. His hair was now badger grey, his face had lost its tan and was a pallid yellow and altogether he looked much older than his fifty-five years.

"Well, I'll be damned." Freeland stood up and pumped his outstretched hand, then waved him to a chair. "You're the last person I expected to see, Frank. When did you leave Shanghai?"

"The end of June this year. I was glad to see the back of the place."

"I imagine life must have been pretty difficult by then?"

"It was. Things went from bad to worse after the Korean war broke out. Every business enterprise went bust; workers' co-operatives usurped the functions of management and the Communists taxed the turnover at a hundred and ten per cent. Under the Nationalists, bars, restaurants, nightclubs and dance halls had to close at nine p.m., under the Communists they never opened. Shanghai became a prison everyone wanted to escape from."

"How about Nina Burzova, the woman Teale named as a Communist?"

Matthews raised a quizzical eyebrow. "Fancy you remembering her, Harry."

"I promised Teale I would get her out of jail; I didn't keep my word."

"She was still in Ward Road prison when the PLA marched in, but you needn't feel guilty about that. Teale did Nina Burzova a favour when he denounced her; a heroine of the Soviet Union could not have been treated better. Nina's only worry was the possibility that they would send her back to Moscow in triumph.

166

But she's a survivor and married a Filipino before the Chinese authorities discovered she was a phoney. Rumour has it she is now the joint-owner of one of Manila's most expensive nightclubs."

"You and I should be so lucky," Freeland said drily. "What are you doing these days?"

"Same as I was before, only this time it's in Bonn." Matthews tugged the lobe of his right ear, apparently embarrassed. "Acland asked me to run my eye over this place to see what protective measures are needed."

"Who's Acland?"

"He's Head of Security, has an office at 54 Broadway. An ex-Guards officer, six feet one or two, slim, about fifty, though you'd never think it to look at him."

Freeland shook his head. "Never heard of the man," he said tersely.

"He literally made a flying visit to Bonn yesterday. You can phone London if you don't believe me."

"Hey, Frank, when did I ever doubt your word?"

"Well, that's okay then. Truth is, I don't like this any more than you do but Acland said we didn't want another case of arson like Magnus Strasse." Matthews gazed at him thoughtfully. "It was arson, wasn't it?" he asked.

"Most people are satisfied it was, including me."

The fire had started in the library on the ground floor and had been initiated by a phosphorus grenade detonated by a time-delay pencil and a minute amount of plastic explosive. Whoever had started the conflagration had also soused the bookshelves with several gallons of petrol for good measure.

"Acland would like to believe the fire was the handiwork of some neo-Nazis," said Matthews.

"Both the *Kölner Stadt Anzeiger* and the *Kölnische-Rundschau* received a phone call from a man describing himself as the spokesman for the New National Socialist Party. He is alleged to have said that what happened in Magnus Strasse is only the beginning."

"But you don't attach much credence to the caller?"

"He wasn't a practical joker," said Freeland, "and I'm equally sure he wasn't a neo-Nazi either."

"So what's left, apart from your fruit-and-nut case who enjoys setting fire to things?"

"The NKVD."

"You've got to be joking, Harry. According to Acland, the editors of both newspapers are certain the man they spoke to was a German."

167

"I never said he wasn't."

More than a million refugees had entered the Federal Republic from East Germany in the last two years. Not all of them had been motivated by the desire for a better way of life; based on the number of clandestine radio stations known to be operating in West Germany, the Bonn Government had estimated there were some fifteen thousand Hostile Intelligence Agents among the refugees. They were Moscow's advance guard and took their instructions from the men in Dzerzhinksy Square and they wouldn't question it if ordered to fire-bomb the offices of the British Council in Cologne.

They were the professionals; there were also the reluctant amateurs who could be blackmailed into performing the same service for the NKVD because a mother, father, sister, brother, wife or girlfriend still resided in East Germany. The knowledge that if they failed to co-operate, someone very close would be charged, tried, convicted and sentenced to a long term of imprisonment on some trumped-up offence against the State was often enough to bring the most reluctant volunteer to heel.

"Are you saying your cover has been blown?" Matthews asked.

"I've always worked on that assumption. Why else would I carry a Colt .38?"

To infiltrate his organisation was not an impossible task for the NKVD. Group commanders like Gunther Altmüller recruited the cell leaders who, in turn, recruited their own individual cell members. If Joachim Hausser could pass the entry checks and join the highest echelon of the Gehlen Bureau, what chance did a cell leader have of discovering that the veteran of the Eastern Front he'd recruited had been turned while a prisoner-of-war in the Soviet Union? Once the NKVD agent had been accepted into the resistance network, it was only a question of time before he discovered who Freeland was, where he lived and worked.

"All right, for the sake of argument, let's say the NKVD were responsible. What exactly did they achieve?"

"A hell of a lot," said Freeland. "Amongst other things, they destroyed our card index."

The card index, which listed every member of the resistance network by individual codenames, had been kept in the combination safe in his office. After the fire, the safe had been found in the basement buried under a heap of rubble but seemingly unharmed. However, the Manufoil combination had been distorted and he'd had to call a locksmith to open it up, only to find that the intense heat generated by the fire had reduced the contents to ashes.

"There were other spin-offs," Freeland continued. "For instance, I'm left wondering just how many Fifth Columnists we've recruited."

But it was in attributing the arson to a group of neo-Nazis that the NKVD had shown a real stroke of genius. Anthony Eden was trying to use the treaty which had brought the European Defence Community into being on the thirtieth of May as a means of raising a West German Army, Navy and Air Force. German rearmament was, of course, a sensitive and emotive issue with the French; anything which suggested the National Socialist Party was still alive and kicking could lead them to reject the whole concept of a multi-national defence force.

"You must also be questioning your own future, Harry. I mean, if the Russians have got your number, they've only to follow you around and they'll know every cell leader in the Zone."

Freeland didn't care for the implication. "Is that what they're saying in London?" he asked coldly.

"I'm just a humble security officer," said Matthews. "How would I know what the high-priced help in Broadway are thinking?"

"I thought Acland might have told you."

"No, we only talked about this building."

"Well, make yourself at home, Frank, it's all yours." Freeland got up and moved towards the door. "I'm off to Münster," he said. "I think we may have a lead on one of those Nazis Acland would dearly like us to find."

*   *   *

Altmüller eased his way through the lunch-time crowd in the Gasthaus Leve and found himself a place at the bar. There were two entrances to the Gasthaus, one in Alter Steinweg, the other on Arztkarren Gasse; Altmüller wondered if this was the main reason why Herr Northover had chosen the restaurant for an RV. He could understand the change of venue because they never used the same one twice running, but of all the locations the Englishman could have selected in and around Münster, the Gasthaus Leve was the least convenient from his point of view. It was eleven kilometres from the timber yard in Hiltrup and unlike shop assistants and white-collar workers whose break was from one to three, he was only allowed an hour and a quarter for lunch. Subtract the time it took him to get to Münster and back on a bus and he was left with less than three-quarters of an hour. As a general rule though, you could set your watch by Herr Northover.

There would, in fact, be no need for this meet if it was possible to contact the Englishman direct instead of leaving a message for him on a wire recorder. You had to give him a phone number where he could reach you between specified hours; then, when he finally condescended to get in touch, he would give you an RV and a time to be there. The Englishman said it was simply basic security; it just happened to be a very one-sided arrangement.

Altmüller managed to catch the barman's eye at last and ordered a small beer. He had just begun to savour it when the Englishman tapped him on the shoulder as he moved on through the restaurant to leave by the exit into Arztkarren Gasse. He allowed almost half a minute to pass to check if anyone was tailing him, then followed on. Hurrying now to catch him up, Altmüller walked to the end of the alleyway, turned left on Winkelstrasse and got into the waiting Mercedes.

"So what have you got on the von Nebes, Gunther?"

Altmüller sighed. Herr Northover was a hustler, never even gave a man a chance to get himself settled before he was up and away, weaving in and out of the traffic as if the devil were on his heels.

"The father and mother were killed in an air raid on Osnabrück on the eleventh of October 1944. Their daughter, Elisabeth, was a Luftwaffe Auxiliary serving with the night fighter control station at Enschede in Holland at the time. She was given seventy-two hours compassionate leave formally to identify the remains and make any private arrangements she considered desirable for their burial. It couldn't have been a particularly heavy air raid, nor could there have been many victims, otherwise her parents would have been interred in a mass grave. That was the usual procedure . . ."

"You can skip the peripheral information," Freeland said, cutting him short. "What else have you got on Elisabeth Hausser?"

"Not a lot. Her unit was disbanded after it was withdrawn from Holland and the girls were sent home. They were, after all, completely superfluous; the Luftwaffe had virtually run out of trained night fighter pilots, there was a chronic shortage of aviation fuel and little means of distributing what stocks were in reserve."

No matter how many times he was told, Altmüller could never resist these little embellishments. Turning right into Hindenburg-platz, Freeland started to double-back on his tracks. From time to time, he glanced into the rear-view mirror to make sure he wasn't being tailed. Although he had always observed the basic rules of personal security, the destruction of the British Council offices had underlined the need for vigilance.

"No one knows where Elisabeth Hausser went; the family home

in Osnabrück had been reduced to a pile of rubble, there were no surviving relatives on her mother's side, and her father's younger brother had married a Jewess in 1935 and had then emigrated to America a year later. It's thought she may have gone to Nuremberg where Hausser was born. The one thing we can be sure of is that she didn't return to Osnabrück."

"And that's it."

"Not quite."

Freeland noted the suppressed elation in his voice and knew there was more to come. He also knew he would have to curb his impatience because the German wouldn't allow himself to be hurried by anyone. This was his success story and he would tell it his way and enjoy every moment of it.

"The girlfriend of one of our boys is a clerk in the Bürgermeister's office and we asked her to do a little snooping for us. Specifically, we wanted her to go through the Missing Persons Register." Altmüller lit a foul-smelling cigarette and drew the smoke down into his lungs; it didn't have the slightest effect on him. "Germany was in complete chaos when the war ended, Herr Northover. Unless you were there at the time, you can have no idea what it was like. Millions of homeless people, families broken up and scattered to the four winds, public records lost or destroyed. Every bomb site in every street in every town became a missing persons bureau. There were chalk messages on every wall left standing, like – 'Hans, in case you are looking for me, I am now living in Flat 4 Goethestrasse 78' and 'My wife, Erika Schroeder, used to live here. Anyone who knows where she is now, please contact Pauli Schroeder, Basement Dorfstrasse 119'. It wasn't until towards the end of 1945 that steps were taken to organise a proper Missing Persons Bureau."

Freeland smiled. The Germans were a very methodical people and loved things to be 'Alles in Ordnung'. The haphazard and entirely spontaneous method of tracing missing relatives would have seemed highly inefficient to the bureaucrats and something they would wish to rectify as soon as possible.

"In May 1949, the Bürgermeister's office received a letter from a Frau Elisabeth Dietz whose maiden name had been Elisabeth von Nebe. It was several pages long."

Freeland thought they were getting somewhere at last and didn't mind if Altmüller took all afternoon to tell him about it. "Take your time, Gunther, I'm in no hurry," he said, and for once he meant it.

"I'll just give you the salient facts," Altmüller told him as though determined to be contrary. "She said that her first husband,

171

Joachim Hausser, had been killed in action in April 1945 during the battle for Berlin. A year later, she had married an American serviceman called Dietz whom she had subsequently divorced in New Mexico. Having just returned to her native land, she was anxious to trace one of her oldest and dearest friends, a woman called Charlotte Koch. Apparently, this Dietz woman had terminal cancer and as she had no surviving relatives, she wished to leave all her money to Charlotte. I guess it must have gone to the State because her lifelong friend was killed by a hit-and-run driver in 1947."

"Did the Bürgermeister's office inform her of this?"

"Oh, yes." Altmüller stubbed out his cigarette in the ashtray and reached inside his jacket. "This is her original letter . . ."

Freeland took one hand off the wheel and opened it. The address was in the top right-hand corner of the page. In 1949, Elisabeth Dietz had been living at Wildenmayerstrasse 44 Munich.

"Do you think she's still alive?" Altmüller asked.

"I'm bloody sure she is," Freeland said.

*　　*　　*

Matthews found it hard to believe that in three weeks time, Anthea Clowes would be forty-two. Neville Acland, in his somewhat avuncular and old-fashioned manner, had likened her to a typical English rose, a description which though poetic was not inaccurate. A natural blonde, she was also blessed with the kind of complexion which needed the minimum of make-up. Her face was strikingly attractive and if her figure was a little fuller these days, she still drew admiring glances.

According to Acland, there had been three men in Anthea's life, all of whom had died violently. Her father, when Master of Foxhounds, had been thrown from his horse and killed at the Boxing Day meet of the Quorly Hunt in 1934. Barely a year later, her then fiancé had lost control of his Sunbeam Talbot on an icy stretch of road and had ploughed head-on into a double-decker bus. Anthea had walked away from the crash with nothing worse than a sprained wrist and a bruise on her forehead, while the man she was to have married in six months time had died on the way to hospital. At the behest of the Secret Intelligence Service, Anthea Clowes had spent the next three years in Germany where she had been employed as a secretary in one of I.G. Farben's subsidiaries. Returning to England in August 1939, she had spent the war years in London on loan to the German department of the BBC. In the spring of 1942 she had got engaged again, this time to a captain in the South Saskatchewan Regiment who had subsequently been killed in the Dieppe Raid.

Matthews did not find her an easy person to converse with, yet it was essential to strike up some kind of rapport if he was to do his job properly. Neville Acland hadn't sent him to Cologne to look at a building; the Head of Security wanted to know if Freeland or Anthea Clowes had been identified by the opposition. So far, all his questions had drawn a 'yes' or 'no' answer; unless she was more forthcoming, London would end up none the wiser.

"Mr Acland is concerned only for your safety," Matthews told her quietly.

"I'm flattered, but he shouldn't worry about me, I'm not in any danger."

"Would you know if you were being followed?"

"I like to think I'm pretty observant, Mr Matthews. And I do know what it's like to be under surveillance."

"You've had some previous experience?"

"Yes, with the Gestapo before the war."

Had she wished, Anthea Clowes could have made him feel small but clearly the idea had never entered her head. She had answered his question in the same matter-of-fact voice as she had with the others.

"I understand you collect the mail every morning from the British Consulate?"

"Yes, I have a flat in Leverkeusen which is on the way to Düsseldorf."

"Maybe so, but the round trip must be all of what? Fifty miles?"

"Less, and there's never much traffic about when I leave the flat."

"Do you always take the same route?"

"There isn't much scope for varying it, not that it would make any difference if there were." She smiled fleetingly. "The opposition could always latch on to me by keeping an eye on the Consulate. But even if they did follow me to the house on Magnus Strasse, they wouldn't know that we were using the British Council as a front unless someone told them."

"You mean an insider?"

"I suppose I do, Mr Matthews."

"Frank," he said, and was rewarded with an enigmatic smile.

"All the locally employed personnel have been with the British Council for years."

"Let's talk about Mr Freeland."

173

"No."

The vehemence of her reply startled him.

"Look," he said, "I realise you must find this distasteful . . ."

"You're so absolutely right, Mr Matthews."

In the circles Anthea Clowes moved in, you took people on trust. Loyalty to one's country did not mean you betrayed your friends and acquaintances to a common little snooper. Well, he had news for Anthea; they were now living in a different world to the one she had grown up in and there were British men and women who did not believe civilisation began and ended with the White Cliffs of Dover and whose loyalty lay elsewhere. As tactfully as he knew how, Matthews tried to open her eyes to the unpleasant facts of life. It took him some time to get his message across and even then she was not wholly convinced.

"Mr Freeland doesn't strike me as the sort of man who would put some abstract political theory above loyalty to his country."

"I agree with you," Matthews said, "but neither did Maclean. And yet, with hindsight, there were a number of pointers which should have warned us that he was a very disturbed man. I just wondered if you'd noticed anything strange about Mr Freeland's behaviour recently."

She had noticed something, he could tell it by the far-off look in her eyes and the way her brows met in a brief frown.

"Look," he said patiently, "if you know anything, it's your duty to tell me."

"I'm the Imprest holder for the Secret Account," she said hesitantly. "Does that mean anything to you?"

Matthews nodded. Every Station was allotted a slice of the SIS vote for the purpose of buying information. As the Imprest holder, Anthea Clowes merely kept the books; Freeland would give her a receipt for whatever money he needed, how he spent it was his concern, not hers. Once a year, the account would be audited by an inspector from 54 Broadway who would ask Freeland to explain any entry in excess of fifty pounds.

"Last Wednesday, Mr Freeland went to see his opposite number in Wiesbaden. I don't know what he wanted to discuss with Major Johansen but he drove straight back to the office and asked me for five hundred Deutschmarks before going on to Münster."

"This was from the Secret Fund?"

"Yes."

"Do you usually hold that amount in cash?"

"I'm authorised to keep a float not exceeding the equivalent of seventy-five pounds. Anyway, somewhat to my surprise, he stayed the night in Münster, and I didn't see or hear from him again until he telephoned on Thursday night to say the offices of the British Council were on fire. Mr Freeland implied the NKVD were responsible."

"Did he now?" Matthews said thoughtfully.

"The next day Mr Freeland paid back the five hundred Marks he'd borrowed out of his own pocket."

"How do you know it wasn't the original sum?"

"Because it included a hundred in denominations of twenty and I gave him fifties and hundreds."

"Did he ask you to return his receipt?" Matthews asked.

"It was in the safe with the cheque book, bank statements and accounts."

Not to mention the card index and a number of classified files. No wonder London was worried about Freeland.

"There is something else which perhaps I should mention. Contrary to his normal practice, Mr Freeland didn't claim a subsistence allowance for the night he stayed in Münster."

The way Matthews saw it, Freeland had disappeared for more than twenty-four hours without a word to Anthea Clowes who was supposed to know where he could be contacted in an emergency. Furthermore, he had borrowed public money for some private purpose and Acland wasn't going to like that at all.

"I think you may have to hold the fort, Miss Clowes."

"Oh? I think Mr Freeland will have something to say about that."

"No, he won't," said Matthews. "He'll be going to London first thing in the morning; you'd better get him a seat on the early BEA flight from Düsseldorf."

16

T he Dakota banked, affording Freeland a glimpse of Uxbridge as the pilot began the final approach into Northolt. A vista of lush green fields divided by neat hedgerows flashed past the window; along Western Avenue, a steady stream of traffic was moving towards London. Twelve years ago, Spitfires and Hurricanes of Fighter Command had operated out of the airfield, now it was a temporary satellite of the expanding international airport at Heathrow.

There was a slight jolt as the plane touched down on the runway, then their landing speed dropped swiftly and they taxied round to the prefabricated huts which served as the terminal building. Two men wheeled a flight of steps into position against the exit near the tailplane; then the 'No Smoking' and 'Fasten Seat Belt' signs went out and everyone started to reach for their hand luggage. Freeland moved out into the centre aisle and joined the crocodile of fellow passengers shuffling towards the exit. A pretty airhostess thanked him for travelling with BEA before he went on down the flight of steps and crossed the apron to go through Immigration.

Half an hour later, having cleared his suitcase with Customs, he walked into the Arrivals Hall where he was met by a slight, grey-haired man in his middle fifties.

"My name is Egan," the stranger said, introducing himself, "Tom Egan. I'm from head office."

"Do you have some means of identification?" Freeland asked him.

"Yes, of course, should have shown it to you right away." Egan produced a small brown card with a passport-size photograph on the right-hand side. His name, date of birth and occupation, which was loosely described as government official, appeared on the flyleaf. "My car's outside," he said, swiftly pocketing the ID.

The car was a Standard Vanguard, one of the first post-war models that looked as though its styling owed a lot to Detroit.

Unlike most government saloons, it was not chauffeur driven.

"I hope you're not a nervous passenger, Harry." Egan unlocked the door on his side and got in, then leaned across to release the catch so that Freeland could join him up front. "Not that the traffic is nose to tail at this time of day," he added.

Egan started up and drove through the RAF barracks that had been built in the early 1930s, turned right outside the main gates and headed towards Western Avenue.

"When are you going to tell me what's behind this witch hunt?" Freeland asked.

"It's not a witch hunt," Egan said sharply. "I thought Neville made that perfectly clear when he telephoned yesterday evening. We're simply anxious to hear your assessment of the situation because it seems to us that your operation may have been compromised."

"Oh, come on. Frank Matthews walks into my office unannounced and says he's been instructed to inspect the new premises with a view to improving security, then spends half his time interrogating Anthea Clowes while I'm out. When I return from Münster, I am calmly informed by my assistant that she has booked me on the first available flight from Düsseldorf and has been told to hold the fort in my absence. Now I'd like to know what the hell is going on."

"So would we, Harry. Among other things, we'd like to know why Münster has become such a big attraction. From what we hear, it's practically your second home these days."

"Thanks to Joachim Hausser."

"Who's he?"

"A former Sturmbannführer in the SS who Guy Salusbury and I, as well as a lot of men and women in the French Resistance, have good cause to remember with hatred. He was captured by the Russians and was held in one of their special POW camps in the Urals. Now he's back in the Federal Republic working for the Gehlen Bureau."

"What have the Yanks got to say?"

"They deny he's with their Intelligence organisation; they also say they don't know of anyone who even faintly resembles the description I gave Steve Johansen."

Egan drove on in silence through Greenford, Perivale, Hanger Lane and Park Royal apparently deep in thought. When he spoke again, he didn't exactly come up with pearls of wisdom.

"They could have their reasons for denying his existence, Harry."

"Yes, they could be using him as a double-agent. Alternatively, the information that Hausser takes his orders from Lavrenti Beria, the head of the NKVD, may have come as a nasty shock and they'd rather not be seen with egg on their faces."

"How strong is your information?"

"So-so." Freeland waggled his right hand in a fluttery up-and-down motion. "I've got an eye witness, an ex-Feldwebel in the Abwehr called Karl Heinz Grothmann who knew him in France and was in the same POW camp where he says Hausser was exceedingly well treated by the NKVD guards. Trouble is, Grothmann is far too keen to impress; he's down on his luck and would like to get back into the great game."

"I don't see how we can lean on the Yanks without any corroborating evidence." Egan smiled. "Of course, I'm just thinking out loud you understand."

"I gave Grothmann five hundred Deutschmarks out of my own pocket and sent him down to Munich to see if he could get a line on where Hausser is living. I told him not to spend more than a week looking for him."

"How much longer has he got?"

"Until tomorrow."

"It would seem Grothmann is not having much luck," Egan observed. "Unless of course he's simply a con man."

Freeland had to admit there was that possibility; after all, he only had Grothmann's word for it that the Sturmbannführer was still alive. On the other hand, five hundred Deutschmarks was less than fifty pounds at the fixed rate of exchange, which was a pretty poor return on a confidence trick that could only be used once. There was also the former Elisabeth von Nebe who had taken to calling herself Frau Dietz. After spending three years in America, she had returned to her homeland, the lonely divorcée who wanted to trace her life-long friend, Charlotte Koch. He wondered if Egan would attach the same importance to her as he did, and spent the next fifteen minutes telling him about the woman who had married Joachim Hausser.

"Why is she so important?" Egan asked, after mulling over what he had been told.

"Because if Elisabeth Dietz is still alive, so is Hausser. Don't you see, all that rubbish she put in her letter to the Bürgermeister about wanting to leave her money to her bosom friend, Charlotte Koch, had an ulterior purpose? I've a hunch that this Koch woman was one of the very few people outside the family who'd met her husband, Joachim Hausser."

"And when she learned her friend had been killed in 1947 by a

178

hit-and-run driver, she knew it was safe for the Sturmbannführer to join her?"

"That's the way I see it," said Freeland.

"It's certainly an interesting theory."

Egan continued along Western Avenue through White City to Shepherd's Bush, then turned left into Holland Park Avenue. At Marble Arch, he turned into Park Lane, went on down to Hyde Park Corner and filtered into Constitution Hill.

"Not much farther now," he said, breaking a lengthy silence.

Freeland smiled. Anyone would think he'd never been near 'the firm' before instead of being able to find his way there blindfold. Around Queen Victoria's monument into Buckingham Gate, then along Petty France behind Wellington Barracks and there was the modern-looking office block at 54 Broadway which was connected to the elegant Georgian town house directly in rear.

Egan pulled up outside the entrance and handed the Standard Vanguard over to a Ministry of Defence police constable who parked the car in the underground garage. Entering the building, Egan showed his identity card to the officer on duty in the hallway, then steered Freeland to the reception desk where a middle-aged woman issued him with a Visitor's Pass. The lifts in Queen Anne's Gate were almost as old as the house itself; the one that whisked them up to the sixth floor of the sister building was as new as the office block.

"Do you mind waiting in my office while I have a quick word with Neville?" Egan asked him with an apologetic smile.

"Not a bit."

"Good. I'll only be a few minutes."

Freeland doubted it. Two days ago, he had received a letter from Cyril Upham to say that he'd had a surprise visit from a Mr Thomas Egan. The wartime Principal Administrative Officer of SOE's French Section had also asked him jocularly what he'd been up to. It was a broad hint that he was the subject of a high-level inquiry and the preliminary interrogation had been conducted on the way in from Northolt. Egan would need to brief the Department Head before moving on to the next stage, and that wasn't something that could be done in a few minutes.

*   *   *

The woman who got off the noonday bus from Münster was tall, thin, poorly dressed and careworn. Altmüller didn't see her cross the road and enter the timber yard, nor was he immediately aware of her presence when she walked into his office. It was only when

179

he put the phone down after talking to a potential customer that he really noticed her.

"Herr Altmüller?" she asked timidly.

"Yes. How can I help you?"

"I'm Anna Grothmann. I believe you know my husband, Karl Heinz?"

Altmüller feared the worst and thought it was fortunate that his secretary, Gertrud, had gone down with 'flu and was safely home in bed.

"We've run into one another a couple of times," he admitted cautiously. "Usually at the Bierkeller in Prinzipalmarkt."

"You have heard perhaps of an Englishman called Herr Northover?"

Altmüller frowned. Was there no limit to Grothmann's stupidity? You couldn't tell him anything but it was all over town the next day. One of life's big mysteries was how the Feldwebel had lasted so long in the Abwehr. Of one thing he was sure: the Loiret Bleu circuit must have been the most incompetent Resistance network in Europe for that blabbermouth to have caught them.

"You know I have," he said coolly. "Herr Northover is rather secretive, but I believe he is connected with the British Garrison in Münster."

"Not according to Herr Hauptmann and Frau King."

"Who are they?"

"The Englanders I work for. They live in Gremmendorf." For a brief moment her eyes lit up with something akin to pride. "The Herr Hauptmann is on the staff of the Kommandantur," she added.

To clean the house for someone who was part of the Garrison Headquarters clearly gave her a status she would not otherwise have enjoyed. The observation, however, didn't get him anywhere and was irrelevant.

"Why do you want to find this mysterious Englishman?" Altmüller smiled. "I assume it must be important for you to come all the way out here."

"Herr Northover gave my husband some money and sent him down to Munich. Karl Heinz said that if he was successful, the British would find a job for him with their Field Security."

"When was this?"

"Last Thursday." Anna Grothmann looked even more anxious. "He said he wouldn't be gone more than a week."

"So he should be home tomorrow?"

"Yes. But I haven't heard a word from Karl Heinz since he left and that's not like him, especially as he promised to ring Frau Juttner."

Altmüller didn't have to ask who Frau Juttner was. In the next breath, Anna told him that she was their neighbour across the hall who was fortunate enough to have a telephone.

"I'm sure there's nothing to worry about," he said.

"He's not in any danger, is he, Herr Altmüller? It's just that I can't think why the British would give Karl Heinz a job with their security police unless he was doing something risky for them."

The Englishman who called himself Northover had sent Grothmann down to Munich to look for Joachim Hausser. It was pure guesswork of course but it was the only explanation Altmüller could think of which fitted the known facts. And if he was right, Grothmann could well find himself in all kinds of trouble.

"My dear lady, you're worrying yourself unnecessarily." Altmüller got up and walked round the table to steer her gently but firmly towards the door. "However, to set your mind at rest, I'll get in touch with Herr Northover this evening and ask him if he has any news. How's that?"

"You're very kind, Herr Altmüller." She hesitated, reluctant to impose upon his goodwill. "When do you think you will hear from the Englishman?"

"Tomorrow or the next day; it depends on when I can reach him. He does a lot of travelling and doesn't always go back to his office at the end of the day." Altmüller shook hands with her. "Rest assured, I'll let you know the minute I have news of Karl Heinz."

"I'd better give you our address."

"There's no need, I already know where you live, Gnädige Frau."

A little flattery never did any harm, especially when you wanted to ease a tiresome visitor on their way. He gave her a cheerful smile to speed the parting and waved as she went past the gate on to the road, then he closed the door, returned to his makeshift desk and lit a cigarette.

Grothmann was a dunderhead; four years in a Russian POW camp had addled what few brains God had given him, and the Englishman was no better. The SS hadn't died with the Führer in his bunker; many of them were alive and well with friends in high places. No one in his right mind tangled with those bastards.

*   *   *

The interrogation had begun in a leisurely, very friendly manner with Acland wanting to know how long it would take him to

181

reconstruct the card index which had been lost in the fire; then they had adjourned to the staff canteen in the basement. It became hostile the moment they returned from lunch. At first, there were grounds for thinking that Acland was simply suffering from a bad case of indigestion brought on either by the sausage and mash or the suet pudding he'd chosen from the limited menu. However, once he and Egan began to question him about Nina Burzova, Freeland realised that the friendly reception had been the velvet glove covering the mailed fist.

"What have you got to say about this?" Acland suddenly demanded, handing him a clipping from a magazine. "It appeared in *Esquire*."

"So I noticed." Freeland read the offending paragraphs side-lined in red ink, then returned the clipping to Acland. "Phil Ryan is a good agency man, he's shrewd and has a nose for a story. He can also add up."

"I don't follow you."

"Two and two usually make four. Ryan knew I'd gone across the river into Pootung to collect Howard Teale and he could guess why I had to leave Shanghai in a hurry."

"Evidently you don't feel you committed a serious breach of security?" Egan said.

"When I was ready to go, the only way out of Shanghai was down river. Rightly or wrongly, I thought two men in a kayak looked more innocent than one. Why don't you read the HARVESTER file, it's all there in the Post-Action Report?"

Neither man seemed inclined to take him up on the suggestion. Instead, Acland wanted to know who he thought had sent them the cutting.

"Someone in the US of A," said Freeland. "I wouldn't know his name, I never see a Staff List, assuming such a thing exists."

"Is Guy Salusbury a friend of yours?"

"I like to think so."

"We received the cutting from him. What do you think about that?"

"Guy was only doing his job," Freeland said in a level voice. "The story appeared to indicate that I had been talking out of turn. He had to report it."

"I'm sure I wouldn't be quite so understanding," said Egan.

"Well, you're not me."

"The relationship between you and Guy Salusbury is a bit like David and Jonathan, isn't it?"

"You're making the comparison, Neville," said Freeland.

182

But Acland was right; there was a time when they had been very good friends, more so immediately after the war rather than during it. He wouldn't have been accepted by MI6 if Guy hadn't given him such a glowing write-up. In fact, it was Salusbury who had steered him towards the SIS in the first place and he was duly grateful for that. There hadn't been too many openings in 1946 for a twenty-seven-year-old temporary major with an ear for foreign languages, and he hadn't fancied being a schoolmaster. But above all else, he owed his life to Guy and that was something he wouldn't forget in a hurry.

"You haven't heard from Guy since he was posted to America?"

"Neither of us are what you would call good correspondents."

There was, however, more to it than that. Jenny had taken an instant dislike to Guy Salusbury and he had made it pretty clear that he didn't think much of her either. 'A very attractive young woman, but not our sort,' he'd once observed, though this was before Freeland had asked her to marry him. Guy had also done the Para course at Ringway and Freeland had sometimes wondered if he had made a pass at Jenny and been rebuffed. If so, it would account for their mutual antagonism.

"I understand that Guy was best man at your wedding?" Acland said.

"You understand correctly," Freeland told him.

Jenny hadn't been overjoyed at the idea but in the end she had given way gracefully enough and there hadn't been a noticeably strained atmosphere on the day.

"How did you and Guy become friends?" Egan asked.

It wasn't an easy question to answer. There was an age gap of fourteen years between them and they came from very different social backgrounds. Guy was an Old Etonian and had married money. When it came down to it, they really had few interests in common.

"SOE threw us together," said Freeland, "and there was the shared experience at the hands of the SS. I thought Guy was a very brave man. He was thirty-eight when I met him in November '43 and he could have had a nice, safe war driving a pen, like most of his contemporaries. Instead, he chose to go in harm's way. But Guy wasn't a fool; he had a healthy regard for the enemy and didn't take unnecessary risks. We were talking about courage one day and he said it was like a bank account; you could draw on it once too often and then, before you knew it, you were in the red."

"Did he have anyone in mind?"

"We were comparing notes about Chantal Kiffer at the time.

This would be a few weeks after the war had ended in Europe and I had just learned that she had been executed by the French Forces of the Interior."

"Let's talk about your fixation with Joachim Hausser," Acland growled.

"Fixation? Well, obviously, I don't have your emotional detachment but I like to think I'm not consumed with hatred. I believe Hausser is alive and well and working for the Gehlen Bureau under an assumed name."

"Some people might think the whole thing is simply a smoke-screen."

"What exactly are you implying?"

"You break all the rules," Acland said coldly. "Before you set foot in Shanghai you were told not to contact the British Consulate except in an emergency . . ."

"Teale was missing and his Chinese secretary had been murdered. If that doesn't constitute an emergency, I don't know what does."

"You didn't know where to look for Teale so you asked all and sundry where you might find him . . ."

"I talked to Phil Ryan because no one at the British Consulate seemed to know a damned thing about Howard, which you have to admit was pretty odd considering our SIS representative in Shanghai wanted him removed because he was such a menace . . ."

"You allowed yourself to fall into the hands of the PLA, then killed one of their soldiers in order to escape from the house where you were confined."

Apparently he was responsible for a whole catalogue of disasters. In his determination to prove culpable negligence, Acland had exhumed all the old SOE files relating to the activities of the French Section. Without disclosing the source of his information, he was satisfied that the destruction of the Loiret Bleu network had been due, in part, to Freeland's affair with Chantal Kiffer. There was a lot more nonsense in the same vein, culminating with the fire in Magnus Strasse.

"It is very obvious to us that the NKVD managed to infiltrate your organisation," Acland said in conclusion.

"I have to agree with you there," Freeland told him.

"And the Americans will say that your allegations concerning Joachim Hausser are simply a face-saving exercise."

"Is that also your opinion?"

"I'm not interested in Hausser; I'm more concerned to know what we should do with you. I suppose you'd make a useful decoy if we sent you back to Cologne, but I wonder if it's worth all the expense?"

If they did replace him, they would have to replace Anthea Clowes as well. The NKVD would expect them to do that and would go flat out to identify their successors. But if they remained in place, the new team could set up shop in a different location and might even be able to run down the Soviet agent who'd infiltrated the network. Unfortunately, it would mean paying four people to do the work of two, and money was tight.

"Happily, it's not my decision."

"So what are you going to recommend?" Freeland asked. "Or am I not entitled to know?"

"I think we should send in a new face but that's up to the D-G. You'll just have to cool your heels in England until he makes up his mind. If you've nowhere to stay, Tom can always get you into Dolphin House."

"That won't be necessary, I'm going home to Lichfield."

"Do we have your address?"

"I'll be staying with my father-in-law, Sidney Vail, at 32 Chestnut Close. Failing that, you could try Warley Farm Prep School."

"Good."

"Can I go now?" Freeland asked.

"There is one other thing . . ." Acland avoided his eyes. "I'm afraid I must ask you to surrender your passport." He smiled apologetically. "You know how it is."

"I'm beginning to," Freeland said.

*   *   *

The house was across the Isar River from the Englischer Garten and was situated in the fashionable Munich district of Bogenhausen. Number 8 Schiller Platz where Joachim Hausser resided under the name of Doktor Ernst Winkler, was at the top end of the green, facing the narrow approach road to the exclusive cul-de-sac. For added privacy, the house was tucked away behind a high, pebble-dashed wall.

It had taken Grothmann six days to track down Hausser and discover his new identity. If he now gave the address to Herr Northover, the Englishman might give him a job with the British Field Security Section in Münster, but nothing was certain. No promises had been made and when he'd hinted about a reward, the Englishman had laughed and told him not to worry because he would get it, but in a way that implied it was unlikely to happen in this world. Well, that was not good enough for Karl

185

Heinz Grothmann; he wanted some of the good things in life while he was still here on earth, and Sturmbannführer Joachim Hausser was going to provide them. The bastard could afford it for he had seen the woman of the house prancing around in her finery.

Frau Winkler, or whatever she called herself, was a tall, arrogant-looking, dark-haired bitch. With her slender figure, she was the perfect clothes-horse for the expensive haute-couture models which were beginning to appear in Munich's fashionable salons and were part of that German economic miracle which Grothmann knew would pass him and Anna by in the normal run of things. Well, he had news for the Gnädige Frau; from now on she wouldn't be able to have a new dress whenever the fancy took her.

Grothmann heard a car approaching and moved back into the shadows. An Opel Kapitan entered the cul-de-sac, went round the one-way circuit to number 8 Schiller Platz and disappeared into the drive. A few moments later, the driver returned to close the wrought-iron gates before entering the house. Grothmann allowed five minutes to elapse, then crossed the central green, his coat collar up, his breath vaporising in the cold night air. He let himself into the grounds by the small side gate and walked boldly up the front path to ring the bell. The woman who eventually answered the door was in her mid forties and was obviously the live-in maid.

"Good evening," Grothmann said briskly. "Please tell Herr Doktor Winkler that Joachim Hausser wishes to see him."

The woman looked him over from head to toe, her eyes taking in his shabby appearance. The way her lips pursed told him that she was not favourably impressed.

"We have known each other since 1944," Grothmann added, "and I assure you that the Herr Doktor will want to see me."

The door still closed in his face but it did not remain so for long. When the maid returned, she removed his coat, hung it up in the cloakroom, then showed him into the study directly opposite where Hausser was already waiting. The Sturmbannführer was a lot fuller in the face and he'd had a nose job but no amount of cosmetic surgery could disguise the sloping forehead and steely eyes.

"Thank you, Erika," Hausser said. "That will be all for the time being."

Grothmann waited until they were alone before he pretended to admire the heavy, mahogany writing desk.

"I presume you didn't come here merely to talk about the furniture," Hausser growled.

"Quite so." Grothmann sat down uninvited. "The last time we came within hailing distance was in Special Punishment Camp

129 where you were being treated like an honoured guest by the NKVD. Now, three years later, you have a different name and you are working for the Gehlen Bureau. Need I say more?"

"Yes."

Grothmann shook his head. "I'm very disappointed in you, Herr Sturmbannführer. I credited you with some intelligence. However, it's simple enough; you are a Russian spy and please don't give me any nonsense that the Americans are using you as a double-agent."

"Well, clearly you don't propose to turn me in, otherwise you would not have come here tonight. Perhaps you have some business proposition you would like to put to me?"

"I knew you wouldn't disappoint me," Grothmann said happily. "I'm not a greedy man, Joachim, but I do want to enjoy a few luxuries in my old age. So I'd like ten thousand Deutschmarks in cash and five hundred a month for life, commencing first of January 1953."

"And what do I get in return?" Hausser asked quietly.

"My continued silence."

"I could break your neck; that would be a cheaper way of doing it."

"You might know that I would have foreseen that possibility and taken steps to protect myself."

"But of course." Hausser smiled. "And you might know that I don't keep ten thousand Deutschmarks in the house."

"But you can get it from your bank tomorrow?"

"You have my word on it."

"Good." Grothmann almost sighed aloud; it had been easier than he'd dared to hope in his wildest dreams. But he would still need to keep his wits about him just to stay alive. "I'll phone you tomorrow evening and let you know where and when the initial payment is to be made."

"It's going to seem a long twenty-four hours," Hausser said and touched the electric bell on his desk to summon the maid. "This gentleman is leaving," he told Erika when she entered the study. "Please fetch his coat."

Grothmann was on his feet when he heard the hollow cough of an air pistol behind him. Simultaneously, he experienced a sharp pain below his right ear as the dart buried itself in his neck. Roaring like a wounded animal, he staggered round the study, cannoning into the furniture; then the drug took effect and he sank down on to his knees and rolled over.

187

17

The cold finally got to Freeland, chilling his exposed shoulder to the bone. Jenny had ended up with most of the bedclothes, which happened roughly fifty per cent of the time. Sidney Vail, his father-in-law, didn't believe central heating was healthy and 32 Chestnut Close was like an ice box in winter. Sidney Vail did, however, believe in fresh air and proper ventilation which was why he opened all the top windows at night and enjoyed a perpetual cold from late October to early May. Slowly and very carefully so as not to disturb Jenny, Freeland slid down the bed and pulled the eiderdown up to cover his bare shoulder.

Jenny Vail, ex-Sergeant Jenny Vail; it was funny how they had got together. They'd grown up in the same town and yet the first time they met was up at Ringway when he'd drawn his parachute for the initial jump from a captive balloon. He had noticed that the sergeant behind the counter had a faint Staffordshire accent and he'd asked her where she came from.

For security reasons, SOE agents under training were required to keep pretty much to themselves but some rules were unenforceable, especially when an attractive young woman was involved. They had had a quiet drink in one of the local pubs a couple of times and once he'd taken her to the cinema to see Lloyd Nolan in *Dressed to Kill* as he recalled. Jenny had allowed him a chaste kiss on their second date but she had drawn the line at heavy petting when the house lights were down. French kissing was okay but no man was going to put a hand inside her blouse or up her skirt unless they were very serious about each other, and he'd left Ringway thinking Jenny was just a prick tease.

He had bumped into her again in Lichfield in June 1943, a few weeks after he had returned from his first mission in the south of France. Jenny had also been on leave and had gone to the mid-week hop in the town hall and he'd grabbed her as soon as the MC announced that the next dance would be a gentleman's excuse me. It hadn't mattered what his previous opinion of Jenny had been; from thereon he had monopolised the last five days of her leave, taking her out to dinner at The George, to both cinemas in town, the Repertory Theatre and on more long walks in the countryside than he'd done in years. By the time he saw her off from Lichfield Trent Valley station on the Sunday evening, they had reached the heavy petting stage.

In the November of that year, he had wangled a thirty-six hour pass to Manchester and they had spent the night in a crummy hotel near the station. She had not been the sexually inexperienced young woman he'd imagined and her amorous response in bed had both surprised and perversely disillusioned him. It had come as something of a shock to discover that he was not her first lover and his youthful ego had still been bruised when SOE had sent him in to Chartres.

Chantal Kiffer had reflated his ego, and it had been what he thought was their love for each other that had kept him alive when he was in Flossenburg concentration camp. He had refused to accept the possibility that she might not survive the war, and the news that Chantal had been executed by her own countrymen had left him totally devastated.

It had been Jenny who had picked him up off the floor, starting on VJ Day when they had come face-to-face in a crowd celebrating the end of the war with a large bonfire in the field surrounding Stowe Pool behind the cathedral. Sympathy, love and understanding; she had given him all of those while he tried to explain why he would always feel guilty about Chantal. And what had he given her in return? Precious little when you came right down to it, but Jenny had always been there whenever he had needed her. No one else had been allowed to take her for granted, especially her father for whom she had now become the son he'd lost when his plane had crashed into the Brecon Beacons. 'Come and fetch me when you've finally got Chantal Kiffer out of your system.' That is what Jenny had said to him the night before she had left Cologne. Yesterday, he had telephoned her from Euston and she had been there to meet him when he'd stepped off the train at Lichfield. No questions, no recriminations; she had simply been glad to see him.

"Are you awake, Harry?"

Jenny did not wait for him to answer but turned over on to her right hip and snuggling close, drew the bedclothes over his head, cocooning them both. She kissed him on the mouth, wiggled even closer, then lay perfectly still waiting for him to make the next move.

"So when are you going to tell me what those people in head office have against you?" she murmured presently.

"It's nothing."

"What do you mean, nothing?"

"Exactly that."

"Rubbish. I can read you like a book, Harry, and I know when you've got something on your mind."

Freeland sighed; he had never been able to hide anything from Jenny and there was little point in trying to do so on this occasion. If things went badly for him, the story was likely to appear on the front page of every national newspaper.

"I'm supposed to have committed a major breach of security," he said in a low voice. "That's their diplomatic way of putting it; in plain English, everyone from the D-G downwards suspects I'm a Communist agent."

"They've got to be crazy," Jenny whispered fiercely.

"There are certain grey areas in my background they don't like."

He told her why the SIS were uneasy about the time in Shanghai when he had been detained by a guerilla unit of the People's Liberation Army and the inference they were drawing from the fire-bombing of the British Council offices. He told her about Hausser and the deadpan reaction he'd had from Steve Johansen and how Acland had openly said that the Americans would regard his allegations as a face-saving exercise.

"You want my advice, Harry? Tell them what they can do with their lousy job."

"What do you suggest we do for money?" he asked her softly.

"We'll manage."

"Yes, I could become a schoolmaster; the old man would give me a job teaching French and German."

"No, that wouldn't be right for you." She placed a finger against his lips to persuade him to hear her out. "Pa will give you a partnership. I know business is slack at the moment but it will pick up. Harold Macmillan is going to build the 300,000 houses in a year he promised the Conservative Party, and the private sector will begin to move now that the building controls are being scrapped."

"I don't know the first thing about selling a house."

"I can teach you."

Jenny could too. Sidney Vail hadn't seen any sense in spending good money on a girl's education. It had been all right for her brother to go to Denstone College but she had had to leave the

Grammar School, to which she had won a scholarship, immediately after matriculating at sixteen and had been sent to a secretarial college to learn shorthand and typing. She had then worked for her father at less than the going rate until she had learned everything there was to know about the real estate business.

"If that doesn't appeal, you can always sound out Joe Lander; he's always telling you that America is the land of opportunities."

Always was putting it a bit strong. Lander had sent him a Christmas card in 1949 care of the Foreign Office and they had worked up to a letter a year since then. In any event, Jenny wasn't serious about going to America; that was just so much pillow talk.

Pillow talk: Acland had implied that much of the damage sustained by the Loiret Bleu network stemmed from what he had told Chantal Kiffer in bed. But how would he know? And who had made the allegation in the first place? – Cyril Upham, the French Section's Chief of Staff?

"Are you listening to me, Harry?"

"Of course I am," he whispered hastily.

"So what do you think of my suggestions?"

"I'm going after Hausser first. If things don't work out the way I hope they will, you'll have to teach me how to sell a property that's urgently in need of renovation."

"Haven't you forgotten something? They confiscated your passport."

"Only the one issued to Harry Northover; the other is in a deed box at Lloyd's Bank. Of course, there is one small problem; I'm not exactly flush with cash at the moment." He smiled in the darkness, then whispered, "Do you suppose the manager will give me an overdraft?"

"I've got two hundred on deposit, we can borrow against that."

"I don't know what to say . . ."

"Then don't; just be sure you come back to me in one piece."

"Don't you worry, I'll be very, very careful."

"Then mind you are because I think I'm pregnant again."

"Are you sure?" he whispered.

"We can always make certain," she murmured and started to move against him.

*   *   *

Matthews wasn't sure whether it was Anthea Clowes or himself who felt the more awkward in each other's company. Their mutual embarrassment stemmed from the fact that, having led her to

191

believe that she would have to hold the fort in Freeland's absence, Neville Acland had decided otherwise and had placed him in charge of the office instead.

The tape simply made an already difficult situation worse. Anthea had collected it when she had gone to Düsseldorf to pick up the mail from the British Consulate on her way to work. Both of them knew he had been cleared to see all Foreign Office cables up to and including 'Secret'; neither of them was too sure whether this meant he could hear the messages on the answering machine.

"We could check with London if you like?" Matthews suggested.

"I don't think that's really necessary; most of the messages would seem very innocuous to an outsider." Her face turned a delicate shade of pink as she realised how the observation must have sounded to him. "I'm sorry," she said hastily, "I didn't mean to be rude."

"You weren't," Matthews assured her. "And you're right, I am an outsider." He smiled. "My German also leaves a lot to be desired, which should put your mind at rest."

"I rather think it does."

Anthea Clowes placed the wire recorder on the machine and wound the tape on, then depressed the play button. Speaking slowly and clearly, Freeland gave his phone number, invited the caller to leave a message after hearing the tone signal and promised to get back as soon as he could. Matthews had no difficulty in understanding him; the next two callers, however, spoke at machine-gun speed and he only caught the odd word here and there. Then a voice in halting English said, "Here is Gunther. Today Frau Grothmann came to see me at the timber yard. She say you gave her husband money and sent him to Munich. Grothmann told her you would give him work if he had success. Now she is worried because he has been gone almost one week and she has heard nothing. I ask you to do something because this woman can make big trouble for me and for you also."

The caller broke off and the tape ran silent for almost a minute. Then just as Matthews was beginning to think the German had run out of things to say and was about to hang up, he came alive again.

"She did not say why her husband went to Munich but it is not difficult to guess he is looking for Joachim Hausser and if the Sturmbannführer is still alive, I think things will go badly for our friend . . ."

Another pause followed, then Gunther put the phone down with a loud clunk. There were no other messages on the tape.

"Any idea who Gunther is?" Matthews asked.

"I'm afraid not."

"Did Harry ever mention this Joachim Hausser to you?"

"No, this is the first time I've ever heard of him."

"Well, at least we know where the five hundred Deutschmarks went." Matthews eyed the Grundig tape recorder. Munich was in the American Zone and he sensed a diplomatic incident in the offing. "Does the Consulate have a secure telephone?" he asked.

"Yes."

"Then I'd better get over there."

If he was right and Joachim Hausser was the flashpoint for a political storm, the sooner London heard about him the better.

*　　*　　*

Grothmann surfaced again and slowly opened his eyes. His headache hadn't got any better since the last time he'd woken up, and the curtain of mist was still there obscuring his vision, though it wasn't as dense as it had been. His lips were dry and he wanted to lick them but for some reason this was impossible. Gradually it dawned on him that someone had forced a wad of cloth between his jaws and taped it in place, effectively gagging him.

Someone had also stripped him to the waist and removed his shoes, socks and trousers, leaving him in just a pair of woollen long johns. With growing awareness came the discovery that he was tied to a chair by his wrists, arms and ankles. The room was lit by a single naked bulb dangling from a long flex and there was a huge bank of coke stacked against the wall on his right. The large boiler which provided the central heating as well as the hot water was directly to his front.

Suddenly, everything began to fall into place. The woman called Erika had put him to sleep with a tranquillising dart fired from an air pistol, from which simple fact it was possible to make two positive deductions. Long before he had called at 8 Schiller Platz, Hausser had known that someone was looking for him and had taken steps to deal with any visitor who proved unwelcome. And Erika hadn't attacked him out of loyalty to her employer; she had to be an NKVD watchdog.

Munich was close enough to the Czech border for Hausser to cut and run at the first whiff of danger. Grothmann thought the fact that he had decided to stay put made his own position exceptionally hazardous. Knowing what he did, they couldn't afford to let him go. What was it Hausser had said when they were discussing the price of his continued silence? It would be cheaper to break your neck? Next time he wouldn't be joking, but Hausser would hold off until he discovered what measures Grothmann had taken to protect himself.

He had written to Anna hinting that their financial problems would soon be over and informing her he would be coming home a day or so later than expected. Saturday was therefore the earliest his wife would start to worry about him, and he wondered how long Anna would wait before she opened the envelope he'd enclosed with his letter. That envelope was his life insurance policy; unfortunately, he had neglected to tell her how or when it would be necessary to cash it in. The omission nagged at him until Erika walked into the cellar when he then had a much bigger problem to worry about.

The bigger problem was a hypodermic syringe which she produced from the pocket of her smock along with a small bottle containing an amber-coloured fluid.

"Scapolamine, Herr Grothmann," she said, answering his unspoken question.

Grothmann watched her push the needle through the porous cap on the bottle and draw the plunger to fill the syringe. She expelled a tiny jet of the fluid to make sure the hypodermic was working properly, then pinched a vein in his right arm and injected him.

Scapolamine, the so-called truth drug. Grothmann remembered hearing that the Gestapo had used it experimentally during the final months of the war. It was said to be slow-acting and the interrogator had to be careful not to put words into the suspect's mouth because the drug made the subject responsive to auto-suggestion. He had also been given to understand that the drug tended to make some victims almost incoherent. He hoped it would do the same for him.

"Not much longer now, Herr Grothmann, then we can begin."

He had wondered why she kept looking at her wristwatch like some staff nurse in a hospital, now he knew the reason. The bitch had been waiting for the drug to take effect before she removed the gag. She wanted to be sure he couldn't shout the place down in case the neighbours heard him. Well, at least that proved they hadn't moved him from 8 Schiller Platz and since Hausser wasn't present, he must have already gone to work.

Erika reached out, ripped the sticking plaster from his face and pulled the wad out of his mouth.

"I will tell you how you found Joachim, you will tell me what you did with the information. That's fair, isn't it?"

194

Grothmann nodded instinctively, realised he was already beginning to respond to auto-suggestion and sought to correct it.

"No," he said in a thick, strange-sounding voice he didn't recognise as his own.

"Yes? No? Unable to make up our mind, are we?" Erika laughed. "No matter, I will help you."

"Go to hell."

"You are so very obvious in everything you say and do. You hang around the Special Camp at Pullach and take down the number of the car Joachim is driving. Then you go to the licensing bureau in Munich and tell the clerk you want to trace the owner of Opel Kapitan 21774 MU because he forced you off the road into a ditch and you wish to claim damages in respect of the front wheel of your bicycle which is buckled. Didn't you realise the police would inform the Gehlen Bureau that someone was making enquiries about a highly-placed member of their staff?"

"It was a risk I had to take."

His chest felt as though it was being compressed in a vice and he found it difficult to breathe. He was also sweating profusely which was another sign that the drug was really beginning to take effect.

"And in order to protect yourself," Erika continued remorselessly, "you sent the information to someone for safe-keeping. Am I not right?"

Silence was the only way to combat the drug but he found himself nodding in agreement.

"So who did you send it to?"

"I'm not going to tell you." There was a definite lisp now and he sounded like a fractious child.

*   *   *

Cyril Upham was still the same pugnacious-looking man with jet black hair and dark eyes whom Freeland remembered. There were no streaks of grey, no lines, no wrinkles, nor any sign of flabbiness around the waist since their last meeting six years ago, even though, as the sales director of Bond and Hales, he was now following a much more sedentary occupation.

"This is the first time you've been here, isn't it?" Upham said as they shook hands.

"Yes, you were still ensconced in St Michael's House when I last saw you. You haven't changed a bit."

"Neither have you, Harry," Upham said, waving him to a chair. "Now tell me how I can help you."

"I received your letter the other day . . ." Freeland said, feeling his way.

"Yes. I got the impression from your Mr Egan that several question marks had appeared in your file."

"They've multiplied since you wrote to me. They're now blaming me for the fire."

"What fire?"

"The offices of the British Council in Cologne were burned down a week ago yesterday."

Upham snapped his fingers. "Of course, I remember seeing a paragraph in the *Guardian*; some neo-Nazi group was responsible."

"That's what the NKVD would have you believe."

"Well, they didn't get a lot of publicity this side of the Channel. Why are you to blame?"

"Egan and his superiors reckon I led the opposition to the Council offices."

"And did you?"

Freeland shrugged. "I've been doing the same job for over two years and my face could have become known. However, they maintain this wasn't the first time I'd committed a major breach of security. It was my pillow talk with Chantal Kiffer which enabled the SS to inflict so much damage on the Loiret Bleu network."

"Pillow talk?"

"That's the expression they used. I'm curious to know where they got it from."

"Why ask me?"

"You headed the Court of Inquiry on the network, Cyril."

The Court had been convened by the Ministry of Defence to investigate the circumstances which had led to the destruction of the Loiret Bleu network and to apportion responsibility for the disaster where appropriate. It had met *in camera* on the fifteenth of January 1946 and had taken evidence over the next two days from the Director of Operations, Guy Salusbury and Freeland. Before reaching their conclusions, the Court had also read the proceedings of the Military Tribunal which had tried and convicted Chantal Kiffer. No one had ever told Freeland what the Court of Inquiry had decided.

"There was no mention of pillow talk and no one blamed you for what happened," Upham said. "You held out for three days, Harry, and none of us could ask for more than that."

"Chantal and I were lovers."

"The Court of Inquiry took that into account. We also noted

196

the date you arrived in Chartres and how long you were operational."

The RAF had flown him into the Chartres area in one of their Lysanders on Thursday the sixth of January 1944, a month after Guy Salusbury had gone in. Chantal Kiffer had been a member of the reception committee waiting for him at the improvised landing strip that night, and he had gone to bed with her a fortnight later. On the twenty-second of February, he had been picked up by the Abwehr at a road block outside Chartres.

"You lasted six weeks and five days, Harry; you barely had time to meet all the cell leaders in your area of responsibility, let alone anyone outside it. Chantal Kiffer was the weak link, she was the network's hub, the post office for all the other groups in the Loiret Bleu organisation. She knew all the bloody couriers."

Freeland nodded, vaguely aware of what Upham had said to him. His papers had been scrutinised by other soldiers at other road blocks and he'd never had any trouble until that fateful morning.

"The network was too big and there were too many overlaps. In the months leading up to D-Day, the French Resistance multiplied like rabbits and with the influx of recruits, the principle of self-contained cells went by the board. We took risks we would never have taken before."

What was it Grothmann had said to him the night they'd driven out to Ostbevern? St Aubin des Bois was a very small village and some of the malicious gossip about the number of lovers Chantal Kiffer was alleged to have entertained in her cottage reached my ears. That's how we got on to you.

"Anyway, you weren't the only one who talked, Harry. Several of the witnesses who testified against Chantal Kiffer admitted they had broken under hostile interrogation."

"Guy never talked."

"No, Guy was one of the exceptions, but then he pretended to be related to the Marquis of Salisbury and the SS handled him with kid gloves. Hausser didn't put him through the meat grinder."

'I never turned Chantal Kiffer . . . the SS were calling the tune in '44 and they ordered me to be nice to her after the network had been rounded up . . .' Karl Heinz Grothmann again, and he had led the Abwehr Feldwebel to all his French contacts. So why had Hausser wired him up to a 12-volt battery and subsequently amputated his little finger a joint at a time?

"Hausser was an animal," Upham continued. "One of his first acts was to butcher fifteen prisoners-of-war several days after Warsaw had surrendered. He then went on to murder God knows

197

how many Jews in the Ukraine before he finally got to France where at least a dozen members of the Resistance died at his hands while under interrogation. If he hadn't been killed in the battle for Berlin, the Poles, the Russians or the French would have strung him up for war crimes."

"He's still alive," Freeland said quietly. "He's working for the Gehlen Bureau, probably under an assumed name."

"Are you sure?"

"I mean to get him, Cyril."

"Mind you do it by the book then," Upham warned.

"I've already tried to; unfortunately, the Americans don't want to know, and neither do we."

"But that's not going to stop you, is it?"

"Absolutely not."

He had his original passport and a hundred pounds in cash which Jenny had borrowed against her deposit account. He had deliberately caught a train from the City station to Birmingham in case the staff at Lichfield Trent Valley had been warned to keep an eye out for him. And, as far as he could tell, Special Branch hadn't been waiting for him at Euston. Just in case anyone had followed him to Bond and Hales, he would double back to Victoria when he left the department store to give the impression he intended to catch the boat train to Dover. Then he would make his way to the BEA terminal in Cromwell Road and book himself on the first available flight to Munich or any other airport that was within reasonable distance of the city.

"You make sure you look after yourself, Harry," Upham said, rising to his feet.

"I intend to."

"All the luck in the world."

"Thanks."

Freeland knew he was going to need a large slice of it in the next few hours, otherwise he could see himself stranded in England. The temperature had barely risen above freezing point all day and now it looked as though the fog, which had always been there on the horizon, was beginning to close in.

18

Hausser lit a cigarette and sat down on one of the steps leading to the cellar. Breaking Grothmann had taken Erika, whose real name was Raya Yasnev, far longer than either of them had anticipated. The former Abwehr Feldwebel had proved unexpectedly resistant to Scapolamine but, in the end, he had told Raya about the envelope he'd enclosed with a letter to his wife, Anna. He had also disclosed her address and the only major problem facing them now was how to recover the envelope before Frau Grothmann decided to open it. At least, that was how Hausser saw it. In Raya Yasnev's view, however, there were several questions that needed to be answered.

"I would like to know how and when this piece of filth discovered you were working for the Gehlen Bureau."

"I thought we'd already covered that." Hausser stared at the wisp of grey smoke curling into the air from his cigarette. "You asked him how long he had been in Munich and he said a week."

"That's what bothers me."

"Why?"

"The timing is all wrong. He recognises you, presumably from a distance because you are not aware that your paths have crossed. Then he learns about your new identity, traces you to this house and comes here demanding money for his continued silence. I find it inconceivable that he could have done so much in the space of seven days. What made him go out to Pullach in the first place, a village in the middle of nowhere?"

"You'd better ask him," Hausser said.

Raya turned to face their prisoner, placed a hand under Grothmann's chin and raised his head to look him in the eyes. Grothmann had received two boosters since the initial injection and was only marginally in possession of his faculties. For this reason, Hausser left the interrogation to Raya Yasnev, believing that if he joined in, it would only confuse him even more. Grothmann's voice was slurred, his speech almost incoherent; nothing he said made any sense with the exception of a nickname.

"Who is this 'Felix'?" Raya asked.

"An English officer who fell into our hands during the war," Hausser informed her. "The British Strategic Operations Executive sent him into Chartres to work with the French Resistance. His real name was Freeland and he was a temporary major in the Royal Artillery. I questioned him when he was captured; after he had given me the confession I needed, I sent him on to Flossenburg concentration camp where he was subsequently executed."

"Are you sure he was killed?"

"I wasn't there when the guards marched him into the execution shed and hung him, but he was a spy, and in his case there was no reason why the sentence should not have been carried out."

"Grothmann is very confused . . ."

"I can see that for myself," Hausser said irritably.

"I think he is saying that he has been in Munich before . . ."

"When?"

"Perhaps a long time ago." Raya shrugged. "It is very difficult to pin him down to dates and places when his mind is wandering. According to the papers we found on him, he's employed as a labourer by the British Army in Münster."

"They can't be paying him much judging by the state of his clothes." Hausser flicked his cigarette, spilling ash over the cellar steps. "Maybe he came south looking for work, spotted me and tried to peddle his information to the highest bidder? Perhaps Grothmann only came here because no one else was interested in what he had to offer?"

"Who, for instance?"

"The Americans. Let's suppose he told them that ex-Sturmbann-führer Hausser was working for the Gehlen Bureau. They wouldn't find that name on their wanted list of war criminals because I never harmed a single American. It's you Russians, the Poles and the French who wanted my head, but the NKVD provided incontrovertible proof that Joachim Hausser was killed in action during the Battle of Berlin in April 1945."

"You forgot to mention the British," Raya informed him coldly.

"I only ever dealt with two British agents. Freeland is almost certainly dead and the other, whose name is Salusbury, does not have an axe to grind. He certainly wouldn't have sent Grothmann after me, if that's what you're thinking. Besides, we know from

200

Whitaker's Almanack that he's in charge of the British Consulate in New York."

"Would you recognise Freeland again if he was still alive?"

"Of course I would, I never forget a face."

"And he has good cause to remember yours."

"What's the point of all this . . . ?"

"The point is, Herr Sturmbannführer, we have invested a lot of time and money in you and I have to satisfy Moscow that you are still a valuable asset."

She didn't have to say any more. The NKVD had spared him in 1945 because he had known where a lot of the skeletons were buried and had been able to put flesh on the bones. He had also given them one potentially major source and then, when his usefulness to the NKVD was obviously coming to an end, he had managed to persuade the Commandant of 129 Special Punishment Camp that with a little investment, he too could become an equally valuable asset. The task of furnishing him with a new identity had been given to Wilhelm Zaisser, Head of the Stadtsicherheitsdienst in the Ministry of State Security. After he had wormed his way into the Gehlen Bureau, the East Germans had provided a stream of high grade information to establish his reputation and make him the up-and-coming star of the American-backed Intelligence organisation. All that hard work would count for nothing if he had to disappear behind the Iron Curtain because of Grothmann. Worse still, the Russians wouldn't hesitate to liquidate him once he became unemployable outside the Soviet Bloc.

"We should recover the incriminating envelope while time is still on our side. If we wait for instructions from Moscow, it may well be too late. I'll handle things in Münster; you'll have to dispose of Grothmann." He dropped his cigarette and stepped on it. "Can you manage that?"

He could see from her tight-lipped expression that Raya Yasnev resented taking orders from him. She was the watchdog the NKVD had installed to make sure he remembered who his paymasters were, and she was used to calling the tune.

"I think my wife should spend the next few days in Switzerland . . ."

"No." Raya shook her head vehemently. "She will stay here with me; we do not want any misunderstandings."

Elisabeth was to be a hostage to ensure he wasn't tempted to make a deal with the other side.

"It's a matter of supreme indifference to me . . ."

201

"Frau Grothmann will also have to be eliminated," Raya said, interrupting him.

"Naturally."

"So tell me how you intend to go about it."

"I shan't go anywhere near her in broad daylight, you can depend on that."

He would give the neighbourhood a quick once-over, then wait until it was dark before making the next move. Persuading Anna Grothmann to invite him inside would not be difficult, but unless he was exceptionally lucky, she was unlikely to hand over the envelope. It would be enough, however, to learn that the incriminating evidence was somewhere in the house. He would kill her at the first opportunity and make it look as though she had slipped and fractured her skull.

"I'll try to arrange for a back-up team to be in place," Raya Yasnev told him.

A back-up was the last thing Hausser wanted but it wasn't politic to say so. "Good. I'll call you from the first Raststätte north of Cologne so that you can let me know what's happening."

"Will they miss you at Pullach if you don't go in this morning?"

"I'll phone my secretary and make some excuse." Hausser smiled. "When you're as highly placed as I am, you don't have to account for your movements. Provided your PA thinks she knows where you are, that's all that matters." He glanced at his wristwatch and saw that it was a few minutes after two a.m. "I'd better grab a couple of hours sleep," he said, standing up.

Hausser climbed the steps from the cellar and went into his study off the hall. Unlocking the centre drawer of his desk, he took out a Walther 7.65mm PPK automatic and checked the magazine to make sure it was loaded with seven rounds. Anna Grothmann wouldn't give him any trouble but in the event that Freeland was still alive and was somehow involved, he wasn't going to be emptyhanded should they chance to meet face-to-face. The same went for the back-up team.

*   *   *

Freeland got off the Rhineland Westphalia express at Münster Hauptbahnhof and walked down the flight of steps leading from the island platform to the main concourse at street level. Nothing had gone right for him from the time he'd left Bond and Hales. The only flight to Munich had departed at 1400 hours and the fog had thickened up during his detour to Victoria. Poor visibility over the

Continent had led to the cancellation of all BEA flights to Frankfurt, Stuttgart and Cologne. Düsseldorf had still been open but it was too close to the office for comfort and he didn't want to bump into anyone from the Consulate. In the end, Freeland had booked himself on a flight to Hannover, only for the plane to be diverted to Hamburg because of deteriorating weather conditions.

He had spent the night in a small hotel in the St Pauli District and had intended to catch the first train to Munich via a connecting service at Frankfurt, but his taxi driver had skidded on an icy patch on the way to the station and had wrapped the Mercedes round a tree. Rather than hang about in Hamburg, he'd decided to stop off in Münster to see if Grothmann had returned from Munich. The odds against him having run Hausser to ground were astronomical in his opinion, but all the same, Freeland thought there was a chance that the former Abwehr Feldwebel might have stumbled across something which he would find helpful.

There were no taxis in the yard. Turning left outside the station, Freeland walked down Bahnhofstrasse and turned left again to pass under the railway bridge into Albersloher Weg. Ten past seven: a dark, cold winter's morning, the street lights still burning and a small dispirited queue of workmen waiting at the bus stop for a number 6, 8 or 331 which would take them to the military barracks in Loddenheide or the brickworks eight miles out of town.

Both hands thrust deep into the pockets of his duffel coat, Freeland walked on towards the Halle Münsterland, then turned right into Lippstädter Strasse opposite the bombed-out skeleton of what had once been the town's gasworks. The night trade had dispersed and gone home; there were no kerb-crawling motorists on the look-out for a flashy trickster in high heels, no MPs waiting to pounce on an eighteen-year-old squaddie hoping to find a girl who would show him what sex was all about for the price of the loose change in his pocket.

Freeland pushed open the gate to number 64, walked up the weed-infested front path and was about to ring the bell when one of the tenants left the house on his way to work. Freeland nodded good morning and stepped past him into the hall.

The Grothmanns had two rooms on the ground floor to the right of the entrance. He pressed their buzzer and when that failed to have any effect, he hammered on the door.

A woman behind him said, "They're not in."

"What?" Freeland turned about and found himself confronting a middle-aged Hausfrau.

"Herr Grothmann is away on business and Anna didn't return

203

home last night. The English officer she works for asked her to stay on."

"Actually, it was Herr Grothmann I wanted to see," Freeland said and edged towards the door. "Perhaps I'll try again this evening."

"Who shall I say was calling?"

"My name is Northover but that won't mean anything to Frau Grothmann. We've never met."

Freeland bid the Hausfrau goodbye, walked briskly down the front path and closed the gate behind him. He had told Grothmann to spend no more than a week looking for Hausser and now the man was already a day late. The Field Security detachment could get him the name and address of the British family Anna worked for, but he didn't want to involve them while there was still an alternative source of information as yet untapped. Acland had probably discovered that he had slipped out of the country by now and would have put out an all stations alert for Harry Freeland, also known as Harry Northover. It was therefore reasonable to assume that Special Branch had already traced him to Hamburg; if he contacted the Field Security detachment in Münster, Acland would get to hear about it sooner rather than later.

Freeland returned to the Hauptbahnhof and rang Gunther Altmüller from a pay-phone in the concourse. Having his telephone bill paid for by the British was one of the few perks Altmüller enjoyed from being a recruiter for Special Forces. It was also a fact that but for this concession, he could not have afforded a phone on the salary the owner of the timber yard paid him. Freeland caught him as he was on the point of leaving for work.

"I won't keep you long," Freeland assured him. "All I want is the name and address of the British officer Anna Grothmann works for."

"His name is King, Hauptmann King; he's a staff officer at Garrison Headquarters and lives somewhere in Gremmendorf. You'll have to ask the Civil Labour Office for his exact address."

"Thanks, Gunther, I knew I could rely on you."

He wouldn't have to go to the Civil Labour Office or Garrison Headquarters. Army families invariably lived on a 'cabbage patch'; with a name, all he had to do was knock on a few doors and one of the wives would tell him where he could find the Kings.

"Did you get my messages, Herr Northover?"

"What messages?"

"Frau Grothmann came to see me the day before yesterday. She said you had given her husband some money and had sent him

204

down to Munich and she was anxious because she hadn't heard a word from him since he left. The next day, she shows up at the timber yard again and is all smiles because she has had a letter from Karl Heinz. He is going to stay on in Munich for another day or so to attend to a few minor points and then it seems their money worries will be over." Altmüller paused, then said, "You wouldn't like to solve my money worries, would you, Herr Northover?"

"You wouldn't thank me, Gunther, if you were in Grothmann's shoes."

Freeland put the phone down and backed out of the kiosk. Grothmann was staying on to sort out one or two little matters and then it seemed they would no longer have to pinch and scrape. The sudden change in the family fortunes could only mean that he had found Hausser and was planning to put the bite on him. Freeland supposed there were more dangerous ways of making a fast buck but offhand he couldn't name one.

He walked into the Café Diercksen, sat down at a corner table and ordered rolls and coffee. Although it was vital to find Anna Grothmann as soon as possible, he didn't want to go knocking on any doors before all the husbands were on parade.

*   *   *

Egan thought the sequence of events would read like an indictment for gross negligence when they came to write their report, no matter how hard they tried to gloss over the salient facts. Entirely of his own volition, he had telephoned Freeland yesterday morning shortly after eleven and had found himself talking to the father-in-law instead. From Sidney Vail he had learned that Harry was out shopping and wasn't expected back before lunchtime. Promptly at two o'clock he had phoned again, only to find he had Jenny Freeland on the line. He had known she was lying the moment she told him that Harry had dropped by the Prep School to see his parents.

Even though he had obtained the number of Warley Farm Preparatory School from Directory Enquiries, Acland had been reluctant to do anything about it. To placate Egan, he had eventually phoned Warley Farm and had learned from the school secretary that the headmaster and staff were attending the end of term carol service in the assembly hall. She had also led Acland to believe that Freeland was present. Subsequently, he had spoken to Jennifer Freeland and extracted a promise that she would get her husband to call the office the minute he returned.

"He's trying to make us sweat," Acland had opined after five o'clock had come and gone without any word from Freeland. "But it isn't going to work because we've got his passport and he can't skip the country."

One hour after making this confident assertion, Acland had decided to alert Special Branch. It wasn't until Egan was brushing his teeth prior to retiring for the night that it suddenly occurred to him that Freeland might still have the passport which had been issued to him in his real name. Acting on his own initiative, he had immediately called the Deputy Commissioner at his home to advise him that the man Special Branch was looking for might be travelling under the name of Freeland. Some four hours later, the duty officer at 54 Broadway had informed him that Freeland had departed for Hannover on BEA Flight 412 which had been diverted to Hamburg.

Acland had had all the time in the world to digest the information while he was lying in bed at home, over breakfast and on the train to London; now here he was still vacillating at five past ten in the morning.

"I don't see what else you can reasonably expect me to do, Tom," he said plaintively. "I've already informed Cologne of the situation."

"With respect, that's just passing the buck," Egan said in a voice that was anything but deferential. "What do you expect Matthews and Anthea Clowes to do? Chase all over West Germany looking for him? We've got to bring MI5 in on the act; they're responsible for counter-espionage and they have their own security people in BAOR."

It wasn't difficult to tell what Acland thought of that suggestion. His nose wrinkled as though his nostrils had detected an unpleasant smell and was complemented by the sour expression on his face.

"It's too late to go cap in hand to the other 'firm'. Freeland will be across the border by now."

Egan saw it for the transparent excuse it was. The SIS had lost face over the Burgess and Maclean affair, their 'in house' personnel security procedures had been seen to be a joke and no one in authority had paid much attention to the obvious character defects of the two men. To inform MI5 that the SIS might have another rotten apple in the barrel was the very last thing Acland wanted to do.

"I don't believe he has defected, Neville."

"I wish I could share your optimism."

"Look at it this way," Egan persisted. "If he was going to bolt, why did he come back to England when we sent for him?"

206

"Search me."

"I think he's gone after Hausser. I don't know why he didn't fly direct to Munich and I'm not prepared to waste valuable time on speculation. We know he ended up in Hamburg and that's where we should start looking."

They had to trace Freeland's movements from the time he'd left the airport and to do that quickly, they would need to enlist the aid of the German Civil Police. At the same time, it was essential to obscure the reason why they were anxious to find him.

"We do it on the old boy network," Egan continued. "We'll get Innes Dalwood, the British Resident in Cologne, to ask the Police President to do him a small favour. We'll make Freeland a civil servant in the Ministry of Supply and hint at a number of irregularities which have come to light in some of the contracts he okayed."

"Bribery and corruption," Acland said eagerly.

"Precisely. We can also credit him with a German girlfriend for good measure. That should do the trick."

"I like it." Acland frowned. "Of course, I shall have to clear it with the Old Man first," he added.

Egan nodded. He had never known Acland to sanction a tricky course of action without first seeking the prior approval of the D-G.

*   *   *

Mrs Susan King, Sue to her friends as she quickly informed Freeland, was in her early twenties and was still full of suppressed energy even when she was feeling hung over. Her husband was the Staff Captain 'A' and 'Q' at Garrison Headquarters, responsible for discipline, courts martial, welfare and logistics, which gave her a certain amount of reflected kudos among the other wives on the patch. The Kings occupied a large house opposite York Barracks which, before the war, had belonged to the Luftwaffe. So too had their house, purpose-built in a manner befitting an Oberst in the newly created Air Force. The Garrison Commander lived near Wolbeck in a much grander place whose owner, a former industrialist and member of the Nazi Party, had been evicted to make way for the Brigadier.

The Kings were invited to and attended all the best parties in town. Yesterday evening, they had been to the Moodkee Ball, a social occasion commemorating a battle honour, which she informed him dated back to the Sikh War of 1845–1846 and was shared by the Royal Norfolks, the South Staffordshire Regiment and the 3rd Light Dragoons.

207

Freeland had had little difficulty in persuading Susan King to invite him in. His passport, where the occupation was shown as government official and the magic words 'Foreign Office War Crimes Section', had done the trick. Getting her to tell him where he could find Anna Grothmann without hearing the ins and outs of being an army wife was proving an Herculean task.

"Our cook-housekeeper is on a week's leave which is rather tiresome, so we asked Anna if she would babysit for us." Susan King waxed indignant. "You would have thought she'd have been glad to earn a few extra Marks, but not a bit of it. She came within a whisker of saying no, but then my husband pointed out that there are plenty of German women of her age who would give their right arm to work for the British, and she thought better of it."

"I had noticed there was no scarcity of domestic servants," Freeland said drily.

"Quite. Anyway, we made a bed up for Anna in the attic because obviously we weren't going to be back before the last bus to Münster departed. Good thing we did make Anna stay the night; we were both rather worse for wear when we got home in the early hours."

"So where is Frau Grothmann now?"

"At the Krankenhaus. She's been having dizzy spells lately and her doctor referred her to a specialist. I don't know why they couldn't have given her an appointment in the afternoon. Anna only works mornings for me."

"Any idea which hospital she's gone to?" Freeland asked, containing his impatience with difficulty.

"'Fraid not."

"Never mind, I'll find her."

"You're not leaving, are you, Mr Freeland? Do stay and have a cup of coffee. I'm expecting some of the other wives at ten thirty and I'm sure they'd love to meet you."

A hen party was the last thing Freeland wanted to get enmeshed in. There was a distinct possibility that he wasn't the only one looking for Anna Grothmann and it was vital he found her before the opposition did.

"There's nothing I'd like more," Freeland told her, "but you know how it is – duty calls."

"Yes, indeed."

She offered him her hand and he held on to it a bit longer than necessary to give her the impression he was genuinely sorry to leave. The time was exactly ten twenty-eight and the next bus to Münster wasn't due until two minutes after eleven. There were of course no taxi-cabs plying for hire in Gremmendorf.

208

19

Cologne 8 Km: Hausser took his eyes off the road for a split second and glanced at the dashboard. He had left Munich at five o'clock in pitch darkness and it was now fifteen minutes after midday, which meant that it had taken him more than seven hours to cover approximately five hundred and seventy kilometres. He'd had to contend with poor visibility and icy conditions as far as Frankfurt and it was only in the last hour or thereabouts that he had really been able to put his foot down. But he would need to do even better if he was to arrive in Münster in time to give 64 Lippstädter Strasse the once-over in daylight. That, however, was easier said than done; as soon as he turned off the autobahn on to the paved surface of Route 51, he would be lucky to average eighty kilometres in the hour.

He flattened the accelerator, felt the car leap forward and instinctively gripped the steering wheel a bit tighter. The rhythmic drumming of the tyres on the concrete slabs began to have an hypnotic effect on him and he lowered the window a fraction to make sure he didn't fall asleep.

The autobahn was one of the lasting achievements of the Third Reich, a strategic highway that ran all the way from the old Polish frontier to the Alps. It was one piece of engineering the Americans, Russians, British and French were going to leave intact. They'd done everything else to destroy every vestige of the National Socialist Party, from removing the swastika from public buildings to dynamiting the flak towers, some of which had proved extraordinarily resilient. There was one tower he knew of near Wesel which had defied every effort by the British Army to demolish it.

Thinking back, Hausser remembered the fourteen storey G Tower in the Berlin Zoological Garden, one of six massive emplacements in the Humboldthain and Friedrichshain districts of the city. Each flak tower had been a self-contained fortress with its own water supply, generating plant, five hundred bed hospital, operating theatre, command centre, barracks and battery of 88mm AA guns on the roof. The reinforced concrete had been thick enough to withstand a direct hit from a ten-ton blockbuster that could level an entire street.

On the morning of the twenty-fifth of April 1945, approximately thirty thousand Berliners had been sheltering in the tower which was under intense tank and artillery bombardment. The entire firepower of two Soviet divisions had been concentrated on the building and the continuous hailstorm caused by thousands upon thousands of 7.62mm rounds striking the steel-protected embrasures had driven three civilians to commit suicide. From his lofty observation post on the twelfth floor, Hausser had had a commanding view of the Zoological Garden itself. Although the big cats and reptiles had been destroyed before the Red Army had besieged Berlin, the other species had continued to attract visitors right up to the moment when the first shells had fallen on the city. In the final stages of the battle, the Zoo had resembled a lunar landscape of overlapping bomb craters seen through a haze of brick dust from the pulverised buildings in Charlottenburg. Once, during a brief lull, he'd spotted a lone chimpanzee wandering aimlessly among the corpses of wildebeest, Thompson's gazelle, warthog and ostrich; then another incoming salvo had landed and the animal had vanished without trace.

He had seen the incident as an omen of what could happen to him. Rumour had it that the Ivans were shooting every SS man who fell into their hands. Yet if he attempted to escape from the flak tower and go into hiding, there was a very real danger that he would encounter one of the numerous SS death squads who were roving the city busily hanging every deserter they caught from the nearest lamp post. In the end, he had taken a uniform off one of the medical orderlies at gun point, then shot the Gefreiter in the head and stuffed the half-naked body into one of the hospital linen baskets. A few hours later, the senior surviving officer had surrendered the tower and Hausser had been marched into captivity with the rest of the garrison.

According to the papers in the breast pocket of his uniform, he was Gefreiter Horst Trenzler of the Medical Corps; the blood group tattooed on the inside of his left upper arm told the Soviet interrogator at the screening camp in Potsdam that he was someone else.

The NKVD guards had worked him over and would have shot him on the spot had he not convinced the political commissar that he would be of more value to him alive rather than dead. In the next few months he had proved that contention over and over again and had lost count of the number of men who had kept a rendezvous with a firing squad because he had denounced them as war criminals.

The NKVD had rewarded him by taking care of his wife. Elisabeth had fled to Oberammergau in the Bavarian Alps when her unit of Luftwaffe Auxiliaries had been disbanded in the autumn of 1944. Her parents had owned a chalet in the village and Hausser had agreed she would be safer there than anywhere else in Germany. In 1946, the NKVD had spirited her into the Soviet Zone of Occupied Austria where she had been installed in a villa at Ebenfurth under virtual house arrest. It was only when they had shown him a photograph of Elisabeth taken in the grounds that he had known his own survival was assured.

Hausser pulled off the autobahn into the Reststätte south of Duisburg. After filling up, he parked the Opel outside the restaurant and called Raya Yasnev in Munich from a pay-phone. It took the operator less than a minute to connect him with the number he wanted in Munich.

"Have there been any messages for me?" Hausser asked.

"Only one," Raya Yasnev told him. "Head Office would like you to call on a prospective client at Goethe Strasse 43. His name is Arnim, Viktor Arnim."

"When is he expecting me?"

"Between 1700 hours and 1815, if that's convenient?"

"I don't see any difficulty." Hausser paused, then said, "Does he have a phone number in case I should be delayed?"

"You can contact him on 513278 up to 1830. After that, he has another appointment and won't be available."

Hausser thanked her and put the phone down. He would not find Goethe Strasse on any street map of Münster, but his back-up team was in place and he had been given a code-name and contact number. In a roundabout fashion, he had also been given to understand that he would be in serious trouble if Herr Arnim hadn't heard from him by 1830 hours.

*　　*　　*

Freeland hadn't realised just how many hospitals there were in Münster until he started looking for Anna Grothmann. Since hospitals were not listed under a collective heading in the local telephone directory, he had hired a cab driver from the rank outside the Bahnhof who'd claimed he knew every Krankenhaus in town.

211

They had started with the Clemens Hospital in Duesberg Strasse, then moved on to the University Clinic on Kardinal von Galen Ring, steadily working their way round the city in a clockwise direction. It had proved to be a time-consuming business.

From what Susan King had told him, there were grounds for thinking that Anna Grothmann had been referred to a heart specialist. Alternatively, her dizzy spells might have something to do with her hearing and Anna's doctor might have wanted an ear, nose and throat man to have a look at her. Freeland played it safe and tried both specialists at each hospital he visited. It was easy enough to get the names of the consultants from the duty receptionist in the Out-Patients Department; finding out whether a Frau Anna Grothmann had an appointment with either of the specialists was a vastly different proposition. Every secretary he'd encountered had regarded that as privileged information and had been reluctant to disclose it to him.

"My name is Northover," he had told each secretary in turn. "I am the account holder of the German Civil Labour Office. As one of our employees, Frau Anna Grothmann is entitled to have her medical expenses paid by the British Army." Then he had smiled and added, "Unfortunately, she forgot to collect the requisite forms from the office."

The ploy had worked with every other secretary, but the dark-haired woman at the Franziskus Hospital off the Hohenzollern Ring was less trusting than the others. Her hostile manner suggested to Freeland that she was not overly fond of the British either.

"You have the necessary papers?" she asked.

"They're for Frau Grothmann."

"You may give them to me, Herr Northover."

Freeland looked round the waiting room. There were only three out-patients, a small fat man in his mid sixties and a worried-looking mother with her eight to ten-year-old son.

"Is Frau Grothmann with the doctor now?" he asked.

"She left some twenty minutes ago. The Herr Doktor does not keep his patients waiting."

"Ah, well, that's it then," Freeland said. "I'm sorry to have troubled you."

"What about the papers?"

"Frau Grothmann has to sign them first." He smiled. "Don't worry, I'll be back as soon as I've got her signature."

It was past one o'clock and except for the department stores in the city centre, all the shops were closed for an extended lunch hour. The Gasthofs were open, but he wouldn't know where to start looking for her, and it was only logical to assume she had gone home. Anna Grothmann, however, was not behaving in a logical fashion; when he again failed to get an answer at her door, the same chatty neighbour whom he'd met earlier that morning informed him that she must still be with the English Hauptmann's Frau in Gremmendorf.

"Anna's left there," Freeland told her. "She had an appointment to see the heart specialist at the Franziskus Hospital."

"She is ill?"

"They haven't admitted her so she can't be too poorly. I just wondered if she might have gone somewhere for a drink?"

"Who knows what Anna does? She keeps herself to herself. You want to come in and have a cup of coffee while you wait for her?"

"That's very kind of you, Frau . . . ?"

"Jüttner."

Neighbourliness had very little to do with the invitation. The Jüttner woman was a nosy busybody and he knew he would have to deal with a barrage of questions, but anything was preferable to walking the streets on a miserably cold day.

*   *   *

Geoffrey King liked to socialise. On his way home to lunch, he always called in at the Officers' Mess to have one for the road and pass the time of day with the bachelor officers on the staff. It was, he frequently told his wife, simply a means of keeping himself abreast of what was going on in the garrison. He also saw it as part of his job to ensure that any visitors to the headquarters were being properly looked after. As a result, he usually had lunch at one fifteen. Today, however, the Garrison Headquarters had had more than its fair share of visitors from Corps and Division and he had arrived home a good half an hour later than usual to a burnt lamb chop and a very irate wife who'd refused to speak to him after the initial blast. The strained atmosphere had persisted to the coffee stage.

"I'm truly sorry," he said for the umpteenth time.

"So you should be."

"But I don't see what else I could have done. The place was stiff with visiting firemen and I couldn't very well leave the Brigadier to cope with them on his own."

The Brigadier hadn't been anywhere near the Mess, but Sue was not to know that.

"You could have telephoned me."

213

There was no answer to that and he didn't attempt one. "How did your coffee morning go?" he asked, changing the subject.

"Why should you care?"

"Because I'm interested."

There was a longish pause before Sue finally began to tell him the usual tittle-tattle before announcing that Valerie thought she was pregnant.

"Who's the father?" King asked and roared with laughter.

"I don't know," Sue told him, "she's still compiling the stud book."

"Let's hope she doesn't forget to include past and present members of the Guards and Cavalry Clubs."

"You'll never guess who came to see me before the coffee party."

"The Brigadier's wife?"

"No."

"The British Resident?"

Sue shook her head. "But you're getting warmer."

"I give up."

"A Mr Freeland from the Foreign Office."

"Foreign Office? Are you sure he wasn't having you on?"

"He showed me his passport where it said government official."

"What did he want?"

"It seems Anna's husband is a Nazi war criminal. Apparently, he was a Warrant Officer in the Intelligence Branch of the German Army and the French are now saying that he personally murdered at least eight members of the Resistance in cold blood."

King didn't care whether there was any truth in the allegation or not. What did concern him was the fact that, as far as he knew, no one in Garrison Headquarters had been warned about Freeland's impending visit.

"I'll have to look into this," he said, voicing his thoughts.

"Look into what?"

"This Freeland business." King folded his napkin and stood up. "The Foreign Office should have warned us before they sent him sniffing around the Married Quarters."

"Don't tell me you're going back to the office? You've only been home twenty minutes."

"Half an hour more likely. Anyway, it's more than my job is worth to sit on this."

Once back in the office, King made two phone calls, one to the Field Security Detachment, the other to the Military Police. Both

214

units denied all knowledge of a Mr Freeland; no one in Garrison Headquarters had heard of him either. The matter was therefore referred to the British Resident in Münster to investigate, the first link in a chain that would eventually reach back to London.

*   *   *

"Such things you have never seen in your life, Herr Northover. The sky was full of four-engined bombers – amerikanisch, you understand?"

"They had to be, the RAF didn't mount any daylight raids on Germany in 1943."

They had started talking about the war because Frau Jüttner had asked him how he had met Karl Heinz Grothmann. Freeland had told her that Anna's husband had been a Feldwebel in the Abwehr and had actually taken him prisoner in France. It had proved a useful diversion and had satisfied her curiosity in a way no other explanation could have done.

"We lived in Schiller Strasse in those days and I remember it happened on a Sunday because my husband was on leave and we had gone to the show ground south of Münster to see the Police Horse Trials. Most people threw themselves flat when the bombs began to fall, but I looked up and saw two planes collide and vanish in a big fireball. A third bomber was spiralling towards the ground, one of its engines smoking. I counted seven parachutes in the sky before it crashed in the woods near Wolbeck. About ten minutes later, the whole of Münster seemed to be burning."

Freeland glanced at his wristwatch surreptitiously. Three twenty-six: where the hell was Anna Grothmann? There was no way she could have returned without his knowledge because he and Frau Jüttner were sitting in the front room and he could see the gate through the net curtains even though the window-sill was a jungle of potted plants.

"Our house had gone of course but at least we survived, which was more than could be said for a lot of people we knew. When the sirens sounded, the audience watching the film at the Apollo Theatre in Königstrasse were told to leave and go to the nearest air raid shelter. The civilians did, the soldiers in the audience didn't; they stood around outside and were still watching the flak bursts when this huge bomb demolished the Apollo and killed all eighty of them. The Military Police post outside the Bahnhof took a direct hit too and the building and everyone in it vanished without a trace except for the crater. Next morning, the army brought in gangs of Russian prisoners-of-war to clear the blocked streets."

215

Freeland heard the gate squeak on its rusty hinges and half rose in his chair. The woman he saw was thin and round-shouldered, her face partially hidden by a shawl.

"I presume that's Anna?" he said.

Frau Jüttner stood up. "That's her all right; she doesn't look too steady on her feet either."

When Freeland caught up with her, Anna Grothmann was having trouble getting into her flat. Each time she aimed for the keyhole, she managed to hit the metal surround, which caused her to mutter a few choice expressions to herself.

"Here, let me help you," Freeland said, relieving her of the key.

"Who the devil are you?"

"My name is Northover; I'm a friend of your husband's."

"Yes?"

"I'm the one who sent Karl Heinz to Munich."

"Ah, Herr Northover," she said, then hiccupped and quickly placed a hand over her mouth. "Excuse me . . ."

Freeland opened the door, removed the key and followed Anna Grothmann into her minute apartment. The front room had been turned into a bed-sitter, while the kitchen-diner was obviously at the back. He assumed the bathroom and lavatory were down the hall and were shared by the other residents on the ground floor.

"But what are you doing here, Herr Northover?"

"I went to see Frau Hauptmann King and she told me you had an appointment at the hospital. When I got to the Franziskus, you had already left."

"I needed a drink."

"Bad news?"

"My heart is not good; the specialist said I should rest more . . ." Anna scowled. "What nonsense. I ask you, Herr Northover, how can I afford to rest? It is not possible . . ."

"I'm afraid I've got some more bad news for you."

"Nothing you can tell me can be worse than I've heard already."

"It's about Karl Heinz," Freeland said. "I think he could be in real trouble."

Anna Grothmann flopped into a shabby armchair. Her face was grey and there were dark hollows under her eyes. "With whom? The police?"

"With a man called Joachim Hausser, a former Sturmbannführer who is supposed to be dead but isn't."

"I've never heard of him."

216

"Karl Heinz was going to find him for me; that's why he went to Munich."

"So why have you come to me?"

"You went to see Gunther Altmüller on Wednesday because you hadn't heard from Karl Heinz; the next day you got a letter from your husband and you went to Hiltrup again to let him know that everything was all right after all. Only it isn't. Your husband didn't think I was paying him enough so he went to Hausser and asked for a small fortune in return for his silence, which was his big mistake."

Freeland showed her the mutilated stump of the little finger on his left hand and explained precisely how and why going to Hausser was the biggest and most disastrous error Karl Heinz Grothmann would ever make. He told her step by step what the SS Sturmbannführer had done to him, from the water treatment and the electrodes to the final amputation. Freeland wanted her to understand that Hausser wouldn't stop until Karl Heinz told him everything he wanted to know. Then he would come looking for Anna Grothmann.

"If you want to see your husband again, you'd better show me the letter he wrote to you and whatever else was enclosed with it."

She stared at him glassy-eyed, jaw sagging, until with something of an effort, she eventually managed to find her voice.

"I don't know what you're talking about, Herr Northover."

Anna Grothmann was drunk but not so drunk that she was going to part with a scrap of paper that Karl Heinz had told her was worth a king's ransom. Her stupid intransigence angered Freeland and he wanted to shake her until her dentures rattled.

"Give me the letter," he snarled. "Give me the bloody letter or Hausser's going to kill you."

Anna blinked at him; then, like a robot, she opened her battered handbag, took out an oblong-shaped envelope and gave it to him without a word. There was a smaller envelope inside which had been folded in two. Ripping it open, Freeland found a sheet of lined notepaper on which Grothmann had written – 'Doktor Ernst Winkler, Schiller Platz 8, Munich 44. Real name Joachim Hausser, former SS Sturmbannführer wanted for war crimes by France, Poland and Israel.'

"Now listen to me," Freeland said. "I'm going across the hall to ask Frau Jüttner if I can use her telephone. Lock the door after me and don't let anyone else into your apartment while I'm gone."

He would make two phone calls; it could even run to three if he

217

felt he could trust Frank Matthews, but a lot would depend on the outcome of the first two. Right now, his first concern was who to contact first – Altmüller or Steve Johansen.

* * *

Altmüller walked over to the window and gazed out at the timber yard. Last week's snowfall had partially thawed, then frozen over, so that it now looked dirty and in need of a fresh layer to make it shining white again. The sky was a slate grey but it wasn't going to snow; it was too damned cold and raw for that. The roads and sidewalks would freeze when the sun disappeared below the horizon, which it was going to do in the next quarter of an hour or so, and they would probably have some sleet. But it wouldn't snow, no matter what the weather forecasters said.

He had learned to read the sky that first winter before Moscow when the army had had its collective arse frozen solid. Summer uniforms in a Russian winter; he'd wrapped himself in newspapers to keep warm and he hadn't changed his clothes or dropped his pants in five months. Instead, he had unpicked the stitching on his pants from just above the crotch to the base of the spine, then clipped the seams together with safety pins. It had been crude and unhygienic, but at least his backside had never frozen to the thunder box which had happened to some poor bastards in the division. Christ, he had forgotten more about weather patterns than these university *Dummkopfs* would ever know with their piddling balloons and barometric pressures.

The telephone rang behind him and he instinctively waited for Gertrud to answer it, forgetting for the moment that she was still off work with influenza. Altmüller turned about, returned to his desk and picked up the phone to find that he had Herr Northover on the line.

The Englishman said, "This is for your ears only, Gunther, so be careful what you say in reply. You understand?"

"But of course, Herr Northover."

"I'm calling from 64 Lippstädter Strasse. That bloody old fool Grothmann has tried to make a deal with Hausser, with all that that entails. You follow me?"

"I think I'm ahead of you," Altmüller told him.

"In that case, you will appreciate why I don't want to be empty-handed when he calls on us."

"I'll get a delivery to you as soon as I can, Herr Northover."

"Good, I was hoping you would say that, Gunther."

Altmüller slowly replaced the receiver. The Englishman wanted

218

him to get an automatic from one of the arms caches they'd established in Rhineland Westphalia. The nearest one to Münster was on a farm near Ostbevern and the local switchboard operator had a reputation for eavesdropping on calls routed through her exchange. He just hoped she would rapidly lose interest when he started talking about special agricultural implements.

20

Freeland hung on to the phone, waiting impatiently for the operator to connect him with the Wiesbaden number. Come on, come on, come on: what was the Bundespost doing out there, laying a goddamned line? Frau Jüttner smiled at him, her currant-bun eyes almost disappearing into her plump cheeks.

"You are having difficulties, Herr Northover?"

"A slight delay," he told her.

At long last, the operator informed him she had the Wiesbaden number and Steve Johansen's Midwest accent had never sounded so good. Better still, Frau Jüttner didn't understand a word of English which meant he could speak freely without having to disguise everything in veiled speech.

"So how's the world treating you, Harry?" Johansen enquired after he'd said hello. "How's Jen and the boy?"

"They're both fine." Freeland gave Frau Jüttner a tight little smile to let her know that everything was all right, then said, "Remember me asking you about Joachim Hausser, the man who was supposed to be working for the Gehlen Bureau?"

"Will I ever forget?"

"Well, Grothmann's found him, only now he calls himself Doktor Ernst Winkler and he's living at 8 Schiller Platz in Munich. Make a note of the address, Steve, because I want you to . . ."

"Now see here, Harry . . ."

"No, you listen to me," Freeland said tersely. "I want your Counter-Intelligence people to go round there with whatever tame number they can dig up from the Kriminalpolizei. And please don't give me any bullshit about it being outside your jurisdiction because every minute you try to stall me makes it that much worse for Grothmann."

"What was the address again, Harry?"

"8 Schiller Platz."

"Okay, I got it."

Freeland glanced at the disc on the dial where the subscriber's number was displayed. "One last thing," he said. "Please call me back on Münster 21691 the moment you have anything. The lady's name is Frau Jüttner and she'll bring me to the phone if you ask her nicely in German."

Freeland hung up, wondered if he should call Matthews, then decided he would wait until Altmüller had arrived before he put Frank's loyalty to the test. He took out a twenty-Mark note, gave it to Frau Jüttner and told her what he wanted her to do. She was happy to oblige him; he got the impression that for twenty Marks she would have performed cartwheels in the city centre if he'd asked her to.

*   *   *

Hausser continued on Hindenburg Platz as far as the university, then made a left turn into the parking lot facing the Administrative Building. The University was winding down for the Christmas vacation and, since most of the students had already departed, fewer members of the faculty needed to use the car park. It also meant he didn't have to queue for one of the pay-phones on the sidewalk. Entering the nearest one, Hausser fed twenty Pfennigs into the coin box and dialled 513278, the number Raya Yasnev had given him. It rang only half a dozen times before a gruff voice answered with a monosyllabic grunt.

"Herr Viktor Arnim?"

"Yes, who's calling?"

"My name is Winkler," Hausser told him, "and I'm an insurance broker. I understand you'd like me to give you a quote on 64 Lippstädter Strasse."

"Have you seen the property?"

Not a Russian who'd learned to speak the language fluently but an honest-to-God German from the East Zone. He would be one of the fifteen thousand infiltrators Wilhelm Zaisser, Head of State Security, had slipped across the border with instructions to remain dormant until they were needed. Hausser fancied he could tell all this from the accent.

"I've had a look at the house from the outside," he said cautiously.

"It isn't necessary to be quite so circumspect, Herr Winkler. I can assure you no one is monitoring this line."

"If you're sure . . ."

"I am positive."

"Well, okay then, it looks a quiet enough street to me."

"The locals call it Whore Alley. You can't park your car in that street while you call on Frau Grothmann; it will cause too much comment. You should leave your vehicle in the car park opposite the British Army Kino in Friedrich Ehart Platz and walk back from there."

"But . . ."

"No buts, Herr Winkler, we know this town better than you do. We'll cover Lippstädter Strasse from Albersloher Weg. You will therefore call on the lady at six fifteen which will give us time to get into position."

Hausser didn't like it. The man in charge of the back-up team was giving the orders and that wasn't right. He was about to object when the phone started to bleep and he hastily fed a one-Mark coin into the box.

"What is the make and number of your car, Herr Winkler?"

He wondered why they should want to know, then realised that all they had was a name, not a face. They had told him where to park his car; once they had the number and make, they would be able to identify him.

"I'm waiting, Herr Winkler."

"I'm driving a black Opel Kapitan," Hausser said and rattled off the number.

"I'll be waiting in a DKW licence number DO 5912. Have you got that?"

"What?"

"The number of the DKW. It's DO 5912."

"Oh, right."

"If you run into trouble at Grothmann's place, double-back to Albersloher Weg and make for the DKW. I'll be parked on the bomb site where the gas works used to be."

"Right."

"And don't hang about waiting for Anna Grothmann to show up if she isn't at home. Just walk away from the house and leave everything to us. We'll clear up the mess."

"And what do I do meanwhile?"

"You get into your Opel Kapitan, Herr Winkler, and drive like hell for the border."

The phone died on Hausser. There had been no prior intimation from the man that he was about to hang up. They had been conversing more or less normally one moment and suddenly there had been this decisive clunk followed by the usual burring noise.

Hausser slowly replaced the receiver. Grothmann had destroyed his cover; if he didn't plug the leak, the NKVD surrogates would clean up the mess. Just what was that supposed to mean? Was he part of the mess? Did those men in Dzerzhinsky Square intend to cut their losses and have him liquidated? Where was the percentage in that? Maybe after he was dead, the NKVD would use him to smear the Gehlen Bureau as the last refuge for the SS man on the run?

Well, then, he would beat them to it and do a deal with Reinhard Gehlen and his CIA backers. In return for a guarantee of immunity from prosecution, he would tell them everything he knew about the East German Sichterheitsdienst. But – and it was a big but – Zaisser had made sure that he was kept in quarantine while he was being trained and he didn't know a great deal about the State Security organisation, at least not enough to satisfy the Americans. And not enough for Bonn to stand up for him if the Israelis applied for his extradition.

This damned paranoia has got to stop, Hausser told himself. The NKVD are not going to eliminate you; if they did, people like Burgess and Maclean and who knows how many other Communist agents would never trust Moscow again. Forget the ifs and buts, do it their way and don't look beyond the next couple of hours.

Hausser backed out of the kiosk. Although it was below freezing, his shirt was damp with perspiration.

*   *   *

Freeland glanced at his wristwatch. Twelve minutes to six and still no sign of Altmüller. He could afford to wait another five minutes before he contacted the office but any later and Frank Matthews was unlikely to be there. As a last resort, he could always get in touch with Anthea Clowes but he didn't want to involve her if he could possibly help it. Anthea was a professional middle grade Intelligence officer to her fingertips, the kind of operative who did things by the book. If London had put out an all stations alert for him, she would contact the duty officer at 54 Broadway the minute he had finished talking to her.

Frank Matthews was different; he wasn't going anywhere in the Service and didn't have to keep one eye looking over his shoulder. He had gone out of his way to help him in Shanghai despite the instructions the Consulate had received from the Foreign Office, and there was a chance he would do it again. There was another important difference; Frank Matthews was a straight-up ex-colonial policeman who didn't know how to be devious. Simply by his tone of voice, Freeland would know whether or not he could count on

223

him; but you couldn't say the same for Anthea for she had been trained to hide her feelings.

Anna Grothmann heard the faint tap on the door before Freeland did and she was out of her chair and halfway across the room by the time he reacted. She was about to turn the key when he caught up with her and asked the caller to identify himself.

"It's me – Gunther," Altmüller said.

Freeland signalled Anna to move back into the room, then unlocked the door and let him in. The German stooped down, picked up the brown carrier bag between his feet and stepped past him.

"You're a sight for sore eyes," Freeland said.

"Bitte?"

"An English expression, I'm glad to see you."

The carrier bag contained two standard issue 9mm Walther P38 automatics and a box of twenty-five cartridges. Protected by an old newspaper, the arms and ammunition were hidden under a red cabbage and a kilo of potatoes.

"Two Walthers, Gunther?"

"Yes, one for you, one for me. I can of course load the magazine myself but it would be quicker if you did it for me, Herr Northover."

"You go on home, Gunther, this isn't your quarrel."

"I may only have one arm, but I am still a good shot, better perhaps than you."

"I'm sure you are . . ."

"And you need all the help you can get," Altmüller continued.

Freeland broke the seal on the waxed carton, took a handful of 9mm and thumbed eight rounds into one of the magazines. "What gives you that idea?" he asked.

"Because I think you are in trouble with your own people; if this was not so, you would not have asked me to provide you with a gun."

Freeland loaded the second magazine, tapped it home into the butt and pulled the slide back to chamber a round. Then he applied the safety catch and handed the Walther to Altmüller.

"Thanks, Gunther, I'll be glad of your help until the police arrive."

"You are going to call them?"

"I only wish it was that simple, but they are not likely to do it my way unless the British Resident makes an official request. And persuading him to contact the Police President may take a little time."

224

"Well, at least you won't have to worry about Anna while I'm around."

"As long as we don't have any false heroics."

"I'm too old for that sort of thing," Altmüller told him.

Frau Jüttner was surprised to see Freeland again so soon and assured him a dozen times over that she would come and fetch him the moment his friend in Wiesbaden telephoned. Freeland told her he wanted to make a private call to his office, then gestured towards the kitchen and slipped her a ten-Deutschmark note. Herr Jüttner had only just got home from work and was understandably reluctant to leave his comfortable armchair by the stove, but money was always a convincing argument.

Freeland waited until both Jüttners had left the room before he called the operator and asked her to connect him with Cologne 6132. The time was eight minutes after six and he was surprised to find that Matthews was still in the office.

"Is Anthea with you?" he asked.

"She put you through."

He wondered if Frank Matthews was trying to warn him that she would be listening to their conversation on the party line, but it no longer mattered. He wanted to take Hausser alive and he couldn't do that on his own.

"You've been causing a lot of heartburn, Harry," Matthews continued. "Head Office has got a bad case of indigestion and now Headquarters Münster Garrison wants to know what an official from the Foreign Office was doing questioning one of the dependents without first informing them."

Susan King had obviously told her husband and he had dutifully passed it on to a higher authority.

"I need your help," Freeland said, cutting him short. "Hausser has broken cover and I'm expecting him at any moment."

"You're with Anna Grothmann?"

It was either a shrewd guess or else King had informed all and sundry that the Foreign Office official had been looking for his part-time housemaid.

"I'm at 64 Lippstädter Strasse."

"Right, I'll get in touch with the police straight away."

"Keep the MPs out of it, Frank, I don't want them clumping all over the place in their hobnailed boots."

"Who said I was going to telephone the Provost Marshal?"

It was the kind of thing Anthea would suggest on the scratch pad she had probably stuck under his nose. Getting the Military Police to arrest him would be a neat way of keeping things in the family.

"You've got it all wrong, Harry . . ."

"Hear me out," Freeland said tersely. "This is a job for the Kriminalpolizei and I want them to provide unmarked cars at either end of Lippstädter Strasse. Two armed plainclothes officers should then join me inside the house to arrest Hausser, alias Doktor Ernst Winkler, the moment he steps across the threshold."

"What makes you think the Germans will take any notice of me?" Matthews asked.

"I don't. Get Innes Dalwood to talk to the Police President of Rhineland Westphalia."

"Suppose Hausser doesn't put in an appearance?"

Freeland smiled. Anthea Clowes had tired of being the silent eavesdropper and had voiced the question that had been nagging at her since he had mentioned the ex-Sturmbannführer.

"I'll still be here at this address," he told her. "You can pick me up whenever you like after midnight. Now, just do as I ask because time's running out."

Freeland hung up, called to Frau Jüttner to let her know that he'd finished his private call, and let himself out of the flat.

*   *   *

Hausser tucked the Opel Kapitan into a vacant space on the parking lot adjoining the Friedrich Ehart Platz, tripped all the interior catches bar one, then got out of the car and locked the offside front door. Across the way, the Globe Kino belonging to the British Army was showing *High Noon,* starring Gary Cooper and Grace Kelly. From the box office in the entrance a queue stretched round the corner almost as far as the railway bridge over the Albersloher Weg. The soldiers were mostly eighteen-year-olds, callow-looking youths in ill-fitting battledress made from coarse serge which some of them had shaved with a razor to make the creases in the sleeves of the blouse and down the front of the slacks that much sharper when pressed with a hot iron on brown paper.

Several obviously didn't give a damn about their appearance and shuffled forward, hands in pockets, beret tucked under one of the epaulettes on the blouse, the inevitable cigarette clinging to the lower lip. Decadent weaklings, unfit to bear arms, the kind of trash the SS Leibstandarte in their heyday would have swept aside with contemptuous ease. It sickened him to observe how many German girls were consorting with this rabble that called itself an army. Perversely, he felt disappointed when a Red Cap pounced on one of the worst offenders and hauled him out of the queue.

Hausser walked on down Albersloher Weg towards the Halle Münsterland. A freight train drawn by a Pacific Class locomotive thundered over the bridge above his head, the might of Germany on the move again, steel plate from Krupp of Essen destined for the Blohm and Voss shipyards of Hamburg. One day, with his help, Germany would be reunited under the Communists and that old fool Konrad Adenauer would be sent packing; then, when the new-born army was strong enough, they would turn on Walter Ulbricht and his fellow-travellers whom Moscow had installed. For that to happen, he had first to deal with Anna Grothmann.

Heels clacking on the cobblestones, he marched on, his right hand closed round the Walther 7.65mm PPK in the pocket of his leather trenchcoat. Approaching the bomb site where the gas works had been, he could just make out the shape of a DKW.

*　　　*　　　*

"Herr Northover." Frau Jüttner banged on the door of Anna Grothmann's flat and raised her voice. "Telephone for you."

"Coming." Freeland tucked the Walther P38 into the waistband of his slacks and buttoned his jacket. "You know what to do," he said, looking at Altmüller.

"Don't worry about us, we're fussy about the company we keep. Isn't that so, Frau Grothmann?"

Freeland opened the door and stepped out into the hall. Frau Jüttner positively beamed at him and pointed to her flat as though he'd never been there.

"Your friend from Wiesbaden," she said before he had a chance to pick up the phone.

Johansen did not sound best pleased. He said, "That was some wild goose chase you started, Harry."

"You didn't find Grothmann?"

"Damn right we didn't."

Grothmann couldn't have got it wrong. Unless . . . unless . . . unless the letter he had written to his wife had been a ruse to cover his tracks.

"Are you sure no one by the name of Winkler is living at 8 Schiller Platz?"

"No, there is a Doktor and Frau Ernst Winkler living at that address and they have a maid called Erika but I'm telling you the police searched the house from top to bottom and there was neither sight nor sign of Grothmann."

"What does this Winkler do for a living?"

"He has an office in Pullach." Johansen found it impossible

to disguise his embarrassment even though his voice was barely audible.

"You mean he's with the Gehlen Bureau?"

"This isn't a secure line, Harry . . ."

"Fuck security," Freeland exploded, "we're talking about a man's life, for Christ's sake."

"Hey, take it easy, fella . . ."

"I'm trying to . . ."

"Losing your temper won't solve anything."

Freeland took a deep breath, counted slowly up to ten. "You are absolutely right."

"I'm glad you see it my way."

"What did Ernst Winkler have to say for himself?"

"He wasn't at home."

"So where did Frau Winkler say he was?"

"That's classified information, Harry."

Freeland gritted his teeth in a supreme effort to curb his anger which was bubbling to the surface again. "Could you describe him? I mean, you must have seen his photograph somewhere in the house."

"I wasn't there, Harry. G2 Intelligence at V Corps Headquarters sent a Liaison Officer but the search was actually conducted by the security boys from the Gehlen Bureau."

"Dear God."

"What do you mean by that?"

"Do me a favour, Steve. Get one of your Counter-Intelligence Corps guys to call at the house again and obtain a photograph of the Doktor. Tell him to give you a verbal description over the phone, then if it matches the one I gave you, pick up the whole damn menagerie including the maid." He paused, then added, "Will you do that?"

"No promises," said Johansen, "but I'll see what I can do."

Freeland thanked him and replaced the receiver. Right on cue, Frau Jüttner reappeared from the kitchen to ask him if everything was all right and collect another ten-Mark note for her trouble. Still chattering brightly, she opened the door for him. There was, he thought, something very familiar about the man in the leather trenchcoat whose back was towards him. Then the German turned about and he saw it was Hausser.

"Good evening, Major Freeland," Hausser said and creased his mouth as if to smile.

Freeland saw his right hand start to come out of the trenchcoat pocket and instinctively sidestepped to his left, using the wall to shield himself as he unbuttoned his jacket to get at the Walther. In the confined space of the hall, the small automatic Hausser was holding sounded like a cannon. The bullet struck the door jamb, chipped a splinter from the woodwork and sent it lancing into Freeland's right eye. There was a momentary numbness before the pain hit him and every gutter word he'd ever heard spilled out, triggered by a combination of shock and anger. Beside him, Frau Jüttner stood rooted to the spot, her mouth wide open, giving voice to a high-pitched scream.

Freeland thumbed the safety to fire, transferred the pistol to his left hand and pointing it vaguely in the right direction, squeezed off a round. Then he changed position to the right side of the door, bundling Frau Jüttner ahead of him to take her out of the line of fire.

Although presented with a fleeting target, there had been no response from Hausser. From where he was now standing, Freeland could see only the rear part of the hall from the staircase to a point just short of the door to Anna Grothmann's two-room apartment. There was no sign of the former Sturmbannführer and all he could hear was the clamour of voices on the landing above. He came round the door fast because there was no other way of doing it. If Hausser was still inside the building, he would be watching the doors on both sides of the hall and speed of movement was the one chance Freeland had of surprising him.

Nothing happened. The front door was wide open, so was the gate. Then there was the sound of two shots somewhere outside on the street and the noise made by a vehicle as it crashed into an immovable object. Yelling to Altmüller to stay put, Freeland ran out of the house.

Hausser was on the opposite side of the road, doubling back towards the railway tracks. He had been heading towards Albersloher Weg when the Military Police jeep had turned into Lippstädter Strasse. No one had sent for the MPs, but Hausser was not to know that. They appeared to be bearing down on him and he had reacted accordingly. The jeep had mounted the pavement and rammed into a lamp post opposite number 64 which, except for a four foot stump, was now some thirty degrees out of true. The driver was slumped over the wheel; not so his companion who sat bolt upright staring straight ahead as though mesmerised by the two bullet holes in the windscreen.

Freeland reached the front gate, yelled after Hausser to stop where he was and saw the muzzle flash of the automatic as the German halted just long enough to swing round in his direction

229

and get off a snap shot. The bullet passed high and to his right, clipped the tenement building somewhere between the first and second floors, and ricochetted into the night. Farther up the street, a kerb-crawling motorist in a Volkswagen saw a gunman closing on him in his rear-view mirror and took off like a rocket with the blonde hooker, whom he'd stopped to pick up, still half in, half out of the car. The nearside door swung to, crushing her left leg; a few seconds later, it swung back again and she fell head first into the road as though the driver had shoved her out.

Freeland ran on; he had seen too many people die to know there was nothing he could do for her. It was also a fact that Hausser was a good twenty yards ahead of him and was stretching the gap with every stride. Blind in one eye and half crazy with pain, the only thing which kept him going was his hatred for this man who had made him betray God knows how many people in the French Resistance.

Hausser reached the bend in the road directly behind the Halle Münsterland and made for the railway embankment. Freeland went after him into the lunar landscape of the bomb site, scrambled over the grass-covered mounds of bricks and fought his way through the tangle of brambles. On the embankment above, an eight-car passenger train headed south towards Dortmund. As the red light on the last coach disappeared into the distance, he heard the crack of gunfire; glancing back over his left shoulder, he saw that Altmüller had joined him. He thought Gunther was at least fifty yards behind Hausser which should have meant that his chances of hitting the former Sturmbannführer were about zero. But sometimes the million to one fluke comes off and Hausser had just reached the top of the embankment and was silhouetted against the night sky when the 9mm smashed into his left shoulder to spin him round like a top. The impact also knocked him off balance and stumbling forward, he went down flat.

Freeland got to the foot of the embankment and started climbing. His face and hands had been lacerated by the brambles but he was unaware that he was bleeding from half a dozen scratches. He was only a few feet away from his quarry now and he meant to take him alive, provided Gunther didn't kill him first.

"Cease firing," he roared. "Cease firing, he's mine."

But Hausser was up and moving again, weaving unsteadily across the railway tracks like a man who'd had several drinks too many. Freeland could hear a train hurtling towards Münster Hauptbahnhof on the fast up-line and attempted to cross the tracks before it arrived. In his haste, he tripped over one of the rails and

230

fell on the ballast. By the time he'd picked himself up, the express was only a few yards off and he was forced to stand back while it thundered past.

One, two, three, four: he counted off the cars, buffeted by the turbulence as they flashed by. How many were there, for Christ sake? Hausser was the other side of the train and he was going to lose him thanks to the Bundesbahn. Night blindness; he closed his one good eye against the glare of light from the compartments, then realised he had left it too late and opened it again.

The turbulence ceased with the eighth and last coach and there was Hausser making his way towards the marshalling yards south of the Bahnhof. Another train: this time a freight leaving the yards to head north. The bloody place was almost as bad as Clapham Junction in the rush hour. Worse still, Hausser had seen the train and had made sure he was the right side of it. Or had he?

The 4-6-2 German Pacific Class 01 locomotive clattered across the points and suddenly changed direction to head straight for Hausser. It wasn't doing much above ten miles an hour but the engine weighed in excess of a hundred and forty tons and Hausser didn't have time to get out of the way. Either the driver or the fireman saw him at the last moment and did what they could but what was left of the former Sturmbannführer was under the seventh freight car when the train finally ground to a halt. In the unnatural silence which followed, Freeland could hear the blee-bah of a police siren in the distance.

"You're too late," he shouted, "you're too bloody late."

1954

QUEBEC,
NEW YORK,
CAMDEN, MAINE.

Wednesday 25 August

to

Friday 27 August

21

The apartment Freeland had rented was on the corner of the Avenue Bougainville and the Boulevard St Cyrille Ouest in downtown Quebec. The upper half of the two-storey house was conveniently situated as it was just over a mile on foot from his office at the Militia Barracks in the Parc Des Champs De Bataille. In winter, however, when he sometimes drove to work, it was nearer two miles thanks to the number of one-way streets. Like all the neighbouring properties in the street, the house was noted for its Dutch-style roof and external spiral staircase. There was no garage, and the back yard wasn't much larger than a nine-by-twelve carpet, but summer visitors to the city found the Avenue Bougainville picturesque and cute. Freeland certainly didn't find it cute in winter when his Chevrolet was buried under two feet of snow and negotiating the icy steps of the spiral staircase was a distinctly hazardous business.

On this particular summer evening however, the only cold front he expected was likely to arrive with Tom Egan. Acland hadn't forgiven him for the damage he had supposedly done to Anglo-American relations arising from the Hausser affair and Egan was His Master's Voice in most things. There was no telling when Egan would turn up. He had said to expect him at six and he was already half an hour late. Twice in the last five minutes the noise of a vehicle slowly cruising down the avenue had enticed Freeland to the window and he wasn't about to be drawn a third time. He switched on the television, adjusted the volume, then sat back to watch *I Love Lucy*. The credits were still rolling when he heard a car stop outside the house, followed some moments later by the sound of footsteps on the iron staircase. Killing the programme, Freeland went to the front door before his visitor could ring the bell.

Egan hadn't changed since they'd last met in December 1952 and appeared to be wearing the same double-breasted dark blue pinstripe even though the temperature was touching eighty-two

Fahrenheit. He was carrying a leather briefcase which looked brand new.

"Sorry I'm late, Harry," Egan said and smiled apologetically. "I hadn't allowed for the road works in the city centre and made the mistake of checking into my hotel first."

"Where are you staying?"

"The Château Frontenac."

Well, where else? Freeland thought. If the copper-roofed hotel overlooking the St Lawrence was good enough for Churchill at the time of the Quebec Conference in 1943, it was good enough for Egan eleven years on.

"Come on through," Freeland said, and led him into the living-room. "Can I get you a drink, Tom? Gin, whisky, beer?"

"Whisky with a little soda, please. Where are Jenny and the children?"

"Holidaying in Camden, Maine, with the Landers," Freeland told him. "I took the family down there last weekend."

Route 173 to the US border, then 201 as far as Augusta before heading cross-country on 105 to Camden. A round trip of five hundred miles which would have seemed twice as far in England.

"Lander?" Egan frowned, then snapped his fingers. "The American you met in China."

"I didn't tell you about him, you must have read the HAR-VESTER file." Freeland poured two whiskies, added a splash of soda to each and handed Egan one of the tumblers. "Anyway, we've stayed in touch ever since and I've seen quite a lot of him since you people sent me to Canada."

"Talking of China, there's something I'd like you to see." Egan placed his drink on an occasional table, opened his leather briefcase and took out a batch of glossy photographs. "Recognise this chap?"

The Chinese was wearing a pair of khaki shorts, a bloodstained singlet and a pair of sandals made from an old tyre from a truck. He was lying flat on his back, teeth bared, lips stretched in a caricature of a smile.

"He looks vaguely familiar," Freeland said.

"So he should, Harry. His name was Lau Kai Wu; he used to be Chiang Kai-shek's Assistant Military Attaché in London. You met him on a number of occasions between October '48 and March '49."

"Half a dozen times to be precise. I was working for Guy Salusbury and we were passing the Nationalists transcripts of various radio intercepts between Moscow and Peking. Even though we were acting on instructions from the D-G, we had to be very discreet because the information wasn't really ours to give away. It had been collected by the Government Communications and Cipher School."

"Quite."

Freeland glanced at the other photographs. Taken at different angles, they showed Lau Kai Wu lying inside a shack built from empty tins of kerosene and old packing crates.

"Any idea who killed him?" he asked.

"The Communists in all probability. The Hong Kong Police believe he was running some kind of cross-border operation and Peking decided to make an example of him. Lau Kai Wu wasn't hard to find; he was living amongst a lot of other Nationalist refugees in a shanty town above Happy Valley, practically opposite Tiger Balm Garden. Perhaps you know the place?"

Freeland nodded. The Tiger Balm Garden was an exotic folly of garish pagodas and brightly-coloured stone dragons. It had been built in the late 1930s by Aw Boon Haw who had marketed a patent medicine called Tiger Balm which had made him a millionaire. The medicine was a cure-all for the common cold, headaches, rheumatism, gout, scorpion bites, toothache and most other ailments. Apart from the brand name, it had nothing whatever to do with the tiger.

"As a gesture of defiance, Lau Kai Wu used to fly the Nationalist flag from a large bamboo pole that had been stolen from a building site."

"Really?"

"The police found a metal box in a hidey-hole under his bed," Egan continued. "He kept all his papers in it, official as well as personal. There were also transcripts in Mandarin of all the radio intercepts he got from us. Pinned to them was a note dated the eighteenth of April 1949 naming you as a Communist spy."

"Well, now we know where Colonel Li got his information from."

"Did you tell Lau Kai Wu you were going to Shanghai?"

"More or less. We talked about Howard Teale a good deal of the time because we were hoping that Wu would get his people to persuade him to leave Shanghai as a *quid pro quo* for all the stuff he was receiving from us. I recall telling him that if the worst came to the worst, I might have to go out there and bring Teale home whether he liked it or not."

"What gave him the idea that you were a Communist spy?"

237

"Search me. Maybe he thought the Intelligence produced by our radio intercept stations was deliberately misleading."

"And was it?"

"I didn't think so before I went to Shanghai; afterwards I came to the conclusion that the Russians had been feeding us a load of rubbish. Alternatively, Lau Kai Wu might have been told by Shanghai that Teale was a Communist and, *ipso facto*, I had to be one too." Freeland drank some of his whisky, then put the glass down again. "Is this why you wanted to see me?" he asked. "To talk about a dead Chinaman I knew briefly in London six years ago?"

"No, that was just the *hors-d'œuvre*." Egan gathered the photographs together and slipped them back into his briefcase. "You're leaving for New York tonight."

"You're joking."

"I couldn't be more serious. Guy Salusbury is about to pull a top-ranking defector and you are going to watch his back from the shadows."

"You mean I am to be his bodyguard?"

Egan nodded happily. "A very discreet one. Guy shouldn't even be aware of your presence."

"I may not be aware of his," Freeland said grimly. "The surgeons did the best they could for me but I'm still practically blind in one eye."

"Nevertheless, you're the best man for the job."

"What's the name of this Russian? I presume the defector is a Russian?"

"He is. Do you remember when Petrov defected?"

Who didn't? – it had been front page news. Vladimir Petrov had been a Third Secretary at the Soviet Embassy in Canberra when he'd suddenly defected back in April after being informed that he was being recalled to Moscow. His wife, Yevdokia, had decided to go back without him and she had appeared in all the newspapers flanked by a couple of KGB heavies who'd practically frogmarched her on to the plane at Sydney. She had looked so anguished that none of the reporters could believe that she was returning voluntarily, but Yevdokia had maintained she was until the stop-over in Darwin when she had suddenly asked for political asylum.

"Vladimir Petrov was one of Lavrenti Beria's protégés," Egan said. "He didn't want to go back to Moscow because he thought he was going to be executed."

Stalin was dead but it seemed things remained pretty much the

238

same under Malenkov, Bulganin and Khrushchev. The NKVD was now calling itself the KGB but it was still the same killing machine.

"Our defector in New York is a member of the Soviet delegation to the United Nations. He thinks Petrov may have compromised him, which is why he's coming across."

"Do the Americans know about this?"

"They will in good time," Egan said cheerfully.

"They'd better, because they won't take kindly to us playing games on their turf."

"Well, it goes without saying that you will need to keep a low profile, Harry."

It was Egan's way of informing him that the CIA had neither forgotten nor forgiven him yet. When the Counter-Intelligence Corps people had arrived at 8 Schiller Platz with their tame German policeman, the house had been in total darkness. No one had answered the doorbell and the garage had been empty. With considerable reluctance, the Kripo had gone round the back, broken into the house and opened the front door to the Americans. There had been no sign of Elisabeth Hausser or her live-in maid but the open wardrobes and chests of drawers had provided silent testimony to her hasty departure. The house had not been completely deserted however; after looking around for some considerable time, they had eventually found the body of Karl Heinz Grothmann buried under a huge pile of coke in the cellar.

Grothmann had been given a massive overdose of morphine. Had Gehlen's people found him when they'd called at the house earlier on in the evening, there was a chance that he might have been saved. But what had really pissed everyone off was the fact that Hausser had ended up under a freight train. With Hausser dead, the CIA had no way of knowing how much disinformation they had been fed and they couldn't forgive Freeland for denying them the opportunity to interrogate the former Sturmbannführer.

"This should take care of your expenses," Egan said, handing over a brown envelope. "Fifteen hundred US dollars in used notes of varying denominations. Careful how you spend it."

"Have you got any other surprises in that briefcase of yours?"

It transpired that he had several, one being a Canadian passport in the name of Harry McIver complete with a photograph of Freeland. It was followed by a New York City driver's licence in the same name, a used billfold that had been purchased from Saks sometime in the dim, distant past, and a dog-eared social security card.

"Someone's been busy," Freeland said drily.

"We can get a move on when we have to." Egan produced one further item from his briefcase, a .38 Police Positive with a three-inch barrel. "You may need this if things get a little hectic."

The serial number on the side of the frame had been removed. The FBI claimed that it was impossible to obliterate every trace and that their scientists could identify the original number from the most minute indentations. But whoever had doctored this revolver had done more than use a grindstone on the frame and they wouldn't find a damned thing.

"Does this firearm have a record?" Freeland asked. "Has it ever been used against a live target?"

"Of course it hasn't."

"I hope you're right because I wouldn't be at all happy if ballistics were able to match it."

"Nor would we, Harry."

"Okay, what do I do for ammunition?"

In answer to his question, twelve loose rounds appeared in a child's sweetie bag.

"Magic," said Freeland. "All you need is a wand."

Egan didn't smile. "Let's save the humour till later," he said.

"That sounds ominous."

It was. The briefing which followed reminded Freeland of the one he had received from SOE before he was sent into Chartres.

*   *   *

Matthews disliked few people on first acquaintance but Guy Salusbury was rapidly becoming one of the few exceptions. His innate air of superiority and the condescending way he had treated him grated on Matthews like a hacksaw cutting through a steel pipe. His charm, thoughtfulness and hospitality, which Acland had enthused about, were obviously reserved for those whom he considered were his social equals or were in a position to do him some good.

It soured Matthews to admit that, at forty-nine, Salusbury looked at least ten years younger. An inch under six feet, he had weighed eleven stone eight pounds at the time of his last physical and obviously hadn't put on an ounce since then. Furthermore, his dark hair showed no sign of receding and there were no worry lines on his forehead or anywhere else for that matter. To cap it all, nature had endowed him with the kind of face that had people reaching for such phrases as distinguished, handsome, well bred and dignified.

Although Salusbury was listed as the passport control officer at the British Consulate in New York, members of the public never came into contact with him. Most evenings he left the office promptly at five thirty for the timber-frame house his wife had bought in New Canaan, the most exclusive suburb in Connecticut's Fairfield County. Thanks to Matthews, this evening was one of those occasions when Salusbury would not be wending his way homewards with the other commuters. Irritated by the knowledge that he was going to be late home, Salusbury didn't want to hear the latest news about Neville Acland, Tom Egan or anyone else in V Section.

"London gave me to understand I was to receive a special briefing from you, Mr Matthews," he said coldly.

"Yes. It concerns a Mikhail Orlenko. Perhaps you've heard of him?"

Salusbury frowned. "The only Mikhail Orlenko I know is one of the interpreters for the Soviet Ambassador to the United Nations."

"We're talking about the same man. According to Petrov, he was the chief interrogator at 129 Special Punishment Camp in 1945. Joachim Hausser was one of the SS prisoners he questioned and subsequently recruited into the NKVD. Of course, this was before the Sturmbannführer became Doktor Ernst Winkler and went to work for the Gehlen Bureau."

"He must have been one of the few people to have mourned the death of that poisonous bastard. I know I opened a bottle of champagne the night I learned that Hausser had ended up under a freight train."

"Had I been you, I think I would have done the same," Matthews said quietly.

"Smiling Death – that's what the other SS officers at Gestapo Headquarters in the Rue des Saussaies used to call him behind his back. He knew more ways of torturing a prisoner than ever the Spanish Inquisition devised. He kept me trussed up like a chicken for seven long days and nights; I was crying like a baby when they finally took the ropes off me, couldn't move a muscle."

"But he never broke you."

"No, I managed to convince Hausser that I was related to the Cecils; it's a good job he didn't think to look me up in *Burke's Peerage*." Salusbury smiled briefly. "Still, that isn't the reason you brought up the subject of Mikhail Orlenko, is it?"

"No. We've reason to believe he wants to defect."

"Who says so?"

"Petrov; at least, that's what he gave the Australians to under-stand. The KGB is being purged of its Beria faction and Orlenko thinks he could be a candidate for the firing squad."

"So what's holding him back? All he has to do is walk into the nearest Precinct House and ask for police protection."

"He wants to come over to us," Matthews said.

"Orlenko must be crazy, the Americans would pay him a small fortune."

"According to Petrov, he doesn't trust the CIA. So it has to be us or no one. Furthermore, you will have to make the initial approach."

"I'm to do what?" Salusbury stared at him as though he had taken leave of his senses.

"Without the Americans getting wind of it," Matthews finished.

"Now I know Acland has gone potty."

"The D-G has given it his blessing."

"Perhaps he would also care to advise me how I should make the initial approach?"

It was the opening Matthews had been waiting for and he made the most of it. Salusbury's bailiwick was the UN and he had cultivated a number of valuable sources among the delegates representing the Third World and non-aligned countries. The best Intelligence on the Soviets was provided by a Yugoslav code-named 'Chetnik'. In looking for an intermediary, London considered he was the obvious choice.

" 'Chetnik' will be finished as a source if I use him in the way you suggest." Salusbury took a cigarette from the silver box on his desk and lit it. "I presume London has taken that into account?"

"They have, and they are prepared to sacrifice him."

"Does that also apply to me, Mr Matthews?"

"No, sir, you're far too valuable."

Salusbury had made his name in New York. Any question marks about the way he had handled the Teale affair had been more than erased by his subsequent performance in the States. Rumour had it that when he was relieved in post in January 1955, Salusbury would be moved up a couple of grades to head the Intelligence Co-ordinating Committee. Such a move would put him among the contenders for the D-G's chair when the present incumbent retired.

"We don't anticipate the initial approach will provoke a hostile reaction from the KGB," Matthews continued. "The situation could however become very violent should Orlenko decide to take us up on our offer. That's why it's Freeland's job to give you close protection."

"You mean Harry will be watching my back?"

"Do you have some objection?"

"Good heavens, no," Salusbury said quickly. "I know Harry has been under a bit of a cloud lately but I'd trust him with my life."

"You may have to. Eliminating Orlenko is unlikely to be the sole aim of the KGB; they may try to create a major diplomatic incident by taking you out as well. The Yanks wouldn't take kindly to the idea that British Intelligence is waging a private war in their back yard."

"I should think there would be a bloody great explosion." Salusbury leaned forward and stubbed out his half-smoked cigarette in a silver ashtray. "Where's Harry now?"

"Still in Quebec; he'll drive down overnight and will contact you sometime tomorrow. He'll be very discreet."

"And you can be damned sure I will."

"Yes, sir."

Matthews realised this was the second time in as many minutes that he had metaphorically touched his forelock to Salusbury. One might dislike the man on sight but there was an aura about him which would make a lot of people feel inferior and Matthews could understand how he had been able eventually to impose his will on Hausser.

"What am I allowed to offer him, Mr Matthews?"

"Who? Orlenko?"

"How many other defectors are there?"

Matthews flushed. He had allowed himself to be caught out and the bloody man had squashed him again.

"You can go up to a hundred thousand pounds without reference to London. If he asks for a larger sum, you will have to get the D-G to okay it. He can live in whatever country he likes provided it is within the Commonwealth and you can also throw in a detached four-bedroom house."

"What about Mrs Orlenko? Will she want to come across?"

"Petrov says it's a marriage of convenience and Orlenko will be happy to dump her."

"That will simplify matters. Is there anything else you want to tell me?"

"No, we've covered just about everything."

"Good." Salusbury emptied the contents of his ashtray into the wastepaper basket, then checked to make sure he had thrown the tumblers on the combination safe behind his desk. "Where are you staying?"

"The Berkshire. I fly home tomorrow, first thing in the morning."

"Can I give you a lift?"

"That's very kind of you."

Outside on Third Avenue, Salusbury flagged down a passing cab and told the driver to take him first to the Berkshire on Madison and 52nd Street, then on to Grand Central. Apart from wishing Matthews a pleasant journey when he dropped him off, Salusbury didn't say another word to him.

*   *   *

He had called himself Max Reissenburg because most people couldn't get their tongues around the family name of Zygmunt Szczesliwicka. He was sixty-two years old and had arrived in America with his parents, his younger brother and two older sisters in 1910 from Lvov in Poland where he had spent the first twelve years of his life in the Jewish ghetto. His father had been a cobbler and the whole family of six had lived in two rooms above a poky little shop on Manhattan's Lower East Side where the head of the household had found employment for the princely sum of two dollars a week.

His formal education had ceased the day the family had left the ghetto and if he hadn't learned to use his fists to make a living, Max Reissenburg would never have amounted to anything more than a glorified errand boy. In later life he was to say that he would never have become a fully-fledged citizen of the United States but for the First World War. Max had had no quarrel with the Kaiser, nor had he understood why Woodrow Wilson had declared war on Germany. But the US Government had offered instant citizenship to anyone who enlisted in the armed forces, and joining the army had seemed a good idea at the time. Sixteen months later and after he had been through the slogging match of the Argonne with the 77th (New York National Army) Division, he hadn't been quite so sure.

Max Reissenburg might not have been the greatest lightweight to duck through the ropes but he had been a fighter with heart and getting him a bout had never been a problem for his manager. He would probably have ended up as a punchdrunk old pro if it hadn't been for Esther Rabin. They had met on Central Park South near Columbus Circle one spring morning in 1923 when Esther had been distributing leaflets to anyone within arm's reach. He had

244

never heard of Nicola Sacco and Bartolomeo Vanzetti, the two anarchists who had been condemned to death for murder and armed robbery on the flimsiest of circumstantial evidence. But a couple of bully boys had and they had taken exception to the political tract she had pressed on them. Under the benevolent gaze of one of New York's finest, they had manhandled Esther, then invited her to eat the leaflets. Max had stepped in, flattened both assailants with combination punches to the head and body and had promptly been arrested with Esther by the patrolman.

As soon as the desk-sergeant at the 18th Precinct heard her speak, he'd known the patrolman had made a big mistake. Esther Rabin was a nice, middle-class Jewish girl and nice middle-class Jewish girls had fathers who could afford to hire a smart-assed attorney. Their lawyer had arrived roughly an hour after they had been arrested; he had actually been retained to represent Esther but she had refused to leave without Max. Eight months later they had married despite strong opposition from her parents who had not considered Max a suitable husband for their only daughter.

Thanks to Esther, he had left the Lower East Side for a brownstone on East 147 Street near St Mary's Park. He had also quit the ring and, under the tuition of his father-in-law, had become a moderately successful businessman to the point where he had owned two liquor stores, a delicatessen and a newsvendor's. He had also become a father, Esther presenting him with a boy and a girl.

In 1944, after twenty years of marriage, Esther had suddenly died from a cerebral haemorrhage and the bottom had dropped out of his world. Not long afterwards, both children had left home, his son eventually settling on the West Coast, his daughter moving to Chicago with her doctor husband. Although the neighbourhood was no longer what it used to be, he still lived in the same old brownstone and though he had sold both liquor stores and the delicatessen, he had held on to the newsvendor's near United Nations Plaza. He said it gave him something to do, and every morning he caught the first subway from Third Avenue and 149 Street and did not return much before seven p.m.

That particular evening, he was enjoying a well-earned rest in front of the TV when the telephone rang. Muttering to himself, he shuffled out into the hall and lifted the receiver.

The Englishman said, "When our mutual friend collects his *New*

York Times tomorrow morning, tell him to call me at nine thirty. He knows the number."

"Okay." Max cleared his throat noisily. "Anything else?"

"Yes, you can say it looks as though a thunderstorm is on the horizon."

22

Freeland lowered the window to its fullest extent and leaned against the door to catch the slipstream. At ten after seven, the temperature was already in the low sixties and the air was no longer as fresh as it had been during the small hours of the night when its cooling draught had kept him awake on the long drive south. He had left Quebec at eight fifty-five p.m.; now, some ten hours later, he was approaching the Triboro Bridge. He had crossed the border below Stanstead on Route 55, then driven south on 91 through Hanover, Brattleboro and Hartford until it merged with Interstate 95.

Shortly after crossing the border, Freeland had pulled off the road to retrieve the .38 Police Positive and the child's sweetie bag containing twelve rounds which he had concealed under the bench seat of the Chevrolet. No Canadian or US Customs officer had ever asked him to open his suitcase, but there was always a first time and he didn't believe in taking unnecessary chances. He had transferred the revolver to the suitcase, tucking it under a spare pair of slacks and a layer of clean shirts.

The .38 was an embarrassment and he had been tempted to ditch it. Harry McIver was a fake Canadian passport, a New York City driver's licence and a dog-eared social security card, none of which would hold good if there was a major foul-up. London would deny all knowledge of him and Ottawa would be anxious to prove that Harry McIver was not working for them. However, remembering what Egan had told him, he had decided to hang on to the revolver if only for his own protection. He had debated whether or not to load the .38 with six rounds and had come to the conclusion that keeping the ammunition separate from the weapon was unlikely to lessen the offence if the police found it.

He had stopped twice to fill up and had eaten a plate of ham and eggs at the first filling station which happened to have an all-night diner. He had thought of phoning Jenny but it was after midnight by then and he had been reluctant to disturb her.

Freeland crossed the Triboro Bridge, found himself in Harlem on West 125th Street and headed south on Eighth Avenue. Although the morning rush hour was still some time off, the traffic density was starting to build up. At the intersection with West 66th Street, he turned right and headed across town to West End Avenue, then drove south again.

The parking lot was sandwiched between a large book depository and a row of small shops comprising a hardware store, a druggist, a dry cleaners and a delicatessen. The uneven surface and the buttresses on either side were obvious signs that the buildings in between had been demolished. The steel mesh security fence and the wooden shack which served as an office looked impermanent; when the site value increased or some entrepreneur put enough money together to start building again, the parking lot would vanish. Meantime, a sign above the gates said, 'Hendrik's Long Term Parking – Open Twenty-four Hours A Day'. A tall, thin, black man emerged from the hut as Freeland drove into the lot and stopped immediately beyond the gates.

"Four bucks a day, twenty a week. How long you wanna stay heah, suh?" he asked in a thick Southern accent.

"A week," Freeland told him.

"Cash in advance."

"That's okay."

The black attendant nodded. "You wanna park yo automobile top of the lot left side and leave the keys in th'office?"

"Right."

Freeland found a vacant space for the Chevrolet, removed his suitcase and locked all the doors, then walked back to the shack. Apart from twenty dollars, all Hendrik's Long Term Parking wanted from him was his name, make of vehicle and licence number. The black attendant then gave him the duplicate copy of the invoice and hung the car keys on a board behind the counter.

Freeland walked outside, flagged down a yellow cab and told the driver to take him to the Kayser Hotel on West 42nd Street. The Kayser was Egan's choice and its general run-down appearance suggested that he had been concerned to save the Treasury money. The pile had worn off the wall-to-wall carpeting in the lobby, the woodwork looked in need of a lick of paint and the air-conditioning plant sounded as though it was about to expire.

The night desk clerk, who was still on duty, was a near-sighted, plump, ginger-haired man in his late twenties. He was wearing a blue shirt with short sleeves, a red, polka-dot bow tie and pale grey slacks held up by a snakeskin belt around his ample midriff. Freeland couldn't see what kind of shoes he was wearing, neither could the desk clerk.

"Do you have a single room with private bath?" Freeland asked.

The desk clerk glanced over his shoulder at the row of pigeon holes. "One on the eleventh floor back, corner room on the sixth. How long are you planning to stay in New York, Mr . . . ?"

"McIver. A week, perhaps longer, depending on how things work out. Is there a phone in the room?"

"Naturally. 1117 has a TV as well."

"1117 it is then."

"The room rate is seventeen fifty. Will you be paying by cheque or credit card?"

"Cash."

Freeland completed a registration card, took out his billfold and gave the clerk one hundred and twenty dollars. The change came slowly, so did the hall porter.

The eleventh floor room was furnished on simple lines – single divan, wardrobe, chest of drawers, small bedside locker, upright ladder-back chair, table and easy chair. The twelve-inch TV was on the table, the phone on the bedside locker. There was an ice-making machine and water cooler at the far end of the landing. When he drew the curtains which had been closed to keep the room cool, the window offered a peep view of the Hudson and the Weehawken Ferry at the bottom of 42nd Street.

Freeland unpacked, placed the empty suitcase inside the wardrobe and for want of somewhere better to leave it, tucked the .38 Police Positive under the pillow along with the dollybag of six spare rounds. Then he rang the operator, asked for long distance and called the Landers in Camden to let Jenny know where he was and when he might be seeing her and the children again. Before the day was much older, he would have to ring Guy Salusbury to arrange a meeting and he would need to rent a car from Hertz. But right now, he was too damn tired to keep his eyes open a minute longer.

Freeland kicked off his shoes and lay down on the bed. He slept fitfully and dreamed that Joe Lander and Avril, the girl he'd married on his return from China, were giving a barbecue in the grounds of their Inn. Jenny was there with Mark and fourteen-month-old Veronica who had been born in Quebec. So were Egan, Acland,

249

Frank Matthews, Guy and Caroline Salusbury, which he thought was strange because Joe had never met any of them. Nor had he been introduced to Gunther Altmüller, Sturmbannführer Hausser and Feldwebel Karl Heinz Grothmann but they were there too with Chantal Kiffer. Everyone was getting a little drunk and for some reason, Guy Salusbury suggested they should play Blind Man's Bluff and Chantal Kiffer volunteered to go first. And then, as Chantal was stumbling around the lawn with a blindfold over her eyes, Jenny suddenly appeared with a pump-action rifle and shot her in the head.

*   *   *

They met on the Staten Island Ferry. At nine twenty-five, Salusbury had walked into the RCA Building on Rockefeller Center and had made straight for the bank of pay-phones inside the entrance. Had the fourth kiosk from the left been occupied, he would simply have killed time until it was vacant and 'Chetnik' would have kept on ringing the number until he got through. As it happened, the booth had been free and 'Chetnik' had rung him promptly at nine thirty in accordance with the message he had received from Max Reissenburg.

Their conversation had been brief and to the point. Leaving the RCA Building, Salusbury had walked two blocks west to the 50th Street Station of the IRT Broadway-7th Avenue subway and had caught a local train to South Ferry. He had walked round Battery Park to give 'Chetnik' time to get to their rendezvous, and had then made his way to Whitehall Terminal. The Yugoslav had met him some eight minutes later and they had boarded the Staten Island Ferry. Although the rush hour had long since finished, there were still enough tourists visiting New York even this late in the season to provide them with the anonymity they needed.

'Chetnik' was thirty-two years old, short and stocky. He had dark brown hair, brown eyes and a face shaped like an inverted triangle that was at odds with his otherwise compact physique. His real name was Josip Cabrinovic; acquaintances called him Pauli.

Distancing himself from the other passengers, Salusbury found a space on the upper promenade above the car deck where no one would overhear their conversation. "Orlenko," he said quietly, "how well do you really know him, Pauli?"

"Better than any other interpreter in the pool."

"I hear he's getting itchy feet."

"Who told you that?"

"A friend of his in Canberra who decided to leave his present

250

firm and go to work for the Australians because he was out of favour with Head Office. He believes Head Office is planning to fire Orlenko."

"I don't think that's likely."

"Well, neither do I, Pauli, but London is convinced that your fellow-interpreter would like to join us. I've been authorised to offer him up to a hundred thousand pounds as an inducement but I daresay my superiors would double it if he really pushed them."

Pauli folded his arms and leaned against the rail, his gaze seemingly fixed on the Statue of Liberty as he contemplated what he had just been told.

"The Americans would pay him more," he said presently.

"True. However, Orlenko doesn't like their business methods."

"A lot of people don't."

"I'd like you to put our proposition to him, Pauli."

"When?"

"Today."

"Impossible."

"Think about it," Salusbury told him. "Nothing's impossible."

Pauli's indecisiveness was infuriating. On the other hand, it would take the ferry twenty-five minutes to cover the five miles to the port of St George on Staten Island and he could afford to be patient for a little while longer.

"Orlenko and I used to have a mutual acquaintance, Pauli."

"Oh? Who was that?"

"Joachim Hausser of the SS. I met him in 1944, over a year before Orlenko did. The Sturmbannführer was killed in December 1952, but I expect he already knows that."

It was difficult to tell if Pauli was even listening to him. The Yugoslav continued to lean against the rail, his entire interest apparently captured by the Circle Line pleasure boat steaming towards Liberty Island.

Salusbury kept his voice down. "He will also have heard of Mr Freeland, the man London has detailed to protect him from his former colleagues."

Pauli took out a pack of cigarettes, then made a great show of going through his pockets to find a box of matches, a charade which was intended to give himself time to think.

"This Englishman called Freeman . . ."

"Freeland, Harry Freeland. Tell Orlenko he's the one who put Hausser out of business. That should encourage him to make up his mind."

"We'll be finished, you and I, if I pass this message on."

"I don't like it either but London wants Orlenko and they are prepared to accept the consequences."

The ferry was no more than two hundred yards from the landing stage now and they would be docking in a few minutes. Time was running out and they were still deadlocked. Salusbury wished he could order the Yugoslav to do what he was told instead of having to rely on friendly persuasion.

"What consequences are your people talking about?" Pauli asked.

"The probable destruction of my network of informers, though I gather Acland refuses to believe it."

"Who's Acland?"

"The man at Head Office who is running this particular project."

"Am I allowed to mention his name to Orlenko?"

Salusbury nodded. "It may prod him into action if he knows who's in charge. One other point; since Mikhail Orlenko doesn't trust the Americans, we'll ensure that word of our little arrangement doesn't reach their ears."

Pauli tossed his cigarette overboard. "How should he get in touch with you?" he asked.

It was settled; they could walk off the boat and go their separate ways. Salusbury almost sighed aloud with relief.

"Through Uncle Max," he said. "Who else?"

*   *   *

Egan looked at the meter and winced. The Treasury would pay his air fare from Quebec to New York because he had the flight ticket to prove it; whether they would reimburse him for the taxi fare from La Guardia to Nassau Street was a different matter. Putting a brave face on it, he paid off the cab driver, walked into the Potter Building and took a lift up to the Zenith Technical Corporation on the fourth floor. A front organisation for the CIA, Zenith's activities were directed towards the UN. Like Guy Salusbury, they were in the business of gathering Intelligence from those Third World countries which received aid in one form or another from the Soviet Union.

Steve Johansen was the Executive Vice-President in charge of Market Research. As such, he had an office on the fourth floor and a personal secretary, one of whose tasks was to maintain the fake graphs displayed on the wall behind his desk. Egan had an appointment to see him at three thirty.

"It's good of you to see me at such short notice," Egan told him as they shook hands.

In fact, his appointment had been arranged through Allen Dulles, the Director of the CIA. Although Johansen therefore had no option but to see him, Egan was a firm believer in pouring oil on the waters before they became troubled.

"It's always a pleasure to do business with the British Secret Intelligence Service," Johansen said with equal conviction.

"Even if it means working with Harry Freeland?"

The smile slowly disappeared from Johansen's face. "He's here in New York?"

"Only temporarily. He's stationed in Quebec."

"Yeah? Doing what?"

"Analysing the data captured by the Canadian listening posts on the Distant Early Warning Line. It's not much of a job."

"Is that a polite way of saying that he's been put out to pasture, Mr Egan?"

"I suppose it is. Anyway, we're bringing him back into the fold now because his involvement with the late Joachim Hausser, alias Doktor Ernst Winkler, is known to a third party in the Soviet Delegation at the United Nations."

"A third party?" Johansen pursed his lips. "That's kind of coy, isn't it?"

"A purely legal expression. I'm not averse to disclosing his identity." ·

As succinctly as he could, Egan told him about the information Petrov had given the Australians and then outlined the leverage the SIS were hoping to exert on Mikhail Orlenko. In considerably more detail, he also explained the tenuous relationship between the Russian, Hausser, Salusbury and Freeland.

"You think Orlenko will defect?" Johansen asked.

"He may do if we can persuade the Federal Bureau of Investigation to stay out of it when the balloon goes up."

"It's that delicate?"

"Put it this way, Salusbury and Freeland don't know that I'm here in New York keeping an eye on things."

"Perhaps you'd better tell me what you have in mind?"

Egan did just that.

*　　*　　*

Freeland turned into Henry Thoreau Avenue and cruised slowly past the white timber-frame houses, each one separated from its neighbour by a sloping lawn planted with evergreen shrubs. A little over fifty miles from the city, New Canaan was the fashionable suburb for Manhattan's bankers, lawyers, investment brokers, advertising executives and businessmen. The surrounding area was noted for its general farming and livestock, its fir, spruce, maple and birch trees. Local colour was provided by the Silvermine Guild of artists who maintained a complex of studios, classrooms, galleries, a library and a photography laboratory. He suspected the Salusburys were venerated as the town's resident English aristocrats, though only Caroline Salusbury whose grandfather had been ennobled for political services to the Liberal Party by William Ewart Gladstone, could claim such a connection.

Freeland spotted the Salusbury's mailbox too late to make the turn; stamping on the brakes, he shifted into reverse and backed up into the driveway. The garage was wide open and empty, but the sprinkler was playing on the lawn and a child's bike was lying on the front path where Helen had abandoned it. Helen was nine, the youngest of their three children and very much an afterthought. She was also the only one living at home.

Salusbury met him at the door before he could ring the bell. If his smile appeared mechanical, there was no lack of warmth in his voice.

"It's good to see you again, Harry," he said. "Come on in."

"Thanks."

"How long is it since we last met?"

"Almost four and a half years," Freeland said, following him into a large sitting room on the left side of the hall.

"Never."

"'Fraid so. I know you were posted to New York in March 1950. That was just after the HARVESTER inquiry when I was sent on a German language course."

"My God, how time flies." Salusbury walked over to the drinks trolley. "Let's see now, whisky's your tipple, isn't it?"

"Please."

"Ice or soda?"

"Both."

Salusbury nodded, then said, "I'm sorry Caroline isn't here to meet you but she's a member of the New Canaan Literary Appreciation Society and they always meet on a Wednesday evening. You know how it is."

"Yes."

"Jenny and the family keeping well? What do you have now – a daughter as well as a son?"

Salusbury wanted to prove that out of sight was not out of mind.

254

Answers to his questions were unnecessary; all Freeland had to do was smile at the appropriate time.

"I was sorry to hear about your eye. Any chance the sight will eventually be restored?"

"No, but I'm not totally blind."

"I'm glad to hear it, Harry."

"And I can shoot pretty straight for someone who isn't naturally left-handed."

"Which brings us neatly to Mikhail Orlenko." Salusbury held his glass up to the light and inspected the slice of lemon in his gin and tonic as though it wasn't as fresh as it might have been. "Would you recognise our friend if you saw him?"

"Egan didn't have a photograph and he was unable to describe him very graphically either. I gathered he was relying on you to identify Orlenko."

"Did he happen to mention that London doesn't want the Yanks to know what is going on?"

"Yes."

"Did you ever hear anything like it?" Salusbury scowled. "This so-called defection has all the ingredients for a monumental cock-up and you and I will be left holding the shitty end of the stick. How long has V Section been in the Intelligence-gathering business for Christ sake? They're the official watchdogs and every last one of them is a has-been. I can't think what the D-G is playing at; no one in his right mind would allow that bunch of cretins to run an operation."

"Would you rather have someone else as a back-up?" Freeland asked.

"What?"

"I seem to be a jinx; a guy called Lander once said that people have a habit of dying around me."

"Rubbish. I can't think of anyone I'd sooner have in a tight corner."

Outside on the lawn, a little girl told Debbie she would see her in the morning, then the front door opened and daughter Helen wheeled her bicycle into the hall.

Salusbury said, "Come and say hello to Mr Freeland, darling."

Helen was all arms and legs, a gangling little girl with her mother's blonde hair and blue eyes. She had her father's instant smile which unfortunately showed the braces on her teeth. She shook hands with Freeland, said she was pleased to meet him, then asked her father if she could have some crackers and milk while she watched television in the den.

255

"I am afraid Helen is becoming very American," Salusbury observed after she had left them.

"Does it matter?"

"No. What does matter is pulling Orlenko and that has to be done quickly, otherwise he's likely to get cold feet and change his mind."

"You've already contacted him?"

"Let's say I've put out a feeler, Harry. I had a long talk with my Yugoslav this morning and spelled out our offer. He'll relay it to Orlenko."

"When do you expect to get a reaction?"

"Some time tomorrow or not at all. If Orlenko does decide to accept what's on the table, he'll come straight across."

Salusbury thought there would be no preliminary moves; the Russian would simply appear at a pre-arranged rendezvous and expect everything to go like clockwork. Within a matter of an hour or so, his absence would be reported to the KGB Resident who looked after the Soviet Delegation at the United Nations and steps would be taken either to recover Orlenko or to have him terminated. There was an additional complication; agents from the local FBI Field Office kept the Soviet Delegation under surveillance and at the first hint of any unusual activity, certain precautionary measures would be put into immediate effect. One such measure required all airlines to inform the FBI of any last minute bookings on flights departing from La Guardia and Idlewild.

"We shall have to drive Orlenko across the border into Canada before we can put him on a plane," Salusbury continued. "And those five hundred miles could be exceptionally hazardous. Make no mistake, diplomatic niceties don't mean a thing to the KGB. What their predecessors, the NKVD, did to Leon Trotsky in 1940, they can do to us fourteen years later."

In May 1940, twenty NKVD men armed with machine pistols had assaulted Trotsky's villa in Mexico, pouring more than two hundred rounds into his bedroom. Although miraculously he had come through the attack unscathed, his luck had run out three months later when Ramon Mercader, also known as Jacques Mornard, had stuck an ice pick into his brain.

"We shall have to outfox them, Harry – switch cars, that kind of thing." Salusbury twisted round in his chair to look at the driveway. "Matthews told me you were driving down from Quebec, but I see you hired a Ford from Hertz. What happened to your own car?"

"Nothing. I garaged the Chevrolet in New York, the one out front is a blind. Egan said I was to cover my tracks."

"Oh?"

"I'm also travelling on a Canadian passport under the name of Harry McIver."

"That's an unexpected bonus."

"I'm surprised Matthews didn't mention it when he briefed you," said Freeland.

Only the Brits had to produce their passports when crossing the border into Quebec Province. The Chevrolet was already registered in Canada; to complete the deception, Freeland had removed the GB plate from the rear fender before he reached the border. Unless he had the bad luck to run into an Immigration officer who remembered his face from when he'd taken Jenny and the children to stay with the Landers, he and Orlenko should sail through the checkpoint.

"I'll meet Orlenko at whatever RV he chooses and bring him to you." Salusbury got up, took Freeland's glass and fixed them both another drink. "Then I'll move off and draw the opposition away from you. What do you think?"

"Egan said I was to cover your back. I can't do that if I'm waiting at some switch point."

"My face is too well known to the opposition, Harry. If you're anywhere in the vicinity of the RV when Orlenko comes across, they'll make you."

"Two people start out in your car, suddenly there's only one. What makes you think the KGB will continue to follow you after we've made the switch?"

"I could tell Orlenko to get in the back and lie down on the floor."

"Suppose he comes over in broad daylight? People are going to think it's damned odd if they see a grown man crawl into a vehicle on his hands and knees, aren't they?"

"All right, Harry, what do you suggest we do?" The rasp in Salusbury's voice was a sign of his growing irritation.

"We use the subway to run a check," Freeland told him.

Instead of allowing Orlenko to choose the RV, Salusbury would instruct the Russian to walk out of the UN Secretariat Building and make his way to Grand Central where he would be waiting for him on the Lexington Avenue Line. Freeland would pick them up at the first free transfer station and then, having satisfied himself that Orlenko was not being followed, he would break off and head for the switch point. In order to give him time to get into position, Salusbury would continue to ride the subway for a further thirty minutes or so.

"Use a cab when you bring Orlenko to me, then you can leave the subway at whichever station you like."

"I could park my car somewhere else as a decoy," Salusbury murmured.

"Right."

"I like it, Harry."

"Good. You know the town better than I do so I'll leave the detailed planning to you."

"Well, I can't begin to do that until I know where you're staying." Salusbury paused, his eyes narrowing thoughtfully. "Why the frown, Harry?"

"No reason. I'm staying at the Kayser Hotel on West 42nd. My room number is 1117." He could almost hear Egan clucking his tongue in disapproval, but what the hell did that matter? The instructions he had received from him were no longer relevant.

"I can see you're not happy about this job either." Salusbury shook his head. "I don't mind telling you I've had a sinking feeling in my gut ever since Matthews briefed me yesterday evening. We'll be taking a leap in the dark, like we did at Ringway during the war. Remember all those instructors who'd made over a hundred jumps and reckoned parachuting was the second greatest sensation in the world? Well, I never cottoned on to it, Harry. I died a thousand deaths on the way up and another thousand on the way down. And that bloody night jump was one of the most terrifying experiences of my life."

The wind had been Force 3 to 4 gusting to 6 that night, which was stretching the safety limit to breaking point, but Salusbury had been with a very gung-ho course and they had taken off despite the risks. When he'd jumped with the rest of the stick, the slipstream had damn nearly slammed him into the tail and he'd thought his parachute was never going to open. When finally it did, he'd found himself hanging upside down, one foot entangled in the rigging.

"I was spinning like a top, Harry, and I knew the canopy was likely to collapse at any moment. It was pitch dark. There was no moon, the black-out was practically a hundred per cent, and if the stars were out, they were hidden by the overcast. Cutting my leg free seemed to take an eternity; a few seconds later, I plunged into the Manchester Ship Canal and bloody nearly drowned."

"Look at it this way," Freeland said. "Compared with that nightmare, getting Orlenko to London will be a piece of cake."

"It won't be unless we do our homework."

Salusbury went into the study across the hall and returned with a street map of Manhattan and Hagstrom's New York Subways.

Freeland had given him the germ of an idea, now he proceeded to develop it lucidly and in meticulous detail. The self-doubt of a few minutes ago had evaporated and he was his old self again – cool, methodical, efficient.

"First Grothmann, then Hausser, and now Orlenko; odd that all three should meet their nemesis through you, Harry."

"Life's full of coincidences."

"I suppose it is." Salusbury walked him to the door and out into the driveway. As they stood there in the gathering dusk, the street lights came on in Henry Thoreau Avenue. "I'm sorry Caroline will have missed you," he said. "She must be having a good old chinwag at the Literary Society. You know how it is . . ."

"Never mind, give her my regards." Freeland got into the car and started the engine, then wound the window down on his side. "Purely out of interest, when did Orlenko join the Soviet Delegation?"

"Early in 1950, must have been in the April."

"About the same time you were posted to New York."

"Yes, well, you said it, Harry, life is full of coincidences."

"I missed my vocation as a philosopher," Freeland said with a smile.

Shifting into gear, he drove out on to the road, turned left and headed back to New York.

23

The phone rang on the dot of nine a.m., some fifteen minutes after Freeland had returned to his hotel room from the breakfast bar across the street from the Kayser. Mouth suddenly dry, he lifted the receiver and grunted a hello.

"Harry?"

He recognised the voice immediately. "Yes, Guy."

"Good news, we've clinched the deal with Eastern Electrics." Salusbury cleared his throat. "Thing is, they want to see what our operation in Ottawa is like."

"When do we leave?"

"There's an Eastern Airlines flight out of La Guardia at 1105. Can you make that?"

"No problem. I'll meet you at the check-in desk."

Freeland obeyed his instinct and held on to the phone a fraction longer than was necessary and heard a faint click before he finally hung up. An eavesdropper on the line, but who? The FBI? Only Egan and Salusbury knew he was staying at the Kayser Hotel and he couldn't think of a single reason why either man should want to tip off Hoover's people. More to the point, he couldn't afford to waste time on an imponderable question. Orlenko was coming across and his first priority was to shake off anyone who might be tailing him before he parked the Chevrolet at the pre-arranged switch point. He lifted the phone again, called Reception and told the desk clerk that he would be in Ottawa for a couple of days on business but wished to retain his room. Then he opened the bedside locker, took out a screwdriver and went into the bathroom.

Between checking into the hotel and driving out to New Canaan yesterday evening, Freeland had not been idle. Apart from the screwdriver, he had also purchased a chamois-leather, a pair of scissors, needle and thread and some adhesive tape. Kneeling by the bath, he removed the side panel, reached inside under one of the supporting cradles and brought out the .38 Police Positive and dollybag containing six spare rounds, then screwed the panel back in place. The revolver was now tucked inside a home-made holster fashioned out of the chamois-leather.

Freeland hoiked his right trouser leg above calf level, then holding the holstered revolver in place with one hand, he taped it into position above the ankle by winding the adhesive several times around the barrel and chamber of the .38. When he straightened up, there was no tell-tale bulge but it was going to be a painful business if he had to get at the revolver in a hurry.

He returned to the bedroom with his shaving tackle and packed the suitcase, then checked all the drawers to make sure nothing had been left behind before he went down to the lobby. When he handed in his key, the desk clerk felt constrained to inform him that the hotel management were unable to allow him a part refund on the room rate while he was away in Ottawa. The hall porter wanted to get him a cab and was disappointed to learn that Freeland didn't need one.

The Ford which Freeland had rented from Hertz was parked in an open air lot between Ninth and Tenth Avenues, diagonally across the street from the McGraw Hill Building. The temperature was already touching seventy; by the time he'd walked the better part of two blocks, his shirt no longer looked fresh and clean on that morning.

Freeland paid off the attendant, dumped the suitcase in the trunk and drove out of the lot. Somewhere on the street a surveillance team would be waiting for him but he didn't bother to look for them. The quickest way to draw the opposition out into the open was to do the totally unexpected. Turning right, he headed towards the Weehawken Ferry at the bottom of West 42nd. No prowl car in sight, no patrolman on the beat; he eased the Ford into the outside lane and waited for a gap in the oncoming traffic. Shortly after crossing Eleventh Avenue, he got the break he wanted. Slamming the gear shift into second, he made a U-turn, taking up all of three lanes to complete it. A rig coming up fast on the innermost lane blasted an angry warning but his foot was already hard down on the accelerator and he immediately pulled away from the juggernaut.

Beyond Tenth Avenue, he moved across into the middle lane to overtake a Pontiac, then began to slow down as he approached the next set of lights at the intersection with Ninth Avenue. Behind him, another angry driver vented his spleen on the horn. Timing was everything and he got it right, the vehicle in front clearing the intersection moments before the lights changed to red. He was also in exactly the right position, top centre of the grid with an

261

unrestricted view of the crossing southbound traffic and far enough from the kerb to give himself a bit of leeway when the pedestrians started across the street.

He shifted into first, revved the engine, saw the crossflow begin to move and let the clutch in. Tyres screaming on the asphalt, Freeland cut in front of the solid phalanx bearing down on him and wheeled right into Ninth Avenue. No one thanked him for it, especially not the cadaverous, elderly man in a cloth cap who had to jump out of his way.

"Goddamned meathead . . ."

He had the windows part way down on both sides and caught the opening words as he shot past. Two successive left turns and he was heading north on Eighth Avenue. Crossing 42nd Street, he saw a vacant space at the kerbside up ahead on his left and slotted the Ford into it. He closed both windows, tripped the catch on the passenger's side, then got out and locked the door. He walked on up the Avenue, distancing himself from the Ford before he began looking for a cab. The morning rush hour was over but it was his lucky day and one came along just when he needed it. Flagging down the cab, he told the driver to take him to West End and 64th Street which would leave him within easy walking distance of Hendrik's Long Term Parking. As they moved off, Freeland looked back over his shoulder; no one appeared to be following him.

*   *   *

The operational display board in Johansen's office had impressed Egan when he had first seen it. Utilising a large-scale map of Manhattan, it showed the deployment of the CIA surveillance team in and around the Kayser Hotel on West 42nd Street. Different coloured pins indicated the positions of both men and vehicles in the target area.

Johansen had been given two cars and a team of eight to play with; in deploying them, he had put one man on the hotel switchboard, another in the lobby and two out on the street, one of whom was to cover the parking lot between Ninth and Tenth Avenues while the other acted as a long stop in the vicinity of the Empire Theatre in case Freeland headed east on 42nd Street. One car was parked around the corner from the hotel in Eleventh Avenue, facing south; the second was in Tenth Avenue below 42nd Street, facing north. With the exception of the two agents inside the Kayser Hotel who had been on duty since the previous evening, the surveillance team had moved into position at six a.m.

262

Within fifteen minutes of Freeland leaving the Kayser Hotel, the operational display board was a shambles and Johansen was working himself into a fine old temper. Forewarned by the man watching the parking lot, the car waiting on Eleventh Avenue had moved out and turned towards the Weehawken Ferry some three to four hundred yards ahead of Freeland. As soon as the lights were in their favour, the second vehicle in Tenth Avenue had tagged on behind him. Although Freeland's U-turn had left the lead car high and dry, the driver of the second had been far enough back to swing round at the Eleventh Avenue intersection. Unfortunately he had found himself boxed in some distance behind the Ford when Freeland had jumped the lights and swung into Ninth Avenue.

"What do you mean, he's vanished into thin air?" Johansen held the radio handset close to his right ear and paced back and forth, his freedom of movement restricted by the umbilical cord leading to the remote control unit. "Jesus H. Christ, we're dealing with a human being, not some goddamned ethereal spirit." He broke off, cupped his hand over the mike and looked at Egan. "Can you beat it? The guy outside the Empire Theatre sees Freeland heading uptown on Eighth Avenue but doesn't think to move his ass some place where he can keep him in sight. No, he just passes the information to the mobiles and figures he's done his good deed for the day. Now your man's abandoned the Ford between 44th and 45th Street and there's no sign of him. Got any idea where he's gone?"

"Freeland has his own car . . ."

"Yeah, that's right – a Chevy with Quebec plates, I remember you telling me. What was the licence number again?"

"8512964."

"Where did you tell him to garage it?"

"I didn't."

"Why not? You told him where to stay in New York, what he was to do, when he could eat, sleep and go to the can . . ."

"Some things had to be left to his own initiative," Egan said unhappily.

"That's terrific."

Johansen lifted the handset, instructed all stations to wait out for further information, then called his secretary into the office and told her to look up the address and phone number of every parking lot in the classified directory for Manhattan. Ten minutes later, she was back with a list of a round dozen.

"Let's hope we're not too late," Johansen said grimly.

Egan wondered what the hell he was going to say if, as he suspected, Freeland was already one jump ahead of them.

*　　*　　*

The switch point Salusbury had chosen was outside Hunter College on East 68th Street between Park Avenue and Lexington. Hunter had been his first choice for two reasons; finding somewhere to park would not be a problem because the College was still closed for the summer vacation and it was close enough to the 19th Precinct to deter the opposition.

Freeland had studied the street map Salusbury had given him until every detail of the route was firmly in his mind. Collecting the Chevrolet from Hendrik's Parking Lot on West End Avenue, he went on up to 65th Street and headed for Central Park West and the Transverse road through the park. At East 65th and Madison, he drove north to 68th Street. Hunter College was not totally deserted but as Salusbury had confidently predicted, finding a slot for the Chevrolet did not present him with an insuperable problem. After locking the car, he continued on foot to the IRT subway station on the Lexington Avenue Line. The time was coming up for ten fifty; in another fifteen minutes, Orlenko would arrive at Grand Central where Salusbury would be waiting for him.

Freeland bought a token from the ticket office, fed it into the turnstile and went on down to the southbound platform. Two express trains, one going to Bowling Green, the other to Atlantic Avenue, went through the station before a local from Pelham Bay Park arrived. Fifty-ninth street was the next stop down the line but the enforced wait had eaten into the time Freeland had had in hand and it was now touch and go whether Salusbury would arrive at the RV ahead of him. He watched the second hand on his Ingersoll bite away the minutes until only five were left when the train pulled into 59th Street. There was no crowd to mingle with; the rush hour had long since ended and less than a dozen passengers got off the train. Feeling slightly conspicuous, Freeland made his way to the northbound platform and moved to the far end to be roughly in line with the second car.

The Russian who left the Woodlawn Express with Salusbury was about five and a half feet, weighed under ten stone, had mousey-coloured hair and pointed features. For a KGB man, Orlenko looked about as menacing as a hamster. Freeland gave the two men a head start, then tagged them to the BMT's 60th Street station where they boarded a Broadway and Fourth Avenue local going to 95th Street in Brooklyn. Freeland entered the adjoining car,

264

found he had a patrolman from the New York Transit Authority for company and had to wait until Seventh Avenue before the police officer left the car and he was able to join Salusbury and Orlenko up front.

A young mother with her two small sons, a Marine Corps sergeant, two black men, a nun and three teenage girls; Freeland looked round the car, then walked up to Salusbury and greeted him like a long lost friend in case any of the other passengers wondered why he had come through the connecting door while the train was in motion.

"How does it look?" Salusbury asked.

"No one seems to be interested in you two. I wish I could say the same for me."

"Problems?"

Freeland nodded. "A nosy switchboard operator at the hotel. But they wouldn't have gleaned anything from your phone call unless someone had told them what was in the wind."

"They?"

"A rival firm."

"Friendly?"

"Too friendly," said Freeland. "Fortunately I managed to lose them before I picked up the Chevrolet."

Salusbury frowned. "Whether you did or didn't shake them off is immaterial. Mikhail has put his life on the line and there's no turning back now."

"I know that." Freeland took a bunch of car keys out of his jacket pocket and palmed them surreptitiously to Salusbury. "The Ford Mercury I rented from Hertz is on Eighth Avenue between 44th and 45th Streets. The licence number if 9Y 86.47."

"9Y 86.47." Salusbury repeated the number, committing it to memory.

"I had to leave my suitcase in the trunk."

"I'll see to it, Harry, soon as you take Mikhail under your wing."

"Better wait a day or so before you go near the car; the FBI, or whoever, could be watching it."

Freeland shook hands with both men and moved towards the doors. At Times Square, he would take the shuttle to Grand Central, then catch a northbound local to his original start point at East 68th Street.

*   *   *

Egan knew what was coming long before Johansen ordered both mobiles to return to base. The increasingly angry expression on

265

the American's face said it all, but forewarned was not forearmed. There were some questions London would not allow him to answer no matter how tough things got.

Johansen said, "I don't suppose I have to tell you that Freeland had already collected his Chevrolet by the time our people arrived at Hendrik's Parking Lot?"

"It was always on the cards," Egan murmured.

"You want to tell me what else is on the cards? Like where he may have gone for instance?"

"I only wish I knew, but Salusbury's handling the Orlenko defection and in the interests of security, he's been allowed to play it close to his chest."

"And you didn't want us to keep an eye on him in case we frightened Orlenko off?"

"That was our thinking," Egan said carefully.

"You should have told Freeland what the score was, then maybe we wouldn't have spooked him."

Egan found it hard to quarrel with that observation but he could scarcely tell the American that Acland didn't altogether trust Freeland. Such a disclosure would only raise more questions than it answered.

"The only lead we have is the licence number of the Chevrolet," Johansen said in a quieter tone of voice.

"So?"

"Well, suppose I suck up to the Police Commissioner and get the whole of the New York Police Department looking for the Chevrolet? All we want from them is the location of the vehicle. If the Chevy is on the move, they're to keep it in sight until we can take over. The one thing they don't do is arrest the driver. What do you say?"

Egan didn't have to give it much thought. "It might work," he said.

"It had better," Johansen told him, "otherwise I am going public."

In simple terms, going public meant that every law enforcement agency, every airline desk, every bus terminal and railroad station would be given a detailed description of a man calling himself Harry McIver, also known as Harry Freeland.

*   *   *

The Chevrolet had gone. Freeland walked the length of East 68th Street between Lexington and Park Avenue and back again but there was no doubting the evidence of his eyes. Some car thief had stolen it in broad daylight and there wasn't a damned thing he could do about it. The need for absolute secrecy which Salusbury and Egan, to a lesser extent, had impressed upon him meant that he couldn't even report the loss to the police. Worse still, he didn't have time to rent another vehicle; in less than fifteen minutes from now, Salusbury would arrive at the switch point expecting to deliver Orlenko into his safe-keeping.

He glanced left and right; Dodge, Chrysler, Pontiac, Buick, Plymouth, Oldsmobile, Ford, Cadillac, every make that had rolled off the production lines of Detroit. With so many different models to choose from, why had the thief singled out his Chevrolet? It was more than three years old, for God's sake; there was over sixty thousand on the clock, the chrome was pitted with rust from the harsh Canadian winters and some months back Jenny had creased the rear nearside mudwing against a fire hydrant. And another thing, not thirty feet from where he was standing, there was a two-door drophead coupé for the taking, the nearside window fully retracted.

A yellow cab turned into East 68th Street from Park Avenue and came slowly towards him. On time almost to the minute. Freeland moved out from the cars parked by the kerbside to make it easier for Salusbury to spot him. As the driver brought the Dodge to a halt, Salusbury leaned across Orlenko in the back to open the door for him.

"Where have you left your car, Harry?"

"It was right here."

"Was?"

"Someone borrowed it without my permission."

"How very inconsiderate of them," Salusbury said calmly. "Looks as though we shall have to go by train after all." He leaned forward and tapped the driver on the shoulder. "Sorry about this but we've had to change our plans. You'd better take us to Penn Station."

The driver grunted, shifted into gear and went on up to Lexington Avenue, then headed downtown.

"Why do you suppose the thief stole your car, Harry? Did you forget to lock it?"

"No. What's more, there was a newer model going begging not thirty feet away."

"He must have had a set of Chevrolet keys, saved him the trouble of hotwiring the ignition or whatever they call it."

"Yes, I suppose that must have been it."

They fell silent. After a while, Salusbury began to hum the hit number from *Oklahoma* to himself as if to demonstrate that it would take more than a stolen car to faze him. His *sang froid* failed to have the desired effect on Orlenko. Far from being relaxed, the Russian sat between them, hunched up, his face pasty and sweating profusely. At Lexington and East 33rd Street, they turned right and drove by the Empire State, across Herald Square and on past Gimbel's, then south on Seventh Avenue to Pennsylvania Station.

Salusbury paid off the cab driver and led them into the main waiting room, a vast Roman temple of triumphant arches and marble columns. Leaving Freeland to look after Orlenko, he went over to the information desk. A few minutes later, he returned with a copy of the train schedules of the New York, New Haven and Hartford Railroad Company.

"You and your jinx, Harry," he said, smiling. "Going by train is about the only way you can leave town now."

"What is happening please?" Orlenko asked.

Freeland thought the Russian sounded nervous, and with some justification. The KGB were going to use Orlenko for target practice if they ever caught up with him and he was painfully aware that there had been a major foul-up.

"We're making alternative arrangements to get you out of the country," Salusbury told him. "Nothing you need worry about." He turned to Freeland. "Somehow I don't see you making it across the border today, Harry."

"Somehow neither do I."

"So what do you think? Would your friend, Lander, provide a temporary bolthole for the two of you while I try to straighten things out with the Yanks?"

"Not if he knows the score."

"Then you'll have to lie in your teeth to him, won't you, Harry?"

"I don't like it."

"Neither will Mikhail if he gets splattered all over the pavement. The next train out of here is the 1310 to Boston, arriving 1753. I suggest you board it."

"I still don't like it," Freeland told him, "but you're the boss."

The boss, it transpired, had several other suggestions to make before they went their separate ways. Within the SIS, Salusbury had always enjoyed a reputation for clear and decisive thinking; it did not desert him in this particular crisis.

*   *   *

They were working the two-to-ten shift. For the past hour and five minutes they had been checking the streets either side of

268

Lennox Avenue looking for witnesses to a domestic fracas which had culminated in a near fatal stabbing. If there hadn't been a victim lying unconscious in the Columbia Presbyterian Medical Centre with multiple stab wounds in the stomach, chest and back, they would have written off the anonymous 911 call as a hoax long ago.

The injured man had been found on a patch of waste ground near the IRT Yard some eight blocks north of where the informant had alleged the incident had occurred. Just how he had managed to stagger there from West 140th Street was a mystery none of the residents were willing to help solve even though, unlike his partner, Officer Jerome H. White had been born in Harlem.

"You think we should give up on this no-hoper, Pat?" White asked his partner.

"Why not, I could do with a change of scenery."

White picked up the mike and informed Despatch that they were extending the search in the hope of finding an eye-witness. Continuing on West 140th, they crossed Eighth Avenue and headed towards Edgecombe Place. The derelict tenements in this part of Harlem reminded White of some of the war-torn German towns he'd seen in 1945 when his MP outfit had been attached to 1st Army. Same tired people living in the ruins, same kind of rubbish littering the area; only the abandoned vehicles were different.

"Hold it, Pat."

"What?"

"Pull up." White reached for the clipboard on the shelf under the dash and ran his eye over the notes he'd made when the shift had mustered for briefing. "They told us to keep a sharp look-out for a 1951 Chevrolet sedan. Right?"

"So?"

"So there's one in an alleyway about fifty yards back."

White got out of the car and started walking. The Chevrolet had Quebec plates and was resting on its brake drums. Apart from the wheels, the thief had also taken the battery, air cleaner and car radio.

24

Orlenko was clearly the worrying kind; almost three hours after leaving New York, the Russian still looked drained of all colour. They were sitting in the end coach where the conductor rode most of the time; no one was behind them and Freeland only had the communicating door up front to watch. There was no safer place on the train, but Orlenko wouldn't have it.

"Not much farther now," Freeland said. "The next stop is Westerly, Rhode Island."

"How much longer to Boston?"

"Another hour fifty."

"And then what?"

It wasn't an easy question to answer. Salusbury expected him to switch to the Boston and Maine Railroad and go on to Portland via Portsmouth, New Hampshire. If he made the connecting service with the Maine Central Railroad, he was supposed to end up at Augusta, but that was too restrictive for his liking.

"You let me worry about that," he told Orlenko.

Lander had had to cope with some pretty strange house-guests since he and Avril had acquired Seaview Lodge in Camden but Mikhail was going to take some beating. Freeland had thought of calling Lander when the train had stopped at New Haven for ten minutes but he'd no idea how long it would take him to find a pay-phone and he couldn't risk leaving Orlenko on the train by himself. He would have to ring him from Boston's South Station; by then he ought to know whether Salusbury had managed to square the Americans and would therefore have a much clearer idea of what he was going to do.

"What is he like, this friend of yours?" Orlenko asked.

"Which one?"

"The American we are going to see."

"Joe's all right."

"He is an important man?"

"No."

"Rich?"

"I guess you'd have to say he's wealthy."

In fact, the money belonged to Avril. Her father had had his own construction company in California and had also been pretty big in real estate when he'd died. The sole beneficiary, Avril had retained a minority holding in the construction company but had got out of real estate. Freeland had no idea what she was worth, but the twelve-bedroom inn set in the Camden Hills above the town had been purchased with her money. So too had the fishing boat, the schooner, the Cadillac, the Ford pick-up and the Aeronca four-seater plane which was needed for the business.

"What does this Mr Joe do for a living?"

"Some people would say he's a gentleman of leisure."

Thanks to Avril, Lander could afford to be selective about his clientèle and could close Seaview Lodge whenever he felt like it. It wasn't so much a business he was running as a hobby. Right now, the house was empty and was likely to remain that way until the 'leaf peepers' arrived in the Fall.

Lander had met Avril just over four years ago in San Francisco when she had been going through a bad patch and was in a bar on Fisherman's Wharf drowning her sorrows. Her father had died some nine months previously, the man she had expected to marry had jilted her for someone else, and she had just had the results of her annual check-up in which a routine X-ray had revealed a shadow on her left lung. At first, Joe had simply provided a shoulder for her to cry on; a few weeks later, a casual relationship had grown to a bond of love and understanding. When further tests had shown that Avril had pulmonary tuberculosis and not the cancer she had feared, Lander had celebrated the good news by giving up drinking altogether.

"I don't like these arrangements, Mr Freeland."

"I'm not wild about them either."

"Mr Salusbury should have taken me straight to the airport and put me on a plane to England. This way is dangerous."

"You worry too much."

"How long will we stay with your friend?"

"Only the one night. And try to keep your voice down; we don't want the whole damned coach listening in on our conversation."

Freeland lit a cigarette. The more he thought about it, the less he liked the idea of Orlenko spending the night at Seaview Lodge, and certainly not while Avril, Jenny and the children were there. Maybe Lander could get some hotel in town to put them up.

271

Whatever he did, he would have to leave a message with Lander so that Salusbury would know where to find them.

"Excuse me." Orlenko stood up and moved past him.

"Where do you think you're going?" Freeland asked.

"I need to take a leak."

The toilets were at the opposite end of the day coach. Orlenko had almost reached them when a slim, mean-looking blond in his early thirties left his seat and followed the Russian up the centre aisle. He was wearing a pair of tan-coloured slacks and a pale blue shirt with the sleeves rolled above the elbows, but it was the jacket carried over the left arm that Freeland didn't like. Reacting swiftly, he stubbed out his cigarette and went after the blond man. As soon as he was within touching distance, Freeland deliberately stumbled into him as if caught off balance by the swaying motion of the train.

"Sorry about that." Freeland smiled apologetically, raised both hands shoulder high to show he had no aggressive intentions and backed off a pace. "I tripped over something."

The blond man bent down and picked up his jacket which had fallen to the floor. "You want to watch it, fella," he growled.

"Oh, I certainly will."

The man was unarmed, nothing hidden under the jacket or on his person. Freeland thought it symptomatic of his growing paranoia that he found it difficult to accept the evidence of his own eyes.

Orlenko entered the first toilet on the right, the blond man made for the one immediately opposite. The fact that it happened to be vacant did nothing to set Freeland's mind at rest. He walked on past the remaining cubicles, then turned about, his back to the communicating door. The conductor watched him like a hawk just in case he took it into his head to molest the young girl in white ankle socks who emerged from the other cloakroom on his right. Then Orlenko reappeared and he quickly changed places with him.

Freeland locked the door behind him, searched under the wash-basin, behind the pedestal toilet and checked the used paper towels in the disposal bin. Although he didn't find anything amongst the garbage, the feeling that something was not quite right persisted.

Ten minutes after he had returned to his seat, the train pulled into Westerly, Rhode Island, and the blond man got off.

*   *   *

The cable which Salusbury had drafted was addressed to Beta Tech Limited, 257 Western Avenue, London NW7. It read: With reference to yours of the 16th instant (.) Have obtained sample as requested and despatched same today's date (.) Assume you will arrange collection in Quebec (.)

Beta Tech Limited was only one of a dozen companies whose registered offices were at the same address. Sharing the same clerical staff, it was, like the other bogus firms, a receiving station for the Secret Intelligence Service. It enabled agents who could not use diplomatic channels for one reason or another, to pass unattributable information by commercial cable. In this instance, the sample referred to Mikhail Orlenko.

Salusbury was about to leave his office to despatch it when his secretary informed him that he had a visitor. Although he had not been told who would be meeting Orlenko in Quebec, he had assumed it would be Egan and was therefore a little surprised to find that this was not the case.

"I'd no idea you were in New York, Tom," he said lamely when Egan walked into his office. "What are you doing here?"

"Keeping an eye on things, liaising with our friends. Steve Johansen from the Zenith Technical Corporation kindly ran me over here from their offices on Nassau Street."

"You've been talking to the CIA?" Salusbury glanced at the cable he'd drafted. "You haven't told them about Orlenko, have you?"

"I had to."

"I don't understand. Matthews told me we had to play it close to our chests. He said Orlenko didn't trust the CIA and wouldn't come across if he thought they . . ." Salusbury broke off, suddenly aware of the implications. "Jesus Christ," he breathed, "they were keeping tabs on Harry and he lost them."

"Yes."

"You didn't trust Harry; in fact, you've had your doubts about him ever since that business in Shanghai. But why have you waited so long to do anything about it?"

"We didn't have anything to go on until Vladimir Petrov defected to the Australians."

Salusbury was willing to bet that all the Russian had given the SIS were a few signposts. Had he named someone and provided chapter and verse, Egan would not be running a half-baked surveillance operation in New York.

"What are you hoping to get from Orlenko, Tom?"

"Has he come across?"

"Well, of course he has." Salusbury waved the cable at him. "Why else do you suppose I drafted this?"

273

"Describe him."

"He's a nondescript little man, knee high to a grasshopper, shouldn't think he weighs more than a hundred and forty pounds . . ."

"Is this the man?"

Salusbury studied the photograph which Egan had placed on the desk. Although the picture had been taken in poor light and was blurred, there was no mistaking Orlenko.

"It certainly is. I never saw a man look so frightened when I . . ." His voice tailed off, leaving what he had started to say tantalisingly incomplete.

"When you did what?" Egan said impatiently.

"When I left him at Penn Station with Freeland."

"You think Orlenko was frightened to be left alone with him?"

"Yes . . . perhaps . . . hell, I'm not really sure. It's not as though he knows what we do, that people around Freeland have a habit of dying violently. I don't mind telling you there have been times when I've wondered just whose side Harry was on and lately I've been asking myself if it really was Chantal Kiffer who betrayed the Loiret Bleu network. Then I recall that stump on Freeland's left hand and there's no explaining that away."

"Unless the mutilation was inflicted at a later date," Egan suggested ominously.

"You mean when he was in Flossenburg concentration camp?"

"Well, look at it this way, you convinced Hausser you were related to the Salisburys and would ensure he wasn't prosecuted for war crimes. But what did Freeland have to trade, apart from a list of names?"

"Do you suppose Hausser told the Russians that Freeland betrayed the Loiret Bleu network and they used that to blackmail him?" Salusbury blinked. "My God, that's it. According to Matthews, Orlenko was the chief interrogator at Special Punishment Camp 129."

"Never mind all that," Egan said tersely. "What train was Freeland planning to catch when you left him at Penn Station?"

"The 1310 to Boston, gets in at 1753. He will then be going on to Camden to stay with the Landers."

Egan glanced at his wristwatch. "We might just catch him at Boston."

"We?"

274

"Johansen's chartered a Cessna from Independent Airspeed in Newark. I think you'd better come with us, Guy."

*　　*　　*

The train pulled into Boston Back Bay Station at 1748 exactly on schedule. In another five minutes they would arrive at the South Station and there was no telling what sort of reception committee might be waiting for them at the terminus. It was illogical, even stupid, but Freeland couldn't put the blond man out of his mind, but when the CIA, as well as the KGB, were breathing down your neck, anyone whose behaviour was the slightest bit unusual was automatically suspect.

"This is where we get off," Freeland said in a low voice. "No arguments, no questions, just do as I say."

He stepped out into the centre aisle, walked towards the door at the rear of the car and squeezing past the conductor, climbed down on to the track. Orlenko halted on the bottom step, glanced left and right as though expecting to see a familiar face.

"Are you getting off here, sir?" the conductor asked him.

"He is," Freeland said and virtually hauled the Russian off the train.

In common with every other defector who'd asked for political asylum, Orlenko knew that he would be a dead man if the KGB ever caught up with him. From the moment Freeland had met him, the Russian had given a very lifelike impression of a man who was frightened of his own shadow, yet he now seemed hell bent on making things as difficult as possible for the one person whose job it was to protect him.

"It's a bit late in the day for second thoughts," Freeland said quietly.

"I don't know what you mean."

"You think the comrades will welcome you back with open arms? The hell they will; it's a pine box or the Gulag for you, Mikhail."

He steered Orlenko through the entrance hall and out into the yard. Grabbing the first cab on the rank, Freeland bundled the Russian into the back and got in beside him.

"Where to?" the driver asked.

"I want to rent a car," Freeland told him. "Do you know where the nearest agency is?"

The driver nodded. "Whether it's still open is something else."

They started out on Columbus Avenue, skirted Boston Common on Charles Street, then headed roughly north-east, parallel with

275

the river. The cab driver was a talkative Italian and a mine of irrelevant information. Boston's economy, he informed Freeland, was founded on banking, insurance and shipping. The Irish used to live in the North End until they were replaced by the Italians and the Black community, once centred in the downtown area, had moved out to Roxbury. He knew the best eating places and the cheapest hotels in town but he couldn't find a rental agency that was still open. On the other hand, he had a brother in the used car trade who might be persuaded to rent one to Freeland.

The brother was equally friendly and outgoing but unfortunately, owing to a slight misunderstanding with the insurance company, he'd had to suspend the rental side of the business. However, he did have an automobile on the lot which Freeland could have for six hundred for a trial period of seven days. The deal included his personal guarantee that he would then buy the vehicle back for not less than fifty per cent of the original purchase price.

The bargain of the week was a 1947 model Ford V8 Super de Luxe sedan. The paintwork had lost its sheen, the tyres were practically bald, the engine was burning oil and sounded as if it was only firing on six of the eight cylinders. Six hundred was going to make quite a dent in what was left of the fifteen hundred US dollars Egan had given him in Quebec, but Camden was roughly a hundred and sixty miles from Boston and Freeland could only hope the bargain of the week wouldn't expire halfway there.

*   *   *

They weren't on the train. The frantic dash to Newark, the charter flight to Boston and the hair-raising drive from Logan International Airport had all been for nothing. The last passenger on the 1310 from New York had passed through the gate and the cleaners had boarded the empty train. Salusbury had waited at the exit with Egan while Johansen questioned the conductor; observing the American closely as he walked towards them, Salusbury noted his grim expression and guessed what was coming.

"They left the train at the Back Bay Station," Johansen said angrily.

"Are we sure of that?" Egan asked.

"The conductor identified Orlenko from the photo I showed him. He also gave me a pretty good description of Freeland. He thought Harry was either a dip or a faggot. Seems he had some kind of set-to with a blond guy; the conductor wasn't sure whether he was after his billfold or was getting overfriendly with him." Johansen half smiled. "Well, we all know Harry isn't a pickpocket and I've never felt uncomfortable in his presence. So we are left with the possibility that the blond guy is with the opposition."

Salusbury rubbed his chin. "Did the conductor say where he left the train?"

"Westerly, Rhode Island. His ticket wasn't valid beyond there."

"He wasn't KGB then, but Harry thought he was and got off one stop down the line in case they were waiting for him at the South Station."

"Freeland could have left the train at Kingston or Providence, Rhode Island, which would have given him an extra hour to play with. Question is, why didn't he?"

"Search me." Egan turned to Salusbury. "Any ideas, Guy?"

"Maybe Harry decided to rent a car. He'd have a better choice in Boston and he'd be a damned sight less conspicuous in a big town."

Johansen nodded. "I'll buy that. Do you think he's still making for Lander's place in Camden?"

"You ought to address that question to Egan," Salusbury told him. "He's better equipped to answer it than I am. There was a time when I thought I knew Harry Freeland, but not any more. Tom here thinks he may belong to Moscow."

"Is that why you wanted us to keep an eye on him?" Johansen demanded furiously.

"When Petrov defected back in April, he told the Australians that the KGB were nurturing the career of an SIS officer whom the Germans had first used as a double-agent during the war. In the absence of any further information, we had to compile a list of suspects; Freeland happened to be one of the prime candidates."

"So now you've got your proof."

"Except I'm not happy about the theft of the Chevrolet. It doesn't fit the pattern."

"There is no connection; some punk happened to steal his car, that's all." Johansen jabbed a finger in Egan's chest. "We've played it your way long enough, so now I'm changing the rules. If Orlenko is still alive when we catch up with him, he belongs to us. In return for this concession, you get to keep Freeland and we don't make a song and dance about him. Agreed?"

"Yes."

"There is one small proviso. It's now six thirty-four; if Freeland hasn't contacted Lander by eight, we go public with the FBI."

"Do you have to?"

"I've no choice, you know that."

If Freeland had rented a car, he could reach the Canadian border in under six hours. To put a road block on every possible crossing place was going to be a major task and it was doubtful if Johansen was giving Hoover's people enough time as it was.

"You're right," Egan told him.

"Okay, we'll pick up a few reinforcements from the Boston office, then we'll return to the airport and hire ourselves a couple of helicopters. Meantime, Zenith Corporation can run a check on Mr Lander."

*   *   *

The sign on the outskirts of town said 'Welcome to Hampton Beach'. The map, which Freeland had picked up from a filling station in the suburbs of Boston, indicated that the resort was roughly a third of the way along the eighteen mile coastline of New Hampshire. The bay on his right stretched as far as the eye could see to Strawberry Banke beyond Portsmouth. A few hours ago, the beach would have been crowded; now, with the sun dipping below the horizon, it was almost deserted. Up ahead, Freeland spotted a couple of pay-phones outside a large cafeteria on the promenade and pulled into a vacant parking space by the roadside.

"Get out," he told Orlenko, "we're going to stretch our legs."

Freeland led the Russian into the nearest kiosk, called long distance and asked the operator to connect him with Camden 184; the phone rang just half a dozen times before Lander answered it.

Freeland said, "How do you feel about three unexpected house-guests?"

"Depends who they are, Harry."

"Me, Guy Salusbury and a little man from Moscow who fancies a change of scenery."

"Sounds like an interesting combination."

"I think it would be best if Avril, Jenny and the children spent the night in town," Freeland continued. "Things could get a little rowdy."

"Where are you making for?"

"Canada."

"I could fly you across the border. My plane's at Rockland Field which is only a few miles from here."

"Thanks for the offer, Joe, but I don't want to involve you any more than I have to. As a matter of fact, I don't think we should even be spending the night under your roof. I had a run in with the FBI and had to throw some dust in their eyes for the sake of my Russian friend who you might say is basically anti-American.

Anyway, I don't suppose I'm exactly popular with Mr Hoover, and some of his acrimony could rub off on you."

"I'll worry about that when it happens."

"Yes, well, hopefully nothing will come of it. Guy Salusbury is still in New York endeavouring to smooth things over. He'll be joining me later."

"When do I expect you, Harry?"

"Roughly two and a half hours from now, I'm about a hundred miles away." Freeland paused, then said, "Do you think I could have a word with Jenny?"

"Surely."

He heard Lander call to her, then Jenny picked up one of the extensions in the house and he went through it all again, explaining why he wanted her and the children out of the house.

"Are you going to be all right, Harry?" she asked when he'd finished.

"Of course I am, it's a piece of cake."

A brittle laugh crackled down the line. "I've heard that one before. Just mind you take care, and no heroics."

"And I think I've heard that one before."

"Well, try listening to me for once, darling."

Freeland promised he would and slowly hung up. Then, lifting the receiver again, he called the long distance operator and gave her the number of Salusbury's office in New York. Before they'd separated at Penn Station, Guy had said that someone would be there no matter what time he telephoned. That same someone would also be able to tell him in veiled speech how they stood with the FBI, but the operator told him she was unable to raise anyone.

He replaced the receiver and escorted Orlenko back to the car. Shortly before joining the Expressway beyond Portsmouth, Freeland pulled off the road and stopped. Hoiking his right trouser, he bent down and ripped off the adhesive tape that held the holster and .38 Police Positive to his leg. Then he withdrew the revolver from the home-made holster and placed it on the shelf below the glove compartment where Orlenko couldn't reach it.

"Never forgotten the old Scout motto," he told the Russian. "Be prepared."

*   *   *

Lander stood in the large sitting-room gazing out at the dark shapes of the islands in Penobscot Bay. In the harbour way below Seaview Lodge, sleek yachts and motor cruisers lay at anchor in the

279

gathering darkness amidst two-masted windjammers and coastal schooners. To his left, he could see coloured lanterns strung between the trees around the Bok Amphitheatre where a travelling theatrical company were staging *A Midsummer Night's Dream*. Down there, just off the waterfront park, Avril, Jenny and her children were spending the night on board his schooner, *The Gooney Bird*; without them, the lodge seemed unnaturally quiet, almost menacingly so. In the eerie silence, the sudden jangle of the telephone made him jump.

Crossing the room in a few strides, he picked up the receiver and said, "Camden 184."

"Mr Lander?"

The caller was brusque and overbearing, arousing his instant hostility. "Yeah, who wants him?"

"Mr Johansen asked me to call you . . ."

"I've never heard of him," Lander said.

"How about a Mr Guy Salusbury?"

"What is this, some kind of quiz game?"

"You have a mutual acquaintance called Harry Freeland."

"So what?"

"Has he been in touch with you, Mr Lander?"

"You want to give me your name and phone number?"

"This is a matter of national security . . ."

"Bullshit."

"We know a great deal about you, sir. For instance, you are the owner of an Aeronca four-seater monoplane Federal Registration Number N2031B. Your wife's name is Avril, you were one of Chennault's Flying Tigers and you met Freeland in May 1949 when you and George Berringer flew him from Kweilin to Shanghai in a C46 belonging to Civil Air Transport. Now, sir, I repeat, has Mr Freeland been in touch with you this evening?"

"What are you – FBI?" Who the hell else would know so much about him? Unless he was prepared to end up in jail with Freeland, he'd better co-operate. Besides, it was time he put Avril first.

"Has he been in touch, Mr Lander?"

"Yes, dammit."

"Thank you, sir."

"I'd like to say you're welcome."

"I can understand your hostility, sir, but there's nothing for you to worry about. Mr Johansen is on his way by helicopter with several of our officers and they should be with you a little after nine. Matter of fact, my next call will be to your Chief of Police to ask him to meet them at Rockland Field with a couple of prowl cars."

Lander started to tell him that the Camden Police Department only had two cars but the line suddenly went dead as if the operator had pulled the plug on the connection. He put the phone down and went into his study at the side of the house. Freeland had warned him that it could be a rowdy night and it was beginning to look as if he might be right. Unlocking the gun cupboard, he took out a Remington 12-gauge pump shotgun, broke the seal on a new carton of buckshot and loaded five cartridges into the magazine, then fed a round into the breech and applied the safety.

He checked all the windows and doors to make sure they were closed and locked, then switched on the floodlights under the trees which provided a backdrop to the lawn fronting the house and drive. Finally, he activated the burglar alarm before returning to keep watch in the dark of the sitting-room.

Seaview Lodge was perched high above the town on the forward slope of the Camden Hills, a narrow winding track its only access to the main road three-quarters of a mile away. Consequently, Lander saw the headlights of the approaching vehicle winking at him through the trees long before he heard the familiar note of the Cadillac engine. Avril; what the hell did Avril think she was playing at?

But the woman who alighted from the Cadillac had a rounded chin, a small upturned nose and dark curly hair. One thing all women seemed to have in common; they never did as they were told. Muttering to himself, Lander put the shotgun down, went out into the hall and de-activated the burglar alarm. Switching on the light above the porch, he opened the front door to Jenny Freeland.

"What's the matter, Jen?" he asked.

"Nothing. Avril's fine, so are the children."

"Then why have you left *The Gooney Bird?*"

"Because I want to be here when Harry arrives. I don't pretend to know the ins and outs of the Orlenko business, but if what's happened in the past is anything to go by, Harry will be left holding the dirty end of the stick." She smiled. "You're not going to keep me talking on the doorstep, are you, Joe?"

"No, of course not." He stepped aside, closed the door behind her and just managed to reach the switch and put the lights on before she walked into the sitting-room. "Can I fix you a drink?"

"Please. Something long and cool." Her eyes fell on the shotgun Lander had left on the floor by his chair. "Expecting trouble, Joe?"

"No, just a sensible precaution." He stepped behind the bar

next to the chimney breast. "Lime and lemonade, or something stronger?"

"Lime and lemonade. You're enjoying this, aren't you?"

"Enjoying what?"

Jenny drew the curtains in the sashcord windows. "This whiff of danger."

What she had said was true enough but he wasn't going to admit it. To do so would somehow be disloyal to Avril and the kind of life she had made possible.

"What danger? Someone called Johansen will be arriving at any minute with a Mr Guy Salusbury and a small army of law enforcement officers."

"Now I know I was right to come back," Jenny said drily.

*   *   *

The cable had snapped on the speedometer and the needle was now resting on the zero mark. In addition to being sluggish, the engine was also displaying a tendency to overheat which meant Freeland had to keep an eye on the temperature gauge. The clock, however, was still functioning accurately and the luminous hands showed eight minutes to ten.

The Expressway was a long way behind them now and they were heading north-east on US Route 1. Some time back, Freeland had noticed two relatively slow-moving winking lights in the night sky and had wondered if the helicopters were making for Rockland Field. Ever since then, he had also spent an inordinate amount of time wondering if the FBI would be waiting for him when they arrived at Seaview Lodge. One thing was certain, he would know the answer soon enough; the road to Augusta was only a hundred yards or so beyond the slight rise ahead and Camden was less than seven miles from the T-junction.

"Not much farther now," he told Orlenko.

"What's that flashing light?"

"Where?"

"There, directly to our front."

Freeland leaned forward over the wheel as they breasted the rise. Orlenko was right, someone was standing in the middle of the road waving them down with a red flashlight.

"It's the police," Orlenko said.

The man in the centre of the road was wearing a khaki uniform, his flat-brimmed hat shaped like a pyramid. Some twenty yards to his rear, a second officer covered him from behind the hood of a sedan parked on the left side of the road.

282

"You have to stop," Orlenko shouted.

State Troopers. Freeland recognised their uniforms, stamped on the brakes and skidded to a halt some eighty odd yards beyond the road to Augusta. The trooper with the flashlight moved towards the verge on Orlenko's side as if to give his partner a clear field of fire. At the same time, his free hand dipped towards the unbuttoned flap of the pistol holster on his right hip, and suddenly everything that had happened to him in the last fourteen hours made sense to Freeland. Grabbing the .38 Police Positive from the shelf under the dashboard, he tracked the nearest trooper and squeezed off two shots through the windshield, then threw himself sideways on top of Orlenko. Holding the Russian down on the bench seat, he leaned across him and opened the nearside door by using the barrel of the revolver to raise the lever. He went out head first, dragging Orlenko with him by the scruff of his collar and wriggled into the overgrown ditch bordering the road. A lingering doubt that he might have acted precipitately was dispelled by the hollow cough of an automatic fitted with a noise suppressor. As far as he knew, police officers were not issued with silencers for their personal firearms.

Still holding Orlenko face down in the ditch with his right hand, Freeland raised his head. The gunman whom he'd shot was sitting in the road nursing his left side, his .45 calibre automatic levelled straight at him. Sighting with his good left eye, Freeland shot first and saw in the headlights of the Ford the fine spray of tissue and shattered bone as the bullet exited high up on his back. Then the man toppled over on to his left side and lay still.

The hollow cough of a silencer and the crack of a round passing close above his head sent Freeland diving for cover again. A second bullet thumped into the verge to his front, a third struck the base of a tree beyond the ditch. The sound of footsteps coming towards him, two more shots in quick succession, a door slamming, the whirr of a starter motor and the engine catching first time. Orlenko squirmed and kicked out in a frantic attempt to break loose; Freeland cracked the barrel over his head hard enough to stun him, then scrambled out of the ditch to empty the .38 at the receding lights of the sedan. The brakelights came on just short of the T-junction as the driver stopped to pick up the look-out who had obviously warned him that they were coming. A few moments later, the lights disappeared over the rise.

Freeland tucked the revolver into his jacket pocket, stepped down into the ditch and grabbing hold of Orlenko, dragged him over to the Ford. Leaving the unconscious Russian by the roadside, he switched off the engine, removed the keys from the ignition, unlocked the trunk and bundled him inside. Then he hauled the dead gunman into the woods and drove on, his limbs trembling as the adrenalin dissipated and he went into shock. To reach the private road which led to Seaview Lodge seemed to take for ever.

Orlenko came to and started kicking the bodywork as Freeland drove round the last bend in the track. In addition to Lander's Cadillac, there were two prowl cars from the Camden Police Department parked in front of the house and the whole drive was lit up like the fourth of July by the floodlights under the trees. He stopped in front of the porch, switched off the engine and got out of the car. A harsh voice from the darkness ordered him to freeze.

"Piss off." He roared it at the top of his voice, venting his anger and fear in two explosive words, then the front door opened and he saw Johansen standing in the hall. "Hullo, Steve," he said conversationally, "fancy meeting you here. What is this, a reunion party?"

Egan, Salusbury, Joe Lander and a stranger who looked as though he'd been dressed by Brooks Brothers were waiting for him in the sitting-room. So was Jenny. In all the years they had known each other, Freeland could not recall a time when he had been so glad to see her.

"Are you all right, Harry?" she asked quietly.

"Never felt better," he told her, striving to appear cool, calm and collected but sounding nothing like it.

"What have you done with Orlenko?" Johansen demanded behind him.

"He's in the boot of my car."

"Let's have the keys then."

"You'll find them in the ignition," Freeland said, glancing over his shoulder.

"Good." Johansen nodded. "He's all yours, Mr Egan. Just get him the hell out of America before I change my mind."

"You get Orlenko in exchange for me? Is that the deal, Steve?"

"Yeah. No two ways about it, I've got the best of the bargain."

"There's a dead Russian in the woods up the road about a hundred yards from the turn-off to Augusta. Before you start celebrating, Steve, I suggest you give him a quiet burial, otherwise the FBI may want to know why you've been poaching on their territory."

Johansen gave a fair impression of a drill sergeant, used most of

284

the four-letter words common to every army, then told the man in the Brooks Brothers suit to attend to it.

"We'll use that broken-down heap of yours as a hearse," he told Freeland, "so you needn't expect to see it again."

"This must be your lucky night," Freeland said, poker-faced. "You've got a real bargain there."

They parted the worst of friends, Johansen slamming the front door behind him as he stormed out of the house. Freeland heard him call to the man who had been positioned somewhere in the wooded area beyond the lawn to close on the vehicles, then the drivers started up and they moved off in convoy.

"It would seem you blew it, Harry." Salusbury paused before adding, "Yet again."

"Yes, well things never do quite work out the way you intend, do they, Guy?"

"What do you mean?"

"You set me up. I was supposed to be killed in that ambush down the road."

"Oh, Harry . . ." Salusbury gazed at him with something like pity in his eyes as well as his voice. "We all know you're tensed up and on edge, but you're not thinking straight. You can't shift the blame for your own mistakes . . ."

"Shall I tell you what your big mistake was?" Freeland interrupted. "You were too damned calm when I told you the Chevrolet had been stolen. The whole operation was coming apart but it didn't faze you one bit."

"Your car was found in Harlem minus all four wheels, the battery, air cleaner and radio . . ."

"And you were the one who told me to park it outside Hunter College on East 68th Street. That's how your Russian friends knew where to find it."

"Dear God, did I also know you would rent a car in Boston?"

"That was the clever part; it wouldn't have mattered if I had caught a connecting train to Portland or even Augusta, I would still have had to come through the roadblock to reach this place."

Jenny made as if to say something but Egan put a restraining hand on her arm.

"It all started when you sold out to Hausser," Freeland went on.

"What nonsense. You were the one who caved in, Harry."

Freeland closed his eyes. There was his own confession to support the allegation, but it wasn't the whole story. Somehow he had to convince Egan that Salusbury had been picked up by the SS and

285

made a deal with them long before Grothmann had arrested him. Everything stemmed from that.

"When the war was over, Guy recruited me into the SIS because I was making a nuisance of myself in France, asking too many questions about Chantal Kiffer, and he wanted to keep me on a tight rein."

But only until Salusbury could find a way of eliminating him, and the Teale affair had presented just such an opportunity.

Salusbury laughed. "Are you seriously suggesting that I told the Nationalists you were a Communist?"

"It was a neat way of solving your problem, and a whole lot safer than hiring a freelancer to silence me. Unfortunately, your problems were only just beginning. You sold yourself to Hausser and to save his own skin, he then sold you to the Russians."

Egan's expression was still sphinx-like and it was impossible to know what he was thinking. But Salusbury was beginning to sweat and Freeland sensed that what little courage remained in him was fast ebbing away.

"Tell me something, Harry, if what you say is true, why did Hausser bother to chop off your little finger?"

"It was part of an insurance policy to protect you. I was to be known as the one who cracked and gave the SS an entry into the Loiret Bleu network. Chantal Kiffer was the double indemnity clause."

"Next thing I know you'll be telling me that I arranged for someone to torch the British Council Office in Cologne."

"No, the NKVD did that when they learned from Hausser that I was looking for him. They wanted to discredit me by making it clear to the SIS that they knew we, and the Americans, were organising a national resistance movement throughout West Germany. It's called killing two birds with one stone."

"Do you believe any of this garbage?" Salusbury asked Egan in a cracked voice.

"I do," Jenny said icily. "I believe every word."

"Well, we all know you're prepared to accept any explanation that will lay the ghost of Chantal Kiffer. You've always been aware of just how much Harry loved her and the knowledge has been gnawing at you like a cancer all these years."

"That's enough," Freeland grated.

"You've also hated me ever since I made it clear that marrying you was the last thing I had in mind."

"You lying bastard . . ."

Salusbury ignored her outburst and concentrated on Egan

286

instead. "Sergeant Jenny Vail did a lot more than pack my parachute when I was up at Ringway." He shook his head as though it pained him to say it. "I believe she threw this in Harry's face a few days ago when they were having one of their periodic fights. It would certainly account for his strange behaviour tonight."

'A very attractive woman, but not our sort' – Freeland recalled Salusbury's words and not for the first time wondered if he had made a pass at Jenny and been rebuffed.

"I'm not listening to any more of this." Jenny walked purposefully towards the telephone on the bar. "For ten years, Harry gave you his total, unquestioning loyalty because he believed you'd saved his life during the war. No one was allowed to say a word against you in his hearing, and now it turns out you betrayed him time and time again. I'm going to call the police."

"Oh no, you're not," Egan told her sharply. "We'll handle this."

"How? By sweeping it under the carpet?" Her voice rose in anger. "That would be about par for the SIS, wouldn't it?"

"Some things are better done quietly, Mrs Freeland."

"I bet they are." Jenny walked behind the bar and picked up the shotgun which Lander had concealed there when Johansen and the others had arrived. "But this isn't one of them," she continued and tucked the butt amateurishly under her right armpit. "Somebody just lift the phone and call the police."

The barrel was pointing somewhere between Salusbury and Egan and wavering. Lander sidestepped out of the line of fire, just to be on the safe side.

"Take it easy, love," Freeland said quietly.

"Put that gun down, you stupid bitch," Salusbury yelled. "You obviously don't know how to handle it safely."

"You could be right."

The shotgun bucked in her hands and sounded like a cannon. The range was less than twenty feet which meant the buckshot hadn't even begun to spread when it hit Salusbury in the stomach and almost cut him in two.

"Christ. Jesus H. Christ . . ." Lander stared at the shattered corpse, then looked at Egan. "It was an accident," he said deliberately. "The safety wasn't on and that damned Remington has a hair trigger. Right?"

Egan clenched his hands in suppressed anger. Thanks to Jenny Freeland they would never know just how much damage Salusbury had done to the SIS, nor could they use him against the Russian

Intelligence Service. Watching Freeland as he removed the shotgun from his wife's grasp, Egan also knew that he would be forced to participate in a cover-up.

"Joe's still waiting for an answer to his question," Freeland reminded him gently.

"Yes, it was an accident," Egan agreed reluctantly, but he believed he had seen Jenny move the safety off and thought different.